PRAISE FOR *THE WATER RAT OF WANCHAI*

WINNER OF THE ARTHUR ELLIS AWARD FOR BEST FIRST NOVEL

"Ian Hamilton's *The Water Rat of Wanchai* is a smart, action-packed thriller of the first order, and Ava Lee, a gay Asian-Canadian forensics accountant with a razor-sharp mind and highly developed martial arts skills, is a protagonist to be reckoned with. We were impressed by Hamilton's tight plotting; his well-rendered settings, from the glitz of Bangkok to the grit of Guyana; and his ability to portray a wide range of sharply individualized characters in clean but sophisticated prose."

— Judges' Citation, Arthur Ellis Award for Best First Novel

"Ava Lee is tough, fearless, quirky, and resourceful, and she has more — well, you know — than a dozen male detectives I can think of... Hamilton has created a true original in Ava Lee."

— Linwood Barclay, author of *No Time for Goodbye*

"If the other novels [in the series] are half as good as this debut by Ian Hamilton, then readers are going to celebrate. Hamilton has created a marvellous character in Ava Lee... This is a terrific story that's certain to be on the Arthur Ellis Best First Novel list."

— *Globe and Mail*

"[Ava Lee's] lethal knowledge... torques up her sex appeal to the approximate level of a female lead in a Quentin Tarantino film."

— *National Post*

"The heroine in *The Water Rat of Wanchai* by Ian Hamilton sounds too good to be true, but the heroics work better that way...formidable...The story breezes along with something close to total clarity...Ava is unbeatable at just about everything. Just wait for her to roll out her bak mei against the bad guys. She's perfect. She's fast." — *Toronto Star*

"Imagine a book about a forensic accountant that has tension, suspense, and action...When the central character looks like Lucy Liu, kicks like Jackie Chan, and has a travel budget like Donald Trump, the story is anything but boring. *The Water Rat of Wanchai* is such a beast...I look forward to the next one, *The Disciple of Las Vegas*." — *Montreal Gazette*

"[A] tomb-raiding Dragon Lady Lisbeth, *sans* tattoo and face metal." — *Winnipeg Free Press*

"Readers will discern in Ava undertones of Lisbeth Salander, the ferocious protagonist of the late Stieg Larsson's crime novels...she, too, is essentially a loner, and small, and physically brutal...There are suggestions in *The Water Rat of Wanchai* of deeper complexities waiting to be more fully revealed. Plus there's pleasure, both for Ava and readers, in the puzzle itself: in figuring out where money has gone, how to get it back, and which humans, helpful or malevolent, are to be dealt with where, and in what ways, in the process... Irresistible." — Joan Barfoot, *London Free Press*

"*The Water Rat of Wanchai* delivers on all fronts...feels like the beginning of a crime-fighting saga...great story told with colour, energy, and unexpected punch."— *Hamilton Spectator*

"The best series fiction leaves readers immersed in a world that is both familiar and fresh. Seeds planted early bear fruit later on, creating a rich forest that blooms across a number of books... [Hamilton] creates a terrific atmosphere of suspense..." — *Quill & Quire*

"The book is an absolute page-turner... Hamilton's knack for writing snappy dialogue is evident... I recommend getting in on the ground floor with this character, because for Ava Lee, the sky's the limit." — *Inside Halton*

"A fascinating story of a hunt for stolen millions. And the hunter, Ava Lee, is a compelling heroine: tough, smart, and resourceful."
— Meg Gardiner, author of *The Nightmare Thief*

"Few heroines are as feisty as *The Girl with the Dragon Tattoo*'s Lisbeth Salander, but Ian Hamilton's Ava Lee could give her a run for her money... Gripping... [Ava is] smart, gutsy, and resourceful." — *Stylist UK*

"With Ava Lee comes a new star in the world of crime-thrillers... Hamilton produced a suspenseful and gripping novel featuring a woman who is not afraid of anything... Captivating and hard to put down." — *dapd/sda*

"Thrillers don't always have to be Scandinavian to work. Ava Lee is a wonderful Chinese-Canadian investigator who uses unconventional methods of investigation in a mysterious Eastern setting." — *Elle* (Germany)

"Ava has flair, charm, and sex-appeal... *The Water Rat of Wanchai* is a successful first book in a series, which will definitely have you longing for more." — *Sonntag-Express*

"Hamilton is in the process of writing six books and film rights have already been sold. If the other cases are similar to this first one, Ava Lee is sure to quickly shake up Germany's thriller-business." — *Handelsblatt*

"Brilliantly researched and incredibly exciting!" — *Bücher*

"Page-turning till the end of the book!... Ava Lee is the upcoming crime-star." — *dpa*

"Exciting thriller debut with an astonishing end." — *Westdeutsche Zeitung*

"Seldom does one get a thriller about white-collar crime, with an intelligent, independent lesbian and Asian protagonist. It's also rare to find a book with such interesting and exotic settings... Readers will find great amusement in Ava's unconventional ways and will certainly enjoy accompanying her on her travels." — *Literaturkurier*

PRAISE FOR *THE DISCIPLE OF LAS VEGAS*

"I started to read *The Disciple of Las Vegas* at around ten at night. And I did something I have only done with two other books (Cormac McCarthy's *The Road* and Douglas Coupland's *Player One*): I read the novel in one sitting. Ava Lee is too cool. She wonderfully straddles two worlds and two identities. She does some dastardly things and still remains our hero thanks to the charm Ian Hamilton has given her on the printed page. It would take a female George Clooney to portray her in a film. The action and plot move quickly and with power. Wow. A punch to the ear, indeed."

— J. J. Lee, author of *The Measure of a Man*

"This is slick, fast-moving escapism reminiscent of Ian Fleming, with more to come in what shapes up as a high-energy, high-concept series." — *Booklist*

"Fast paced . . . Enough personal depth to lift this thriller above solely action-oriented fare." — *Publishers Weekly*

"Lee is a hugely original creation, and Hamilton packs his adventure with interesting facts and plenty of action."

— *Irish Independent*

"I loved *The Water Rat of Wanchai,* the first novel featuring Ava Lee. Now, Ava and Uncle make a return that's even better . . . Simply irresistible." — Margaret Cannon, *Globe and Mail*

"Hamilton gives his reader plenty to think about... Entertaining." — *Kitchener-Waterloo Record*

PRAISE FOR *THE WILD BEASTS OF WUHAN*

"Smart and savvy Ava Lee, a Toronto forensic accountant, returns in this slick mystery set in the rarefied world of high art... [A] great caper tale. Hamilton has great fun chasing villains and tossing clues about. *The Wild Beasts of Wuhan* is the best Ava Lee novel yet, and promises more and better to come."
— Margaret Cannon, *Globe and Mail*

"One of my favourite new mystery series, perfect escapism."
— *National Post*

"As a mystery lover, I'm devouring each book as it comes out... What I love in the novels: The constant travel, the high-stakes negotiation, and Ava's willingness to go into battle against formidable opponents, using only her martial arts skills to defend herself... If you want a great read and an education in high-level business dealings, Ian Hamilton is an author to watch."
— *Toronto Star*

"Fast-paced and very entertaining." — *Montreal Gazette*

"Ava Lee is definitely a winner." — *Saskatoon Star Phoenix*

"*The Wild Beasts of Wuhan* is an entertaining dip into potentially fatal worlds of artistic skulduggery." — *Sudbury Star*

"Hamilton uses Ava's investigations as comprehensive and intriguing mechanisms for plot and character development."
— *Quill & Quire*

PRAISE FOR *THE RED POLE OF MACAU*

"Ava Lee, that wily, wonderful hunter of nasty business brutes, is back in her best adventure ever... If you haven't yet discovered Ava Lee, start here."
— *Globe and Mail*

"A romp of a story with a terrific heroine."
— *Saskatoon Star Phoenix*

"Fast-paced... The action unfolds like a well-oiled action-flick."
— *Kitchener-Waterloo Record*

"A change of pace for our girl [Ava Lee]... Suspenseful."
— *Toronto Star*

"Ava [Lee] is a character we all could use at one time or another. Failing that, we follow her in her best adventure yet."
— *Hamilton Spectator*

"Crackling with suspense, intrigue, and danger, your fingers will be smoking from turning these pages."
— Terry Fallis, author of *Best Laid Plans* and *Up and Down*

"Ava Lee returns as one of crime fiction's most intriguing characters. *The Red Pole of Macau* is the best page-turner of the season from the hottest writer in the business!"
— John Lawrence Reynolds, author of *Beach Strip*

THE SCOTTISH BANKER OF SURABAYA

Also in the Ava Lee Series

The Water Rat of Wanchai
The Disciple of Las Vegas
The Wild Beasts of Wuhan
The Red Pole of Macau

THE SCOTTISH BANKER OF SURABAYA

AN AVA LEE NOVEL

IAN HAMILTON

This edition published in 2013 by
House of Anansi Press Inc.
110 Spadina Avenue, Suite 801
Toronto, ON, M5V 2K4
Tel. 416-363-4343
Fax 416-363-1017
www.houseofanansi.com

Distributed in Canada by
HarperCollins Canada Ltd.
1995 Markham Road
Scarborough, ON, M1B 5M8
Toll-free tel. 1-800-387-0117

17 16 15 14 13 1 2 3 4 5

Library and Archives Canada Cataloguing in Publication

Hamilton, Ian, 1946–
The Scottish banker of Surabaya / Ian Hamilton.

(An Ava Lee novel)
Issued also in electronic format.
ISBN 978-1-77089-234-7

I. Title. II. Series: Hamilton, Ian, 1946– . Ava Lee novel.

PS8615.A4423S26 2013 C813'.6 C2012-905950-1

Cover design: Gregg Kulick
Text design and typesetting: Alysia Shewchuk

Canada Council for the Arts
Conseil des Arts du Canada

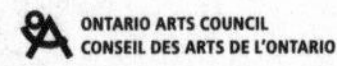

We acknowledge for their financial support of our publishing program the Canada Council for the Arts, the Ontario Arts Council, and the Government of Canada through the Canada Book Fund.

Printed and bound in Canada

For my aunt, Margaret Burns, and in memory
of her husband and a good friend to me,
Dr. Archie Burns

PROLOGUE

REVENGE WAS NOT AN EMOTION SHE WAS ACCUSTOMED to managing.

In the course of business there were times when things came unstuck and she found herself on the wrong end of an outcome. But in her mind it was still business, and the people who were causing her grief were simply exercising their own right to do business as they saw fit.

This was different. He had made it personal, more personal than she could have imagined possible.

She lay in the dark, cold despite being wrapped in a thick duvet, and she thought about the day that was about to dawn.

She was going to get him. She was going to hurt him. The thought of it didn't bring peace. It ran unchecked in her mind, bouncing from pain to pain.

She prayed she would be calmer and in control when the moment came. It might be revenge she sought, but she still wanted it to be quiet, and private.

(1)

IT WAS THE FRIDAY BEFORE THE LABOUR DAY WEEK-end, the last weekend of Canadian summer, and Ava Lee woke with the realization that her two months of relative seclusion were about to end.

She lay quietly for a moment, listening for the sounds of birds that greeted her every morning through her open bedroom window. She heard the leaves rustling and lake water lapping against the dock, and she knew the wind was up.

She moved her legs and felt a burning sensation in her right thigh. Two and a half months before, she had been shot there during a house invasion in Macau. Luckily the bullet hadn't struck bone or cut through an artery. She had flown back to Canada two days later, using crutches that had evolved into a cane and then a limp. To her surprise she had been able to start a modest workout regime soon after getting to the cottage. Given that she was supremely fit and that the bullet hadn't done any structural damage, it was all about pain management. Most mornings she felt nothing in the leg, only to have the pain reappear randomly, burning and throbbing; it seemed to twitch, to almost be alive.

Ava was a debt collector. It was a job often fraught with peril, and over the ten years she had worked with her Hong Kong partner, Uncle, she had been stabbed, kicked, punched, hit with a tire iron, and whipped with a belt. None of them had left a permanent mark; none of them revisited her like the muscle memory of that bullet.

She pulled down the sheets and glanced at her leg. The doctor in Macau had done a good job getting the bullet out of her thigh and treating the initial wound, but he was no cosmetic surgeon. Her girlfriend, Maria, had gasped when she first saw the raw red scar, which eventually turned into a less ugly long pink worm.

She slid from the bed, slipped on her Adidas training pants, and left the bedroom. She walked softly down the hallway so as not to disturb her mother and went into the kitchen. The hot water Thermos she had brought from her Toronto condo sat ready on the counter. She opened a sachet of Starbucks VIA instant coffee and made her first cup of the morning.

The sun was well over the horizon, but she could still see the last remnants of morning dew glistening on the wooden deck. She opened the kitchen door and felt a slight chill in the air. She put on her Adidas running jacket, slipped her cellphone into a pocket, grabbed a dish towel, tucked her laptop under one arm, and, balancing her coffee, walked across the wet grass to the dock.

Ava started every morning on the dock with her coffee and her electronic devices. She wiped the dew from the wooden Muskoka chair and eased herself into it. One broad arm held her coffee, the other comfortably accommodated the laptop. She turned on her computer and then her phone.

It was just past nine o'clock, and the emails from the part of her world that was beginning its day were first in line. Maria had emailed at eight. I have a seat on the Casino Rama bus leaving the city at 4 this afternoon. I should be at Rama by 5:30. Do you want me to take a cab to the cottage?

Ava started to reply and then reached for her phone. Maria would be at her desk at the Colombian Trade Commission office by now. She called her direct line.

"Hi, honey," Maria said.

"I'll pick you up in front of the casino hotel," Ava said.

"Your mother is staying at the hotel again?"

"Yes."

"She doesn't like me."

"That's not true."

"She never wants to be in my company, and when she is, the only two things she ever says to me are that I have nice manners and that I look good in bright colours."

"Those are compliments."

"I make her uncomfortable."

"No, *we* make her uncomfortable. Although we've never discussed it, I know she can't stay in the cottage when you're here because she wouldn't be able to stop herself thinking about what's going on in our bedroom. She's very Chinese and very Catholic, and as understanding as she tries to be, there are limits to what she can handle. Is your very Colombian, very Catholic mother any different?"

"No," Maria said softly.

"So I'll see you tonight. The weather forecast for the weekend is fantastic."

Ava returned to the computer. Her sister, Marian, had sent one of her typical newsy emails. The girls go back to school on Tuesday. New uniforms for them this year. I bought them over a month ago, and when I did I couldn't help but remember how Mummy always left doing that until the very last minute, and how we ended up in long lines that took hours to process and were lucky at the end to find uniforms in the right size.

Ava sighed. Her mother and her sister had personalities that didn't mesh well, a fact made even more contentious when Marian married an uptight *gweilo* civil servant who was incapable of understanding a woman like Jennie Lee.

And I can't believe that she actually stayed at the cottage with you for two months, Marian wrote. She came to our cottage in the Gatineaus once and barely lasted the week. She said she didn't like blackflies, squirrels, raccoons, horseflies, mosquitoes, dirt roads, and cold lakes.

Give the girls a hug for me, Ava replied. I'm sure they'll have another great year at school. As for Mummy, well, she initially came to the cottage because she knew I needed her help, and she stayed because I stocked the fridge with Chinese food, brought in Chinese cable TV, told her to invite her friends from Richmond Hill to play mah-jong, and most evenings I drive her over to Casino Rama to play baccarat.

The cottage was on Lake Couchiching, near the town of Orillia, about an hour's drive from Toronto's northern suburbs and only fifteen minutes from the casino. She had found it online, surprised to find something that could give her the privacy she wanted and still be close to good restaurants and the services she was used to.

She worked down her email list, deleting most messages until she got to the part of her world that was ending its day. There were emails from Amanda Yee, her half-brother's fiancée, in Hong Kong, and from May Ling Wong in Wuhan. Ava had met Amanda during the Macau affair and they had become friends. She was Jack Yee's only child. Jack owned a Hong Kong trading operation that occasionally — something common enough for traders — ran into problems with suppliers or customers. Twice he had hired Uncle and Ava to get his money back. Twice they had succeeded, once saving his life in the process.

Ava hadn't known that Amanda and Jack were related until after she had met Amanda as her half-brother's fiancée. It had been a difficult introduction, made in the middle of a kidnapping and the financial fiasco that threatened her half-brother Michael's business and the entire family's well-being. But Amanda had been a rock throughout it all, earning Ava's respect. In her email, Amanda was fretting about wedding dates and venues; friends or not, and respect or not, those were two subjects Ava had no interest in.

May Ling's message was long and colourful. Ava had met May Ling as a client. She and her husband, Changxing, were the wealthiest couple in Hubei province, and among the wealthiest in China. They had hired Ava and Uncle to find the people who had sold them some fake Fauvist paintings and to retrieve their money. It wasn't a simple job and had been made even more complicated when the Wongs decided they also wanted revenge. Lies were told, some vicious acts ensued, and the early relationship between Ava and May Ling devolved into mistrust and anger. But fences had been mended and May had been supportive and, indeed, integral to Ava's success in Macau. The two women were now friends, and perhaps becoming more than just friends. May's emails were chatty, full of news about her business and other things going on in her life. She asked questions, sought advice, but mainly wrote to Ava as if she were writing in a diary. The first few times that May became intensely personal, Ava had been taken aback. She didn't need to know, she thought, about May's fears, the details of her marriage and sex life. Then she became accustomed to May's openness and even found herself — tentatively — sharing more of herself with May. They had not been and never would be physically intimate, but there was an emotional connection. May Ling, a Taoist, said it was *qi* — the life force — flowing between them.

About once a week May would phone. She was smart, tough, and funny and could buck up Ava's spirits in no time. It was during one of those calls that May had asked Ava if she would be interested in joining her business. It was time she and her husband made some North American investments, she said, and they needed someone to spear-head the initiative.

"I wouldn't be a very good employee," Ava said.

"A partner, then," May said.

"I have a partner, and I have a business."

"Ava, you know that Uncle can't keep doing this for much longer, and I can't imagine you would want to do it without him."

For ten years Ava and Uncle had been partners in the collection business. They had met when both were sepa-rately pursuing the same thief and had bonded almost at once. He was now in his late seventies or maybe his eighties — Ava didn't know — and he had become more than a partner. He was a mentor, almost a grandfather, and the most important man in her life. That was the source of her dilemma. She was tired of the stresses of the job, fed up with the kind of people she had to pursue, and she was beginning to wonder how much longer her luck could hold out when it came to dodging bullets and knives.

As she mended, she had waited for the urge to get back to work to return. It hadn't. She then began to ask herself if it was possible it never would.

During her recuperation Uncle had stayed in constant touch by phone. He didn't discuss business or ask when she was coming back; his only concern was her health and her family and friends. He did talk about May Ling, whom he knew well. He had urged Ava to make up with her when their relationship went sour, and his judgement of May Ling's character had proven to be correct.

"The woman has *guanxi*, influence, and could be a very powerful ally for you in the years ahead. You need to stay close to her," he said during one call.

Ava didn't know if Uncle knew about May's offer, and she wasn't about to tell him. "I have a business partner," she said.

"Yes, one who is not going to be here forever."

"I have a business partner," she repeated.

"I am not suggesting otherwise," he said.

Ava thought that over time she could grow as close to May Ling as she was to Uncle, the kind of closeness where trust is absolute and forgiveness is never necessary. The chance to do real business, to build a company, was an attractive proposition. Ava was an accountant with degrees from York University in Toronto and Babson

College, just outside Boston, and she liked the idea of using her education for something other than locating and retrieving stolen money.

But no matter how she spun things, it all came down to one fact: she couldn't leave Uncle. He loved her, she knew, and she realized that she was the daughter — or, more likely, granddaughter — he had never had. She loved him in return. Neither of them had ever mentioned the word *love*. Their relationship was built on things that were never said, and never needed to be said.

Ava finished her coffee and weighed the options of having another or starting her workout. At the beginning of her second week in the north, Ava had begun to exercise again. She started with just a morning walk, advanced to a walk/jog cycle, then a full jog, and now she was able to run some distance at close to her normal pace. Every second day she limited her run and instead went down to the lakeside to do bak mei drills in slow motion, as she had been taught. Only a handful of people in Canada practised this martial art. It was taught one-on-one, traditionally passed down from father to son, or in her case from teacher to student. It wasn't pretty to watch but it was effective, designed to inflict the maximum possible damage. Ava had become adept at it.

"Ava, do you mind if I join you?"

The voice startled her. She looked up and saw her mother standing to one side with two cups in her hands.

"I made you another coffee," Jennie Lee said.

"Thanks. I'm surprised to see you up this early."

"I couldn't sleep."

"Is something bothering you?"

Jennie passed a coffee to her daughter and then sat in the other Muskoka chair, ignoring its dampness, her eyes fixed on the lake. "I need a favour," she said.

Jennie was close to sixty years old, but even without makeup and with her face lit by the morning sun, she looked like a woman in her forties. "What is it?" Ava said.

"I'd like you to drive me to the casino at three o'clock."

"That's early, Mummy. Maria doesn't get in until five thirty."

"I know, but I need you to talk to someone there."

"Who?"

"Theresa Ng."

"Who is Theresa Ng?"

Jennie Lee took a pack of du Maurier extra-mild king-size cigarettes from her housecoat pocket, lit one, and blew smoke towards the lake. "She is a baccarat dealer at Rama."

"Why would I talk to a baccarat dealer?"

"She has a problem."

"I'm not a counsellor."

Jennie took two more long puffs and then threw the cigarette to the ground. "She has a money problem."

"How do you know that?"

"I asked her why she looked so troubled."

Ava knew that her mother made friends as easily as other people changed clothes. There wasn't a store she went into or a restaurant she ate at where she didn't ask the server or the sales associate what their name was and how they were doing.

"How does this involve me?" Ava said.

Jennie leaned her head against the back of the chair and then slowly turned towards her daughter. "Just because I never talk to you about what you do for a living doesn't mean I don't know."

"Really?"

"Yes, really. I've always had suspicions that you didn't make all that money you have by being a good accountant. I also found it strange that you work with Uncle, but I ignored all the rumours about his Triad connections by telling myself he's an old man who's moved on to other things. But any doubts I had were put to rest after you went to Hong Kong and Macau and saved Michael's partner's life, and their business."

"Michael wasn't in Macau."

"Ava, please don't treat me as if I'm an idiot or can't handle the truth."

Ava sipped her coffee and stared out at the water, which was dotted with people quietly fishing from canoes and small boats. The jet skiers usually invaded the lake after lunch and then departed before dinner, leaving the lake to the fishermen again until dusk. "Macau was hard on me emotionally as well as physically," she said. "I don't like talking about it."

"Other people in the family, including Michael, have done enough talking for everyone to know what happened."

"And I'm sure it's been exaggerated."

"What, you didn't save the partner and the business?"

"I had help."

Jennie waved her hand dismissively. "You led; we all know you did. When your father heard the story, he couldn't handle his emotions. It was the first time I've seen him cry. And then I cried, because I knew you had not only saved Michael, you had saved the entire family.

If you hadn't recovered all that money, your father would have emptied his bank accounts to cover Michael's losses. And then where would we be? His years of labour gone, and my security and that of the other wives and children completely at risk."

"I did what I had to do."

"You mean you did what you chose to do, and that's why I'm so proud. When I was raising you and Marian, that was my prayer — that my girls would become women capable of being true to themselves."

"Some days that's harder to do than others," Ava said. "When it is, I often think of you and how you have persevered."

"Ava, you don't have to —"

"I'm not. I mean it."

"Well, it's true that my relationship with your father has tested me. When I married him, I knew what I was getting into: the second wife of a man who wouldn't leave his first. I thought I could handle it, but all of us being in Hong Kong was too much. So I moved us to Canada. That was my choice, Ava, not his. And once we were here, I re-established my marriage on a basis that suited me and was designed to look after you girls... I would have done anything to look after you girls."

Ava reached over and touched her mother's hand. "We know."

"And your father and I have somehow made it work for more than thirty years."

"I know it wasn't easy."

"No, it wasn't, and it isn't. I know what people, particularly non-Chinese, say and think about my so-called marriage. They don't understand our culture and traditions, and in their eyes I'm sometimes a mistress and sometimes a whore. I just pretend I don't hear them and I go about my business and my life, knowing that it is a life I chose and not one that was imposed on me."

"We're the same that way. Neither of us can stand being told what to do."

"Your father sees that as a blessing in you and a curse in me," Jennie said.

Ava closed her eyes. She wasn't up for a discussion about her father or the complicated family he had created — her mother and sister and her alone in Canada; her father with his first wife and four sons in Hong Kong; and a third wife with two young children in Australia.

"This Theresa Ng, she's a friend?" Ava said.

Her mother sipped her coffee and took out another cigarette. Ava saw her jaw relax. "By now she is."

"And you say she has a money problem?"

"Yes, and I told her you were good at sorting out that kind of thing, so she asked me to see if you would talk to her."

"Uncle and I don't normally take on Canadian clients."

"She's Vietnamese Chinese."

"But her problem is in Canada?"

"Yes, I think it is."

"Well, there are other options she can pursue here. She could get a lawyer, a good accountant, even a local collection agency. This is a country with laws that actually work."

"She wouldn't feel comfortable with them. Besides, from what I can gather, the problem she has is complicated."

"How so?"

"She's vague about the details. She just shakes her head and moans every time she starts to talk about it."

"Mummy, very honestly, I don't think this is a job for me."

Jennie Lee took a deep drag on her cigarette, and Ava saw her jaw muscles tighten again. "The thing is, I told her that you would talk to her."

"I wish you hadn't."

"Well, I did, and it's too late to undo it."

"Why?"

"She wasn't even scheduled to work today. She's driving up from Mississauga for the sole reason of meeting with you."

Ava sighed. "I wish you wouldn't do this kind of thing."

"I'm sorry, but all you have to do is listen to her and then point her in the right direction."

Ava put her hands over her face and rubbed her eyes in frustration. "You cannot tell anyone again that I'll meet with them. Uncle and I have our own way of operating, and I don't freelance."

"Does that mean you'll drive me to the casino early?"

"Yes, I'll drive you to the casino early."

"Thank you. And you will take the time to speak to Theresa?"

"Yes, I'll talk to the woman, but that's all. You didn't promise anything else, I hope."

"No."

"Good. Now, how large is the problem this baccarat dealer has?"

"Between three and thirty million dollars."

"What?"

"Like I said, she's vague about the details."

(2)

THE CASINO PARKING LOT WAS GETTING FULL ALREADY, and by six it would be jammed for the long weekend. "Go around to the side. I told Theresa we'd meet her near the bus drop-off area."

There wasn't a vacant spot to be seen, and cars were circling like vultures. Ava joined the carousel, beginning to get irritated at her mother's randomness. "I'm going to wait five more minutes before I drop you off and leave," she said.

Jennie Lee kept her attention on the front of the casino, pointedly ignoring her daughter.

"Did you hear me?"

"There she is," her mother said. "The short woman in jeans and a red blouse."

Ava drove as close as she could to the casino entrance and stopped the car. Jennie opened her door and ran over to Theresa. They chatted for a minute, Jennie motioning to go inside the building, Theresa shaking her head. The two of them walked back to the car. Jennie climbed into the front seat, Theresa into the back.

"Theresa says she can't talk to us inside the casino. Employees aren't allowed to mingle with customers," Jennie said. "There's a Tim Hortons coffee shop on Highway 12 just before Rama Road. Why don't we go there?"

Ava tried to contain herself. If Theresa knew they couldn't talk in the casino, why ask them to meet her there? Why not go directly to Tim Hortons? And second, her mother knew she didn't like Tim Hortons; her choosing it was her way of making Ava pay for being grumpy in the parking lot.

"I'm so sorry to put you to this trouble," Theresa Ng said.

Ava looked back at Theresa's round face: pale lips; no makeup; hair pulled back in a tight ponytail, highlighting eyes that were nervous and timid. The woman smiled, flashing beautiful white teeth, and her right hand tugged at the bottom of her red silk blouse.

"No problem," Ava said.

Tim Hortons was peculiarly Canadian, like curling and like donning shorts as soon as the spring temperature reached ten degrees Celsius. The country was in love with the chain, a fact reinforced when her Audi A6 came within sight of the store on Highway 12. There was a line outside the drive-through window that snaked almost all the way to the main road. This was hardly a phenomenon; it was probably happening at every Tim Hortons in Canada at that very minute.

She found a space in the crowded parking lot. She got out of the car and walked quickly to the coffee shop, her mother and Theresa trailing behind, deep in conversation. Ava could hear Theresa apologizing to Jennie for putting her to all this trouble. The apologies were misdirected, Ava thought, but they did seem sincere, and the woman seemed nice enough.

Theresa insisted on paying for Ava's bottle of water and Jennie's tea. They found a table at the back of the shop and wiped off doughnut crumbs and splashes of coffee with a napkin.

"Theresa is Vietnamese Chinese; her mother is originally from Shanghai," Jennie began. "They came here in the 1970s when the communists invaded the south — she, her mother, and three sisters."

"My two brothers came later," Theresa said.

Jennie said, "They are all Catholic, like us."

Catholic and part Shanghainese. Little wonder my mother wants to help, Ava thought.

"We all live in Mississauga, on the same street," Theresa said. "At first we lived in the same house, my sisters, my mother, and me. We all got jobs, paid off the house, and then bought another one, which my older sister moved into with her new husband. When we got that one paid off, we bought another, and so on and so on. We now own six houses on the street. Everyone is close by, so it's perfect."

"You've done very well."

Theresa lowered her head, worry lines bracketing her mouth. "We were doing a lot better."

Ava waited for her to continue. When she didn't, Jennie tapped the back of Theresa's hand. "Don't be embarrassed," she said.

"Yes, tell me what happened, and take all the time you want," Ava said.

Theresa looked up, anger showing through the onset of tears. "My family invested money in a fund run by a guy who was a friend of a friend of my oldest brother. It was supposed to be safe, with returns of around ten percent a year."

The word *Ponzi* flashed into Ava's head.

"For the first two years the cheques came to us like clockwork every month, so we put more and more of our money into it," Theresa continued. "Then the trouble began, and it all happened so fast. The fund was late with a payment one month—maybe by two weeks—and people were starting to panic. But then the payment came in and we got a note saying there had been a small technical problem at the bank. But the next month it was late again. My brother went down to the company's office to complain and found the office closed. That was it. Gone. Finished."

"What was the name of the company?"

"Emerald Lion."

Ava searched her memory and came up blank. "I don't remember reading or hearing anything about this."

"It was mentioned in *Sing Tao* and the other Chinese newspapers," Jennie said.

"And the Vietnamese ones," Theresa added.

"When?"

"About six months ago now."

"And what did the papers have to say?"

"What do you mean?"

"How was it reported? As a scam?"

"They sort of hinted at that, although they were being careful because none of them had talked to Lam Van Dinh."

"He ran the fund?"

"Yes."

"What did the authorities say?"

Theresa's face went blank.

Ava asked, "The fund was registered, wasn't it? Surely the securities and exchange commission looked into it."

"I never heard about any commission, and I have no idea if it was registered."

"Theresa, the Ontario Securities Commission has an investment funds branch. In order to operate legally in the province, Emerald Lion had to be registered with them."

"I don't know anything about that."

"Well, then, there are the police. Surely you went to them?"

"One of the other people who lost money did, but then decided not to pursue it."

"And why not?" Ava asked.

Theresa's face was pinched. She glanced at Jennie, questions in her eyes.

"They were scared," Jennie Lee said.

"Of what?"

Jennie said to Theresa, "You can trust Ava, I told you that. She's helped people with bigger problems than yours and she knows how to keep her mouth shut. Don't you, Ava."

"Mummy, I'm not sure —"

"Theresa, tell her what happened," Jennie insisted.

"Cash," said Theresa.

Ava blinked. "Now I'm past confused."

"They all gave this Lam cash," Jennie said.

"It was my brother's idea," said Theresa. "He was talking to a friend who owns some Vietnamese grocery stores with dead cash registers that he was taking the cash out of. The problem was, he had too much cash to spend without raising attention. I mean, try buying a car with cash, or a house. And then he was afraid of Revenue Canada and the police. You just can't put it in the bank anymore without them asking a hundred questions. So he hooked up with Lam."

"And what did Lam do with the cash?"

"He said he had an arrangement with Bank Linno, from Indonesia, I was told. They had a branch in Toronto. He would deposit the cash into the fund account there. He told them he had hundreds of small investors in the fund and that he collected cash from them every week. So, according to him, he could deposit it regularly without any of the fuss or bother he'd get from the Canadian banks."

"How many investors were there?"

Theresa shrugged. "I don't know for sure, but not hundreds, because you had to be able to put in at least one hundred thousand in cash to start."

"Everyone put in cash?"

"Of course. That was the purpose."

"You mean money laundering was the purpose?"

"We just wanted to be able to spend our money without having the government on our backs."

"So you put cash in and you got cheques back from a supposedly reputable financial fund, right?"

"Yes."

"And those cheques were deposited into the bank in Indonesia?"

"Yes."

"So no questions from the bank, and you could withdraw the cash as you wanted, without any worries."

"Yes."

"Did you report that income to Revenue Canada?"

"No. Lam said we didn't have to," Theresa said, fidgeting with her napkin.

"That's nonsense. The fund would have had to issue T5 slips for all the payments it made."

"They didn't send us anything. Just a monthly report of how much money we had in the fund."

"Did they tell you how it was invested?"

"No."

"These people don't have much trust in the government or the banks," Jennie said to Ava, as if Theresa weren't sitting next to her.

"No, I guess not, but putting their faith in a fund that was probably unregulated and unregistered, and whose main attraction was that it was run by a fellow Vietnamese, doesn't seem to have worked out so well," Ava said. She saw Theresa's face flush. "I'm sorry, I don't mean to be harsh," she added.

"No, you are just speaking the truth."

"Theresa, just how long were you in the fund?"

"More than two years."

"How much were you paid over that time?"

"More than two hundred thousand dollars."

"My God. Just how much money did you have in it?"

"Close to three million dollars."

Ava thought she hadn't heard correctly. "Do you mean the fund had three million in it?"

"No, it had more than thirty million, from what we can figure. My family had three million in it."

"How did you —" Ava began.

Jennie said, "Theresa, I'd like another tea. Do you think you could get me one? And Ava, how about you? Another water?"

Theresa seemed only too happy to get away from the table. When she was out of earshot, Jennie said to Ava, "I know what you're going to ask, and I don't think you should.

Does it really matter how they got that kind of cash? They all work hard and they save hard. Accept it at that. This is embarrassing enough for her."

"Mummy, by not declaring income they were already breaking the law. Laundering the money compounds the severity."

"When did you become so Canadian?" Jennie asked. "Is it only the big and the rich who are allowed to do whatever they want to avoid paying taxes?"

"That's not the point."

"No, the point is that Theresa and her family worked for years and put everything back into the family, and now the money is gone and they want you to help them get it back. That is what you do for a living, isn't it?"

"You know it is."

"And when you do it in Asia, are you and Uncle always so fussy about how your big-shot clients came by their money, and how they hang on to it too?"

Ava sat back and stared at her mother. "You don't know who most of my clients are, or the kind of due diligence we do," she said.

"I know about Tommy Ordonez, because you needed my help, remember? You needed to get to his sister-in-law in Vancouver. When you called me, did I ask you how Ordonez became the richest man in the Philippines? Did I ask you about due diligence? All I remember is that my daughter needed my help."

Ava and Uncle had recovered more than fifty million dollars for Ordonez, money from his businesses that his brother had lost in an online gambling scam. Arguments lined up in Ava's head about the difference between that case and Theresa Ng's situation, and just as quickly they dissolved. She didn't win many arguments with her mother anyway, particularly when Jennie decided she wasn't going to back down, regardless of whatever logic Ava threw at her.

Theresa came back with two mugs and a bottle of water on a tray. She couldn't look Ava in the eye, and Ava felt a twinge of sympathy for her.

"So, Theresa, as I calculate, this character Lam stopped paying you dividends and has been gone for the past six months," she said as the woman passed out their drinks and then sat down.

"That's about right."

"And neither you nor any of the other people who lost money went to a government authority, other than that one person who approached the police and then backed off."

"Yes, that's true."

"So you've done absolutely nothing to try to get your money back?"

"We tried to find Lam."

"How?"

"We hired a private detective, a Canadian. I don't think he took us very seriously."

"And what did he find?"

"Nothing."

"So what makes you think I can do any better?"

"We think we know where Lam is now."

"You think?" Ava said.

"I got a phone call four days ago from my sister, who's visiting relatives in Saigon — they call it Ho Chi Minh City now, but to us it is still Saigon — with my mother. They took our cousins to dinner at the Hyatt in the city, and when they were leaving, a big BMW pulled up at the hotel entrance. My sister swears she saw Lam get out of the car and walk into the hotel."

"How did she know it was him?"

"His picture was all over the local Vietnamese newspapers when the company got into trouble, and my sister said she recognized him from there. And, of course, she yelled his name. She said he turned around right away, looked at her, and then ran into the hotel."

"It was him," Jennie said, nodding at Theresa.

Theresa nodded back and then looked at Ava. The uncertainty that had been in her eyes had vanished, replaced by anger that verged on hatred. "I was upset and happy all at the same time. I talked to the rest of my family, and we told my sister to go back to the hotel every night and see if she could talk to him. He never showed again. While this was going on, I was telling your mother everything, and she was kind enough to suggest that maybe you'd help us."

"I didn't say you would," Jennie stressed to Ava. "I told Theresa that you and the man you work with in Hong Kong are very good at recovering money. That's true enough, isn't it?"

"Yes, that's all she said," Theresa added.

Ava felt the pressure all the same. "You have to understand, I don't decide which cases we take and which ones we don't take. I have to talk to my boss in Hong Kong. You haven't given us very much to go on. I mean, one possible sighting at a hotel—"

"My sister wrote down the licence number of the car, so you have that too."

"Well, that's helpful, but there is also the amount of

money involved. I don't mean to be insulting, Theresa, or minimize its importance to you, but it's less than what we'd normally consider."

Theresa glanced at Jennie, her eyes begging.

"You will talk to Uncle, though, won't you?" Jennie asked.

Ava sighed. She knew there wasn't any way her mother would accept no for an answer. "Okay, I'll talk to him. No promises, though."

"Thank you," Theresa said.

"And then there is our fee. We pay all our own expenses — all of them — but we keep thirty percent of everything we collect. Are you okay with that?"

"What if you don't get anything back?"

"The expenses are still our cost, not yours."

Theresa nodded. "Getting seventy percent of something is better than one hundred percent of nothing."

"Do you need to talk to your family?"

"No, I can make the decision, and I think you're being fair."

"Okay, then. I still need to talk to Hong Kong to get the go-ahead."

"Ava, can't you just tell her now?" Jennie said.

"Mummy, I can't."

"You'll do your best with Uncle, though?"

"My best, but I'm not making any promises."

"Ava," Jennie persisted.

"No promises," Ava repeated.

(3)

LABOUR DAY WEEKEND HAS A PECULIAR IMPACT ON the Canadian psyche, and Ava wasn't immune to it. The weekend represents the end of summer, the start of a new school year for virtually every child in the country, and the turning of new pages in many lives. It marks, very specifically, the time for play to end and for work to recommence in a dedicated way. Having a plan in mind would be a good start, but Ava didn't have one. She was all loose ends, suffering from the same kind of melancholy that January 2 often induces in people.

She met Maria at the bus drop-off at Rama on Friday night. They lazed their way through the weekend, eating, drinking, walking, reading, and making love. Maria was one of the least demanding people Ava had ever met. She seemed content with doing little things — in fact, doing nothing at all — as long as it was in Ava's company. It made Ava feel guilty at times, and she found herself overcompensating by planning activities she wouldn't consider if she were on her own. So it was that on Sunday she drove them north to Midland, to the Martyrs' Shrine.

They were both Catholic, both wore crucifixes, and, in their own quiet ways, both often prayed. Maria, like Jennie, rarely missed Sunday Mass, but knowing Ava's aversion to the official structure of the Church, forewent it on her weekend trips to the north. So it came as a surprise when Ava suggested they drive to Midland. Ava debated asking her mother to join them but, knowing that the three of them would be sharing a car ride back to the city on Monday, decided one trip together was all she could handle.

They left the cottage just after eight, and the roads were so quiet they reached the shrine just before nine, in time for the ten-o'clock Mass. They wandered the spacious grounds and then stood at the back of the church reading the grisly details of the martyrs' deaths. Most of them had been tortured at length by the Hurons. Maria was especially taken by the suffering endured by Jean de Brébeuf, and insisted on reading the details aloud to Ava.

Maria was Colombian, a graduate in English and business from the University of Bogotá. She was an assistant trade commissioner at Colombia's office in Toronto, on a four-year assignment with two years left to go — a fact they didn't discuss. Ava couldn't understand how, with all that education, Catholicism still flowed so vigorously through Maria's veins. For her own part, Ava had never had a true passion for the religion, and the Church's position on sexual orientation watered down any other emotional pull she might feel. Still, she found comfort from time to time in prayer, and she was completely tolerant of other people's religious beliefs.

The church filled quickly, mainly with summer visitors, Ava assumed. The church was built almost entirely of wood in the manner of the great longhouses the Hurons and Algonquins had once built. Even the roof was patched with enormous sheets of dried birch bark. The service began and Maria quickly fell into its rhythm, her face beaming, her voice loudly echoing the refrains, her arms held out, palms turned up. Ava's mind began to wander five minutes in, as she replayed the options in her life.

She thought again about May Ling and her offer. It was flattering, and the money would certainly be great. But she didn't need the money, and she had been working basically on her own for so long she wasn't sure how well she would adapt to a more structured occupation. It was not that she didn't believe in structure, but the idea of its being imposed upon her rather than self-imposed bothered her.

Maybe I should go into business for myself, she mused. *But what would Uncle do?* she thought for what seemed like the tenth time in ten days. He had never discussed retiring, and she wondered if the day would ever come when he would walk away from work. What else did he have? He had no family. He had no hobbies except betting on horse racing, and that wasn't enough to occupy a man whose mind was still sharp and whose sense of adventure was still keen.

Well, I could always keep doing nothing for a while, she thought. And then an odd feeling gnawed at her. Was she really built to do nothing? Her best friend, Mimi, had a good job. Maria loved her work. Even her mother qualified as being employed, if playing mah-jong for money could be considered a profession. The only person she knew who actually did nothing was Mimi's husband and her own best male friend, Derek. Like Ava, Derek practised bak mei. That's how they had met—as the only two bak mei students of Grandmaster Tang. Derek was the only child of a wealthy Hong Kong family, and after graduation he had chosen to stay in Toronto and live a life of complete idleness, interrupted only by odd jobs he did when Ava needed him. But even those jobs had ended now. Mimi was pregnant, and Ava couldn't ask her husband, a father-to-be, to put himself at risk.

Ava's thoughts of Derek were interrupted when Maria leaned over and whispered, "That woman is staring at you."

"What woman?"

"The one to the right a couple of aisles down."

Ava saw only the backs of heads, and then she noticed one whose hair was pulled tightly back in a ponytail secured by a red rubber band. As the homily ended, the woman turned and looked back. It was Theresa Ng. Ava acknowledged her with a smile.

She hadn't thought about Theresa since turning off her computer on Friday evening. After returning from their meeting, Ava had opened the computer with the intention of checking emails, but almost subconsciously she typed "Emerald Lion" into the search engine. There was a small story about the company in the *Globe and Mail*'s business section, but it lacked any kind of detail.

She went to the *Sing Tao* website and tracked several stories there. The first one was longer than the *Globe*'s but also surprisingly vague on specifics. It mentioned that Emerald Lion was a private investment fund that had run into problems. No numbers were mentioned, and the story consisted mainly of quotes from unnamed investors asking that the fund's management come forward.

The same photo of Lam accompanied every article. Long, thin face. Sad, droopy eyes. A thick head of hair combed straight back and a thick, bushy moustache — unusual for an Asian. He was certainly distinctive-looking, and if Theresa's sister thought she had seen him, she probably had. Not that it mattered. There was no reason for Ava to take on the job other than to appease her mother. She had decided to call Uncle on Tuesday, because keeping her word was important to her, but she knew already he wouldn't want to take on such a minor job. Theresa and her mother would be disappointed. To avoid her mother's sharp tongue, Ava would blame Uncle.

When the Mass finished, people began to file out of the church. Maria lagged behind as always, kneeling for a final prayer. Ava sat patiently, and when Maria was done, she reached for her hand and walked with her to the exit.

The church was dimly lit, and the contrast between its dark interior and the outside world, where the sun shone unfiltered, was almost blinding. As Ava struggled to adjust her vision, Maria said, "There's that woman again."

To their right, Theresa Ng stood with an older woman. Before Ava could react, Theresa was upon her, the other woman in tow. "This is Ava Lee," Theresa said. "She is the woman who is going to help us."

Ava didn't know what to say.

"This is my mother," Theresa continued. "I told her I was coming here today before work to pray, to thank God for sending you to us, and she insisted on coming with me."

Ava still didn't know what to say.

Theresa's mother stepped forward, tears welling in her eyes, and reached for Ava's hand. "Bless you," she said.

"Auntie, please—" Ava said.

"Bless you for helping us."

"Auntie—"

Theresa intervened. "I'm sorry for disturbing you on a Sunday, at church."

Ava was grateful that at least she had restrained the mother. "I'll call you sometime next week, okay?" she said.

Theresa nodded, looking a little confused.

What did Mummy tell her after I dropped them off? Ava wondered.

Ava felt a chill in the air, a hint of autumn, and a reminder that in about twenty hours she would be making the drive south, back to Toronto, back to a life that she had spent two months avoiding.

(4)

AVA LIVED IN A CONDO IN YORKVILLE, IN THE CENTRE of Toronto, surrounded by boutiques, art galleries, restaurants, and stores on nearby Bloor Street that showcased a wide swath of the world's luxury clothing, jewellery, and leather brands. It was early Monday afternoon when she pulled up in front of her building, handed her Audi A6 keys to the concierge, and took the elevator with Maria to her unit.

The drive from Orillia had been slow and uneventful. She had dropped off her mother at her house in Richmond Hill, a northern suburb, and then worked her way down the Don Valley Expressway to the city. Maria lived just off the Danforth, the eastern extension of Bloor, only a few kilometres away, but she spent the afternoon with Ava as she stocked up on instant coffee at the Starbucks almost directly across the street from her condo and bought groceries at Whole Foods on Avenue Road. They ate dinner at a Japanese restaurant and went back to Ava's to have sex. Then Maria left to get organized for her work week.

Ava sat at the window and looked down at Avenue Road. The traffic was moving slowly, and it would be moving even more slowly in the days to come as the city repopulated after the long weekend. *What the hell am I going to do with myself?* Ava thought before going to bed.

She slept well, was up by seven thirty, made coffee, and retrieved the newspaper from the door. She carried paper, coffee, and her computer to the small table by the kitchen window. She glanced outside. The street below was teeming with traffic and pedestrians, everyone with someplace to go, something to do.

She turned on her computer and waded into her emails. May Ling had sent her daily diary and was urging Ava to think more seriously about joining forces. Amanda Yee said her father was impressed with the business she'd constructed with May and was giving her more and more responsibility; for the first time, he was talking about retiring. She made no mention of Michael. Ava had no reason to think this was a bad sign, but she did. Mimi had emailed to say she and Derek were buying a house in Leaside, a neighbourhood filled with professional daddies and yummy mummies. Ava could already feel her slipping away. And then her father, Marcus, had written that the crisis with Michael had convinced him he needed liquidity. He was going to sell all his properties and put the money into some safe interest-bearing bonds. It would allow him to spend more time with his family, he said. *Which one?* Ava wondered.

Everyone in flux, everyone in transition, she thought, her feeling of aimlessness deepening.

She decided to go for a morning run when the traffic

outside settled down, and then later in the afternoon to walk over to the house where she was tutored in and practised bak mei. She wasn't back to full strength yet, but she was getting close, and the pain the exercise brought on was becoming more manageable.

She opened the newspaper, scanned the news section, and then turned to the business section. The word *Ponzi* jumped out at her from the headline on the front page. The article wasn't related to the Theresa Ng situation, but it brought her name back into Ava's head and reminded her there was an obligation she needed to fulfill. She reached for the phone and called Hong Kong.

When Uncle didn't answer his cellphone, she called his apartment. Lourdes, his Filipina housekeeper for more than thirty years, picked up. "Ava, he is lying down," she said. Ava detected a touch of worry in her voice.

"Is there a problem?"

"Food poisoning, he says."

"Again? Didn't he have that just a few months ago?"

"And several times since then."

"Has he seen a doctor?"

"He won't go."

"What are the symptoms?"

"He gets feverish and then the chills, throws up, has the runs. I've been making him sip warm water to stop from getting dehydrated."

Ava hadn't detected anything different about him, but then she hadn't seen him since Macau. He initiated all the telephone contact, and he seemed the same man to her. "Have you talked to Sonny?"

"No, not yet, but I'm going to."

"Well, tell Uncle I called, and if he's up to it, to call me back."

Ava walked to the bathroom to get ready to go out. As she brushed her teeth and then her hair, she thought about Uncle. He had been in his late sixties or early seventies when they met, and even adding on the years they had spent together, she thought of him as ageless. It depressed her to think he might not be.

Her run took close to an hour. She went north on Avenue Road, around Upper Canada College, where the children of Canada's elite were now back in school. The kids were still arriving when she ran past, through part of the affluent neighbourhood of Forest Hill, and then turned east. She trekked over to Mount Pleasant, the western edge of Leaside — Mimi and Derek's new home — and then ran south, dodging around prams and Filipina *yayas*. When she got to Bloor Street, she turned right and headed back to Yorkville.

It was nearly ten o'clock when she walked into her condo. The message light on her phone was blinking. She checked the last number and saw that it was Uncle. Ava debated for a second about showering first, then picked up the phone and called his Hong Kong apartment.

"*Wei*," Uncle said.

"It's Ava."

"Is everything okay?" he asked.

"I was going to ask you the same question."

"I'm fine. It is just that you usually do not call unless there is something pressing."

"Sorry if I alarmed you," she said, pleased to hear his voice sounding robust. "It's just that we have been offered a sort of a job, and I wanted to discuss it with you and get your opinion."

"Sort of a job?"

"A small one, for a Vietnamese woman who knows my mother. She and her family are out of pocket for about three million Canadian dollars."

"Tell me about it," he said.

His request surprised her. She had expected him to reject it out of hand because the amount was so much smaller than the jobs they normally took on. Ava began to explain Theresa Ng's dilemma and Uncle listened without interruption. When she was finished, she said, "I feel obliged to give her an answer today or tomorrow. I don't want her hanging on to false expectations."

Uncle was so quiet Ava wondered if he was still there. Then he said, "The total scam is for about thirty million, you think."

"Yes, that's the number she used."

"Recovering thirty million interests me."

Ava wondered if he had heard her properly. "Uncle, Theresa has lost three million, not thirty."

"I know, but all those other people who lost money, you do not think they want it back?"

"I'm sure they do, but they haven't approached us, have they."

"Maybe because they do not know who we are."

Where is he going with this? she thought. It wasn't like him to complicate matters. "Uncle, I'm not about to start chasing down these people one by one to ask them to hire us."

"But there is nothing to stop Theresa Ng from contacting them, is there? Let her do the work. Tell her to get hold of them and persuade them to sign on with us, organize a meeting if she has to. Three million is of no interest, of course, but if she can deliver commitments for anything over twenty million, then let us take the job."

This was not what she had expected, and it took her a minute to process Uncle's suggestion. On the surface it made sense, at least if her intent was to stay with Uncle. How could she tell him that wasn't entirely where her head was? How could she tell him she was seriously weighing other options? *Sure as hell not in this phone conversation,* she thought. *In fact, in any phone conversation.* When and if the day came for her to part ways with Uncle, she'd tell him face to face. "Okay," she relented. "I'll call Theresa and see if she is willing to do this. If she is, I'll give her a week to pull it together. How does that sound?"

"That sounds reasonable."

Ava paused. "Lourdes told me about the food poisoning," she said as casually as she could.

"It was nothing."

"I find it unusual that you get it so frequently."

"I have to stop eating bargain sashimi."

"Was that it?"

"Every time."

"You have enough money to eat the most expensive sashimi in Tokyo a thousand times a day."

"Old habits die hard."

She knew he meant his careful spending of the Hong Kong dollar. "My mother says, 'Penny wise, pound foolish.'"

"Your mother knows a lot of clichés."

"That doesn't mean it isn't true."

He laughed. "I will be more careful."

Ava hung up the phone, feeling better about his bout

of illness but frustrated that he hadn't told her to let go of the Theresa Ng case. He was supposed to be her excuse for saying no. Now she would have to depend on Theresa's inability to deliver more clients.

(5)

HER MOTHER WAS BARELY AWAKE WHEN AVA CALLED. Her voice was throaty, smoky. "I played mah-jong until six this morning," Jennie said.

"How many hours straight was that?" Ava asked.

"Not so many. We took a break at two and went for fried noodles at Big Mouth Kee."

"Do you want me to call back?"

"What is this about?"

"Theresa."

"No, no, don't call back. Tell me now what you've decided."

Ava couldn't remember the last time her mother had been so eager to talk about anything that early in the morning. "I haven't decided anything. I spoke to Uncle, and he says he has no interest in chasing after three million dollars."

"Ava!"

"Wait, Mummy, don't start having a fit. It isn't what it seems."

"Then what is it?"

"You have to understand that for us to go after three million costs us the same amount in money and time as going after twenty or thirty million. Uncle is suggesting that Theresa contact some of the other people who got ripped off and get them to sign on with us. If we can get enough people, and enough money as a target, then he says he'll agree to take on the job."

Her mother went quiet and Ava knew she was steaming. Ava was now certain that she had told Theresa it was a done deal, and the last thing she wanted to do was eat her words. "Theresa thinks you have taken the case," Jennie confirmed.

"I don't know how that can be, since I never made a commitment. And even if I did, I report to Uncle, and the final decision is his," Ava said, giving her mother the excuse she could use.

"It won't be easy for her to do this, you know," Jennie said. "Outside of their immediate families the Vietnamese are close-mouthed. Even if they want to hire you, they won't want everyone else to know how much money they had, how much they lost."

"I'll keep their secrets. If she can get them to agree to hire us, we'll give them individual contracts. They won't have to disclose anything to anyone."

"I'll talk to her."

"It's the only way."

"You didn't have to say that," Jennie snapped.

"Sorry."

Jennie sighed. "Me too… It's just that she's such a nice woman and I really want you to be able to help her."

Ava felt the first traces of guilt creep in. "I want to help her too. So talk to Theresa and tell her to get some more people onside. When she talked to me before, she said she was getting a monthly statement of affairs from that company. All the other people have to do is bring their last statement so I can confirm what they are owed. I'll also need some basic bank information from each of them — bank name, branch address, and account number. We'll take it from there."

"I wish you didn't have to drag other people into this."

"That's the way Uncle wants it."

"And do you always do what he wants?"

"Yes," Ava lied.

It would take at least a few days for Theresa to locate and talk to the others, Ava knew, and it was by no means certain that they would want to hire her and Uncle. Agreeing to give up thirty percent would be hard for some of them, even though, as Theresa had said, seventy percent of something was better than a hundred percent of nothing.

Uncle had taught her the most basic truth about clients on the day he hired her. "They are always initially overjoyed that we will help them, prepared to pay just about anything we ask. But the moment we actually have the money, they remember that it was all theirs and they begrudge paying us even five percent, let alone thirty." It was why Uncle nearly always moved the recovered funds through their own bank account, so he could subtract the fee before passing on the balance to the client.

Ava showered and dressed. It was getting close to lunch time, and now that she was back in the city, dim sum was on her mind. She phoned Mimi, who worked within walking distance of Ava's condo, to ask if she could join her. Mimi said she had a lunch meeting at her office, so Ava called Maria's office and was told she was at a meeting in Oakville, a suburb just west of Toronto. She didn't feel like any other company, so it was dim sum alone or no dim sum.

The Dynasty restaurant was east on Yorkville Avenue, no more than a five-minute walk for Ava. She ordered hot and sour soup, har gow, chicken feet, and steamed pork wrapped in bean curd. As she started in on the soup her cellphone rang. It was a 905 area code, the outskirts of Toronto, and an unfamiliar number.

"Ava Lee," she said.

"This is Theresa. Your mother called and told me what your boss had to say."

"Yes?"

"It is done."

"Done?"

"Me and my brother contacted some of the people we know, and they did the same. I think we have about twelve people who are willing to hire you now."

"How much money does that represent?"

Theresa hesitated. "I don't really know. We didn't want to start asking people how much they'd lost. Your mother told me what you want to know and we passed that information along. Everyone who is coming to the meeting will bring their own paperwork. You have to keep it secret, though. You know that, don't you?"

"I also told Mummy it had to be more than twenty million, not more than twenty people."

"Ava, I think it is more than twenty million, but the only way to be sure is for you to look at the paperwork. That's why we organized the meeting."

"The meeting?"

"We told everyone to be at the Pho Saigon Ho restaurant on Highway Ten — Hurontario Street — in Mississauga at seven o'clock and to bring their documents."

"When?"

"Tonight."

"That's short notice."

"Our people can all make it. It's too important for them not to. And your mother said you are between jobs right now."

Between jobs, Ava thought. *More like between two women.* Why hadn't she said no when they were in Orillia? Why hadn't Uncle said no? "Pho Saigon Ho?" she said, feeling trapped.

"Yes, it has a private dining room in the back we can use. The owner is one of the people who lost money."

"Okay, I'll be there."

"That's wonderful. Thank you so much."

"And Theresa, just in case, bring me the licence plate number of the car your sister saw Lam get out of in Ho Chi Minh."

"I have it with me. Do you want it now?"

"Why not," Ava said.

As Theresa recited the number, Ava couldn't help thinking about one of the maxims of the great American community organizer Saul Alinsky: *If you don't make a decision, someone else will make it for you.* She had procrastinated, tried to fob off the decision onto Uncle, and in the end had been caught up in other people's expectations. Alinsky had been writing about Boris Pasternak's Doctor Zhivago, caught between his lover, Lara, and his wife, Tonya. He couldn't decide which woman to live with — *Too bad he wasn't Chinese*, Ava thought. *He could have had both* — and as he rode from Lara's house back to Tonya's, filled with doubt and guilt, a Red Army patrol burst from the woods and took him away to serve for years as their surgeon. If he'd made up his mind, Alinsky said, his life would have been entirely different. Ava believed that. Normally, if she was guilty of anything, it was of being too decisive. Now Theresa had turned into the Red Army.

"How many people will be there?" Ava asked.

"At least forty, maybe more."

"How many speak and understand English?"

"Some."

"I'll need someone to translate. I don't want there to be any misunderstandings."

"The restaurant owner is good."

Ava had a copy of their standard contract on her computer but had no idea how many copies she would have to bring. "Theresa, I want one person signing for each family, for each group, so how many of those will there be?"

"At least the twelve I mentioned."

"Okay, I'll bring twenty contracts just in case."

Ava checked her watch and wondered if she should call Uncle, then decided not to. Better to wait until she saw exactly how much money they would be chasing.

(6)

SHE SPENT THE EARLY PART OF THE AFTERNOON GET-ting organized for the meeting. All that really involved was printing up the contracts and going through her closet, pulling out the assortment of skirts, slacks, and shirts she wore for business. They hadn't seen daylight in months. She tried some on and to her surprise found that the skirts and slacks were a bit loose. The shirts, a wide selection mainly from Brooks Brothers, all with French cuffs, fit as snugly as before. Ava had large breasts for a Chinese woman and wasn't shy about making that plain to see.

She laid out a black skirt that came to the middle of the knee and a white linen shirt with a modified Italian collar. Then she looked at the time. She had hours to kill before she had to drive to Mississauga. Her bak mei teacher worked out of a house just north of her condo and just west of Avenue Road. He had only two students of the art, her and Derek. He made his real living teaching other martial arts to large evening classes. Derek and Ava did their training separately — bak mei is always taught one-on-one — and when she was in the city they coordinated their hours. They didn't have to call Grandmaster Tang. The afternoons were always open, and he was nearly always there and happy to see either of them.

Ava decided to forego calling Derek. It was only a short walk to the house, and if Tang wasn't there or Derek was, she could head back home. She had started taking martial arts when she was in her early teens, and had almost immediately shown ability. She was quick, agile, and fearless, and she loved to practise. In a matter of months she was so far ahead of everyone in her class of fellow teens that she was moved up to train with the adults. After two years she was at a level that almost equalled her teacher's. That's when he pulled her aside and asked if she was interested in learning bak mei. Ever since then she had been making the trek to the house in Toronto to learn from Grandmaster Tang.

Bak mei is almost the perfect martial art for a woman. The hand movements are quick, light, and short, snapping with tension at their fullest extent, where the energy is released. It doesn't take a lot of physical strength to be effective. Bak mei attacks are meant to do damage. They are directed at sensitive areas of the body, such as the ears, eyes, throat, underarms, sides, stomach, and groin. Kicks are aimed low, hardly ever above the waist.

It hadn't come completely easily to Ava. Derek was probably a more natural student, but she had persevered. And although she couldn't match his power, her lightning-quick reflexes and her ability to attack weak spots with uncanny accuracy made her formidable.

The Grandmaster lived in an anonymous two-storey brick house. He had no reason to advertise his presence to the neighbourhood or to martial arts students. Anyone in

Toronto who was the least bit serious about the arts knew who he was and where he was.

Ava rang the buzzer at the windowed front door. If he was in, he'd answer. She waited for close to a minute before she saw him coming down the stairs. She had no idea how old he was, maybe in his mid-fifties, but his usual costume of jeans and a white T-shirt revealed the body of a twenty-year-old. He smiled when he saw her and Ava gave him a little wave. Tang opened the door and then bowed his head ever so slightly. "Welcome home," he said.

They worked out for two hours, focusing on all of the core forms. On her own she tended to focus on the panther, the snake, and sometimes the crane. Tang spent close to half an hour on the dragon, and then another long stint on the tiger. He knew her tendencies and he knew her weaknesses, and he saw no reason not to strive for perfection. Ava thrived on the challenge.

It was close to five o'clock when she returned to the condo, her entire body feeling as supple as a rubber band. She showered quickly and dressed. Up north at the cottage, not only had she never dressed in anything the least bit formal, she hadn't worn a single piece of jewellery. Now her Cartier Tank Française watch came out of its case. She fastened the gold crucifix around her neck and then went through her collection of cufflinks, choosing the green jade pair she'd bought in Beijing. Finally she brushed back her shoulder-length hair, jet black and fine as silk, and secured it with an ivory chignon pin. Ava had a large collection of clasps, combs, and barrettes, but the ivory pin had become a good luck charm; she wasn't sure she could ever go on a job without it.

She called downstairs for her car. In normal traffic, Mississauga was no more than thirty minutes away, but it was five thirty and she knew the Gardiner Expressway would be packed.

It took her thirty minutes to edge her way down University Avenue to get to the Gardiner, and then a full forty-five minutes of stop-and-go traffic as she headed west on the Queen Elizabeth Highway, with Lake Ontario on her left. When she got to Hurontario, she turned north.

Mississauga, a city of half a million, bordered on metropolitan Toronto. It was a big suburban sprawl of housing developments, apartment buildings, strip malls, and the occasional larger shopping centre. The restaurant was only a kilometre north of the QEW and was, no surprise, in a strip mall.

Ava gathered the stack of contracts and tucked them under her arm. She was ten minutes early but Theresa was there already, standing at the front door. She rushed over to Ava and said, "Let me help you with those."

As Ava followed her into the restaurant, the aromas of cilantro and nuoc mam wafted through the door. Theresa walked towards the back. There were maybe twelve people in the place, and Ava began to think Theresa had misled her about the turnout. Then she heard the murmur of voices from behind a closed door. "Everyone is here already," Theresa said as she opened it.

There were about sixty people, sitting in four rows. The room went instantly quiet as the two women entered, every eye focused on Ava.

"I have to say I'm surprised you got so many people, and so quickly."

"They're desperate now. They have nowhere else to turn — that's what my brother and I told them."

Theresa walked to a table at the front with two chairs and put down the contracts. A tall, thin man with steel-grey hair got up from his seat in the front row and joined them. "This is Eddie Trinh," Theresa said. "He owns the restaurant and will act as translator."

Trinh shook her hand and then sat at the table, his arms folded across his chest. Ava remained standing as she looked at the assembly. Most of them were middle-aged or older, most likely boat people or the children of boat people — good, hard-working immigrants with old-fashioned Asian values.

"I'll speak slowly and try not to say too much at once," she said to Trinh. "It's really important that everything be explained in full, so if I go too fast or you don't understand something, please let me know right away."

He nodded and then stood beside her.

"Good evening, my name is Ava Lee," she began. She spoke for just under half an hour, explaining who she and Uncle were and how their company operated. She took one of the contracts and went through it page by page. When she mentioned the thirty percent recovery fee, she saw people glancing at one another. She went into great detail about how she and Uncle would bear the cost of expenses, regardless of the outcome.

"Now, one last thing," she said. "If we take this job you have to understand that we work quietly and discreetly. None of you can contact us, and we won't contact any of you unless there is something substantial to report or we need more information. If either of those situations arises,

I'll call Theresa Ng and she will be the go-between. So don't expect any progress reports and don't expect success right away. These things often take a lot of time, so we don't make any promises in terms of job duration or outcome. We will do the best we can as fast as we can, but the reality is that sometimes we fail. Is there anyone here who can't accept that?"

Ava looked out at a wall of blank faces. "Okay, then, let's get the contracts signed. One person per family, and I need to see the last financial statement you received from the Emerald Lion Fund. We'll put that amount in the contract and then you will sign two copies, with your name, address, and phone number. I'll sign the contract for my company. You get one copy, I get the other. So if you could, please come up here one at a time." Ava sat behind the table and took her Mont Blanc pen from her bag.

Trinh and Theresa organized a line along one wall. "I'll go first," Theresa said.

One by one, seventeen people came to the table and handed Ava a statement with a green lion logo and a slip of paper with their bank information on it. She recorded the information in her notebook, and after each contract was signed she wrote the person's family name and the amount owed in a running tally. By the tenth contract she was already over fifteen million dollars. After the last one was signed, the total was thirty-two million. Ava was beginning to realize that Lam Van Dinh had probably scammed a hell of a lot more money than had been reported.

When she had the last signature, Ava gathered together her copies of the contracts and tucked them into her Chanel bag. People were lingering, chatting among themselves and glancing at Ava. She imagined they had all kinds of questions, but she knew most of them would be hypothetical, and she wasn't in the mood for conjecture.

It was past eight o'clock when she left the pho restaurant. Theresa and Eddie Trinh walked her to the door. She saw in their faces that they had questions too, or at least the two questions that every client had: *How long is this going to take? How much do you think you can get back?*

"I meant what I said in there," Ava said. "I have no idea if I'll be able to find Lam, or, if I do, if he'll have any money, or, if he has, how much I can get back. I could be on this for weeks."

Trinh began to speak but Theresa interrupted him. "Thank you, Ava. I'm sure, if something important happens, you'll call."

"Yes, if something important happens," Ava said. "One thing I would like to know is the name of the friend of your brother who is the friend of Lam — the one who got you into this mess."

"Lac, Joey Lac."

"How can I reach him?"

Theresa paused. "I'm not sure he'll talk to you."

"Why not?"

Another, longer pause. "When the troubles began, my brother went to see him and told him he had to do something for us, and for other friends we recommended the fund to. He said he would try, and maybe he did, but nothing happened. My brother got very angry with him and they had words and, well, my brother hit him. He hasn't heard from Joey since."

"Theresa, I need you to call your brother and I need your

brother to call or go to see Joey Lac and make some kind of peace. It's important that I meet with him. Give my phone number to your brother and ask him to pass it along to Lac. I'd like to get together with him right away."

"Maybe I should call him myself."

"If you think that's best."

"I do."

"Okay, but when you talk to him, please be persistent. I'll meet him anytime at all, and I don't care where."

(7)

THE DRIVE BACK TO THE CITY WAS QUICK, AND BY nine o'clock Ava was sitting in the Italian restaurant a few steps from her condo, digging into a dish of linguine with rapini and portobello mushrooms. Her black Moleskine notebook was open on the table, and between bites she began to make a list of the things she wanted to do the following day. She kept a separate notebook for every job she undertook. In it she recorded names, numbers, dates, summaries of conversations, questions to be asked, questions answered, and her thoughts as the case unfolded. When the job was done, the notebook was put in a safety deposit box at her local bank. Ava's friends teased her for being so old-fashioned, but there was something about putting pen to paper that cemented memories and sparked her imagination. It had been three months between notebooks. And as she wrote, the first stirrings of anticipation began to form. *Maybe I've missed working after all,* she thought.

She phoned Uncle's apartment and Lourdes answered. "Is he out?" Ava asked.

"No, he's still in bed."

Ava looked at her watch. When did Uncle ever sleep this late? "Have him call me as soon as he can," she said.

She had finished the linguine and was picking at the remnants of a bowl of mixed olives when Uncle's Hong Kong number flashed on her phone screen. "*Wei*," she said, mimicking his usual response.

"You sound happy," he said.

"We have a job, I guess. We have seventeen clients who've lost a combined thirty-two million Canadian dollars."

"Good, good. It is nice to be back at work again. I was beginning to wonder if you were ready to retire before me."

"Never," she said, knowing full well he had sensed her uncertainty.

"When do you start?"

"Right away. I have things I need to do here tomorrow. And I have a Vietnamese licence plate number I need you to track for me."

"Give it to me."

She read him the number, then said, "How are our contacts in Ho Chi Minh City?"

"Excellent."

"So this shouldn't take too long?"

"One phone call, perhaps two, that is all."

"And if I need to go there?"

"You will have all the help you need. We have some old colleagues there who are still active, and they have friends with the police and the army."

"Then, in addition to the licence plate, could you ask them to come up with whatever they can on a Lam Van Dinh? He was spotted about a week ago in Ho Chi Minh, so there must be a record of his entering the country sometime in the past six months. He would have had to put his local address on the customs entry form. It could be entirely bogus, of course, but you never know."

"I will look after it."

"Thanks."

He paused, then said slowly, "Ava, I really was worried that you might have had enough of our life. I would not have blamed you if you had gone to work with May Ling."

How does he know about May? Ava thought, though the fact that he had mentioned it surprised her more than the fact that he knew about it. "I thought about it," she said.

"And so you should have."

"I guess I'm just not ready for that kind of change."

He paused again and she felt he wanted to add something. Instead he simply said, "I'll call you when I have the information."

It was a cool night, and Ava found herself shivering as she walked back to the condo. It wasn't her imagination anymore — summer was gone.

She phoned Maria to chat but just got her voicemail. She left a message, then turned on the television and found a Chinese soap opera set in the seventeenth-century Ching Dynasty. It was a guilty pleasure of hers. Her mother had been watching this soap for more than twenty years, and it had somehow caught and held Ava's interest. The court intrigue was timeless. This was the soap her mother had most missed when they were at the lake, and although Ava was loath to admit it, she had kind of missed it too.

The show was so predictable that Ava was able to get caught up in ten minutes, even after a two-month absence. As it turned out, it was a marathon night, and Ava was into her third episode when her cellphone rang, just as the provincial governor was trying to explain to his distraught and angry wife why a young woman had been seen draped around his neck. "Where were you?" she said, thinking it was Maria.

"*Wei*," Uncle said.

"Ah, Uncle, I was expecting another caller."

"Do you want me to call back?"

"No, of course not."

"I have the information on the car and on Lam."

"Already? It's been less than three hours."

"I told you we had good contacts in Ho Chi Minh."

"Obviously."

"The car generated quite a bit of interest from that end."

"How so?"

"It is registered to Lam Duc Dinh."

"A relation?"

"Yes, his older brother... and perhaps the leading neurosurgeon in Vietnam."

"That's interesting."

"Our friends think so. They are very curious why I would be asking about a car owned by such a distinguished man."

"And you told them?"

"I explained that our main interest was the brother."

"Did they have anything on him?"

"He landed in Ho Chi Minh about five months ago, and from all accounts he is staying at his brother's house."

"Is he known to them otherwise?"

"Not to any great extent. He left Vietnam twenty years ago to attend university in Canada. Until now he has been back infrequently, and then for only a week at a time, presumably to visit his family."

"So, no criminal activity?"

"Nothing on record."

"I guess I'm going to be visiting Ho Chi Minh."

"If you do, you will come through Hong Kong?"

"Of course."

"It will be good to see you," Uncle said.

He sounds sentimental, she thought, *and that's not like him.* "You too," she replied, wondering what exactly was going on in his head. "But before I book anything, could you get confirmation for me that Lam is still there? You mentioned his brother's house..."

"He is there, in the house. Our people saw him puttering around the garden."

"How did they know it was him?

"Ava, they have his passport photo."

"Of course," she said, feeling silly. "They didn't talk to him, did they?"

"Do not worry. They did not approach him."

"So that settles it. I'll try to leave tonight. I'll catch the Cathay Pacific flight to Hong Kong and connect from there."

"Don't book anything to Ho Chi Minh until late morning or early afternoon. That way we can have breakfast before you leave."

"I'll do that, and I'll email you my flight information once I have it."

"It is good to have you back," he said.

"I'll see you in Hong Kong," she said, ending the call.

I'm going back to work, she thought.

(8)

AVA SLEPT FITFULLY, HER FATHER BACK IN HER DREAMS and her half-brother Michael lingering at the edges. They were in some big city in the United States, staying in a complex of offices and factories and floors of hotel rooms all intermingled, and they had to get to the airport. Her father sent her to get their bags while he checked out. She got lost in a warren of corridors, madly taking elevator after elevator as time ticked away. Doors opened onto rooms filled with conveyor belts, other rooms crammed with desks and office workers who thought she was crazy when she demanded to know where the entrance to the hotel was. As their departure time drew closer, her panic increased. That was when Michael appeared, in an atrium two floors above her, yelling at her to join him. Afraid to try the elevators, she took the stairs. But when she had climbed the two flights, there was no exit door. In fact there was no door at all.

She woke with a start and glanced quickly at her bedside clock. It was just past seven, and she was glad to get out of bed, thinking it odd that the dream, with its recurring theme of a lost father and a distant brother, should come back to her on the second night she was in the city. Up north she had slept like a stone.

Ava went to the door to retrieve her newspaper and then made herself an instant coffee. She sat at the table by the window and read with a bit more urgency than she had the day before. She had other things to do now.

After showering, dressing, and drinking two more cups of coffee, she went through her clothes three times before finally choosing two pairs of slacks, a short skirt, four dress shirts, and two pairs of shoes. She placed them on her bed and then added her travel toilet kit, bras, panties, three T-shirts, running shoes, shorts, and her Adidas nylon jacket and training pants. *I'm going to need a real suitcase if I take all this stuff,* she thought as she looked down at the piles. Two shirts, the skirt, and a pair of shoes went back into the closet. If she wore the runners and the Adidas outfit, she'd get everything else into her Shanghai Tang leather carry-on.

When she'd finished packing, she sat down in the kitchen and picked up the phone. In rapid succession she called Maria, Mimi, and her sister, Marian, and told them she'd taken a job and was leaving the country for at least a few days. None of them seemed surprised. Marian said, "I was wondering how long it would take for you to get back at it." Mimi told her to stay in touch. And Maria, who Ava had anticipated would feel bereft, just said, "That woman at the church?" Ava felt slightly put out by their lack of concern, until she realized that none of them knew the soul-searching she'd been doing the past few months. They thought that it was business as usual, and that meant Ava getting on a plane to somewhere.

She called her mother last. It was still a bit early for Jennie and her voice was heavy with sleep. "You're leaving today?"

"How did you know?"

"Theresa called me late last night. She's very grateful. I'm very grateful."

"I made no promises, and don't you make any either. I'll do the best I can."

"I'm just happy that you're trying."

"*Trying* is the correct word."

"Are you going through Hong Kong?"

"Yes."

"Are you spending any time there?"

Ava hesitated. She knew where this would go. "Just a few hours. I only have enough time to meet with Uncle."

"Call your father anyway when you're there. If someone sees you and tells him you were in Hong Kong and you didn't at least call, he'll be hurt."

"I'll call him."

"Good. When he calls me tonight, I'll tell him to expect it."

Ava started to protest and then caught herself. Marcus and Jennie talked every day, and she was sure there wasn't a day when she and Marian weren't part of the conversation. And if Jennie talked to Marcus, Marcus would mention it to Michael, and Michael to Amanda, and Amanda to May Ling. Ava's life had been much simpler six months before.

Her cellphone rang. "Mummy, my other phone — I need to answer it."

"Keep in touch."

"Only if you promise not to ask me how I'm doing with Theresa's case."

"Ava, don't be so mean."

"Love you," Ava said, hanging up and reaching for her cell.

It was Theresa Ng, sounding depressed. "I just talked to Joey Lac, and he's not sure he wants to meet with anyone."

"Not sure or won't?"

"You'll have to phone him and find out."

"Theresa, when you said your brother hit him, what exactly happened?"

"They argued and my brother lost his temper."

"Did he hurt Lac?"

"A bit."

"What does that mean?"

"He hit him in the leg with a baseball bat."

"Oh, for God's sake."

"I'm sorry, Ava. But he didn't break his leg or anything. He just bruised it, I think."

No wonder Joey Lac isn't keen on meeting, Ava thought. "Give me his phone number," she said, exasperated.

Ava dialled the number, for a Richmond Hill accounting firm, and was put on hold for a couple of minutes. She was beginning to think Lac was going to duck her call when he came on the line with a timid "Hello."

"Mr. Lac, my name is Ava Lee and I'm an accountant. I was given your number by Theresa Ng. She told me that you had an unpleasant conversation with her brother some time ago. I just want you to understand up front that I'm calling you in a professional accounting capacity. I'd like an opportunity to meet with you — just the two of us — for a far more civilized and polite discussion about Lam Van Dinh and his fund. Do you think that could be possible?"

"I don't know anything," he said.

"You don't know anything about what?"

"The Emerald Lion Fund. I told Bobby that."

"Bobby is Theresa's brother?"

"Yes, and I told him I knew nothing about the actual fund."

"But you do know Lam Van Dinh?"

"Of course. We were schoolmates and we were friends."

"Then I really need to sit and chat with you."

"I don't understand."

Ava wondered how much to tell him. "Have you been in touch with him since he left Canada?"

"No. I don't actually know for sure he's gone, although I haven't heard from him, and I know everyone is saying he ran away."

"Well, he almost certainly did leave, and we think we know where he is. My plan is to go to see him to find out what happened to the money."

"Good luck," Lac said sharply.

"Why do you say it that way?"

"I don't think you'll find any money."

"And why not?"

He paused, and Ava knew she had to meet with him. "Look, rather than having this awkward kind of talk, why don't I buy you lunch today? I have to go to Richmond Hill anyway. Do you know where the Lucky Season restaurant is?"

"Times Square?"

"Yes, exactly," Ava said. "I'll meet you there at one o'clock. I'll be wearing a blue nylon Adidas jacket."

When he didn't answer, Ava said, "If you prefer, I can

come to your office... Mr. Lac, I'll be there alone. There is absolutely no reason for you not to talk to me. All I want is to understand the kind of person Lam is — or was — and I think you can help me do that. I have no other motive."

"I can't get away until one thirty," he said slowly.

"Then I'll see you at one thirty. And Mr. Lac, thank you, I really appreciate this."

Ava turned on her computer. There was a long email from May Ling; Ava debated telling her she was headed for Asia and decided against it. May could be emotionally taxing, and now that she was back on the job, Ava knew she needed to focus. The same held true for telling Amanda, with one additional reason: Ava knew Amanda would want to talk about Michael, and Ava wasn't quite ready to get caught up in the complexities of her father's first family.

She closed her laptop and checked her notes from the night before. *Bank Linno* was at the top of the list, right after *Joey Lac*. Ava knew of several Indonesian banks, but Linno wasn't one of them. That wasn't unusual, since there were more than a hundred commercial banks in the country. She logged on to their website and was immediately struck by how sparse it was. As she dug into the information she could access, things became even odder. The bank was headquartered in Surabaya, in East Java. Surabaya had a population of more than three million and was a major city, but it wasn't Jakarta. In fact, the bank had no presence at all in Jakarta, the capital, not even a branch. Its activity in Indonesia was restricted to East Java; from the list of branches the website provided, it seemed to be operating only in Surabaya, Batu, Malang, and Madiun.

What is a small regional Indonesian bank doing with an office in Toronto? she wondered as she clicked the INTERNATIONAL tab on the website. *And what is the same bank doing with offices in New York, Rome, Caracas, and Porlamar?*

She opened the Toronto branch's page and got nothing but an 800 phone number — no address, no contact names, no services. Without thinking, she reached for her cell and dialled the number. It rang twice and then went to voicemail. Ava hung up. *How strange is that?* she thought.

Canada had five major chartered banks and a much longer list of smaller banks and credit unions. The entire system was heavily regulated and perhaps the safest in the world. Linno could be operating without a charter; it could be a "near-bank." Ava knew of several banks that didn't deal directly with the public, that worked through financial advisors, but even they at least posted their services.

She opened the pages for the other international branches and found the same dearth of information. Then she switched back to the Surabaya headquarters. The information on the bank's Indonesian operations was much more detailed; it appeared to provide a full range of consumer and commercial services. Ava copied the branch names, addresses, phone numbers, and email contacts into her notebook. It was noon in Toronto, midnight in Surabaya. Since there was no point in calling, Ava fired off an email requesting a contact name and address for the Toronto office.

When that was done, she packed the laptop and her notebook into the large Chanel bag she used as a briefcase and called downstairs for her car to be brought up from the garage. She looked around the apartment. She had been back for only two days, but it felt like a lot longer.

(9)

THE DRIVE UP THE DON VALLEY PARKWAY WAS LABORI-ous, as usual, and the traffic didn't lessen when she exited at Highway 7 and entered Chinatown North. About 500,000 people of Chinese descent now lived in the city and the Greater Toronto Area. The first big wave had come from Hong Kong, just prior to repatriation, and was quickly followed by an influx from the mainland. The city had Chinese daily newspapers, Chinese radio and television stations, huge shopping centres built Hong Kong style, and restaurants — hundreds of restaurants — offering every known East Asian cuisine, served up by chefs recruited from the best restaurants in Hong Kong, Shanghai, and Beijing and paid huge salaries to relocate in Canada. Jennie Lee maintained that the Chinese restaurants in Toronto were now the best in the world, and Ava couldn't argue with her.

When they had first moved to Toronto, the only Chinatown was located downtown. Every Saturday morning Jennie had bundled Ava and Marian into the car and driven them there for abacus and Mandarin lessons while she shopped for Chinese vegetables and the ten-kilo bags of fragrant Thai rice that she loved. The downtown Chinatown was densely populated, so Jennie had settled herself and the kids in the northern suburb of Richmond Hill, where a wealthy, sophisticated Chinese population was beginning to expand.

Mimi had asked Ava once why so many Chinese people chose to live in Richmond Hill. The answer was simple. For years Vancouver had been the most desired landing spot for Chinese immigrants, and the town of Richmond was where they settled. When Toronto began to supplant Vancouver as the economic hub of Chinese activity in Canada, there was a migration of western Chinese Canadians. And because they—and just about everyone in Hong Kong—knew the name Richmond, Richmond Hill was where they ended up. There hadn't been many Chinese people there when Jennie brought her two daughters east, to get away from what was for her the dreary, rainy climate of Vancouver, which reminded her too much of Hong Kong. But within a few years Richmond Hill, Ontario, was as Chinese as Richmond, British Columbia.

The Lucky Season was in a strip mall named Times Square, which was modelled after a Hong Kong mall of the same name. It wasn't a fancy restaurant, but it served great and cheap dim sum. Jennie had found it years ago and had been going several times a week ever since. Each dim sum serving cost $2.20, about half of what you'd pay at most other places on Highway 7, and maybe a quarter of the tab at trendy downtown restaurants such as Lai Wah Heen. The place sat about four hundred people and was always jammed.

Ava knew the hostess—another of Jennie Lee's innumerable friends—and was immediately led past a knot of waiting customers to a table. No one complained about the preferential treatment; having connections was an accepted part of daily life in Richmond Hill, something to be admired, not envied.

The hostess asked after Jennie. Ava explained that her mother had spent the summer at a cottage. The woman—who was at least six foot two in flat shoes and had been a member of the Chinese women's basketball team—looked down at Ava in disbelief. "I thought she must have gone to Hong Kong or something. I can't see her at a cottage."

Ava shrugged. "She survived."

"Do you want hot and sour soup?" the hostess asked.

"You know I do. I'll order it now and everything else when my guest gets here."

When it came to food, Ava was absolutely biased. She believed that Chinese cuisine, in all its incredible variety and devotion to freshness, couldn't be beat. And if she had to choose just one dish, it would be hot and sour soup. She had eaten it, she imagined, literally thousands of times, in hundreds of restaurants. And every time she ate it, it was different—not just from restaurant to restaurant but even in the same restaurant on different days. Its constant surprise delighted her. The variety of potential ingredients, both necessary and optional, was so vast that minor adjustments here and there could change the entire flavour profile. As the name suggested, the soup was meant to be spicy, so pepper and chilis were a constant. It was also meant to have a slightly sour tang, so vinegar was always added to the chicken-broth base, along with—and this was where chefs got really creative — any combination and amounts of tofu, pork strips, bamboo shoots, wood ear mushrooms, shiitake mushrooms, soy sauce, sesame oil, sugar, green onions, shrimp, scallops, and duck meat.

Any restaurant that could make a good hot and sour soup could count on her business. Lucky Season made a great one, certainly in her top three. Ava liked hers especially spicy, and the chef at the Lucky Season went heavy on ground black pepper and chilis, lighter with the vinegar, and added sliced red and green peppers. His soup was a light brown colour, but Ava had also seen red, pink, and dark brown versions. She dipped in her spoon and pulled out a bright pink shrimp with a strip of wood ear mushroom wrapped around it. She ate it and smiled.

Joey Lac was on time. Ava had finished her soup and was chatting with the hostess when she saw a man hovering near the doorway, eyeing the room. He was larger than she had expected, close to six feet and carrying a lot of weight. Ava stood and waved in his direction. He looked at her and then glanced around, as if trying to make sure she really was alone. *Theresa's brother has made him paranoid,* Ava thought.

He lumbered towards her, beads of sweat visible on his upper lip and forehead. Ava held out her hand. "Thanks for coming."

"You aren't what I expected," he said.

"How's that?"

"I expected someone older, someone Vietnamese. You aren't Vietnamese, are you."

"Well, I'm older than I look, and no, I'm not Vietnamese. I'm Chinese. Why should that surprise you?"

"They don't trust many people who aren't Vietnamese."

"Maybe I'm their only hope to get their money back, or maybe after what Lam did to them they've had to reassess who they should be trusting."

"I would think it's most likely that you're their only hope," Lac said, lowering himself slowly onto a chair.

Ava sat down as well. "Anyway, again, thanks for coming."

"I didn't want to, but this is better than you showing up at my office. There's been enough trouble there, and with my family, because of this. I'm lucky to still have a job."

Questions popped into Ava's head but she caught herself, telling herself not to rush. Lac was nervous enough already. "Let's order some food and then we can chat," she said. "Is there anything in particular you like or don't like?"

"I like chicken feet."

"Duck webs?"

"Those too."

Ava filled out the dim sum menu and held it aloft for a server to take, mark, and carry off to the kitchen. "I added har gow, eggplants stuffed with fish paste, and deep-fried octopus."

"Great," he said, with no enthusiasm.

"Where did you go to school?" Ava asked.

"York."

"So did I. What year?"

"1990."

"Ah, I was a few years behind you."

"No kidding," he said, and then looked directly at her for the first time. "Tell me, just what kind of company do you work for? And what makes you think you can find Lam and, if you do, that you can get some money back?"

"My company is based in Hong Kong," she said, pleased that he wanted to get down to business. "We've been doing this kind of thing for more than ten years. People who lose money and can't get it back through traditional methods turn to us. Our client base is mainly Asian. We have a surprisingly high success rate."

"You said on the phone you know where Lam is. Do you really?"

"Yes."

"It won't matter. I don't think he has any money," Lac said.

"Someone does. The money went somewhere."

"And you'll find it?"

Ava shrugged. "You got in trouble at work?"

"A client put money into the fund."

"And with your family?"

"One of my uncles."

"What is his name?"

"Louis Lac."

The name sounded familiar. Ava pulled out her notebook and checked the entries from the Vietnamese restaurant. There he was, more than two million dollars out of pocket. "Your uncle is now a client of mine. He was one of those who hired us."

The har gow arrived at the table and Joey plunged in. Ava waited until he had chewed most of his first dumpling. "How do you know Lam?"

"We were at school, at York, together. We graduated the same year and worked at the Commonwealth Bank for a few years before going in separate directions. We always kept in touch. There was a group of us, all Vietnamese, who did that. It was a good network until Lam fucked it up."

Ava extracted a har gow from the steamer and slathered it with chili sauce. "So you weren't the only one who referred people to Lam's fund."

"No, but I'm the only one who got hit with a baseball bat."

"That was unnecessary," she said. "People can get overly emotional when it comes to money."

The other dishes began to arrive. While Lac dove into the chicken feet, Ava asked, "What kind of man was Lam?"

Lac paused. "I thought—I thought he was a good man, at least a decent man. He was an accountant, like us, and he took his job seriously. Until this shit happened I would have trusted him with my own money."

"But you didn't?"

"I didn't have enough to buy into the fund."

"Lucky you," she said, and then regretted it. Nothing he had said warranted sarcasm. "Sorry, I didn't mean that."

"I've heard worse. I used to like visiting with my uncle, but not anymore. And Bobby Ng and I were friends for years. Not anymore. Lam ruined it all."

"And you thought he was a good guy."

"Yeah. And deep down, I still do."

"Why is that?"

"If you meet him, you'll find out," Lac said.

"What does that mean?"

"Lam is so small his father tried to get him to be a jockey. And he's as timid as he is tiny. In school he was the guy who was always trying to please everyone else, to be everyone's friend. I kind of felt sorry for him until I got to know him a bit better, and found out how smart he is and how genuine he is. He wouldn't hurt a fly; really, he wouldn't. How he got himself into this mess I have no idea, but I have to tell you,

I don't think it was planned, premeditated."

"What makes you so sure?"

"I saw him after the shit began to come down. The first time was when he was starting to have trouble making payments. He told me he'd invested all the money and that the returns were slow because the bank was screwing around with new systems. He swore to me that the money was intact, and I believed him."

"Why?"

"I don't think he could have been lying. He was obviously troubled about it but he could still look me in the eye. That meant a lot to me."

"You met him more than once?"

"Yeah, about a week later my uncle came to me and asked to talk to Lam about getting his money out of the fund. I met Lam downtown. He was a mess — shaking, stuttering, not thinking clearly, almost disoriented. He told me he couldn't sleep and that he was taking pills and had started to drink. He didn't act like a guy who had salted away millions of dollars and was about to leave with it."

"What did he say about the money?"

"He said his contract required my uncle to give him thirty days' notice before withdrawal."

"Is that true?"

"I didn't know and I didn't care. I pressed him anyway, as a friend. He said he couldn't help me and just got more nervous."

"And you didn't suspect something funny was going on?"

"He said that the way the investors had reacted to one slow payment had really upset him," Lac said. "After what Bobby Ng did to me, I can't blame him."

"Like I said, that was unnecessary."

"So, I don't know, maybe Lam was nervous about someone like Bobby, someone who might use something more deadly than a baseball bat."

"You didn't ask?"

"I wasn't exactly in full control of my own faculties. All I could think about was how my uncle was going to react."

Ava glanced at her notebook. "He collected cash, correct?"

"That's the Vietnamese way."

"And put it into Bank Linno?"

"That's what he told me."

"What do you know about that bank?"

Lac shrugged. "They had one branch here, on College Street. It's closed now."

Ava gaped. "How do you know that?"

"I went there. When Lam disappeared, it was one of the few leads I had."

"And it was closed?"

"I spoke to an accountant who had an office on the same floor and he told me they'd done a weekend flyer. The landlord wasn't pleased."

"Did the accountant know anyone who worked there?"

"No, and I did ask. I also followed up with the landlord to see if he would give me the name and phone number of the person who had signed the lease. He did. It was some guy from Indonesia who the landlord was trying to chase down."

"Did you call Indonesia?"

"I did. The guy wouldn't take or return my call."

"Do you have his name?"

"It's at my office."

"Could you email it to me, with his phone number?"

"Sure."

"And the landlord's name and number as well, if you could."

Lac furrowed his brow and pressed his lips together. "I'll do it, but I think you'll be wasting your time."

Ava shook her head as she passed him her card. "My email address is there," she said. "This thing about the branch closing, how odd is that? Taking all that cash from Lam and then, when he runs into financial difficulties, closing its doors..."

"Of course it's weird, but it was hardly a mainstream bank. The office was on the eighth floor of a rundown building, and from what the accountant told me, there were never many customers coming and going."

"What kind of bank is it? I looked on its website and there was hardly any information."

"The sign on its door said PRIVATE INVESTMENT BANK, so it probably wasn't offering any kind of regular service."

"Did it have a charter?"

"Not that I could find, and I did look."

"I'm sure you did," Ava said.

"It just dead-ended."

"When was the last time you saw or heard from Lam?"

"When I met with him to ask for my uncle's money back."

"Did he ever say anything about the bank?"

"Not a word."

"And you really don't think Lam took off with the money?"

Lac tossed back his head, his eyes pressed shut. "No, and I wish I did. It would be easier that way, because there would at least be some hope of recovering it. But it isn't like Lam to steal. He just isn't that kind of person."

"So you insist," Ava said. "But if he didn't steal it, where did it go?"

(10)

AVA OPENED HER EYES TO THE GLARE OF CABIN LIGHTS. She looked out the window onto the South China Sea, glittering under the morning sun and dotted with ships that would increase in density every kilometre they drew closer to Hong Kong. She stood, stretched, and then went to the bathroom to pee, brush her teeth and her hair, and get her mind settled.

Chep Lap Kok was one of a series of newer Asian airports — Bangkok, Singapore, Kuala Lumpur, Beijing — built simply to move people and baggage as efficiently as possible. It had none of the romance of the old Kai Tak Airport in Kowloon, which was approached through a mountain pass over Victoria Harbour and was surrounded by apartment buildings so close that washing hung out to dry seemed to flutter against the sides of the planes.

Lap Kok was built on a manmade island in the middle of nowhere, about twenty kilometres from Hong Kong. Its virtue in Ava's eyes was that she could deplane, clear Customs, and get her baggage (if it had been checked) in about fifteen minutes. Then, to get to the city, she could ride a high-speed train or take a cab along airport-dedicated six-lane highways. Kai Tak was only a ten-minute cab ride from Uncle's apartment, but by the time she had cleared Customs — many times the lines in the arrivals hall extended into the corridors — and lined up for a cab, it took longer to get to Uncle's than it did from Chep Lap Kok.

As usual, Ava was through Customs and into the arrivals area within minutes. She was starting towards the taxi stand when she heard her name called. She turned and saw Sonny. He was standing beneath the sign that read MEETING PLACE.

She blinked and then looked for Uncle. He wasn't in sight. Sonny waved uncomfortably. Ava started to walk towards him, and as she did, tears welled in her eyes. The last time she had seen him, he was carrying her in his arms from the house in Macau. It had been a one-sided battle: three dead and one badly wounded on the other side, Ava the only one wounded on theirs. Sonny had probably saved her life.

"Hey, boss," he said. He was wearing a black suit, white shirt, and black tie, none of which did much to make him look any less menacing. He was just over six feet, broad, thick, and incredibly agile. Ava couldn't think of another man more fearsome.

"Sonny," she said, holding out her arms.

They hugged, something new in their relationship, something that had been changed by Macau.

"Good to see you. We weren't sure you were coming back."

"Neither was I."

He reached for her carry-on. She resisted, but only for a second. They walked side by side to the exit. She had always felt small beside him, and never more so than now, as memories of Macau came charging into her head. She hadn't thought about it, she realized. Or she had chosen to forget it. Either way, being with Sonny brought it all back.

"I told Uncle not to come to the airport," she said.

"He sent me anyway."

They left the airport and walked almost directly into the silver Mercedes S-Class that was Uncle's new car. It was standing in a no-parking zone with a policeman alongside. He smiled at Sonny, and for a moment Ava thought he was going to open the doors for them. Instead he gave a slight bow of his head and moved away from the car. Ava started to open the front door, but Sonny put his hand on hers and opened the back. "You know Uncle always rides in the rear," he said.

She hesitated and saw Sonny frown. She slid into the back seat and turned on her phone as they pulled away from the terminal. There was one voicemail from Maria, who sounded a lot more downcast than she had when Ava said she was going back to work. It was early evening in Toronto and Ava could have reached her. She decided not to. When she was on a job, she tried to keep her personal life and any distractions it might bring at bay. It was a good habit to get back into.

"We aren't going to the Mandarin," Sonny said, his eyes looking at her in the rear-view mirror. "Uncle said the last time you were here you ate *jook* in Kowloon and that it brought you luck. He'll meet you at the same restaurant."

"That's fine," Ava said.

They drove the first part of the trip to Hong Kong in silence. Sonny wasn't a talker at the best of times and Ava was entirely comfortable with silence, so it was a natural state for them both. But as they crossed the Tsing Ma Bridge and Hong Kong bore into view, Sonny said, "I can't tell you how happy he is that you're here and that you're working on a job together again."

"It will be good to see him too."

"He needed this."

"What do you mean?" Ava asked.

"He needed something to be interested in again," Sonny said. "Lourdes and I have been worried about him."

"You're scaring me," Ava said quickly. "Is there something going on that I need to know?"

Sonny half turned towards her. "We aren't sure."

"Sonny, talk to me, please."

"There is nothing really to talk about, no real reason to be scared. It's just that there have been days when he hasn't left the apartment, and you know that isn't like him. And then there are other days when he's left by himself, without telling me. That isn't like him either."

"Do you know where he goes?"

"No."

"Sonny, this is too strange."

She saw from his eyes in the mirror that he was confused. "Lourdes thinks he's just getting old."

"He is old."

"Of course he is, but he's never acted old. His mind was always so sharp, and physically he was never a man to have aches and pains."

"What's changed?"

Sonny hesitated, and she knew that it was difficult for him to talk about Uncle in any way other than with complete, blind respect. Even suggesting a normal human frailty would seem to him a betrayal of sorts.

"We're like a family, Sonny," she said.

"He's been talking to me about the old days," he said slowly. "We've been together for more than twenty years. He pulled me out of trouble, you know. I had a temper back then, and I never thought twice about anything; I'd just react to whatever got in my face. Well, I went too far when I was running a small gang in the New Territories. Uncle was the boss — the big boss — and it was up to him to decide what would happen to me. He could have just given the order, but instead he sent for me and we talked. I'd never met him before. It turned out we shared a common kind of childhood; there was a connection — rough, of course. He told me he thought I could be useful to him if I could control myself. I said, 'I don't know how to do that.' And Uncle said, 'Just do exactly what I tell you to do. Do not try to think for yourself anymore. Life will be easier for you that way.' And it has been."

Ava felt her cheeks flush. The relationship between Sonny and Uncle had been one she had observed but had never tried to analyze or question. It had a life of its own, closed to outsiders. She had never expected Sonny to be the one to talk about it. She was also taken aback by how long he had gone on for. She wasn't sure she had ever heard him utter more than two or three consecutive sentences. "You say he's been talking about the old days?"

"Yeah, and he never did that before. Oh, when he was with Uncle Fong or some of his old colleagues, they'd reminisce about it, but he never did it with me. Now he does."

They exited the bridge and began the slow crawl through Hong Kong towards the Cross-Harbour Tunnel to Kowloon. "What does he say to you?" she asked.

"It bothers him what's happened to the societies. It all came to a head when he couldn't help you with that asshole in Macau. He told me that when he was chairman, he thought he had brought some structure to them and that the oaths meant something again. But as soon as he left, everything reverted to shit. He feels his time was wasted, that part of his life was wasted."

"He still has so much to be proud of."

"He doesn't seem to want to listen to that."

"Well, I'll talk to him," she said.

Sonny fell silent again and Ava wondered if he'd dismissed her offer. Then he said, "Yes, I think you need to. You may be the only person he actually listens to. Me and Lourdes, we're like old furniture."

There was a lineup of cars leading into the tunnel, and Ava silently wished they had stayed with her plan to meet on the Hong Kong side. "This won't take so long," Sonny said, as if reading her mind.

"Those aches and pains you talked about—anything specific?" she asked.

"He seems to be having stomach problems more often than he should, and he isn't eating as much as he used to. Lourdes says he's lost weight."

"He told me he'd been eating too much cheap sashimi."

"That's bull. He hasn't eaten Japanese in months, unless he's doing it behind my back. He used to have a healthy appetite but now he's picking at his food, and he's cut out a lot of stuff from his diet. That's why I think he wants to meet you in Kowloon. He eats congee every morning now, and sometimes Lourdes says he has it for dinner."

Ava felt a twinge of guilt for even thinking about the inconvenience of the Cross-Harbour Tunnel. "Has he been to see a doctor?"

"We don't know."

"Is it possible that on the days he leaves the apartment without you, maybe he's going to see one?"

Sonny shook his head and sighed. "I never thought of that... Why the fuck didn't I think of that?"

"If he gave you no reason to think it, why would you?"

"But you did."

"I'm as sneaky as he is."

Sonny slapped the steering wheel. "I'm going to park my ass outside the apartment on the days he says he doesn't need me. I'll tail him."

"That's a good idea," Ava said, though she could hardly imagine Uncle not picking up on Sonny's presence. "Another thing you can do is talk to Lourdes and find out who his doctor is. I'd like to know myself."

"I'll do that," Sonny said as they finally made their way into the tunnel and began the last leg to Kowloon.

The restaurant was in Tsim Sha Tsui, near the Star Ferry terminal. The area was jammed with buses and taxis, and even Sonny couldn't find a place to park, legally or otherwise. He dropped her off at the entrance and told her to call his cell when they were done.

Uncle was already there. She couldn't remember the last time she had gone to meet him and had to wait. The front entrance was crowded, but she spotted him between the bodies of the people in front of her. He sat in a booth with a pot of tea in front of him, his legs dangling off the floor. Like Sonny, he was wearing a black suit and a white shirt, closed at the collar. His hair was still mainly black, though there were more streaks of grey than she could remember. His face was almost completely unlined. He was short, no taller than her, and now he looked as if he had shrunk a little and, as Sonny said, lost some weight. Ava stared hard at him. His dark brown eyes seemed as lively as ever, and if he was worried, there was no sign in them.

She pushed through the throng and walked towards him.

He saw her and a grin lit up his face. He stood and reached for her. "As beautiful as ever, my girl, as beautiful as ever."

She kissed him on the forehead. "I'm so happy to see you."

"You do not mind us eating here?"

"Of course not. You know I love congee."

"Truthfully I did not feel like driving to Hong Kong or putting up with the Star Ferry in rush hour."

"And I'm sure the walk did you good."

The waitress hovered, anxious to get their order, get their food, get the table turned.

"Do you know what you want?" Uncle asked Ava.

"Congee with chopped spring onions in it."

"I will have the same, with salted eggs and pickled vegetables on the side," he told the waitress.

"Oh, I also want *you tiao*," Ava said.

"Of course," said Uncle.

It was at their table in a matter of minutes. Congee and *jook* were the same thing, a simple rice porridge. Ava added soy sauce and white pepper to hers and then dipped *you tiao* — a deep-fried breadstick — into it. Uncle left his plain but took bites of egg and vegetable between slurps. "I come here many mornings," he said. "Lourdes would be upset if she knew. She thinks she makes the best *jook* in Kowloon, and I do not have the heart to tell her otherwise."

"I won't say a word."

"I was sitting here waiting for you and thinking about the last time we were here."

"Seems like years ago."

"I was so worried about you."

She glanced up at him from her bowl. There was that sentimentality again, but his face showed none of it. "It wasn't anything we couldn't handle, was it. At the end of the day we prevailed," she said.

"Somehow."

"I'm sorry if I dawdled all summer," she said, trying to get them closer to the present. "It took weeks before my leg began to function anything close to normal, and by then I was at the cottage and feeling lazy. I'm back at work now, so let's put worries aside."

He ate slowly, carefully skimming congee from the top as if it were a hundred-dollar bowl of shark's-fin soup, then emptying his spoon with tiny slurps. He had never been a careful eater, but now he was being deliberate. She found herself resting between spoonfuls so as not to get too far ahead of him.

"I have to tell you, I'm not sure that my going to Ho Chi Minh City will result in anything positive," she said. "This could be a short assignment."

"Why do you say that?"

She detailed her meeting with Joey Lac, emphasizing his belief that Lam was incapable of a theft of that magnitude.

"It is always the ones we never suspect until it is too late," Uncle said, discounting the opinion with a little wave of his hand.

"Still, Lac did know him well."

"You will find out for yourself soon enough."

"What arrangements have you made in Vietnam?" she asked.

"You will be met at the airport by a friend. He will be wearing civilian clothes but he is an officer in the police force, District One. He will do whatever you want him to do... within reason, of course."

"I'm not anticipating that Lam will give me serious trouble. He's an accountant, not a thug."

"Just be cautious. Remember, his brother is a man of substance, and in Vietnam he is also going to have friends. In that country that invariably leads to the police or the army."

"I'm not going to do anything rash," Ava said as she took her notebook from her bag. She tore off a blank page and copied the information on Bank Linno that Lac had emailed her. "Do we have contacts in Indonesia?" she asked.

"Some. Mainly in Jakarta, of course."

She slid the paper across the table to him. "This bank is headquartered in Surabaya. I have only one name attached to it, plus a phone number and an email address. Could you find out what you can about the bank?"

"This is connected to Lam?"

"Very much so."

"Never heard of the bank."

"It was big enough to have a branch in Toronto, and that is where Lam deposited the cash he was collecting. The strange thing is, it shut down its office shortly after Lam ran into trouble."

"Do you think there is a connection?"

It wasn't his nature to leap to conclusions, no more than it was hers. Slow and steady had always been their style: A to B to C until they got to the end, not taking shortcuts, because shortcuts more often than not led to wild goose chases and a waste of time and money. "I don't know what to think," she said. "I need to get to Lam first."

"I will find out what I can from Indonesia," Uncle said.

"Thank you."

He set his spoon aside, the *jook* only half finished. "I have to tell you that I was surprised when you called me to talk about this job."

His face was impassive, but Ava heard the slight tremor in his voice. "Why should you have been?" she asked.

"I thought that after Macau you might have decided the risks were not worth the rewards anymore. I mean, you have enough money never to have to do this kind of thing again, and you are so damn bright you could do anything else you wanted."

Ava reached over and rested her fingers on the back of his hand. "This is about May Ling again, isn't it."

He smiled. "She is not as subtle as you, although she likes to think she is. She called me yesterday, not for the first time, and actually asked me if I had ever thought about returning home to Wuhan. And when I said I had — which was true ten or fifteen years ago — she said that Changxing and she would be honoured if I would take a position in their corporation, some elder-statesman kind of role. This from a woman who resisted hiring us for that job because she did not want their family name associated with mine. She must want you to join her very badly if she is willing to put up with me."

Ava saw no point in being anything other than direct. "Uncle, you helped bring May and I together. Now we're friends. And yes, she has been trying to get me to become part of their firm. Truthfully, I have thought about it, and I have decided that I'm not ready yet. Maybe one day I will be, but not yet. Are you okay with that?"

"Of course. You owe me nothing."

"I owe you everything," she said, more sharply and loudly than she had intended.

His eyes turned away from the table, looking towards the front window. "I see Sonny has been circling. We need to get you to the airport and I need to make some calls to Indonesia, and maybe even the Philippines. My contacts are not so good in Indonesia, but I know Uncle Chang is strong there."

"If you talk to him, send him my regards," Ava said.

"We speak every week," Uncle said. "He is still at Tommy Ordonez's right hand, and I expect he will die there."

(11)

SONNY DROVE HER TO THE AIRPORT. THEY DIDN'T speak until they had cleared the tunnel and were heading through Hong Kong towards the bridge. "You need to keep track of him," Ava said. "He seemed not too bad to me — his mind is still sharp, but physically I see a bit of deterioration. What bothers me most is that he seems to be getting maudlin."

"That's the word I was searching for earlier, when I told you about him wanting to talk about the old days."

"I don't think it's a symptom of anything. We could be overreacting to simple mood swings, so don't press him, eh? If you are going to tail him, be discreet; remember who you're dealing with. He has always been sensitive to his physical surroundings, and unless you're careful he'll spot you in a moment."

"I was thinking of using someone else, a female friend he's never met."

Ava nodded. "That's a great idea, Sonny. Really, a great idea. This woman, though, she's professional enough to pull it off?"

"Yeah."

He said it so aggressively that it triggered a host of questions in her head. She ate them all. "Good. Please keep me posted."

Sonny dropped her off at the VIP departures gate. It took her less than five minutes to check in at Cathay Pacific and only ten minutes more to clear Customs and Immigration on the departures level; she was through security in another five. She had given herself two hours, so she headed for the Cathay first-class lounge. She grabbed a double espresso and copies of the *South China Morning Post* and the *International Herald Tribune* and deposited herself in one of the big easy chairs the lounge provided.

The papers headlined a huge sell-off of stocks in the United States that had evidently been triggered by a computer entry mistake. Some trader selling futures had punched in sixteen billion instead of sixteen million, and the computer had taken over from there. Ava's money was widely distributed — Canadian government bonds, Canadian bank stocks, gold, real estate investment trusts — and she hardly gave market activity a thought, but she found it alarming that so much value could be vaporized through sheer stupidity.

Her cellphone rang. She looked at the screen and saw the name MARCUS LEE. All thoughts about the U.S. stock market disappeared. "Hi, Daddy," she said, kicking herself for not having called him first.

"Mummy said you were going to be coming through Hong Kong," he said.

"I'm in the Cathay lounge at the airport, in transit to Vietnam."

"Back at work, she says."

"Yes, and mainly because of her, in case she didn't tell you. One of her friends lost some money in an investment fund and Mummy put her on to me. A small case, really, and one that I don't think is going to last too long or result in too much."

He paused, and Ava braced herself. Instead he said, "Just be careful."

"I promise I'll be careful."

"Make sure you do. Ava, I know you're entirely capable, but all of us overreach. Look what happened to Michael."

"He survived."

"Speaking of Michael, did you look at your emails today?"

"No, why?"

"Amanda and he have set a wedding date. Our two families had dinner together last night and went over the details."

Ava had an immediate and almost irrational flash of jealousy. Neither Michael nor Amanda had mentioned anything about a specific wedding date to her. And when Marcus mentioned the two families, he meant the Yees and he and his first wife. Ava hadn't paid much attention to the wedding plans, and now that she did, her only thought was whether she would be invited. The instant it came, she just as quickly dismissed it. There was no way, no way at all, she could envision Michael's mother, her father's first wife, agreeing to have Jennie Lee's daughter at the wedding. It was one thing to have a husband with second and third families who were out of sight; it was another to have one of the offspring from those unions at what would be a large, public, and high-profile event. It wouldn't matter what Michael and Amanda wanted. Neither of them would go against his mother.

Jack Yee, Amanda's father, whom Ava knew well and had helped, would be happy enough to invite her if she asked. As soon as that idea came to her she trashed it, and her jealousy began to turn into anger. Her mother understood, accepted, and respected the position that Wife Number One had in the family, and she had passed on that respect and understanding to her two daughters. *But that respect has to cut both ways*, Ava thought. So if she was going to be at the wedding, the invitation would have to come from the Lee side of the family. To accept anything else would be disrespectful to her own mother and downgrade the relationship that Jennie, Ava, and Marian had with Marcus Lee.

"When is it scheduled for?" Ava asked as calmly as she could.

"January. I know it's a bit odd, but it fits their work schedules."

"And where?"

"The Grand Hyatt."

"Nice."

"Jack can afford it, and Amanda is his only child."

"I know."

"So do you think you can get over here for it?"

Ava was sure she had misheard. "What?"

"I wish you had checked your emails; it would have been better that way. But since you haven't, I guess it's up to me to tell you. Amanda wants you to be her maid of honour."

"Daddy, that is crazy," she said without thinking.

"Amanda doesn't think so, and neither does Michael."

"But Michael's mother —"

"Is fine with it."

"How is that possible?"

"Our lives, especially mine, are evolving in unexpected ways. This is just one more twist."

"Don't talk in riddles."

"Elizabeth loves our children to death, and none more than her oldest. They have always been close—almost abnormally so—and they confide in each other. Michael told her about meeting you for the first time at the Mandarin. Michael told her about the problems he was having. Michael told her that he had asked you to help. And when it was all finished, Michael told her you had saved him and his business."

"I see," Ava said, feeling a touch of guilt about her ambivalence towards her half-brother.

"And then Amanda weighed in."

"I don't understand."

"Elizabeth told me that you and Amanda had a conversation during the direst part of Michael's crisis."

"We had more than one."

"This one was very specific. Amanda told Elizabeth that you weren't helping Michael because of what his problems might mean for him. She said you were doing it to protect the family, that Michael had put it at risk, and that you couldn't let him bring down his father, your mother, two aunties you have never met, and two small children in Australia whom you also haven't met."

"I do remember saying that," Ava said softly.

"Elizabeth asked Amanda if she believed that, and Amanda said she believed it with all her heart."

"That was kind."

"No, that was the truth."

"Still."

"So when Michael went to see his mother two weeks ago to tell her about the wedding plans, he asked her point-blank if she could accept having you there as part of the bridal party. And Elizabeth said, 'I can't only not deny her, I should be welcoming her with open arms.'"

Ava experienced an uncommon sensation: she was at a loss for words. "Good grief," she said finally.

"There you are."

"So now what?"

"Tell them you'll be there."

Yes, Ava thought, and then thoughts of her mother loomed. How would Jennie Lee take it? Would she regard it as an act of disloyalty? "Daddy, someone has to talk to Mummy about this. You do understand she could be hurt if I accept."

"Yes, I do, and I'll be the one to talk to her."

"Thanks... I love you."

Ava ended the connection and then felt a surge of conflicting emotions. *What a morning*, she thought. What with Sonny and then Uncle and her father and the complications surrounding the wedding, she had gone through more turmoil that morning than she had for the past two months.

She checked the incoming emails on her iPhone. More than forty had accumulated during the past twenty-four hours. She went directly to Michael's. It was headed WEDDING!!!!!! She read it quickly and couldn't help noticing that he seemed to take her acceptance as maid of honour for granted. Amanda was less effusive and more guarded, simply saying she would be pleased if Ava would agree. Ava replied to Amanda first, drafting an email that started with Have you thought long and hard about this? Then she deleted it and wrote one to both Michael and Amanda, saying she would be thrilled to play any role in the wedding party.

When that was done, she turned her attention to the other messages. The first to catch her attention was from Joey Lac, asking her to let Theresa and Bobby and his uncle know that he had been helpful, then reiterating his belief that although Lam Van Dinh was capable of being stupid and could have lost the money in some ill-timed investment, he couldn't buy into the idea that Lam had stolen the money. He asked Ava to keep that opinion to herself, because he knew it might offend everyone who had lost money in the fund. At the tail end he affixed the names, email addresses, and phone numbers of the contact at Bank Linno in Surabaya and the Toronto landlord.

The other emails were one from Maria, saying that Toronto was already a lonely place; the daily missive from May Ling; and one, dotted with capital letters, from Mimi. We spent the day looking at houses and I can't believe how patient Derek is. All he seems to want is for me to be happy. I've turned into this GAS MACHINE, but he doesn't seem to mind. In fact, he doesn't seem to mind anything connected to the pregnancy, including FOUR TRIPS TO THE BATHROOM EVERY NIGHT, BOOBS THE SIZE OF BED PILLOWS, AND SCREWING DOGGY-STYLE. Lucky me. Thanks to you.

Ava smiled. Thanks was the last thing she deserved. She had been desperate to keep them apart.

She skimmed quickly through the other messages and

then put the phone back into her bag. She hadn't replied to anyone except Michael and Amanda. Toronto seemed very far away, and Ava was beginning to feel the disconnection that took over whenever a job began.

(12)

THE FLIGHT TO HO CHI MINH TOOK TWO AND HALF hours and the plane landed on time, just before three o'clock, at Tan Son Nhat airport. It parked near the runway and waited for buses to ferry the passengers to the terminal. "This is going to be murder," the businessman sitting next to Ava said.

She shrugged, but the same thought had flashed through her head. On her only other trip to Ho Chi Minh, it had taken more than two hours to deplane and clear Customs and Immigration. The airport had been built in the 1950s, and even operating at peak efficiency it couldn't effectively process the massive influx of tourists and businesspeople. The Customs and Immigration staff seemed to be in a permanent state of work-to-rule.

The buses came and the airline made a fuss about letting the first-class and business-class passengers off first. They were conveyed to the terminal, and to Ava's delight it was brand-new. She began to feel more optimistic about their chances of getting through the airport quickly. But as soon as Ava saw the line, her optimism faded. It began almost as soon as they entered the terminal, snaking up the stairs that led to the arrivals hall. "Fuck. We'll be here for three hours or more," the man beside her said.

Ava took some deep breaths. There was no point in getting agitated over something over which she had no control. Then she saw a policeman walking down the stairs holding a cardboard sign over his head that read AVA LEE. *God bless Uncle*, she thought. She stepped out of line and waved at him. He smiled and motioned for her to climb the stairs towards him. As she passed her fellow passengers, she heard muttering. None of it was complimentary.

"My name is Tran," the cop said. He was in his early thirties, she guessed, tall and slim, his dark hair slicked back. He was in uniform, not plain clothes as Uncle had said, a gun on one hip, a phone and truncheon on the other. The bars on his shoulders indicated he was a lieutenant.

"I'm Ava Lee."

He looked down at her. "You aren't what I expected. Younger, and a lot more informal," he said in excellent English.

She looked down at her training pants and Adidas jacket. "These are my travelling clothes. I need to shower and change into something more professional. And I'm older than I look."

"Let's get out of this place," he said. "The air conditioning hasn't broken down yet but it does most days, and then these people in line start getting really cranky. You almost need riot control sometimes."

Ava fought back a sarcastic comment. "I'll follow you," she said.

They walked into an arrivals hall that was filled to

bursting. He pushed his way to the far end, Ava tucked in behind him. There was an empty booth with the words DIPLOMATIC CORPS above it. Tran stepped into the booth and asked for her passport. She passed it to him and then watched with bemusement as he opened it and stamped it with a flourish. "You have that authority?" she asked.

"They know who I am," he said.

They had to fight their way through the throng waiting for the arrivals. It was hot, and as they got close to the door, hotter still. She could only imagine what it would be like for the people inside if the air conditioning did pack it in.

Tran had come in a police car that was parked by the curb. He opened the trunk and she put her bags inside, directly on top of two shotguns. "Front or back seat?" he asked.

"I don't want to pull up at the Park Hyatt looking like I've just been arrested," she said.

He opened the front door and then walked around to his side before she got in.

"I'm not sure what your schedule is," he said as she sat next to him.

"Hotel, shower, change. And then I want to go to the house where Lam is."

"The place is only about a fifteen-minute drive from the hotel, in good traffic."

The words *good traffic* were delivered the same way they were in Bangkok, Jakarta, and Manila — as wishful thinking. "You don't have to wait for me," she said.

"I know, but I will anyway. Your boss in Hong Kong is well connected here. I've been told to make sure you get everything you want, within reason."

"Define *within reason*."

"Lam's brother is a doctor, a famous surgeon, actually. He should be treated with respect."

"I know of no other way of dealing with people," she said.

"Good."

He pulled away from the terminal and started to drive towards the city. The Hyatt was almost in the middle of District 1, only about six kilometres from the airport. Ava saw at once why he had mentioned the traffic. It was brutal: what seemed like thousands of motorbikes, cyclos, and bicycles in one steady, impenetrable stream, cars crawling along in their wake. She remembered the motorbikes. They never seemed to stop coming, and in a city with hardly any traffic lights, crossing the street took agility, guts, and good luck. Ava had quickly learned to attach herself to locals and to follow their every bob and weave. "We may be an hour or so getting to the hotel," Tran said.

"No rush."

"Wouldn't matter if there was, though I could put on the siren and save us ten minutes." He laughed.

"Where did you learn English?" she asked.

"Here. My mother was a language teacher and she taught me French and English at home. I went to university in Australia, so that helped as well."

Ava sat back in her seat and watched the more nimble motorbikes dart around them. Some of them were taxis and had girls perched on their back seats, looking elegant in their *ao dai*s and *ao ba ba*s. It amazed Ava that so many women wore traditional clothing — the *ao ba ba* like silk pyjamas; the *ao dai* a high-necked, long-sleeved, fitted silk and cotton tunic with a mandarin collar and slits down each side, worn over long, wide-legged pants. There were more Japanese and German cars on the street than she remembered from her first trip; fewer of the cars were old Renaults, a hangover from the French colonial days.

They skirted the Reunification Palace, which had been the presidential palace before the fall of Saigon in 1975. There was a tank sitting on the front lawn, a tribute to the communist forces who had crashed the palace gates, and a Huey helicopter on the roof, symbolizing the flight of the Americans and their Vietnamese allies. Tran nodded in the palace's direction. "You should visit there," he said.

Every local she had met on her previous trip had said the same thing. "I have," she lied.

Traffic opened up a little as they neared the Hyatt, and it was just past four when Tran pulled into Lam Son Square and entered the circular driveway at the front of the hotel. "I'll leave my car here. I'll be at the bar when you're ready to leave."

She checked in and managed to get a room on the top floor, the ninth, where she would have a good view of the city and, she hoped, the Sai Gon River. The hotel was advertised as five-star and it didn't disappoint. Her room was spacious; the wooden floors gleamed; the bed was covered in a snow-white duvet that looked as if it could swallow her. She unpacked quickly, leaving her change of clothes on the bed, and then stripped and went into the bathroom. It had a walk-in rain shower that she almost leapt into. She showered for five minutes, maybe longer, luxuriating in the gentle spray and soaping head to foot.

When she came out and reached for a towel, she saw herself in the mirror that took up most of a wall. She was proud of her body. Genes had given her beautiful proportions and breasts that were firm and high despite their size. The rest of it was her doing — more exercise than diet, though. She was lean and muscular. She turned sideways. Her tummy was still completely flat; her bum was hard if not quite round. The only imperfection she could see was the scar on her thigh, and she was even beginning to like it. She pulled her hair back, stretching her body like a cat.

Ava dressed in the bedroom: white bra and panties, black slacks, and a white Brooks Brothers shirt with a modified Italian collar and French cuffs, which she fastened with the green jade links. Her shoulder-length hair was still a bit damp from the shower, so she brushed it with vigour until it felt dry. She pulled it back with the ivory chignon pin, which seemed to sparkle in contrast to her silky jet-black hair. She then took black mascara and red lipstick from her makeup bag and applied them lightly.

She stepped back and looked at herself again in the mirror above the dresser. She hardly recognized herself. More than two months of shorts, T-shirts, tracksuits, no makeup, hair tied back, and no jewellery had created a perception of herself that a five-minute shower, a change of clothes, a little makeup, and her hair properly fixed had crushed. She knew she looked good, and she felt good. Maybe she was ready to go back to work after all.

Tran sat at a small table in the bar, a glass of what looked like sparkling water in front of him. He was positioned so he could see everyone entering the room, and Ava felt his eyes on her the second she stepped into it. However, it wasn't until his attention moved to her face that he seemed to realized it was her. He stood quickly, a sheepish grin on his face. "You've changed," he said.

"Can we go?" she asked. She drew more stares as they walked through the lobby. Her walk was unhurried, her shoulders square, her breasts ever so slightly thrust forward. Tran kept looking sideways at her.

The police car was parked directly across from the main entrance. Tran opened the front door for her, and this time he waited until she got in before closing it after her. As they pulled away from the Hyatt, Ava said, "Tell me everything you know about Lam."

"Which one?"

"Both, I guess."

Traffic was even denser now than the hour before, and Tran had to sit at the curb for several minutes before he could pull out and into Lam Son Square. Ava saw him reach for the siren button. "I'd rather you didn't," she said.

"Just for a few minutes. If I don't use it, we could be in this two-block area for at least twenty minutes."

"Okay."

The screech inside the car wasn't as bad as she had imagined it would be. Outside it must have sounded louder, because cars and even motorbikes began to peel to one side, creating enough of a lane for Tran to scrape through. When they finally reached a boulevard where traffic was moving at a normal pace — which still meant slowly — he turned off the siren.

"Tell me about Lam the surgeon first," she said.

Tran pulled a toothpick from his chest pocket and began to dig at his teeth. Ava wondered if that was a ploy to buy time while he figured out what he should and shouldn't say.

He began to speak in a monotonous, rehearsed voice. "The family is from a village in the south. The father was a farmer and non-political. All he wanted to do was farm and raise his three sons. Sometime in 1973 he decided that Nguyen and his cronies, the Americans, weren't going to win the war, so he began to quietly help his brothers from the north. It was a practical matter, I think, not ideological. But in any event, by the time the famous tank from the north crashed through the gates of the Presidential Palace on April 30 to end the war, Lam had friends on the winning side. And he wasn't a man who was shy about asking his friends for favours."

"*Guanxi*."

"Of course. The family, like many, is Vietnamese Chinese. They know the importance of *guanxi*, and Lam used his. He didn't ask for a lot. His sons were very bright and all he wanted was for them to have as much education as they could manage. The oldest brother is the neurosurgeon. He is a very capable man, and also a great nationalist. He has been offered positions overseas that would pay him ten or maybe a hundred times more money than he makes here, but he has chosen to remain... something that has not gone unnoticed."

"You said three sons?"

"Yes, the middle son died about ten years ago in a car accident."

"I see."

"The father and the mother are dead now as well, so that leaves the surgeon and his younger brother. The surgeon has a wife but no children, so the brother is very important to him."

"I understand," Ava said.

"The brother left Vietnam twenty years ago to attend school in Canada, and he never came back here to live.

He visited from time to time—I have the records with me if you want to see them. He usually stayed for about a week, and it seems all he did was spend time with the family. He has no criminal record: a file that is completely blank," he said, and then glanced at Ava. "I have to tell you, I was a little surprised when my boss asked me to look into him, especially when the request originated with your boss in Hong Kong. The things we normally do for Hong Kong—and for other friends in China—usually involve people who the police know intimately, and for the wrong reasons."

She was slightly taken aback by his mention of "your boss in Hong Kong" again. *Is he fishing for something?* she wondered. "I find you extremely well spoken," she said. "You had a good education, didn't you."

"Australia. I told you."

"BA?"

"Master's."

"So you should be able to understand that I never talk about my boss, or my boss's business, or my boss's friends."

"I wasn't—" he began.

"No need to explain. Let's just drop it," she said. "And as for the Lam brothers, I have no need to speak to the surgeon, but if I do, I'll be respectful. The younger Lam is a bit more of a challenge, since we think he stole or lost more than thirty million Canadian dollars. How many dong is that?"

He looked at her with a touch of anger in his eyes, and she knew she shouldn't have taunted him about the dong, one of the world's weakest currencies. "About fifty-four billion," he said sharply.

"Well, in any currency, it's a lot of money," she said. "He stole it or he lost it—I'm not sure which. I just need to find out."

"He doesn't live or act like a man with a lot of money. We've been watching him for the past few days. He hasn't left his brother's house. He gardens, he goes for walks... One of my men thought he saw him crying."

"I'll try not to bring him to tears," she said.

The house was on a side street in a commercial area just outside District 1. Ava didn't see any street sign where Tran made his turn, and she didn't see anything but warehouse walls and garage doors until they neared the end. The house was sealed off from the main road by the street. It was red brick, two storeys, with a window on either side of the door and four windows across the second floor. Ava looked around and couldn't see any other residences. "What a strange place for a house," she said.

"This street used to house some of the minor officials from the French embassy when we were still a French colony. When the French left, we razed the street on both sides and built those warehouses. Somehow this house survived."

A black wrought-iron fence ran along the property line at the front of the house. There was a red-brick walkway about twenty metres long, flanked by grass, flowerbeds, and what looked like several small vegetable gardens. A small man or boy was working in one of the gardens, his back to the road.

Tran stopped the car well short of the fence. "That's your man, I think," he said.

Ava opened her bag and took out her notebook and a pen. She opened the car door and walked towards the fence, her shoes clattering lightly on the concrete. The figure in the garden didn't move. "Mr. Lam, my name is Ava Lee, and I've come all the way from Toronto to speak with you," she said as she neared him.

She saw his back stiffen. She could have unlatched the gate and walked through, but all her senses told her to wait for him to react. He resumed his gardening.

"I'm an accountant, like you and your friend Joey Lac. I'm not here to do you any harm. I simply want to talk to you."

Now he turned, glancing over his shoulder first at her, then at the police car. A look of panic leapt into his eyes. He started to struggle to his feet. "Mr. Lam, the police simply drove me here as a courtesy. They have no interest in what happened in Toronto, no part in any of this at all."

He began to walk towards the house.

"Mr. Lam, please don't go. I would like you to invite me onto the property so we can speak. And I have to tell you, I won't leave until I get that chance. So let's make this easy on both of us, shall we?" And then she said loudly, "Please."

He stopped. Ava counted to ten and then said again, "Please."

When he turned towards her, she was shocked at how gaunt he was. He had hollows in his cheeks, his eyes were rimmed with shadows. If it hadn't been for his thick moustache she might not have recognized him. One thing was certain: he sure didn't look like a successful con man.

"Come in," he said.

(13)

SHE OPENED THE FENCE AND STARTED UP THE WALK-way. He went on ahead to the front door, opened it, and then stood in the doorway until she reached it. Ava held out her hand.

He looked at it suspiciously. "I knew they'd send someone. I knew eventually they'd find me, especially after I saw that woman at the hotel."

"Who are 'they'?"

"My investors."

"Well, you're right, of course. They did send me."

"And who else?"

"We're not playing a game of bait-and-switch, Mr. Lam. There is no one with a baseball bat lurking in the shadows. I'm all they sent. And truthfully, they don't know exactly where you are, because I haven't told them."

He stood to one side. "Come in," he said.

The house was smaller than it looked from the outside. The main floor consisted of a hallway with a kitchen and eating area to the right and a living room–den combination to the left, with IKEA-style furnishings.

"I need to wash up. Why don't you take a seat while I do," Lam said. "Would you like some tea?"

"I'd love some tea."

"Jasmine?"

"Perfect."

He headed for the kitchen and Ava went into the living room. She sat down in a deeply slanted chair. The room was sparsely furnished and had two walls of bookcases. There was no television, no home entertainment system. Another wall was filled with framed diplomas. She could read most of them from her chair, and it turned out that Dr. Lam's wife was equally distinguished, her medical degree having come from Johns Hopkins University.

She heard a tap running and the familiar sound of water being pumped from a Thermos. Lam came into the living room with a teapot and two mugs on a tray. He put it on the coffee table and then sat in a chair directly across from her. "Are you really an accountant?" he asked.

She took a card from her notebook and put it on the table.

Lam picked it up. "Offices in Hong Kong and Toronto, but no addresses."

"We don't have a walk-in type of clientele."

"What kind do you have?"

"The kind who have lost a lot of money and have exhausted the conventional ways of recovering it."

"Ah."

"Do you mind?" she said, reaching for the teapot. When he said nothing, she poured tea into both mugs.

"So you are here to try to get their money back?" he asked, his hand shaking as he took the mug.

"I'd like to start by finding out what happened to it, and then we'll take it from there."

"Well, it's gone. All of it," he said.

She sipped her tea, her eyes focused on his. He tried to return her stare, but whatever confidence he might have had collapsed. His head dropped to his chest, tears spilling down his cheeks.

"You can take your time," she said. "But I really need to know what happened."

Lam sobbed and his hand began to shake more fiercely, tea splashing out of the mug. She reached over and took it from him and put it back on the tray.

"I've lost my career. I've lost every friend I ever had," he said.

"What happened?" she urged.

He tilted his head back and began to breathe deeply through his nose. Gradually he gathered himself, and after another minute of deep breathing he reached for his mug and took a gulp of tea. "I put the money into a fund," he said.

"Just a moment — you were the fund?" said Ava.

"Yes, I had my fund. But I put all the money I collected into another one — a bigger one. At least I thought it was a bigger one."

"What was its name?"

"Surabaya Fidelity Security."

"Never heard of it."

"Why would you?" he said, the tears returning to his eyes.

Ava thought about what Joey Lac had said, about Lam not being the kind of man to steal or lie. Less than five minutes into her conversation with him she already had the same impression. "Could you start at the beginning?" she asked.

He sipped his tea. "I have — I had a friend named Fred Purslow. We worked for the same accounting firm after school, and even after we went our separate ways we kept in touch. I started my own accounting business, dealing mainly with Vietnamese clients, and he went into banking."

"Bank Linno?"

He didn't seem surprised by the question. "Yeah, that's where he ended up."

"Sorry, I didn't mean to disrupt your train of thought."

"That's not hard these days... Anyway, about three years ago one of my clients, who owns a grocery store, asked me if I could help him with a problem concerning cash. He had been accumulating it illegally and wanted to find a way he could use it without drawing the attention of Revenue Canada or the police or whatever. I couldn't think of any way of doing that and told him so. A few weeks later I was having dinner with Fred and explained the situation to him. He didn't say anything to me right away, but the next day he called and asked to meet me. Over lunch he told me about a fund he administered at the bank. It was private, like everything that bank did, but he thought if he talked to his bosses, they might agree to let me participate."

"Did you run a check on the fund?"

"It was private, not registered, but backed by the bank, Fred said."

"And he was your friend, and you believed him," Ava said.

Lam closed his eyes. "Yes, I believed him."

"So what was special about this fund?"

"Fred told me it would provide a guaranteed return of twelve percent annually. And he told me I could put all the cash I wanted into it, no questions asked. All I had to do was set up a company that I could use to funnel the money in and out of."

"Emerald Lion?"

"Yeah."

"Mr. Lam, would you mind if I took some notes?" she asked, realizing this was getting complicated.

His teeth gnawed at his lower lip as he nodded at her.

She opened her pad and uncapped her pen. "Are you telling me that Emerald Lion was not actually a fund — was never a fund — that it was in reality just an incorporated company?"

"Yeah, and it was a numbered company at that, with no name. It was Fred who put a name to it for bank account purposes, or so he said."

"Mr. Lam, I'm getting very confused, so you're going to have to help me here," Ava said. The connecting arrows on her notebook page were getting jumbled. "Are you saying that this whole scheme was actually concocted by an employee of the bank?"

"Yeah."

"You deposited the cash through him?"

"Yeah, I gave it to Fred. He did the actual deposits."

"But you have receipts and the like?"

He gave her a hard stare. "Yeah. In fact, I brought them with me. They're upstairs."

"So you gave the money to Fred, he put it into your bank account —"

"No," Lam said, his voice rising. "He put it directly into the bank fund account."

"Surabaya Fidelity Security?"

"Yeah."

"Okay, he put your cash into that fund and then, I assume monthly, the fund remitted whatever portion of the twelve percent annual return was due into the Emerald Lion account?"

"That's how it worked."

"And you had promised your people — your clients — a ten percent return."

"Yeah."

"So you pocketed the other two percent for yourself."

"One percent. Fred and I each took one percent."

Ava did some quick math. One percent of $30 million still gave Lam an income of $300,000. "I saw the monthly reports you sent to your clients. They were quite detailed in terms of their returns."

"I just took the reports I got from Surabaya, took off two percent, and then apportioned the money to the clients."

Ava took Theresa Ng's last report from her bag and held it out to Lam. "Is this example pretty standard?"

His head turned away so quickly it was as if she had slapped him across the cheek. "I don't want to look at that," he said.

Ava left it on the table. "What went wrong?" she asked, almost in a whisper.

Lam shook his head and his hands began to tremble again. "You can guess, can't you?"

"I'd rather you told me."

He shuddered, and when he began to speak, his voice

cracked. "It all happened so fast — too fast for me to think clearly. I mean, looking back, I should have acted more quickly than I did."

"There wasn't a bank fund."

He reached for Theresa Ng's fund report, looked at it, and then scrunched it into a ball. "He told me there was a glitch in the bank's system and that the monthly payment was going to be a bit late. I began to worry right away, but Fred was my friend and the explanation he gave seemed plausible enough. He said he'd call me as soon as things were sorted. I waited for about three days before I called him again. He told me we were less than forty-eight hours away from having the funds deposited."

"So you waited some more?"

"Yeah, but when I didn't hear from him, I called again, and this time I got a message on his office voicemail. It was a Thursday, I remember, and the message said he was on vacation and would be out of the office until the following Monday. What could I do? I waited... It was the longest weekend of my life."

"And then on Monday?"

"No Fred."

"Ah."

"I was going crazy. Some of the clients were already calling, and they weren't being polite. I repeated Fred's line about a glitch in the bank's system. No one cared, of course."

"What did you do?"

"I went to the bank and asked to speak to the manager. Actually his title was 'President, Canadian Operations.'"

"What was his name?"

"Aris Muljadi."

"You remember. I'm impressed."

"How could I forget? I had to beg to get in to see him, and even then they made me wait for half an hour outside his office. I must have looked at his nameplate twenty times."

"What did Mr. Muljadi have to say?"

"He just listened at first. I told him I was getting pressured by my people and that I needed the money from the Surabaya fund deposited into my account. But I knew, before I was more than a couple of sentences into my demand, that I was wasting my time. I mean, he sat back in his chair and looked at me like I was demented. I kept talking anyway, mentioning what Fred had told me about the glitches."

"About which he knew nothing, am I right?"

"Yeah, nothing."

"How about the Surabaya fund?"

Ava hadn't thought it possible for Lam to slump even further into himself, but he did. His shoulders collapsed around his chest and his head hung so low she thought it was going to hit the table. "He'd never heard of it," he said, the tears returning.

"What did you say?"

"Nothing at first. I was in a state of shock. It was like a doctor had just told me I had cancer and two months to live. He just stared at me silently. When I did start to talk, I was completely manic, I guess. I cursed the bank and Fred. I threatened to go directly to the police. That's when he finally did something."

"What?"

"He asked me to go into the boardroom next to his office and wait there while he tried to sort things out. I was only in there for about fifteen minutes when he showed up with another man. His family name was Rocca — I never got his first name. Rocca had a tape recorder with him. They sat down and asked me to explain my relationship with the bank and how I had come to put money into the Surabaya fund. I have to tell you, I was really reluctant to do it, but Muljadi said they couldn't do anything to help me unless they knew all the facts. He assured me that if the bank was in any way involved in what had transpired, they would make things right.

"Rocca stepped in then and went even further. He said that if an employee of the bank, even without the bank's knowledge and authority, had done something improper, the bank still had a professional and moral obligation to cover any losses I had incurred."

"That sounds responsible."

"Unless it was bullshit, which it was, of course," Lam said. "All they wanted from me was details about the account and how Fred and I had managed things. After I told them, they asked me to wait in the boardroom while they verified my story. It didn't take that long, maybe half an hour, but to me it felt like an eternity. I was going back and forth between feeling that the bank was going to make things right and feeling like my life was going to end.

"The two of them came back together but it was Rocca who did the talking. He was wearing a black suit with a white shirt and black tie, and I remember thinking that he looked like a funeral director. Anyway, he explained that it appeared that Fred Purslow had put together a rather simple but effective fraudulent scheme. Fred's job at the bank was account manager — he had the authority to open and close accounts. What he had done was open an account for Emerald Lion and at the same time he opened an account for a numbered company, which listed a guy named Barry Lowell as director and sole signing authority. When he said that name, I almost fell over, because Barry had been a classmate of ours as well. He was friends with Fred but not with me."

"So the money you gave to Purslow—he put it into the numbered company's account that he and Lowell controlled?"

"Yeah."

"And then transferred dribs and drabs into your account at month's end?"

"Yeah, and gave me dummy reports on dummy letterhead."

"So Rocca and Muljadi knew it had been a scam."

"They knew."

Ava looked down at the notes she'd been taking and knew there was something wrong with Lam's explanation. "One thing doesn't make any sense to me," she said. "Why would Purslow stop making payments? There had to be tons of cash still available to him, unless of course he was blowing his brains out in Vegas or something. Usually this kind of scheme doesn't unravel for years, unless the fund promises a rate of return that is completely unrealistic. All he was delivering was eleven percent. At that rate he could have kept doing it for years and years, especially since you were putting more and more money into it."

"I'm not a complete idiot," Lam said. "I asked them the same question."

"Did they have an answer?"

"Oh, yeah. The bank had decided six months before to close down their Canadian operation at the end of the calendar year. Everyone was going to lose their job, but to keep things running until then they offered a bonus to any employee who would stay till the end. Purslow signed on to stay. They were into the second-last month when he bolted. I guess he figured there was no way to duplicate this scheme using any other bank, so he took off while he could."

"The numbered company's account was emptied?"

"According to Rocca the money had been transferred offshore. I asked him where and he wouldn't tell me. He said the bank was going to take matters into its own hands and that I wasn't to worry myself."

"Easy to say."

"He said they'd find Purslow, find the money, and return it to me. In the meantime they wanted me to stay quiet. I said that was kind of hard to do when my clients were getting more and more demanding. At that point Muljadi stepped in and said the bank was prepared to advance me the month's payments that were due. That would buy us all enough time to get things sorted out, he said."

"How much was that?"

"Just over three hundred thousand dollars."

"Of course. So you took the money and kept your mouth shut."

"Wouldn't you?"

"I don't know," Ava said, and then regretted it as his face fell.

"What else could I have done?" he said, talking to himself as much as to her.

"Not much, I suppose," she said. "Now, when was the next time you heard from the bank?"

"Never."

He said it so simply that she thought she had misheard. "What?"

"Never. I never heard from Rocca, Muljadi, or the bank, at least not directly."

"I don't understand."

"I saw them on a Monday afternoon, the day Purslow was supposed to be back from his holiday. They put the money they had promised into my account the same day and I paid it out to my clients. Then I sat and waited for them to contact me. A week went by without any word. Halfway into the next week, I was starting to get really, really paranoid again when a brown envelope was slid under my apartment door. I opened it, and whatever bad feelings I had about the way things were going were multiplied by ten — no, make that a hundred. It was a newspaper clipping from a Costa Rican newspaper called the *Tico Times*. The bodies of two headless men had been washed up on shore near a resort, and police were working to identify them. Attached to the clipping were two photos. They were of the heads of Purslow and Lowell, each set up on a wooden chair, with a note that read, *This is what happens to faggots who steal*," he said, fighting for breath.

Ava had stopped writing when Lam mentioned the envelope. He had been looking sideways at one of the bookcases while he talked, so she found it difficult to read his face. "Mr. Lam, look at me, please," she said.

He turned towards her, and she knew immediately he was telling her the truth. "I was terrified," he sobbed.

And you still are, Ava thought. Suddenly nervous, she swivelled her head towards the door to see if someone was there. "You should have been," she said, feeling a deep disquiet.

He began speaking quickly, as if in a rush to get it all out of his system. "I had no idea what to do. I paced for hours. Then I drank some whisky and finally worked up enough nerve to leave my apartment and go to the bank. Of course, when I got there, it was closed — completely shuttered, everyone gone.

"I ran down the stairs to the lobby. I wasn't thinking that clearly, but I thought that if I went to see my lawyer he could at least tell me which police force or government officials or whoever I should go to... I didn't get out of the building. They were waiting for me in the lobby — two of them — they looked like bikers. They were huge. Each of them took me by an arm and almost carried me out the door. They told me to keep quiet if I didn't want to get hurt. Then they bundled me into the back of a big SUV with tinted windows. They sat on either side of me and asked if I'd had a chance to look at the envelope. I couldn't talk, so I just nodded. They said it was time for me to forget that I had seen the photos, and time to forget about the bank and my money. If I opened my mouth to anyone or showed the photos to anyone, they'd come after me and do the exact same thing they'd done to Purslow. The next day I was on a plane to Ho Chi Minh City."

Ava sat quietly, trying to absorb everything he had told her. She had heard his words but had no idea what they meant for him, for her, for Theresa Ng. *What have I gotten myself into?* she thought.

"I knew about the bank's closing. I just didn't know the circumstances or have an exact timeline," she finally said.

"Now you do."

"Have you told this story to anyone else?" she asked.

"No, just you," he said quickly.

"Why me?"

He shrugged. "I don't really know. There you were at the fence and then you were in the house, and you just seemed like someone I could talk to. Besides, I knew someone would come, and that sooner or later I'd have to share this nightmare. I believed you when you said you just wanted to talk...I have to tell you, I feel a bit better for it."

"Well, if I can make a suggestion, don't talk about it with anyone else."

"I have no plans to."

She was still trying to process two dead bodies, their heads on a chair, two bikers in a lobby, a disappearing bank, and thirty-two million missing dollars. All she had were questions that she doubted Lam could answer. She looked at her notebook.

"You said you had a letter from Surabaya with terms and conditions laid out, and you have copies of the receipts. Can I have those?"

"Sure, although I don't know what good they'll do you."

"Do you also have copies of the statements you were sent?"

"I do."

"I'd like to have them too."

"Why?"

"I'm an accountant, like you. I want to know just how much money is involved in case I ever catch up to it." She saw his skepticism and ignored it. "You know, in this day and age it's difficult to hide anything anywhere. Your friend Purslow probably thought he'd be safe in some backwater in Central America, and look what happened to him, and how fast it happened."

Lam shivered. "Will they come after me?"

"Who?"

"The ones who killed Purslow and Lowell. Maybe even the ones who hired you."

"The people who killed Purslow will leave you alone unless you give them a reason not to," she said slowly. "Stay quiet and out of sight and you'll be out of mind. As for my people, I'm it. Assuming you told me the truth — and I think you did — there will be no more visits and there will be no repercussions. Now, I may need to call you in case some detail you forgot pops up, so I'd like a phone number, but that's it."

"Are you really going to chase the money?"

Again she took her time. "I don't know. I really don't know."

He started to say something and then caught himself.

"I'd like to get all the paperwork you have," she said.

He stood, and she saw the sweat stains on his shirt. He left the room and walked to the stairs. She guessed he didn't weigh much more than 110 pounds, and she could imagine how easy it had been for the two thugs to terrify him.

As she waited, the complexity of his story began to spin in her head. Two months at the cottage had made life seem simpler than it was. She had thought that finding Lam and getting him to come clean about the fund's money would start to resolve things for Theresa Ng and the others. Now he seemed to be, if not irrelevant, then at least a minor player in a story that had just taken a dramatic turn.

The thugs in Toronto, the two deaths in Costa Rica, the bank's closing, the missing money — she had no idea what any of it meant.

(14)

IT WAS EARLY EVENING WHEN AVA GOT BACK TO THE hotel. She stripped and got back under the rain shower, fighting jet lag now, her mind a jumble. She replayed Lam's story in her head. It was so far from what she had expected, she didn't know if she had the ambition to deal with it. Revived at least physically, she put on a T-shirt and running shorts and checked the room-service menu. She went pan-Asian: a Vietnamese fresh spring roll and a plate of nasi goreng. She chose a Pinot Grigio that she knew and liked from the wine list.

Her notebook was on the bed. She picked it up, went to the desk and leafed through the three pages of notes from her discussion with Lam, writing comments in the margins. She started a fresh page as other things he'd said came back to her. Then she turned to the back page and taped to it the photos of Purslow's and Lowell's heads and Muljadi's business card. She slid the article ripped from the *Tico Times* between two other pages. It was a rote process, without any clear objective. Her meeting with Lam had left her utterly confused. *Maybe talking to Uncle will help*, she thought.

Her meal came and she drank two glasses of wine rather quickly. They went directly to her head. She knew she needed to make her phone call right away if she was going to be mentally acute.

"*Wei*," he answered on the second ring.

She could hear a television in the background, a voice reciting horses's names and training times. *He's probably watching a Happy Valley Racecourse preview,* she thought. "It's Ava."

"How is Ho Chi Minh City? Did you get the help you wanted?"

"I did, thanks."

"And have you managed to corner Lam yet?"

"Yes. It wasn't very difficult — he was waiting for someone to show up, waiting for someone to talk to."

"Some people cannot carry guilt."

"It was more fear than guilt he was trying to shed," she said.

"Hard to tell the difference sometimes... So, what was his story?"

Ava sighed, trying to group her thoughts in her head, wishing she hadn't drunk quite so quickly. "It's far more complicated than we thought."

Uncle paused. "I am going to turn down the television," he said.

While she waited, Ava turned the pages of her notebook to the photos of the two heads.

"The money is gone?" Uncle asked when he came back on the line.

"I don't know. I don't know anything about the whereabouts of the money. All I know is that Lam doesn't seem to have it, and the people who were the prime suspects are dead."

"Dead?"

"Yes, decapitated, actually. I'm looking at pictures of their heads as we speak."

Uncle said very slowly, "This is not what we expected."

He's like my echo, Ava thought. "It is a bizarre story."

"I am listening."

She went over the events as described by Lam. Uncle didn't speak once, but she could feel his attention. When she was finished, the first question he asked was the most obvious. "And you believe him?"

"I think I do," she said, and then closed her eyes and imagined Lam sitting in front of her. "In fact, I know I do. He told me the truth about as much as he knew. His friend Joey Lac in Toronto told me that Lam can't lie. I feel the same way about him."

"If that is the case, then the people who killed the two men in Costa Rica probably have the money."

"Of course," Ava said.

"And it seems to me that the money is then out of reach."

"I didn't say I couldn't find it," she said defensively.

"Ava, I know if you set your mind to it, you might be able to find it. What I am saying is that it does not appear to be worth the risk. We do not know who is at the other end of the money trail. All we know is that they were prepared to kill two men for it, and were able to reach down to Costa Rica to do it."

She was surprised, even slightly dismayed, by his reaction. They were no strangers to difficult money trails and no strangers to violence, or the potential for it. "I'm not quite ready to give it up," she said. "We still have a link to Lam and the money, and it's that bank. Let's find out what we can about them."

"And then?"

"I don't know. That depends on the information, doesn't it. Did you make those calls to Indonesia?"

"I did."

She waited for him to tell her what he had unearthed. When he remained quiet, she said, "Uncle, you know I'm not about to do anything rash or stupid. What did your people say?"

She sensed he wanted to withhold what he had, and she was preparing to counter when he said, "Our contacts there are not as good as I was led to think. I do not have any information yet."

"How much longer do we have to wait?"

"I do not know."

"I'm finished here," she said. "So I either go home or I pursue this bank lead. I mean, what other options do we have?"

"I will call Indonesia again."

"Thank you."

"Give me an hour."

"I'll wait up until then."

As Ava ended the call she tried to remember a time when Uncle had lacked a sense of urgency, and couldn't. She'd wait for him, she decided, but in the meantime she'd explore one other potential information source.

It was well into the morning in Toronto and Ava knew her friend Johnny Yan would be at his Toronto Commonwealth Bank desk. They had gone to school together and were part of a network of young Chinese professionals who had graduated from York University and who helped each other to advance their careers. They thought of it as *guanxi*, Canadian-style. She sent him an email, knowing that he was in his office, the computer would be on, and he would be monitoring his emails on an ongoing basis. I need to talk to you, she wrote.

In less than a minute he replied. Call my cellphone.

He picked up the phone halfway through the first ring. "Hey, long time, no hear. Where are you?"

"Ho Chi Minh City."

"Thanks for that last piece of business," he said.

Johnny's information had helped her with the Tommy Ordonez case. In fact, without him, she wasn't sure it would have been resolved, or at least resolved so quickly and so well. When the case had been put to bed, she asked Uncle Chang, who functioned as the effective CFO of the Ordonez empire, to divert some business to Toronto Commonwealth and to be very specific that Johnny Yan was to handle their account.

"Did it get you a promotion?"

"Not yet, but it sure as hell got me the right kind of attention in the right kind of places."

"I have another one I'm going to throw your way in a while," she said, thinking of May Ling Wong.

"Is that a prelude to being asked a favour?"

"Of course."

"Then ask away."

"Bank Linno — ever heard of them?"

"Not that I can remember."

"It's Indonesian, out of Surabaya. They had an office on College Street until a few months ago that they closed in a real hurry."

"Still doesn't ring a bell."

"It was private, evidently."

"A near-bank?"

"I think so. It had only the one office and it was on the eighth floor of an older building, so they weren't pandering for business."

"What else do you know?"

"I have two names. A guy named Aris Muljadi, who was the president or something and could be Indonesian, and a Canadian named Rocca."

"First name for Rocca?"

"Don't have one."

"That's helpful."

"Johnny, don't get lazy on me."

He laughed. "When do you need the information?"

"In an hour or two?"

"Of course you do. You always do."

"Exactly, and you always come through for me."

"You're lucky. I don't have my first meeting until ten, so I have some time to work on this now. I'll call Henry Pang—remember him?"

"Vaguely."

"He was two years behind us. He's at the bank now, in the international marketing division. He should know something."

"Thank him for me."

"No, I won't. If he knows you're involved, he'll expect a favour. I'll keep that for myself and throw him a bone of a different kind."

"Your call. Just get me some information."

"I can reach you on your cell?"

"Yes, but if you have problems I'm staying at the Park Hyatt in Ho Chi Minh."

She returned to her computer and emailed her travel agent, Gail, asking her to look into flights to Surabaya and a hotel. She also asked her to hold a seat for her on the next day's Cathay Pacific flight to Toronto. It would be one destination or the other, Ava knew, because there was no way she was going to Costa Rica.

Ava poured herself another glass of wine and eased onto the bed. She scanned the channels, looking for something to kill time. One of the Chinese-language stations was airing *Election*. The movie detailed an election for overall chairmanship of the various Triad societies, and the violent and treacherous tactics used by the candidates. The film was fictional, but that didn't dampen the horror of watching the winner — who until that point had been reasonable and conciliatory — cave in the skull of his opponent with a rock. The act took place on the bank of a river while they were fishing, being watched by the opponent's wife and the winner's young son. It was all the more repellent because of that, and because it was so sudden and so unexpected. Ava shuddered as the scene played out, and she thought of Uncle, who had been society chairman for four consecutive terms. It was a fact that was difficult to equate with the man she knew.

She changed channels before the violence escalated even further, and was just getting into a Hong Kong comedy show when her cellphone rang.

"I made a mistake," Uncle said quickly. "The Indonesians were waiting for me to call them rather than them calling me. They are not quite as useless as I thought."

"*Momentai*, Uncle."

"And they found out some interesting things."

Ava climbed down from the bed and sat at the desk. She opened her notebook and turned to a fresh page. "Go ahead."

"Bank Linno is about forty years old. It was founded in East Java by a family that had a fleet of trawlers, with the idea of supporting the local fishing industry. They started in Surabaya and then slowly began to expand into places like Batu, Madiun, and Malang, all in East Java. In terms of branches and employees it barely breaks into the top hundred in Indonesia."

"So what are they doing in Toronto and New York?" she interrupted.

"Be patient," he said. "Taking three months off has made you edgy."

"Sorry," she said, drawing a deep breath.

"Despite being hardly a blip on the banking scene, Linno is among the top ten Indonesian banks when it comes to capitalization."

"How much are we talking about?"

"Billions."

"Uncle, how is that possible?"

"No one knows. Our contacts were as surprised as you. What they did find out was that about six years ago the bank's ownership and management changed."

"It isn't Indonesian-owned?"

"On the surface it is. The founding family sold their shares to another Indonesian company in Surabaya, but when our people ran that down, they ended up with a law firm that is holding and voting the shares in trust. All legal, I am told."

"And the management?"

"Stranger still. The CEO is a British man by the name of Andy Cameron. He joined the company at the same time the ownership was transferred."

"Where was he before?"

"I don't know."

"This is all very strange," Ava said, writing down Cameron's name and then unconsciously underlining *billions* in her notebook. Whatever doubts she had about going to Indonesia were vanishing. If nothing else, her curiosity was in overdrive. "Uncle, if I go to Surabaya, what kind of help can I get from our people?"

He hesitated, and she wondered if he was preparing to tell her to forget it. Instead he said, "The people I know are in Jakarta. They have associates in Surabaya but they are not well organized — freelancers mainly. They would have to send someone from Jakarta to run things for you, and then of course there is the language gap, so you would need someone to translate anyway."

"These people, are they official?" she asked, meaning police or army.

"No, they are mainly into rent collection, protection money. They kick back a portion to the police and so have some kind of affiliation, but I do not know how much you can count on that."

"They don't sound too promising."

"The man from Jakarta is a different animal. He is a *jago*, a gang boss, and he is tough and smart. He can be there in a few hours if you want him."

"What is his name?"

"Perkasa."

"Can he speak English?"

"Yes, most educated Indonesians can."

"He's not Chinese?" she asked, surprised.

"He is, actually. His Chinese name is Chung."

Ava knew it was common for Chinese people doing business in other parts of Asia, such as Indonesia, Thailand, and the Philippines, to adopt local names. They were often some of the wealthiest people in those countries, and targets for kidnapping and worse. Ava thought it was naive of them to think a name change would offer any kind of protection, but then she wasn't living there. "I think you should ask him to be on standby, to be ready to travel to Surabaya," she said.

"Do you know the place?"

"No, and I hardly know Indonesia," she said. She'd been there twice, both times to Jakarta and both times for only a few days. She had memories of traffic that rivalled the worst of Bangkok and Manila, and the sound of the early morning call to prayer from a mosque near her hotel that had her out of bed with the rising sun.

"It sounds as if you have made up your mind to go."

"Yes, I think I have. That is, if you agree."

He paused, and she wondered if he was thinking about saying no. "Ava, you just need to be careful. I agree this bank is worth looking into, but I do not want you to take any chances."

"I won't."

"And I will make sure Perkasa is on twenty-four-hour standby."

"Okay."

"We have to pay these people. It is not like the usual

exchange of favours. I am going to send him money right away so that he is ready to travel."

"That's perfect."

"And I want to know where you are staying."

"Yes, Uncle, as soon as I know," she said, wondering why he seemed so cautious. "I'll probably make the booking tonight, and if I do I'll forward you the details. In the meantime, could you email me the phone numbers and any other contact information you have on Chung?"

"Better to call him Perkasa. He does not know that I know his Chinese name."

"Huh?"

"It is a little complicated to explain."

"You don't need to."

"I will send you the information you want, as well as everything he told me about the bank and Cameron."

Ava hung up and turned on her computer. Gail had already replied. The quickest route to Surabaya was through Hong Kong. She could take a morning flight there, have lunch with Uncle, and then catch a Cathay Pacific flight at three fifty-five that would get her into Surabaya at seven thirty-five.

Gail recommended the Majapahit Hotel, in the centre of the city. Built in 1910 and with only 143 rooms, it was smaller and older than most of the hotels Ava stayed at. But it was a five-star hotel, built by the same family that owned Raffles in Singapore. Better than Raffles evidently, Gail wrote.

Book the flight through Hong Kong for tomorrow, and the hotel, Ava wrote back. She picked up her cellphone and dialled Uncle's number.

"I was sitting at the computer trying to send you that information," he said.

"I hope you wiped the dust off it first," she said.

"I use it more often now, not that I am any faster."

"I've just booked my flight to Surabaya," she said. "I'm coming through Hong Kong. I'll land around ten thirty and don't take off again until three thirty, so we might be able to squeeze in a lunch. And I'm staying at the Hotel Majapahit."

"I will let Perkasa know," Uncle said. "Are you sure you do not want him now?"

"No, let him stay in Jakarta. If I need him he's only a few hours away," Ava said. She didn't like the thought of having someone hanging around. It added a pressure, however slight, that she didn't need.

"All right."

"And tomorrow you don't have to come to the airport to collect me. Let's have dim sum at Man Wah at the Mandarin. I'll meet you there."

"I will wait in the lobby."

"Perfect. Till then," she said, and ended the call.

She went to the computer again. Waiting for Uncle's email to come through, she scrolled through the messages in her inbox. May Ling had written her nightly correspondence, and Ava read it with feelings that were more mixed than ever. May wrote that she was putting together a business plan she hoped would entice Ava to get on board. She was going to need more time to finish it, and it was the type of thing she wanted to discuss in person. Maybe when we're together in Hong Kong for Amanda's wedding, we could find the time, May wrote.

That's fine with me, Ava replied, not at all surprised that May Ling had already been invited to the wedding. Amanda knew whose bread should be buttered first.

She was beginning to feel tired again, and she was considering turning off her cellphone and getting into bed when the phone rang. It was Johnny Yan.

"Hey, what do you have?" she said.

"And hello to you too."

"Sorry, I don't mean to be abrupt. I'm just tired."

"No problem, I'm used to it," Yan said with a laugh. "I spoke with Henry. He was really curious about why I was asking him about that bank."

"Really? So he knows something about it?"

"Yeah, it turns out that he knows Dominic Rocca. They were in the Commonwealth internship program together and then they sort of kept in touch, even though Rocca went to one of the other Canadian banks before he surfaced at Bank Linno."

"That's convenient."

"According to Henry, this bank had narrow interests. It was primarily a lender and it seemed to specialize in real estate — condos, shopping centres, smaller office complexes."

"My man tells me he had an account there, so it had to offer other services," Ava said.

"Yeah, but on a strictly limited basis, to priority customers."

"So what did Rocca do at the bank?"

"Managed a lot of the real estate business, evidently. He bragged to Henry that in some years he put as much money into the Toronto market as some of the major banks."

"Just Toronto?"

"Yeah, that was the strange part—just Toronto. In the city proper and just northwest of it, around Woodbridge, Vaughan, Kleinburg, Maple."

"Why did the bank close?"

"Henry didn't even know it had. It's been months since he's talked to Rocca."

"Do you think you could ask him to reach out to Rocca? If he doesn't want to, could he get me Rocca's contact information?"

"I'm one step ahead of you. Here, write this down," Yan said, giving her a phone number and a personal email address.

"That's great. Now, how about the other guy?"

"Henry has never heard of him. In fact, he probably wouldn't have heard of the bank if Rocca hadn't been involved. So I did a name search on Muljadi and came up with absolutely nothing."

Ava made a note and then returned to the question that was gnawing at her. "Johnny, why would the bank close?"

"I have no idea," he said.

"Take a guess."

"Not making enough money? I mean, a lot of them come here thinking it's going to be easy going and then find out otherwise. Others have closed, you know."

"They were in real estate. How can you not make money doing that in Toronto?"

"You told me to take a guess and that's what I did. I don't know what else to say."

"Sorry, Johnny, I wasn't picking on you. I just can't help thinking there has to be another reason."

"Talk to Rocca. Talk to that guy Muljadi."

"I'll try, but I'm going to Surabaya tomorrow. I have a small lead there, so that might work out better for me."

"That reminds me," Yan said quickly. "Henry reminded me that we have a mutual friend who lives there. His name is John Masterson. I have to look up his phone number and email. When I do, I'll send him your number and give him a heads-up that you're going to be there and that you're a friend."

"What does he do?"

"He's in the crab business."

Ava's experiences with the seafood business had been mixed, and her opinion of the people who populated it was harsh. "Thanks. I'll reach out to him if it's necessary."

"He's a fun guy. Even if you don't need his help he might be worth contacting."

A seafood guy and a fun guy — it sounded like a deadly combination. "Thanks, Johnny."

(15)

SHE SLEPT FITFULLY, THE JET LAG AND THE STRANGE bed overpowering the wine's effects. Ava dreamt frequently and her father was most often the central figure — always out of reach, a distant figure she chased to no avail, in and out of hotels and airports. That night she dreamt of Maria for the first time. They were in a stranger's house that was filled with people she didn't know. The two of them sat on a couch drinking wine as a party swirled around them. Maria undid her blouse and exposed a breast to Ava, urging her to suck the nipple. Ava did, reluctantly, keenly aware of the eyes that were on them. Then Maria pulled up her skirt and began to masturbate. Despite her embarrassment, Ava was aroused and reached down to touch herself. *Play, play,* Maria said. Ava woke throbbing and close to climax. She slipped her hand beneath the sheets and finished what she had begun in her sleep. *Good God,* she thought afterwards, *what kind of dream was that?*

It was just past six thirty when she hauled herself out of bed. Erotic dreams were foreign to her, as were dreams about Maria, and she couldn't help but be bothered by them. She understood well enough what her father's distant, unavailable presence meant in her nighttime wanderings, but what was her subconscious telling her about Maria and their relationship?

Ava brushed her teeth and then showered quickly. She wanted to spend some time on the computer before heading for the airport. She threw on her casual wear and then packed her bags so she was ready to go. The room had a hot water Thermos; Ava made herself an instant coffee and took it to the desk.

She opened her book and reread the notes she had made the night before while talking to Uncle and Johnny. When she was done, she replaced the SIM card in her cell with one that had a Toronto 905 area code and the name James Lewis as the caller ID. She punched in the number for Dominic Rocca. It rang once and then flipped to an automated message informing her that the number was no longer in service.

Her computer was still on from the night before. Ava logged in as James Lewis and sent an email to Rocca enquiring about investment opportunities. It took only a few seconds for it to bounce back as undeliverable.

She entered a Canadian website she used to track addresses and phone numbers. She input Rocca's name and the phone number she had, and for city references she put in Toronto, Woodbridge, Maple, and Vaughan. It came up completely dry. Then she tried Muljadi with the same locations and again came up empty. Google was equally devoid of any mention of either of them. *Would they both disappear just because the bank office closed?* she wondered. *Or maybe they haven't disappeared. Maybe they were low-key and under the radar from the get-go.* Either way, it felt strange to her.

Andy Cameron wasn't quite so invisible. When he was with the Falkirk Stirling Bank, he had received several promotions that were worthy of news releases but not pictures. His last recorded rise in status had been his appointment as director of the bank's Rome office. He was still in his mid-thirties when he got the appointment, so he was obviously bright, although his education seemed to be limited to a BA from the University of Aberdeen. There was no mention of his appointment to the presidency of Bank Linno. More strangeness, and this time compounded by the fact that Ava couldn't quite see how a Brit working in a bank branch in Rome could — or would want to — manoeuvre his way to Surabaya and become the head of a decidedly provincial and obscure bank.

She circled Andy Cameron's name and then underlined it. She was going to need to talk to him, but under what pretence? She rifled through some of the business cards she kept for these situations and found one that attached her to a real accounting firm in Hong Kong that was close to Uncle. She'd used them for cover before, and they'd been terrific about backing her up. All she needed to do was let them know the when and the how of it, and all that would take was a phone call to Uncle. She called his cell, which went directly to voicemail, so she called his apartment.

"Hello?" Lourdes answered, hesitantly.

"It's Ava."

"That's not the name on the screen."

"I forgot to switch back my SIM card," Ava said. "Can I speak to Uncle, please?"

"He's not here. He went out."

"I called his cell and he didn't answer."

"I don't know where he is, and I don't know why he's not answering his phone," Lourdes said, her voice heavy.

"Has he been doing this a lot?"

"Yes."

"Lourdes, Sonny spoke to me a little about this. I don't want you to worry. I'm going to talk to Uncle when I can, and we'll find out what's bothering him, okay?" Ava waited for Lourdes to respond. When she didn't, she said, "Did you hear me?"

"I don't want him to know that I said anything to Sonny. He would be very angry with me," she said slowly.

"Your name won't be mentioned."

"Ava, I'm afraid."

"He wouldn't be that angry, Lourdes, even if he suspected you had said something."

"No, that's not what I mean. I'm afraid for him."

"Don't leap to conclusions. There could be a completely logical explanation for the way he has been behaving," Ava said, with more conviction than she felt.

"Do you think so?"

"Absolutely."

"I can't tell you how happy I am that you are coming, and how happy he is. When he found out yesterday, he smiled for the rest of the day."

"Lourdes, I am only the second most important woman in his life. Without you, he wouldn't be able to function at all."

"Oh, Ava."

"I mean it," Ava said, thinking, *Please don't cry.*

Lourdes choked it back and said, "When he gets back, I'll make sure he calls you."

Ava ended the call and pushed the chair back from the desk. Hong Kong was now starting to become as important as Surabaya.

(16)

THE FLIGHT TO HONG KONG WAS DELAYED, AND AVA didn't get into Chek Lap Kok until almost two o'clock. She left a message for Uncle on his cellphone, saying she couldn't meet him for lunch. Then she went through the in-transit gate and headed directly to the Cathay Pacific business lounge. She didn't turn on her phone until she was inside; she had missed three incoming calls, from her mother, Maria, and Uncle. She saved the first two messages without listening to them and went directly to his. He just said, "I got your message. Call me."

"*Wei.*"

"It's Ava. I've finally landed."

"You missed a good lunch," he said. "The flight to Surabaya is on time?"

"Yes, it is. Uncle, did Lourdes tell you I called the apartment earlier, before I went to the airport?"

"She did. I thought it was for the same reason."

"No, I need some cover and I'd like to use the business card from Dynamic Accounting. Please call them for me and let them know I'm going to be in Surabaya trying to meet with Andy Cameron at Bank Linno. My story is that we represent a Hong Kong investor who is looking at putting some money into East Java and we thought it might be wise to hook up with a local bank. You never know, Cameron or someone from the bank might call them to confirm."

"It won't be a problem."

"Great."

"Is that all?"

No, she thought, *I'd like to know what you were doing this morning.* "Yes, that's all," she said.

"Be careful over there."

"I'm trying to meet a banker, that's all."

"That is what Lam started off doing."

"Enough said. I'll be careful, and if I need Perkasa I won't hesitate to reach out for him."

"He is waiting."

"That's good to know."

"Keep me up to date on things."

"As always," she said.

As Ava ended the call she thought about phoning Sonny and then decided against it. He'd said he would call her when he knew something. There was no need to pester him.

The Cathay lounge had a noodle bar, and Ava ordered a bowl of rice noodles with har gow. As she waited, she listened to her mother's message. Marcus had called her with the news about the wedding, and Jennie could barely contain her glee. Ava's presence and role at the wedding would be more public validation than their second family had ever received. "You may be the one standing next to the bride, but everyone at that wedding is going to know that you are my daughter. I might as well be standing there myself," she said. Her father had obviously done a good selling job.

The voicemail from Maria was shorter. "I love you so much and I miss you so much. Hurry home."

It was the middle of the night in Toronto, safe enough to call them both and leave messages without worrying about their answering. "Mummy, I am very proud to be your daughter, and when I'm at the wedding I'm going to make sure everyone there knows that." Then, to Maria, "I miss you too." Embarrassed by her display of sentiment, Ava said under her breath, "That's enough of that for this trip."

The flight to Indonesia was four and half hours, landing her at Juanda International Airport on time at seven thirty-five. It was another new airport, built for efficiency, and Ava could have cleared Customs and Immigration and been in a taxi within fifteen minutes if she hadn't needed to buy a visa. Unlike most other countries, Indonesia made visitors buy visas when they arrived. It was a slow process but thankfully a short line. Still, it took twenty minutes before she had a seven-day visa stapled into her passport for a cost of ten U.S. dollars.

She stepped outside the terminal into a beautiful evening, temperature in the mid-twenties, a light breeze. She got into the taxi line and found herself surrounded by smokers. The smell of cloves wafted from their cigarettes — she had forgotten about that Indonesian habit. Ava bypassed one taxi when she saw the driver was smoking, and got happily into the next, which had a big no-smoking sign on its rear window.

"The Hotel Majapahit," she said. "How long?"

"About thirty minutes."

She waited for the usual caveat about traffic but there wasn't any, because there wasn't any need. The cab drove the entire distance at the posted speed. Ava began to wonder if she was actually in an Asian city.

She knew Surabaya had more than three million people and was the second-largest city in Indonesia. It just didn't feel like it. First there was the relative lack of traffic, and they seemed to be driving through quiet residential areas. Ava kept waiting for the downtown skyscrapers to appear, for the wall-to-wall shops, the big hotel complexes. It wasn't until twenty-five minutes into their drive that they began to appear, though in more modest forms than in many other major cities she'd been to.

The driver pointed out the hotel before she saw it. "The Majapahit... It's a hundred years old," he said.

It was already dark, and the floodlit hotel front, all white marble, glass, and dark wood, shone like something out of a dream. As they eased into the driveway, the sprawling gardens became visible. A uniformed doorman came down the steps to greet her. Ava tried to wave off his help, but he either didn't speak English or didn't care. He took both of her bags and led her into the lobby.

Everywhere she looked was marble and a mixture of rich woods. Ceiling fans churned overhead, more ornamental than functional, for she could feel the snap of air conditioning. A stairway carpeted in a deep dark blue slashed with bright gold flowers led from the lobby up to the second floor.

Ava loved hotels that had character, and the Majapahit's elegant colonial style had as much as she had ever seen. She had a standard garden-terrace suite on the third floor. The room was immense, more than forty square metres, she figured, and there was a marvellous sense of balance between the furnishings, the decorative touches, and the gleaming teak floors. The furniture was made of a mixture of hardwoods, mainly mahogany, she thought. Two large windows framed the far side of the room, their wooden shutters opening onto the gardens below. A ceiling fan turned slowly above a giant bed with a large wooden headboard and a sea of crisp white linens and duvet. She threw herself on the bed and sank deep into the covers.

From the bed she could see the bathroom's marble floors, sink, and tub, set off by gold faucets. And tucked in the corner was a modern shower stall with a head that looked as if it could adjust to multiple settings. She glanced across the room at a chest of drawers. On top there was a hot water Thermos, cups and saucers that had to be fine bone china, and an array of teas and instant coffees. No Italian espresso machine.

Perfect, she was thinking, when she heard her phone ring. She hadn't even realized it was on. She leapt off the bed, grabbed her bag, and pulled out the phone. The caller ID showed the Indonesian country code. Perkasa?

"Ava Lee."

"Ava, this is John Masterson."

"Who?"

"John Masterson. I'm a friend of Johnny Yan and Henry Pang. Johnny emailed me that you were coming here and that you're a good friend of his. He gave me this phone number."

"Ah, yes."

"I didn't know when you were arriving, so I thought I'd check."

"I'm here now. I've just arrived, actually."

"Where are you staying?"

"The Majapahit."

"Great choice."

"Yes, I think it is."

"Look, have you had dinner?"

She hesitated and then saw no reason to lie. "No."

"Neither have I. I've been waiting for my wife to get back from a business trip to Jakarta, but it doesn't look like she'll be here for another hour or two. How would you like to get together?"

"Truthfully, John, I'm not sure I really want to eat."

"A drink, then? I don't get a chance to meet many other Canadians here, and certainly none that are friends of friends."

He's pushy, Ava thought, *but polite pushy, Canadian pushy. And he's a friend of Johnny's.* "Sure, why not?"

"Good. There's a very good bar in the lounge at your hotel. Why don't I meet you there? I only live about ten minutes away."

"Call my room when you arrive and I'll come down. I'm in 313."

"See you soon."

That was silly of me, Ava thought as she hung up the phone. All she had wanted to do was order room service, have a bath, and then start getting her thoughts into the day ahead. She looked at her clothes. She was still wearing her Adidas training pants and a Giordano T-shirt. *I better change,* she thought, as much out of respect for the hotel as for Masterson.

She washed quickly, unpacked her travel bag, and was

just putting her cufflinks in when the room phone pealed. He hadn't been kidding about ten minutes. "Be right down," she said.

When Ava exited the elevator, she almost ran into a man who turned out to be John Masterson. He was standing by the doors talking comfortably to someone who looked like security. He was of moderate height and build, with short brown hair and pale blue eyes. He was wearing jeans and a short-sleeved black linen shirt.

"Are you John?" she asked.

"And you must be Ava."

"Pleased to meet you," she said, extending a hand.

"And you," he said, gently shaking it. "The lounge is right over there."

They sat on either side of a small round table. Masterson leaned back in his chair and raised a hand over his head for a waiter. "I'm having beer. What would you like?"

"White wine — something dry, not too fruity," Ava said.

"They have a great burgundy."

"That will do fine."

The waiter approached the table, his head slightly lowered. "Pak John, what can I get for you?"

"San Miguel, and a glass of the Boyer Martenot Meursault for Ibu Ava."

"They obviously know you here," Ava said when the waiter left.

"It's one of the better places in town to hang out, and to meet girls. Before I was married I was a regular. The restaurant on the second floor, Sarkies, is also one of the best in the city. You'll have to try it. It's sort of a combination of Chinese and very good seafood."

"He called you *Pak*, and you referred to me as *Ibu*."

"It's very common here, a form of respect. I could have referred to you as *Bu*, so expect to hear that as well. If you're talking to a female friend or someone like the desk clerk, you'd use the more casual *Mbak*, and if it's a man it would be *Mas*."

"Thank you, that's good to know. You've been living here for a while, I gather."

"Seven years."

"How did that happen?"

He shrugged and then smiled. "I sort of fell into it. When I graduated from the University of Toronto, I joined the Commonwealth Bank entry program. That's where I met Johnny and Henry. I'd been with the bank for just about five years when I came to Asia for the first time. My older brother was running a party boat out of Phuket, and my intention was to help him a bit and have a hell of a holiday." The smile turned into a big grin. "I never went back to the bank. In fact, I didn't even go back to Canada for three years."

"Johnny said you were in the crab business. How did you get from a party boat in Phuket to the crab business in Surabaya?"

Their drinks arrived; Masterson's beer in a glistening bottle, a slice of lime wedged in its throat, and Ava's wine in a glass filled almost to the rim. She took a sip. The waiter hovered, looking down at her. "It's wonderful," she said.

"The twists and turns of my business career in Asia are actually boring. I'm more interested in what you're doing here," Masterson said when they were alone again.

"Business."

"We don't get that many Westerners coming through here, and especially not many Canadians. Despite the city's size, we are a bit of a backwater that way. Most of the Canucks I see are either on their way to Bali or coming back from Bali. You're not going to Bali, are you?"

"I have no plans to."

"It is gorgeous, and worth seeing if you can put up with the Australians," he said, smiling again.

"Like I said, I have no plans to go to Bali."

"Johnny wrote that you're an accountant, like us."

He was going to keep asking questions, Ava knew, and she decided she might as well rehearse the story she intended to spin to the bank. "Yes, I am. I'm here representing a firm out of Hong Kong that has a client who has an interest in expanding his investment portfolio."

"In Surabaya?"

"No, in the Bali area, actually. The client specializes in tourist resorts—three- and four-star mainly, geared towards Hong Kong and Chinese customers. He has several sites in Thailand, one in the Philippines, and now he wants to look at Indonesia."

"I thought you said you weren't going to Bali."

"I'm not. I'm here strictly to assess the investment environment and to help find him a local bank if he decides he wants to come here."

"Do you have a bank in mind?"

Ava paused, the question left hanging. "Several," she finally said.

"I bank at the East Java."

"That's not on my list. One that is," she said, deciding it was time to stick her neck out just a little, "is Bank Linno."

"Linno? They don't have much of a presence here."

"Our Hong Kong office said the president is a Brit. They have a weakness for British bankers."

"Andy Cameron wouldn't like being called a Brit."

"You know him?"

"Of course."

"Of course?" Ava asked, starting to realize that leaving her room hadn't been such a bad idea.

"Like I said, this is a bit of a backwater, and the expatriate community isn't that large. We tend to run into each other and end up socializing. I mean, who do you think goes to a Robbie Burns dinner in Surabaya? Who do you think celebrates Christmas? Not the ninety-nine point nine percent Muslim population." He lowered his voice and leaned closer to her. "And before I was married, I did the single-guy thing with Andy."

"So Andy — Mr. Cameron — is single?"

"Forget the 'Mr. Cameron.' It doesn't suit him, and yes, he is single. He wasn't when he got here, but his wife lasted less than a year before heading back to Scotland with their three daughters. Andy fell into the Asian honey trap, and he's still in it."

"So he likes the girls?"

"Oh yes, he does indeed, and the girls like Andy. And why wouldn't they? He's got money, he's a Westerner, and he's single. He can take his pick, and he isn't shy about enjoying a variety. They come and go about as often as he changes socks. Although I do have to say that his taste leaves something to be desired. In fact he stopped getting invited to some functions because of the girls he was bringing along. Not all cross-cultural encounters are successful, and no matter how badly you want it to work, an Indonesian working girl with her breasts half-hanging out of her dress, her skirt four inches above her knee, and tattoos on her shoulder blades doesn't quite fit in at the British consulate's summer fete."

"Charming."

"Actually he does have charm, in a sly kind of way. He's quick to smile, Andy is, and the girls love that. And he's very confident, to the point of being almost over-the-top cocky. He thinks a lot of himself."

"How did he end up in Surabaya?"

"Who really knows? He says he was recruited, that he was working for a Scottish bank in Rome and was hired to come here."

Ava had finished her wine. Masterson saw her empty glass and then drained his beer. "Another?"

"Sure."

Masterson held his bottle in the air. The waiter was at the table in a flash, taking the bottle and picking up her glass. "Another round," Masterson said.

"How old is Andy?"

"Late thirties, I would guess, though he's starting to look older. He isn't that tall, maybe five six. When he first arrived here, he was whippet thin, or maybe I should say 'weasel thin,' because that's what my wife thinks he looks like. It's his face — it sort of comes to a point, you know, and it's a bit long for his body. He's got a thin nose that sticks out as if he's perpetually sniffing at something."

"That doesn't sound very attractive."

"It wasn't so bad when he was thin, but his lifestyle has wreaked havoc with his body. He's developed this rather large, firm, round belly," he said, patting his own wryly. "I have one too, but I'm tall enough that it gets lost in the shuffle. Andy isn't so lucky. And what makes it worse is that he still insists on wearing tight shirts. He's got a bit of an issue with his self-image. During the week he's in banker suits, but on weekends and party nights he's in ripped jeans and some damn designer shirt made for someone who's fit and in his twenties."

Another San Miguel and glass of Meursault were placed on the table. Ava felt her tummy rumble, and the idea of having dinner with Masterson suddenly became appealing. Before she could speak, his phone rang.

"Hi, babe." He listened intently for a moment and then said, "Okay, see you at home."

"Your wife?"

"Yeah, she's back."

Ava could feel that he was anxious to go. "Is she Indonesian?"

"Yeah. We've been married about three years. She runs an import business. I met her here actually, upstairs at Sarkies. Love at first sight. We were married in Toronto — not that we had a choice. Despite how tolerant this country is, it still wouldn't have gone down too well, her marrying a Christian."

"I'd like to meet her sometime."

"You're here for another day or two?"

"I think so."

"Well, we can have dinner."

"Okay. Just let me know where and when."

Masterson took a deep swig of his beer, and Ava knew she wouldn't have his attention for much longer.

"John, tell me, what would be the best way for me to approach Andy Cameron?"

"You really want to do business with his bank?"

"The Hong Kong client will be upset if I don't at least make the effort to meet with him."

"I'll call him for you."

"You would?"

"Sure."

"That would be great. Where are their offices?"

"Just around the corner from here, near Tunjungan Plaza. No more than a five-minute walk."

"What will you tell him?"

"What do you want me to tell him?"

"That I'd appreciate a meeting — informal or formal, it makes no difference — and the sooner the better, of course."

"Okay, I'll handle it. I'll call him first thing in the morning and then get back to you."

"Thanks."

"My pleasure."

Masterson finished his second beer and then raised his hand towards the waiter, making a signing motion.

"No, please, let me look after the bill," Ava said.

"Okay," he said quickly, and stood, ready to leave.

Ava wasn't used to men letting her pick up a cheque without some fuss. She also wasn't accustomed to their running out on her.

"So you'll call me in the morning?" she asked.

"You got it," he said as he headed for the exit.

(17)

WHEN AVA WOKE AT FOUR THIRTY, SHE KNEW SHE officially had jet lag. She lay still, her eyes closed, her arms limp by her side, trying to coax herself back to sleep. She tried to think of the cottage, the early morning smell of fresh pine, the snap to the air, the lake lapping gently against the dock. But her mind was too active to be seduced so easily. Andy Cameron, a man she didn't even know, kept intruding, her image of him in ripped jeans and tight shirt a compliment to John Masterson's descriptive powers.

She finally gave up and rolled out of bed. She went to one of the windows and levered open the wooden shutters. The sun was inching over the horizon, the gardens below beginning to glint. She listened for a call to prayer and heard nothing.

It was late afternoon in Toronto. Ava thought about calling her mother, Maria, Mimi, and then put them aside. She was back at work and they were best kept at a distance — less distraction that way. She made an instant coffee and then sat at the computer. Uncle had emailed her the information she needed on Perkasa and confirmed that he had sent him enough money to pay for a small gang if she needed it. Amanda had written to say she needed Ava's measurements for her maid-of-honour dress, and was it possible for her to come to Hong Kong for a fitting sometime before Christmas.

Marian had talked to their mother and been told about Ava's role at the wedding. Marian had never met Michael or any of the half-brothers and -sisters; her relationship with their father was far more distant, more neutral—an arrangement encouraged by her *gweilo* civil-servant husband, who had trouble wrapping his head around the complexities of the Lee family. Marian had written, Mummy is over the moon about this. She sees it as a complete validation of her relationship with Daddy. It's like she's won some kind of public moral victory over Wife Number One. I just hope you aren't doing this for her sake, and that it won't be too awkward for you.

In terms of awkward moments in my life, Ava thought, *standing next to Amanda will rank at the bottom of any list.* She wrote back, I understand that Mummy is happy about this, but I have my own relationship with Michael and especially Amanda and my presence at the wedding stems from that. I couldn't be more comfortable with it.

Ava finished her coffee and immediately made another. She checked the door for a newspaper and found none. Back at the computer she pulled up the *Globe and Mail* and read the latest Canadian news. The country was still there, somehow still surviving the ruling Conservative Party and its uptight and thuggish leader.

Light began to stream through the open shutters into the room. Ava went back to the window and saw that the gardens were now fully lit, the grass, leaves, and flowers gleaming with dew that would evaporate in minutes under the full glare of the sun. Traffic was light, with as many street vendors pushing carts loaded with breakfast as there were actual cars.

The hotel had a gym, and Ava debated between going there for a run or outside onto the streets. She was a park girl, liking nothing better than an early morning run in Hong Kong's Victoria Park or Bangkok's Lumpini or New York's Central. But from her window all she could see was pavement. Still, it was better than running indoors, she thought, and it would give her the chance to orient herself. She pulled on her gear, grabbed a bottle of water, and headed downstairs.

The lobby was deserted, occupied only by the desk clerk, a security guard, and the doorman. They all nodded to her as she walked past, mouthing the word *Bu*.

Ava walked out of the hotel onto Embong Malang Street. She stretched, testing her leg. There was still some pain but it was manageable, and she knew she could run at close to full speed. She turned to the right and began to motor. The downtown had an uncluttered look, with offices and shops set well back from the wide streets. The air was humid, thick with the smell of cooking oil, rotting vegetation, exhaust fumes, and garbage left at the roadside for dogs and rats to root through. She gagged a little at first when the smell became especially pungent, but gradually she became acclimatized. After two kilometres straight west, she turned back and found herself breathing normally.

Passing the hotel on the journey back, she found herself on Basuki Rahmat Street, and there, only a few hundred metres away, was Tunjungan Plaza. The complex was massive, with four separate blocks, each five storeys high. A huge SOGO sign advertised the presence of the Japanese retailer. Another promised more than five hundred stores. Ava hadn't seen many shopping centres that large.

She headed east past the plaza, searching for Bank Linno. It was half a kilometre farther on, its name emblazoned in red neon halfway up the eight-storey structure and repeated on the ground level, above double glass doors that led into the customer branch. The building was rather unremarkable: of modest height, the windows small and dusty, the stucco exterior turning yellow in the cracks. It didn't look as if it housed a bank with billions of dollars in capital.

Ava ran for another two kilometres before heading back. The bank didn't look any more imposing from the opposite direction.

She started to sweat the instant she stepped into the air-conditioned hotel lobby. She always sweated when she exercised, but this was different. It was as if her body had been storing heat as she ran instead of releasing it gradually, and the cold air triggered a flood. Her white T-shirt was soaked by the time she was halfway across the lobby, her nipples visible through it in spite of the white athletic bra. The hotel was more active now, and she could feel eyes on her. She wiped her face with the hem of her shirt, briefly exposing her midsection. She should have carried a small towel with her, but after a season of running in Ontario's cottage country—where a normal summer day would have been chilly to any Javanese—she had forgotten about the ravages of humidity.

She stripped as soon as she got to her room. There was no sense showering yet; it would only make her sweat all the more and for longer. She adjusted the air conditioning so it wasn't quite so cold and so strong, and wrapped herself in a robe from the bathroom.

She sat down in a chair by the window and looked out onto the gardens, thinking of the bank and Andy Cameron and trying to come up with an approach that would seem plausible, trying to create a flow of conversation that would throw some light on what was a rather disjointed set of facts. It wasn't an easy transition, moving from questions about the bank and the services it could provide for her fictional Hong Kong company to questions about a defunct Toronto branch, a bogus bank fund, and employees who preferred to be invisible. She was struggling — the connections were almost too tenuous.

When she finally stopped sweating, Ava took off the damp robe and walked into the shower, taking her workout gear with her. When she was done, she wrung out her bra, underwear, T-shirt, and shorts and hung them over the top of the shower stall.

She crawled back into bed and turned on the television. She watched the BBC World News, BBC News from Asia, the BBC world weather report, and BBC Business News. She was just getting into an interview between a presenter and the mayor of London when her cellphone rang.

"Ava Lee," she said, not looking at the ID.

"It's Sonny."

She felt an immediate surge of fear and then caught herself. "Did you find out anything?"

"I had my woman follow him yesterday morning, and

then again today. Both times he went to Queen Elizabeth."

"The hospital?"

"Yeah, here in Kowloon."

So many possibilities, she thought, *and they don't have to be dire*. "Can you figure out why?"

"I'm guessing cancer," Sonny said.

She heard the thickness in his voice and knew he was struggling. "But you aren't positive."

"Ava, it's known as the cancer hospital."

"Still..."

"Yesterday my woman just followed him to the hospital. Today she trailed him right inside. He went to the floor where they give radiation treatments."

"I see."

"Ava, what are we going to do?"

"Well, let's start by not jumping to conclusions," she said with as much force as she could. She moved to the side of the bed, sitting up so she could look out the window at the tops of trees in the garden. Somehow they didn't seem real. "Can you have your woman follow him again?"

"I don't want to push our luck. He's still who he is, and she shared an elevator with him this morning. I'm sure he'd recognize her if we tried it again."

"Can we find out who his doctor is?"

"Which one?"

"What does it matter?" she snapped, impatient more with the situation than with Sonny.

"I don't understand."

She drew a deep breath and forced herself to calm down. Berating Sonny wasn't going to help. "Talk to Lourdes and see if she knows who his family doctor is. If she doesn't, ask around, talk to some of the other uncles...No, no, forget that last bit. For sure they'll tell him. Just talk to Lourdes; she should know. Whatever is going on, his family doctor will have been his first point of contact."

"What if we can't get a name?"

"Then we'll get a list of all the doctors at Queen Elizabeth who do radiation treatment and I'll contact them one by one until I find the one he's seeing."

"He's still at the hospital. I'm going to see Lourdes right away."

"Sonny, don't alarm her."

"She's scared already."

"Don't make it worse. Just tell her you're feeling a bit under the weather and want to see a doctor, and then ask her if Uncle's is nearby."

"She won't believe that."

"Tell her anyway. It's amazing what people are prepared to believe to avoid coping with an uglier reality."

"Okay," he said, without any conviction.

Ava weighed her options. "Sonny, do you want me to come back to Hong Kong today?"

"No, there's no point to that, is there. I mean, we don't know anything for sure, and besides, he's so damn happy that you're back here and you're working a job together. We don't want to ruin that. It's the first time in weeks that I've seen him cheery."

"All right, but if you need me, all you have to do is call. Uncle is more important than any job."

"He's more important than anything," said Sonny.

"I know."

"Than anything," Sonny repeated.

"Yes, Sonny, than anything. Now get over to the apartment and talk to Lourdes before he gets back."

"Okay, boss."

I wish he hadn't called me that, she thought as she ended the call.

She sat on the edge of the bed for another five minutes, her mind spinning. She had known something was wrong, and maybe she had even suspected it was something like cancer. Still, to have it confirmed was different. *Except it isn't confirmed*, she told herself. And then there was the matter of flying back to Hong Kong. It was an emotional reaction, she knew. Get on a plane, go see Uncle, find out what's going on. And then what? What if it wasn't a crisis? How silly would she look then? And she couldn't discount Sonny's logic either. Uncle was happy right now, so why alarm him? Tears welled in her eyes. She wiped them away, but it wasn't so easy to get rid of the knots in her stomach.

Ava slid off the bed and was walking over to her computer to search for the Queen Elizabeth Hospital when the room phone rang.

"Ava Lee," she said dully.

"Good morning, Ava, it's John Masterson."

"Hi, John."

"I just spoke with Andy Cameron and he said he would be happy to meet with you."

"That's good."

"The thing is, though, today his schedule is crammed, and then Saturday and Sunday he has his golf club's annual two-day member/guest tournament. How would dinner tonight work?"

Ava hesitated.

"Actually, Ava, that was my idea. Fay, my wife, and I were going to invite you to join us tonight anyway, and I thought why not throw Andy into the mix. We'll be a foursome, but you can at least have a chance to get acquainted with him, talk a little shop."

That might actually make things easier, Ava thought. *He might be a little more free-wheeling, and with a couple of drinks in him, maybe I can manoeuvre some questions by him.* "Yes, why not," she said.

"Great, I'll let Andy know. We were thinking about Chinese, if that's okay with you. There's a restaurant called X.O Suki not far from the hotel that we like."

"Sounds fine."

"How does that leave your day?" he asked.

Now where is this going? Ava thought. "Reasonably free."

"Because Fay doesn't have to work and she's offered to take you sightseeing if you're up to it."

"I wouldn't want to impose."

"It isn't like that at all. She'd love to do it."

What else was there for her to do? Hang around the room and mope? "Then in that case I'm happy to accept her offer."

"Wait a second," Masterson said, his voice becoming muffled. "I just spoke with Fay. She'll meet you in the hotel lobby at around ten."

Ava checked her watch. It was just nine thirty. The Mastersons weren't people for wasting time.

(18)

AVA HADN'T KNOWN WHAT TO EXPECT IN FAY Masterson, certainly not a near double to Amanda Yee. She was young, maybe in her mid-twenties, not quite five feet tall in her Puma runners, and rail-thin in a pair of tight jeans and a T-shirt with DIOR stitched in beadwork across the front. Her hair was cut into a bob, making her fine-featured face look slightly gaunt. Her dark brown eyes had thick lashes heavy with mascara, and her lips were generously glossed in bright red. She looked, Ava thought, at least partially Chinese.

Fay saw Ava first and waved to her as she came down the stairs. Masterson had obviously given his wife a description. The two women shook hands, gauging each other. Ava was in her training pants and a black T-shirt and wore no makeup. She must have passed initial inspection, because Fay gave her a quick, bright smile and said, "My car is outside." Then she began to chat as if they were lifelong friends — another Amanda trait.

"Have you been to Surabaya before?" she asked as they walked out of the hotel.

"No."

"Then forgive me for doing my tour-guide thing," Fay said. "I took history in college and I'm proud of our city. It's the second-largest city in Indonesia, with a metropolitan population that has to be six or seven million now, but it's manageable, don't you think? Not like Jakarta, with its horrible traffic and pollution. The name is more interesting too. *Suro* means 'shark' and *baya* means 'crocodile.' According to legend, the two animals battled here to see who would have dominance."

"And who won?" Ava asked as they reached the car, an Audi TT.

"I have no idea," Fay laughed.

"I have an Audi at home," Ava said, lowering her head to climb into the sports car.

"What model?"

"An A6."

"Ah," Fay said, acknowledging a peer. "So today I thought we'd visit some museums, maybe lunch near Kalimas Harbour, and then go to the Arab quarter and see some of our beautiful mosques."

"I'm completely in your hands."

"About a month ago John had some visitors here from Boston and I took them on a tour. One of the sites was the Majapahit Hotel, but you don't need to see that, do you."

"It's a great hotel."

"Better than Raffles."

"So everyone keeps telling me."

Fay pulled away from the hotel and into light traffic. "The city was founded in the thirteenth century," she said. "It was a sultanate originally, but then the Dutch came in the mid-1770s and stayed until the Japanese occupied it in 1942. Do you know much about colonial Asia?"

"My family is from Hong Kong."

"There are big differences between the British and the Dutch. The British actually built institutions and infrastructure that were meant to last long after they were gone. The Dutch didn't care about anything other than money. Everything they built in our country was designed for a single purpose: to maximize the outflow of goods and profits to Holland. I mean, when the British left India, Malaysia, Sri Lanka, Hong Kong, they also left behind legal, bureaucratic, and educational systems and some concept of parliamentary tradition. The Dutch were here for more than two hundred years and didn't leave anything other than bad memories."

Ava's family had its own views on the British regime in Hong Kong, and they weren't quite so rosy. She didn't know enough about it, though, to start a debate. Instead she was struck by how much Fay reminded her of Amanda. "I'm sorry, I don't meant to be rude, but I can't help thinking that you have some Chinese blood in you," she said.

"I do. My family has been in Java for more than three hundred years — the family name was Ho. There's been a lot of intermarriage, but even until about fifty years ago Ho was a family name."

"What happened then?"

"Suharto passed a law that forced all the Indo-Chinese to change their names to Indonesian ones. My family's name became Supomo. When Sukarno replaced Suharto, the law was revoked but the name stuck, except for my older sister, who reclaimed our original family name. She's a doctor here, Vivian Ho. She tried to talk me into changing mine back as well, except I had met John, and I liked the idea of being Fay Masterson," she said. "Ava, are you married?"

"No."

"Boyfriend?"

"No."

"And you're such a pretty woman."

"I'm fussy."

Fay nodded. "Me too. I waited for John, and then I made John wait as well. He'd been spoiled by too many women too willing to sleep with him. I made him chase me."

She stopped the car in front of what looked like a colonial mansion. "This is the House of Sampoerna. The building was originally an orphanage, built in the 1800s. It was bought in the 1930s by Liem Seeng Tee and he turned it into a cigarette factory."

"Chinese?"

"Yes, that's why I brought you here. Sampoerna is now the name the family uses, but I prefer to think of it as 'the House of Tee.' It's a great story."

The house was part museum, part art gallery, and still functioning as a cigarette factory. Ava's initial interest was the amazing story of Liem Seeng Tee. After his mother died in China, his father took their three young children to Indonesia, only to die soon after their arrival. Tee was adopted, given a rudimentary education, and then sent out to work. With a bicycle as his only asset, he proceeded to parlay that into a cigarette empire that was now, having passed from the family's hands to Philip Morris, the fifth largest in the world. Smarts, sacrifice, hard work, long-term vision, total commitment, maybe a bit of luck.

Those were the reasons for his success, and the reasons why nearly every economy in Southeast Asia — Malaysia, the Philippines, and Thailand included — was controlled by the Chinese. The house was portrayed as a living, working monument to the company he had built, but to Ava's mind it was all about Tee.

"Have you ever smoked?" Fay asked when they got to the factory and looked out on several hundred people, mainly women, hand-rolling cigarettes.

"No."

"Me neither, but I find this interesting all the same. They make Dji Sam Soe cigarettes here. They're the most expensive and prestigious of all the *kretek* cigarettes. As you can see, they're handmade. We can actually make one here. Want to give it a go?"

"Sure, why not," she said.

The woman who instructed them was more than just hands-on. She had an encyclopedic knowledge of the blends that Tee had developed decades ago and still existed. Ava found the information she imparted on cloves particularly interesting. Who would have known that Zanzibar had the world's best?

Ava dropped her crudely rolled attempt into a garbage can as they left the building. "That was fun. I just can't help feeling a bit sorry that he felt he had to change his family name."

"Well, at least he chose a good one. *Sampoerna* is the Indonesian word for 'perfect.'"

"The House of Perfect... the Perfect House. How clever."

They walked to the car. It was just past noon and the sun bore down on them. It had to be close to thirty degrees.

Fay rolled down the windows while they waited for the air conditioning to kick in. "Is it always this hot?" Ava asked.

"Every day. I don't think the temperature varies more than three or four degrees all year round. And we're on the coast — it's even warmer inland. The only variety we get in weather is rain. We're still in the dry season, at the tail end of it actually. In the next few weeks the rains will kick in and then we'll have the monsoons to contend with. I have to tell you, when John and I got married in Toronto, it was also September, and evidently fine weather for that time of year, but I almost froze to death. I can't imagine how thin my blood is."

Fay pulled out of the parking lot. "We'll go down to the harbour. There's a seafood restaurant there I really like." She turned onto a road that was flanked on the right by a river. "The Kalimas — it runs down to the harbour and feeds into the Madura Strait. We're still a major seaport, as you'll see."

Ava was quite taken with ports and thought she had seen just about every type, but Kalimas Harbour was spectacularly original. It was filled with *pinisis* — two-masted wooden sailing ships — and *praus* — double-hulled ships — their big, colourful sails rippling in the light breeze. These weren't museum pieces; they were real, working ships that filled every berth and lined up three-deep waiting to load or unload an eclectic array of goods.

"This is wonderful," Ava said as they drove past one with Kia sedans on its deck, another with boxes marked HEWLETT PACKARD, and yet more, holding cages stuffed with chickens, live cows, bags of cement, bags of rice.

Fay turned down a side street, drove the car halfway onto the sidewalk, and turned off the engine. They were directly in front of a restaurant that opened onto the street. "We'd better move fast if we want to get a table," she said, leaping from the car.

They sat no more than a yard from the sidewalk, just inside the shade. "John said we're going to X.O Suki tonight, so I thought it might be different for you to eat something local."

"I'm easy," said Ava.

"You want a beer?"

"White wine?"

"They won't have it."

"Then just a sparkling water."

"Bintang, the local beer, is good."

"No, thanks. Beer gives me headaches."

"How about food — any allergies or anything?"

"Order what you want."

Fay spoke in Indonesian to the waiter, then turned to Ava when he left. "John told me you're an accountant."

"I am," Ava said, and repeated the story about the Hong Kong client.

"He's a bit confused as to why you want to meet with Bank Linno. They're not exactly first-class, you know."

"My client gave me the name and asked me to check up on them. It isn't my choice."

Their drinks arrived in bottles with two frosted empty glasses and a plate of lime wedges. "John says you're a friend of a friend."

"That's true — Johnny Yan."

"He lives in Toronto, right?"

"Yes."

"And you're in Hong Kong?"

Ava saw that Fay was trying to connect the dots. She was bright, this one, and more alert than her husband. "I live in Toronto, but I have a client base that's mainly Asian and I'm affiliated with a company in Hong Kong, so I travel there quite often."

"I see."

The waiter brought a plate of plain white long-grain rice piled high in the shape of a cone. "We can spice that up with the sauces that come with our meal," Fay said. "I ordered fried fish, sardines with a tomato sambal, and shrimp in a hot coconut sauce."

"*Sambal* means 'sauce,' doesn't it?"

"Yeah, basically it does. And nearly all our sauces have some amount of coconut milk in them."

"I'm not up to speed on Indonesian cooking."

"Why would you be?"

"Exactly."

The dishes came together, and talk ended as Fay spooned rice onto both of their plates, then placed the tiny whole, cleaned sardines right in the middle and coated them with tomato sambal.

Fay ate the way Ava did, quickly and efficiently, as if afraid to let the food get cold or the flavours dissipate. Halfway through the meal they finished their drinks and ordered another round.

When they were done, Ava sighed. "Those were brilliant choices."

"Did you like your food?"

"Loved it."

"How do you keep so thin?"

"Exercise and genes."

"I'm just genes." The sun had crept sideways and was now starting to encroach on their table. "Time to leave," Fay said.

They hadn't driven far before the streets began to narrow. Fay parked the car on the sidewalk again. "We'll have to walk from here."

"You're not afraid of getting a ticket or being towed?"

Fay looked at her as if she had made a joke. "No, that won't be a problem," she said, opening her glove compartment. She pulled out a plastic sign and placed it on the dash. "That says, *Don't dare give this car a ticket*." And then she took out two scarves. "Let's walk."

Whatever breeze there was in the narrow street was blowing in their direction, and Ava began to pick up faint aromas. She looked around and couldn't see their origin. Then Fay took a hard right and they were on a street lined on either side with shops and stalls. "The Arab quarter," she said.

Fay led Ava through the warren, past shops selling fruit, pistachios, dates, sultanas, rugs, prayer beads, an array of spices, roast lamb, skewered chicken sizzling on hotplates, jewellery. Ava wanted to loiter, maybe shop a little. Fay kept walking. After two more turns they entered a narrow alley and the sky disappeared. The passageway was covered, like a souk in Marrakech, hung about with bright cloths, batiks, and beads in a hundred brilliant colours. Fay handed Ava a scarf. "Here we need to cover our heads so as not to draw attention."

Ava followed her example and tucked in behind her as the crowd began to thicken, forcing them to walk in single file. They shuffled along until Fay moved to one side. Ava found herself in an open courtyard, a mosque in front of them.

"This is the Ampel Mosque. It's the oldest and most sacred mosque in Java."

To Ava's eye it didn't look any different from most of the other mosques she had seen, but she bit her tongue. What was different were the gardens to the side, filled with low frangipani trees and several knots of worshippers prostrate on the ground outside the mosque.

"Those are pilgrims who come to worship Sunan Ampel," Fay said, noting Ava's interest. "He was one of the nine founders of Islam in Java, and he built this mosque. When he died in 1481, he was buried here. They're praying at his grave."

"Most religion is lost on me," said Ava.

Fay glanced quickly in her direction. "Don't say that too loudly here."

"I don't mean to be disrespectful."

"Do you want to go into the mosque?"

"I'd rather not."

Fay turned. "Then let's walk back to the car. I have some shopping to do on the way. I hope you don't mind."

As they walked away, Ava said, "I hope I didn't offend you. You're Muslim, correct?"

"Notionally."

"What does that mean?"

"It means that my family is in business and that one of my many dead relatives decided decades ago that it was easier to do business as a Muslim. None of us actually practise the religion."

"I'm the same kind of Catholic."

"In name only?"

"Exactly."

It was a long, slow journey back to the car. Fay was at the market for fruit and pepper, and every third vendor seemed to be selling one or the other. While Fay haggled, Ava slipped into some clothing and jewellery shops. By the time they got back to the car, Fay had two bags filled with oranges, papayas, and mangos. Ava had twenty-two-karat gold hoop earrings for her mother and Maria, and sarongs in various colours and sizes for Mimi, Marian, and her nieces.

Fay looked at her watch. "We need to get you back to the hotel soon if we're to have time to shower and get dressed for dinner."

"I'm ready to go if you are."

"Just one more stop, I think."

They drove through more of old Surabaya, Ava sensing the river's presence the entire way, to what was obviously the city's Chinatown. "My grandfather used to bring me here when I was a little girl," Fay said as she parked the car, this time almost completely on the sidewalk.

They walked past noodle shops, herbal stores with their baskets of dried twigs, restaurants with barbecued pigs hanging in the window. Ava could have been in Hong Kong, or in downtown Toronto. Fay turned into a narrow alleyway. Ava followed, right into a cloud of incense.

At the end of the alley stood a traditional Chinese temple, fronted by bronze statues and altars meant for worship. There were as many people there as had been at the mosque. They kneeled and bowed in front of the statues and placed fruit on the altars, the joss sticks held between their palms leaching thin coils of sweet smoke. There was a line of candles on either side of the alleyway, each candle about three metres high. "They light those at night," Fay said. "It lends even more of an aura to the place."

"What is this temple called?"

"Kong Co Kong Tik Cun Ong."

Ava looked at the separate groups of worshippers. "Why are there so many altars?"

"My grandfather used to pray at the one on the left—it's Confucian. The one in the middle is Buddhist and the one on the right is for Taoists. I guess it's a multi-denominational temple," Fay said.

"I've never heard of such a thing."

"Well, here it is."

"Do you ever pray here?"

"Yes. I can't help myself; it's like I'm reconnecting with my grandfather."

There were stands to the left of the temple selling various fruits and joss sticks. Ava left Fay and walked over to them. She bought an orange and four joss sticks, which she had the vendor light. When she returned, Fay had moved to the Confucian altar, her head bowed in prayer.

Ava went to the Taoist one and placed the orange at the base of the statue. She slipped the sticks between her palms, the smoke from the incense rising towards her face. Head bowed, rocking ever so slightly, she began to pray. She prayed for her mother and her father. She prayed for her sister and her nieces. She prayed for Mimi and Derek and their unborn child. She prayed for Maria. She prayed for all of her half-siblings. And then she prayed for Uncle. As she did, tears began to roll down her cheeks. *If there is a god, any god—Taoist, Christian, Muslim, Hindu—please look after Uncle,* she prayed.

She wasn't sure how long she had stood in front of the altar, but if it weren't for the gentle tap on her shoulder from Fay, the joss sticks might have burned their way into her flesh. They walked in silence back to the car, each lost in her own thoughts.

Fay was the first to speak on the way back to the hotel. "We don't overdress for dinner here, but you'll need to change."

Ava smiled, relieved that Fay had not asked about her tears. "I have some linen slacks and a dress shirt."

"Perfect."

"What time?"

"We'll pick you up at the hotel around six."

"I'll be waiting."

Ava felt Fay looking sideways at her. "Is anything wrong?"

"No," Fay said. "There's just something I need to say."

"And what's that?"

"Andy Cameron... he's a bit of a pig."

"So John told me last night," Ava said, wondering why it was so important to tell her.

"He's going to hit on you for sure. He can't help himself."

"I can handle it."

Fay gave her a double take. "I had to tell you anyway. I've heard things that I don't like. He can get out of hand, it seems."

"He won't get close enough to try."

"I'm not trying to put a damper on the evening. I'm sure we'll have a good time, and he can be fun. It's just that I don't want to see you put in an awkward position."

"Enough said, Fay. I do understand."

"Just be careful."

(19)

IT WAS JUST PAST FIVE WHEN FAY PULLED UP TO THE entrance of the Majapahit. "Bu Ava," the doorman said as she reached the entrance.

She checked her cellphone as she walked up the stairs to her room. It hadn't rung all afternoon and she couldn't remember the last time that had happened. Out of habit she hit the Missed Calls button and saw two from Sonny. Was her ring mode on? It was. When had he called? She realized it was when she'd been praying at the temple.

Ava waited until she was in her room before returning his calls. His *wei* was brusque. "It's Ava. Sorry I couldn't answer the phone before. I was in a temple."

"I talked to Lourdes."

"Good."

"The doctor's name is Parker."

"*Gweilo*?"

"All I know is his name is Graham Parker."

"Kowloon?"

"Yeah, near the Ocean Mall."

"Thanks."

"You'll call him?"

"Sonny, this is not something I can do over the phone. I'll be back in Hong Kong in a few days, I think, and I'll try to set up a meeting."

"Lourdes is scared."

"I know."

"So am I."

"Me too. But I can tell you now, if I phone the doctor he won't tell me anything. I need to get in front of him, so you're going to have to be patient until I get there. And for goodness sake, tell Lourdes to stay calm. We don't know anything for sure, do we."

"No," Sonny said.

"No. So let's get our facts straight before we jump to conclusions."

"I'll talk to her."

"Thanks."

Ava hung up and sat on the side of bed. Now she had to get calm. This job, which hadn't meant that much to her when she started it, now seemed almost meaningless. She'd have dinner with Cameron and find out what she could about the bank. That was as far as she was willing to commit. And if the dinner yielded nothing of interest, she was getting on a plane for Hong Kong.

There was a smell in the room. Incense. Her hair and T-shirt were imbued with it. She stripped and went into the bathroom, the marble floor cold to her feet. She turned the shower on full blast and jacked up the water temperature to as close to scalding as she could bear. She washed her body quickly and then poured the entire bottle of hotel shampoo into her hair. She scrubbed, her fingers kneading her scalp, washing out the incense and trying to rid her mind of negative thoughts.

When she was done, she stood in the middle of the bathroom, water dripping from her body, and towelled her hair as briskly as she had washed it. *Dinner tonight and then I'm out of here*, she thought. *And if this is my going-away party, then I'm going to look good.*

Ava put on black lace underwear and a black push-up bra. She brushed her hair until she could see it gleam in the mirror, and then fixed it back with her ivory chignon pin. She had packed a pink shirt that was a particular favourite, and she secured its cuffs with the green jade links. She left the two top buttons of the shirt undone to show her gold crucifix. Then she slipped on her fitted black linen slacks and her Cole Haan black leather pumps.

She seldom used much makeup, but tonight she added an extra touch of red lipstick and a little more mascara than usual. The effect was still understated, but the lipstick created a nice contrast to her skin and the mascara magnified her eyes.

She put on her Cartier watch, the shirt cuff sliding over it. It was almost six o'clock. She debated taking her Chanel bag and decided against it. The notebook and her phone could stay in the room as well. She'd go to dinner *au naturel.*

(20)

"I'M WITH THE TWO MOST BEAUTIFUL WOMEN IN Surabaya," John Masterson said from the driver's seat of his Mercedes.

"Well trained, isn't he?" Fay said, turning back to look at Ava from the passenger seat.

They had been close to half an hour late getting to the hotel and Ava had been in the lobby, phoneless, at six. Fay had her paged, so rather than hanging around at the door, Ava sat in the lounge and had a glass of Meursault.

Fay came into the hotel to get her. Ava watched as she crossed the lobby, stilettos clicking. She was wearing a sundress, white with a delicate floral pattern. The dress came just above the knee and had a neckline that exposed the top of abundant breasts. Heads turned as she passed and Ava saw her smile, obviously aware of and enjoying the attention.

"You look absolutely gorgeous," Ava said.

Fay nodded in agreement. "And so do you. I wish I had your elegance."

"Don't be silly," Ava said, pleased all the same with the compliment.

They left the hotel side by side, Fay's stilettos making her almost exactly the same height as Ava. The doorman bowed to the waist. "Bu Fay, Bu Ava," he said, running to open the car doors for them.

"Sorry to be late," Masterson said as Ava got in. "I was on a conference call with New York. And then Cameron got tied up at the bank and phoned to say he wasn't going to be at the restaurant until seven anyway."

They pulled out of the hotel, turned left, and then turned left again into the parking lot of Tunjungan Plaza. "Goodness me, we could have walked," Ava said.

"We are going to walk," Masterson said.

The mall was even larger inside than it looked from the outside, and Ava would never have found the restaurant by herself. Even with Masterson's knowledge of the place it was still close to a ten-minute walk from the car to the restaurant. There was a long line outside that Masterson ignored, moving to the entrance and shouting something in Indonesian to a host. The host waved them inside and took them to a table at the back of the restaurant.

"No Cameron yet," Masterson said as they sat.

"I owe you a couple of thanks," Ava said to him. "Fay was a wonderful guide and hostess today, and you got Cameron for me tonight."

"I'll take the one for Fay. As for Cameron, let's wait until the evening is over."

"Speaking of whom..." Fay said, looking towards the door.

He was in a grey business suit, the large knot of his tie pulled halfway down his chest, the tail swinging right and left as he bounced across the floor. He was shorter than Ava had imagined, maybe not even five foot six, and with the belly that Masterson had accurately described he looked a bit like a garden gnome in a suit. His hair was streaked blond, cut short, and gelled into little spikes. His lips were compressed as if in thought, his eyes darting around the restaurant. Masterson raised an arm and waved lazily. Cameron saw them and a quick grin cut across his face.

Masterson stood and extended his hand. Cameron shook it, turned to Fay, kissed her on both cheeks, and then stood back to stare at Ava. His eyes were blue, almost sparkling. *This is either a very happy man or he's on some kind of medication*, Ava thought.

"John didn't exaggerate. He said you were a real beauty," he said.

"Thank you."

Cameron settled in at the table. "Have you ordered yet?"

"Waiting for you," Masterson said.

"Beer please, lots of beer. It's Friday fucking night and I need to wash the taste of the bank out of my mouth."

"How about you girls?" Masterson asked.

"White wine for me," Fay said.

"And me," Ava said.

"Two beers and a bottle of wine then, and if you don't mind, I'd like to order our food at the same time. I'm starving."

"Order away," Cameron said.

John turned to Ava. "Do you have any preferences?"

"I eat everything. Please order for the table and don't worry about me."

He signalled for the waiter. Masterson spoke to him in Indonesian, the man nodding his head as his pencil scribbled away.

Fay whispered to Ava, "Blue crabs, cleaned, cut in half, and cooked with shallots, chilis, and tamarind. Shrimp steamed with curry in banana leaves. A whole steamed lobster with ginger and garlic. A fish steamed in rice wine with seaweed and cilantro. And nasi goring. John, why nasi goring?"

"What's more Indonesian?"

"No, it doesn't fit. Just get plain steamed rice."

He spoke to the waiter and Ava saw the nasi goring entry get scratched.

"So your name is Ava Lee, I understand," Cameron said.

"Yes, it is, Mr. Cameron."

"Andy."

"Ava."

"Andy and Ava... Has a nice ring to it," he said, the grin returning.

"Thank you for taking the time to come tonight. After your remark about the bank and beer, I can't help but think I'm imposing."

"Just a little, and besides, we don't have to talk about banking."

"That's why I'm in Surabaya."

"And why my little bank?"

"I got your name from my client in Hong Kong. I'm just following through."

"You're an accountant, John tells me."

"I am."

"From where? Your accent isn't like any I've heard from Hong Kong."

"I'm Canadian-raised."

"Ah, that must be the John connection."

"Exactly," Masterson said.

"Who's your Hong Kong client?" Cameron asked Ava.

"Dynamic Accounting."

"No, I mean the investor John mentioned who was interested in Bali."

"I'm afraid I'm not at liberty to disclose that right now."

"Then what do you want from me?"

"I was given the names of several banks by the accounting firm in Hong Kong. They like to use local financing wherever possible, and your bank is a candidate."

"And if we have no interest?"

Ava shrugged. "No matter. We'll find someone."

"Don't throw us overboard so quickly," Cameron said.

"I feel like I'm the one being thrown," said Ava.

"No, no, no, we'll talk, we'll talk," Cameron said. "Just not on an empty stomach."

The drinks were brought by the waiter and an assistant. They seemed awfully eager to please either Masterson or Cameron, as they poured the beers first and then passed the bottle of wine to Ava.

"Let my wife try it," Masterson said.

"Just open it and pour," Fay said.

When four glasses were full, Masterson raised his and said, "*Salut*."

Cameron leaned towards Ava, tapped his glass against hers, and said, "To new friends."

God help me, she thought. She began to speak, but the first word was still on her tongue when Masterson said to Fay, "What did you girls get up to today?"

It took Fay five minutes to get them to the Ampel Mosque, and by then the plate of white rice was on the table and the first of the seafood dishes came rolling out. The men plunged into dinner, scarcely paying attention to Fay's continuing narrative. Ava knew that whatever questions she had were best left for later.

The two men drank three beers during the meal. Fay and Ava hadn't finished their bottle of wine when the last dish was cleared.

"We have to have dessert," Masterson said. "Fried bananas and ice cream all around."

"Why not?" Cameron said.

Ava sat back in her chair. "Andy, do you mind if I ask you a few questions?"

"Of course not," he said, starting on another beer.

"I'm curious. How did a Scot find his way to Indonesia?"

"Did you ask John how a Canadian did?"

"Yes."

"And that's true," Masterson said.

Cameron smiled. "Nosy, is she?"

"Curious," Ava repeated.

"Well, it's a simple enough story," Cameron said. "I was working for a Scottish bank in Rome and Bank Linno came calling."

"How did they find you?"

"I like to think I had developed a reputation. As a breed, Scottish bankers are maybe the best in the world, and I worked harder than most. I had that Rome office humming. Linno wasn't the first offer I had from a foreign bank, you know."

"But you accepted their offer."

"They offered me more money than anyone else, and a chance to be the boss."

It was close to drunken bravado, except that Cameron couldn't seem to maintain eye contact with her. Ava felt the first flutter of doubt.

"Lucky you. Lucky them."

"No regrets from my side, and none from theirs, I can tell you."

"Quite a move, though, from a Scottish bank with offices in Rome to a provincial bank in Indonesia."

"What do you mean?" he shot back.

"In some eyes it could be seen as moving down market."

"Let me tell you something, girlie," he said. "It's all about opportunity. I was given the chance to grow this bank, and that's what I've done. It's twenty times the size it was in terms of assets and deposits since I took over, and it's not just an East Java bank anymore. So you can tell your client in Hong Kong that if he decides to do business with us, he'll be dealing with a first-rate organization."

"I didn't mean to cause any offence," Ava said.

"None taken," he said, his tone belying his words.

"So your bank does business outside East Java?"

"Why does that matter if your client wants to do business here?"

"I guess it doesn't," she said, wondering why he was so defensive.

"Good."

Ava and Fay both passed on the bananas and ice cream. Fay wrapped her arm around John's neck, kissing him on the ear, and watched him eat his share. Ava kept her eyes on Cameron. He was working hard at appearing cool. *There is something there*, she thought. *Maybe nothing important, but there is something.*

"That was a great meal," Ava said as the bill arrived and was quickly picked up by Masterson.

Cameron finished his fourth beer and burped. "Excuse me... Manners," he said, and then grinned the same cocky grin she'd seen when he first walked into the restaurant. "Ms. Lee, why don't I walk you back to your hotel? We can talk banking on the way and I can buy you a nightcap."

"Sure," she said, ignoring the panicked look from Fay.

"I can drive you," Masterson said.

"No, I'd rather walk," Ava said.

They left the restaurant together, Masterson and Fay peeling off right to the car park, Cameron leading Ava to the left.

Just before they exited the mall, Cameron stopped. "Look, I have a toilet kit at my office and it's only a few hundred yards from here. If you want I can go get it."

"I'm sorry?" Ava said, not quite sure she had heard him properly.

"I'll spend the night at the Majapahit if you want. Must get lonely for a girl like you, Friday night in a strange city."

"I don't get that kind of lonely," Ava said.

"I don't make that kind of offer to many girls," Cameron said, smiling at her discomfort.

"Am I to take that as a compliment?"

"Well, I don't do ugly."

"And I don't do with someone I hardly know. I'm an old-fashioned girl who likes to take her time and ease into things, so if you would rather head on home instead of walking me back to the hotel I'll understand."

"Hell no, I'll walk you. And I'll still buy you that nightcap while we talk about your client."

"And your bank."

"Of course."

As they walked she kept waiting for him to say something else or try something else, but he was quiet and polite, even keeping a physical distance between them. His directness had surprised her, even with Fay's warning in mind. Now, she hoped, the moves were over and they could actually talk business.

The hotel lounge was quiet. They found a corner table with no one within hearing distance. "I'm switching to Scotch," he said.

"I'll stay with wine," said Ava.

"Pak Andy, Ibu Ava," the waiter said.

"I'll have Glenlivet, neat."

"The Meursault," Ava said.

"Your client, what is he actually looking to do here?" Cameron asked when they were alone.

Ava took the business card from the Hong Kong accounting firm and placed it on the table in front of him. "He has an interest in real estate either directly or indirectly attached to the tourist trade. He owns several resorts in Thailand and another in the Philippines, and he has interests in various adjacent properties such as shopping centres, restaurants, and the like."

Cameron pursed his lips and frowned. "Ava, do you know — and the client should know — that foreigners can't own land here?"

Shit, she thought, and then started backpedalling. "Of course, it's the same in Thailand. There he took on some Thai partners and then papered himself into total control and effective ownership through the back door."

"He won't find it as easy to do that here."

"Surely it's nothing a good lawyer can't handle?"

Cameron looked dubious, and then his face lit up as their drinks arrived. "Cheers," he said, extending his glass.

"Cheers," Ava said, tapping it with hers.

"Lawyer or not, it can be tricky," said Cameron.

Ava was glad to hear him sticking to the business discussion. "I see from the briefing notes my client gave us that your bank is owned by a local law firm."

"Our ownership is a private matter," he said sharply.

"Sorry, I wasn't prying," Ava said. "I just thought that if my client needed a law firm yours might fit the bill."

"Not a good idea. Don't like to mix things about like that. If he needs a lawyer, talk to John Masterson."

There was that harsh edge to his voice again. *Back off or prod?* Ava wondered. "That's a good suggestion, thank you. Now tell me, Andy, earlier at dinner you didn't want to talk about your non–East Java banking activity. Was there any particular reason for that?"

He swilled back his Scotch and held the empty glass in the air. "Another," he shouted. She waited for him to answer. He said, "You want another wine?"

"Sure, I can handle one more, but first I need to use the ladies' room."

"Right over there," he said, pointing to the door behind the bar.

She peed, washed her hands twice, and then looked in the mirror. *Another ten minutes with the Scotsman and that's it,* she thought and then turned and went back to the lounge.

The glass she had left on the table had been just under half full. Now it was brimming. "I had him top it up,"

Cameron said. "No point wasting."

"That's sensible," she said.

"Scottish stereotype, but true all the same."

"Speaking of which, what makes you Scots such good bankers?"

"We don't trust anyone," he said without hesitation.

"Trust?"

"Everyone lies — about why they need money, about their net worth, about their collateral. It never fucking ends. My old boss at Stirling used what he called the five-check system, and all he meant was check every fucking thing five times."

Ava noticed that his second Scotch was already finished, and that his language was deteriorating in proportion to his intake. "I'll give you all the information you need. You can check ten times and it will still stand up."

Cameron went silent, and Ava wondered if he was going to argue. Then he said, "My turn. I need to use the loo now."

Ava sipped her wine and replayed the evening in her mind. So far it had been almost a complete dud. Cameron had no interest in discussing the workings of his bank. That by itself was a bit unusual. What was there to hide? Maybe nothing; maybe it was nothing more than a private bank retaining its privacy. What bothered her more was his attitude every time she ventured into that area. All he had to say was, *Sorry, we're private.* Instead he seemed nettled. *One more go*, she said to herself, *and then I'm heading upstairs.*

She kept checking her watch and began to worry when more than fifteen minutes had passed. *Five more minutes and I'm sending the waiter into the men's bathroom,* she thought.

As if on cue, Cameron walked back into the lounge, a bounce in his step. He was snapping the fingers of his right hand, and even from a distance she could see the gleam in his eyes.

She finished her wine. "Andy, you okay?" she asked.

"Dandy, just dandy."

She sat back in the chair, her face flushed. *No more wine for you, girl,* she thought.

Cameron stood in front of her. The only problem was that she could see two of him. Jet lag and wine were a bad combination, she knew, and now she was paying the price. She steadied herself and tried to get to her feet. And didn't make it.

(21)

WHEN SHE WOKE, SHE WAS FLOODED BY CONTRADIC-tions.

Light was streaming in through open windows. When hadn't she closed the curtains or shutters?

She was naked.

Her head felt heavy, jumbled.

And then there was the discomfort between her legs.

Before she could sort things out, her eyelids became too heavy and she blacked out.

The next time Ava woke, she shivered. What was that light? Why was she naked? She turned to look at the bedside clock. It read 8:04.

She started to rise and then felt the strangeness between her legs. She settled back into the bed.

She lay there for minutes, trying to remember the events of the night before. All she could recall was drinking wine with Andy Cameron in the lounge downstairs.

She put her hand on her leg and felt something scabby on her thigh. When she looked down, she saw the same kind of caked smear across her chest, between her breasts.

Ava got up and went to the bathroom and took a robe from the hook on the door. She put it on and went back to the bed. She wanted a doctor.

The hotel operator wasn't helpful at first, but by the time Ava had repeated her request for a third time, the number was obtained and the call was made.

"Hello?" a sleepy voice said.

"Is this Vivian Ho?" Ava asked.

"Yes. Who is this?"

"My name is Ava Lee. I'm a friend of Fay and John. I'm visiting from Canada and I've had an accident. Could you please come to my hotel to help me?"

"I don't know you."

"Of course you don't. I could ask you to call Fay, but it would cause me no end of humiliation. Please. I'm at the Majahapit, room 313."

"This is most unusual."

"So is what I think happened to me."

"What did you say your name is?"

"Ava Lee."

"And what do you think happened?"

Ava closed her eyes and heard herself struggling for breath. "I think I was raped."

"Have you called the police?"

"No."

"I think—"

"You're the only person I have called and the only person I will call. So please, just come here."

"I'm about twenty minutes away," she said, her voice now fully alert.

"Thank you."

"But I should stop at my office on the way and pick up some things."

"Things?"

"Would you take a morning-after pill as a precaution against possible pregnancy?"

"Of course, and how about tests for sexually transmitted infections."

"It's too soon. The window for the bacterial type is three days, but for type-specific viruses such as AIDS, herpes, and hepatitis it's at least two weeks. I should take a blood sample to establish a baseline for you, but in terms of knowing anything definite, I'm afraid you'll have to wait."

"I think I was drugged. Can you at least check on that?"

"Yes, I'll take a urine sample."

"Thank you."

"Now, Ms. Lee, I think it's still advisable to call the police."

"No."

"I think—"

"No."

Vivian Ho paused and then said, "With the stop, I should be there in about half an hour to forty minutes."

"Thank you."

"You said room 313?"

"Yes, come right up."

Ava sat down by the window looking out on the gardens. She knew there were trees and shrubs and flowers, but they were a blur. Nothing registered. Nothing mattered.

She heard the phone before she heard the door. "Ms. Lee, Dr. Ho is at your door. She says she's been knocking for a few minutes."

Ava got up and opened the door. She saw a slightly older

and more conservative version of Fay. Vivian Ho was the same height and also thin, but with hair that hung down to her shoulders and not a trace of makeup.

"Thank you so much for coming," she said. "I didn't hear you at the door."

"Are you all right?"

"No, I don't think I am," Ava said, turning away and walking into the room. "Aside from the physical discomfort, my head keeps wandering off."

"I need to examine you."

"I know," Ava said.

"Have you done anything?"

"I don't know what you mean."

"Have you washed? Have you taken any pills?"

"No."

"Then, as awkward as this is, please take off your bathrobe and lie on the bed."

Ava closed her eyes, slipped the bathrobe from her shoulders, and lay on her back.

"You have dried semen on your thighs and between your breasts. There's some bruising around your vagina, and it seems...it seems as if someone was very rough. I would guess that you were penetrated repeatedly. Ms. Lee, how did this happen?"

"Do you mean why am I asking if I was raped?"

"Yes."

"I was unconscious. I think I was drugged. I have no memory of any of it."

"Did you know the man?"

Ava let the question slide. "Do you have the pill you mentioned? Are you ready to take whatever samples you need?"

Dr. Ho pulled the robe back over Ava's shoulders. "Here is the pill," she said, pressing it into Ava's hand.

Ava swallowed it.

"Now go to the bathroom and take this with you," Dr. Ho said, giving her a vial.

Ava sat on the toilet for what seemed like an eternity before she could squeeze out enough urine to fill the vial. When she had, she walked back into the bedroom and handed the vial to the doctor.

"I think I should also scrape off some of that semen, in case at some point in time we need DNA. I would also like to take a blood sample for baseline purposes."

Ava wrapped the robe more tightly around herself. "You can take any sample you want, but I want the urine results back as soon as possible, and I'll pay whatever is necessary to expedite that."

"The lab I use is closed on weekends."

"What will it cost to open it? I'll pay anything."

"Okay, I understand, and I'll do what I can. But Ms. Lee, you can't leave it at this. We need to call the police."

Ava shuddered. "No police. Please don't mention it again. This has to stay between you and me. Not even a word to Fay."

"I'm not sure that's wise."

"This is the way it has to be."

"Ms. Lee—"

"No, there is no other option."

Dr. Ho sat down beside her on the bed. "Well, if we're going to do it your way, then let me get the semen sample I need."

Ava closed her eyes. "Go ahead," she said, and then

grimaced as the blood sample was drawn. She felt a touch of nausea as the doctor scraped her chest.

"There, I'm done," Dr. Ho said. "Now, as I said, in about three days we can run at least some of the STI tests."

"I won't be here."

"You can have them run anywhere. Then, if you wish, you can have the results forwarded to me and I'll compare them to the baseline data."

"Of course."

Dr. Ho reached for Ava's hand. "If you're not going to call the police there is no reason for you to remain in this state. Would you like to shower?"

"Yes, I think that's a good idea."

"Would you like me to stay in the room until you're done?"

"Yes, I think that's another good idea."

She walked into the bathroom and glanced at herself in the mirror. Her hair was still pinned back, the ivory chignon loose but in place. She took it out, slipped off her crucifix, and then turned her back to the mirror as she took off the robe. She stood under the stream of water, her hands by her sides, not able to touch the traces of semen he had left on her body. When she thought they had to be gone, she took a bar of soap and began to lather herself.

Dr. Ho was on her cellphone when Ava left the bathroom, a fresh robe wrapped tightly around her. She saw Ava's look of panic and mouthed, *I'm talking to the lab technician.*

She watched the doctor finish her call. "Thank you."

"They're going to open the lab right away. I'll take the sample there as soon as I leave. We should have the results today."

"I'll know if I was drugged?"

"Yes, you will."

"Thank you for everything, Dr. Ho," Ava said as she climbed back onto the bed.

"Call me Vivian," she said, coming over to her. She sat on the edge of the bed, careful not to intrude on Ava's space. "How do you know Fay?"

"Through John, and only for one day. But I found her to be very considerate, like you."

"My sister and I are very different."

"Not that much... not where it matters."

"Ms. Lee—"

"I'm Ava."

"Ava, is there anything else I can do for you? Would you like me to stay for a while?"

"No, but thank you. I'm starting to feel some sense of normalcy. I'll manage now. Just call me as soon as you get the lab results."

Vivian stood. "I don't like leaving you like this."

Ava swung her legs over to the other side of the bed. "I forgot something. Don't leave just yet," she said.

Her Chanel bag was on the floor next to the desk. Beside it were the clothes she had worn the night before. Her slacks, with the pink shirt on top, two bottom buttons missing, her bra, still fastened, and the black lace underwear, ripped at the waist. She opened the bag and took out a business card and a roll of U.S. hundred-dollar bills.

She handed the card and eight hundred dollars to Vivian. "My mobile number is on the card if you can't reach me at the hotel. And the money is for your fee and the lab tests. Is it enough?"

"It's far too much."

Ava pressed it into her hand. “There is one other thing I’d like you to do for me.”

“What?”

“Those clothes on the floor—could you put them in a laundry bag and take them with you? Burn them, throw them away... do whatever you want with them.”

“Certainly.”

Ava sat on the bed and watched as Vivian Ho took a bag from the closet and stuffed the clothes into them. Then it dawned on her. “Vivian, are there jade links in the shirt cuffs?”

“No, nothing.”

“On the floor?”

“Not that I can see.”

“How about on the dresser or the desk?”

The doctor looked and then looked again. “Nothing.”

“He couldn’t have,” Ava muttered.

“Are you okay?”

Ava nodded. “Maybe they’ll turn up later.”

(22)

ALONE, MORE ALONE THAN SHE COULD EVER REMEMBER being, Ava sat in the chair by the window. The fog that had enveloped her was gone. The world around her was vivid again. Outside, the city was going about its business. She looked down into the garden and watched a woman wearing a cone-shaped straw hat picking up debris from the ground. She pulled herself from the chair, went to the desk, and called the concierge. "This is Ava Lee, could you connect me to hotel security, please?"

"Is there a problem, Ms. Lee?" a female voice asked.

"I need to speak with the head of security. Please put me through."

The woman hesitated. "That is Pak Indra."

"Is he in the hotel?"

The woman paused. "Just a moment, I have to check."

The phone went silent. *If he's not in the hotel then they can go and get him*, Ava thought.

A male voice came on the line. "Indra here, Ms. Lee."

"Are you in the hotel?"

"Yes, I am."

"I need to speak to you."

"Can you give me some idea of what this is about?"

"No, not over the phone."

"What do you suggest?" he asked, caution creeping into his voice.

"Do you have an office?"

"Yes, I'm downstairs on the ground floor, behind the front desk."

"I'll see you there in about fifteen minutes," she said, hanging up before he could reply.

She opened her notebook and found the phone number for Perkasa in Jakarta. He didn't answer so she left a message on his voicemail. "This is Ava Lee. Call me."

Time to get dressed, time to move, she told herself. She brushed her hair and tied it back. She rooted in her bag for a pair of underwear and her sports bra, her hand shaking as she took them out. She struggled to get them on and then climbed into her Adidas training pants and pulled a black Giordano T-shirt over her head. The roll of bills she had taken out to pay Vivian Ho still sat on the dresser. She peeled off five of them and put them in her right pants pocket. Her cellphone went into the left.

She was halfway down the stairs towards Indra's office when her phone rang. "Ava Lee."

"Bu Ava, this is Perkasa. I got your message."

"Uncle spoke with you?"

"I've been waiting for your call."

"Can you get to Surabaya today?"

"Of course. There must be twenty-five flights a day between here and Surabaya."

"Get in this afternoon. There's a Sheraton Hotel attached

to the big downtown plaza. Check in there and then call me."

"Okay."

"Uncle said you had some men in Surabaya you could use."

"How many do you need?"

"Two should be enough."

"No problem."

"They have to be men you really trust, men who know how to keep their mouths shut."

"No problem."

"I'm not sure if we're going to need weapons, but if we do, can you access them?"

"Whatever you need, I can get."

"A picana?"

"What is that?"

"An electric cattle prod."

He paused. "Yes, I'm sure the men in Surabaya can find one of those."

"Fine. Then have them do that today."

"I will do that," he said, this time without hesitation.

"Good. Then I'll see you this afternoon."

Ava ended the call, already feeling good about Perkasa. She liked his confidence, his directness. Men who talked too much or asked too many questions also tended to think too much. She didn't need any thinkers.

As she approached the front desk, she saw a well-dressed man with grey hair standing next to a young female associate. The look he gave her was all she needed to know. "Pak Indra," she said.

"Ms. Lee, I thought it would be less disruptive if we met out here. Maybe sit in the lounge?"

Ava said, "I'd like to meet somewhere where there aren't security cameras. So we can go to your office or we can go outside and stand on the street in the heat."

"My office would be the best of those options," he said, motioning for her to go to the door that led from the lobby to behind the front desk. He opened the door and then stood aside for her. There was another door at the back of the work area, with a security lock. He punched in six numbers and said, "After you."

His office was small, with barely room for a desk, a small credenza, a filing cabinet, and two chairs. There was a picture on the credenza, a much younger Pak Indra with a woman and seven children. "This is my personal space," he said when he saw her staring at the photo. "Next door is the real security office, with our monitors."

"Thank you for seeing me."

"You made it hard for me to refuse."

He was a big man. Ava guessed he'd been a policeman, and from the way he spoke and carried himself, he'd been an officer. "Do you know why I'm here?" she asked.

He began to answer and then stopped when Ava's eyes caught his. She stared, not blinking, expressionless, right into him. Whatever he had been going to say was left unsaid.

"Do you know what happened to me last night in this hotel? I have some idea but I would like you to tell me."

He moved his right hand onto a manila file folder on the desk and slid it in front of him. He took out a sheet of paper, read it, and said, "According to the report from my man on night duty, you and a companion were having drinks in the lounge when you became incapacitated. Your speech was slurred and you were groggy, almost asleep.

Your companion told my man that you had been drinking all evening and that a combination of the liquor and jet lag had hit you quite suddenly. He said he wanted to take you to your room and make sure you were safely in bed for the night. He asked my man to help him take you there. Which he did."

"And then left me alone with him?"

"Yes, that too," Indra said, his eyes shifting away. "When they got to the room, your companion said he would look after you. My man had no reason to stay."

"Have you run the security tapes from the time indicated on that report?"

"Yes, I have. In fact, I did it before you even called. Anytime a report is filed I review whatever I can on video, assuming we have video."

"And what did the video show?"

"Videos. One from the lounge, the other from the elevator. They supported the story that my man recorded."

"*Story* is the right word."

Indra shifted his weight on the chair and put his elbows on the desk, as if he was remembering whose office he was in and who should be in charge. He looked at her. "Ms. Lee, I am quite unclear about what point you are trying to make."

"My companion, you know who he is, right?"

"Of course, Mr. Cameron is a regular patron."

His eyes drifted away. Ava sat quietly, waiting for him to look at her again. When he finally did, she said, "Your regular patron, he drugged me. That's why I was groggy."

Indra slowly shook his head. "All my man could see was a woman who was having difficulty. Under the circumstances, I believe he acted in a responsible manner."

"I'm not here to condemn your man, so you don't have to defend him to me."

"As for Mr. Cameron —"

"He raped me," Ava said.

He flinched, his eyes flickering. "Ms. Lee, that is an incredibly serious charge."

"I don't know for certain about the drug yet, as the lab won't get back to me until later today. As for the rape, well, I had a doctor visit me at the hotel this morning, and if you don't want to take my word for it, you can talk to her."

"I'm not sure that is necessary."

"He also robbed me of some jewellery — a very expensive and valued set of jade cufflinks."

"If this is true, and I'm not saying I doubt you, you should be calling the police. You do intend to call the police, don't you?"

"No, I don't," she said.

Indra cocked his head to one side, as if trying to see her from a different angle. "Ms. Lee, I have to tell you I find your reaction quite strange," he said, his voice acquiring an edge.

He thinks I'm trying to shake down the hotel, Ava thought. "Mr. Indra, you were a policeman, I believe."

"I was."

"An officer?"

"Yes, a senior officer."

"So tell me. I'm here on a two- or three-day visit, a tourist. Cameron lives here. Even if the police are entirely capable, not prejudiced, and not corrupt and I go to them, what kind of investigation will really take place? Are they going to pursue the interests of a fly-by-night tourist or are they going to do everything they can not to offend the local big-shot banker?"

"You seem to be a very intelligent young woman," he said carefully.

"I like to think I am."

"And you're familiar with how things work in this part of the world."

"I think so."

"Then I won't insult you by pretending that Mr. Cameron's status wouldn't have an impact on how this matter would be handled."

"Thank you."

He nodded. "That said, and given that you have already made the decision not to go to the police, I am struggling with the reason why you're here talking to me."

"I wanted to confirm what happened to me in the lounge last night. I wanted to know for certain that it was Cameron who took me to my room."

"I have confirmed that, I believe."

"Yes, you have. And now what I want is for you to supply me with some information."

"I don't understand."

"I want to know about Cameron."

"You're confusing me."

Ava reached into her pants pocket, took out two hundred-dollar bills, and put the money on the desk. "I want to know where he lives; I want to know his home and mobile phone numbers; I want to know what car he drives and what his licence plate number is; and I want to know what he does during his spare time."

Indra looked at the money and then at her. "I still don't understand any of this."

"I'm prepared to pay you two hundred dollars for the

information, and if you can get it for me by three o'clock this afternoon I'll pay you another two hundred."

"Ms. Lee, I'm not sure what you have in mind."

"Does it matter?"

"Yes, it does if your purpose is to do something illegal."

Was he being serious or sanctimonious? Ava couldn't tell. "You have to forgive me," she said. "I've never been raped before, and I'm not sure what the appropriate response is." She looked at the photo on the credenza. "You have three daughters. What would you do if one of them was raped by someone you knew, someone you trusted?"

"I would go to the police."

"Like hell you would," she said, staring him down again.

Ava saw him glance at the money. "Take it," she said, "and get me the information I want."

"And if I can't, Ms. Lee?"

"Then I'll get it elsewhere. I just thought it would be easier to keep everything in-house, so to speak. No reason to involve other people, is there. You don't have to start explaining things to senior management and I don't have to run around the city talking to lawyers and private detectives and the like. I know how to keep my mouth shut, Pak Indra, and it strikes me that you have that quality as well."

He picked up the money.

Ava stood. "Could you send the information to my room when you get it?"

He looked up at her and she saw questions in his eyes. *Don't ask,* she thought, *because I'm not sure you would believe my lies.*

Ava left his office and found her way back to the lobby. Through the hotel door she could see the day was a bit overcast, the rainy season starting to signal its arrival. It was humid but the masked sun made the weather bearable — good enough for running.

She turned right from the hotel and started along the route she had taken the day before. She hadn't run more than a kilometre before the sense of purpose that had energized her when she was speaking to Perkasa and Indra began to dissipate and the realization of what had happened to her began to take a grip. Since she had awakened, she had been operating like Ava: Identify the problem, put together a plan, and execute it. Call the doctor, order a lab test. Start organizing Perkasa. Confirm Cameron's complicity and get the information needed to go after him. Through it all, though, it had been as if she were operating on behalf of someone else. It was as if she were treating herself as a client. Except she wasn't a client.

An image popped into her mind. She shut her eyes and gave her head a brisk shake. The image didn't go away. Then she stopped running, the pictures in her head almost paralyzing her. She was lying on her bed and it was her, not some stranger, not any client. Andy Cameron was on the bed. He had finished with her, but her legs were still open and he was rubbing his penis across her breasts, leaving a trail of semen. He had a grin on his face, and he was happily humming a tune she didn't recognize.

Ava had stopped just outside a coffee shop. She couldn't run anymore. She needed water, she thought, and was starting to walk into the shop when a tear rolled down her cheek. She hesitated, her hand reaching out for a wall. Another tear fell, and she felt a weakness in her legs. She turned and pressed her back against the wall for support as she began to sob, her body shaking uncontrollably.

(23)

AVA DECIDED SHE WASN'T GOING TO TELL PERKASA the real reason why they were going after Cameron.

Earlier that morning, when her run had ended so abruptly and so emotionally outside the coffee shop, it had taken half an hour for her to drink a bottle of water and to stop her hands from trembling. Two women inside the shop had seen her distress and come out to comfort her. They gathered around her, talking between themselves, as one wiped Ava's tears with a serviette and the other gently massaged her neck and shoulders.

The woman Ava had seen earlier with Indra was at the front desk when she returned. As Ava approached, she saw the woman's face take on a worried look.

"I'd like to change rooms," Ava said.

"Is there something wrong with the room you're in?"

"I just want another room, something different."

"Certainly, Ms. Lee," she said, tapping at her keyboard. "There's a suite available on the fourth floor."

"Fine, I'll take it."

Time wasn't moving all that quickly for Ava. The woman

seemed to take forever to finalize the arrangement and pass her a key. When she was finally done, Ava said, "Now I need you to arrange something else for me. Could you please ask one of the room maids to go to my old room and pack all my things and bring them to the new one?"

"Yes, we can do that, of course."

"Thank you. I'll sit over there until it is done."

The hotel was busy. There was a steady parade of people crossing the lobby, about half Western and half Asian. Ava counted them, tried to guess where they were from and why they were in Surabaya and in that hotel. It was a pointless exercise but entirely distracting. She had reached thirty-seven when she heard her name being called.

"Your suite is ready," the desk clerk said.

The suite wasn't any larger than the room she had before but it was configured differently, and the view from her window revealed a new part of the garden. In Ava's mind it was enough of a change.

The maid had left Ava's bags on the floor by the door. Her computer, notebook, and cellphone were on the desk. Ava stepped out of her clothes, threw them on the floor, and got into the shower. When she was done, she rubbed herself dry with a fierce determination, wrapped herself in a bathrobe, and crawled into bed.

She closed her eyes, only to have Cameron's cocksure face flood her mind. *I will get rid of that grin now,* she thought. She would have her revenge. Cameron had taken what should have been just business and made it personal. Now she was going to repay him in her own way — quietly, privately, painfully. She pressed her eyelids tightly together. The face vanished.

When she woke, the room phone was ringing. Ava looked at the bedside clock and saw it was one thirty. She'd been asleep for three hours.

"Ava Lee," she said.

"You changed rooms," Vivian Ho said. "I called 313 and a man answered. I panicked for a second."

"I thought a change of scenery might help."

"Yes, I think that was wise," she said. "I have those lab results you wanted."

"So soon?"

"You were the only priority at the lab this morning."

"Thanks for making that happen."

"You have flunitrazepam in your system."

"I see."

"You've heard of it?"

"I have."

"It would have taken about twenty to thirty minutes to kick in after you ingested it. And judging from the traces, you were given enough to have affected you for eight hours or so."

"I can remember only the first part of my evening in the lounge."

"That's not surprising. It does cause anterograde amnesia."

Ava said, "Maybe it's just as well that's all I can remember, don't you think?"

Vivian paused and then said, "The pill I gave you this morning should look after any chance of pregnancy. Have whatever other lab you go to send me the other results. In a few weeks you should be able to have peace of mind about other possible complications."

"In the meantime, all I have to do is cope with my imagination."

"I didn't mean to make what happened to you seem insignificant."

"I know, and I'm sorry if I sounded ungrateful. You've been wonderful, and I appreciate it."

"Well, look, I'll give you my mobile number and my home phone. If you need anything at all, please don't hesitate to call. Even if you just want to chat, call me. My weekend is wide open."

"Thank you for that."

She hung up the phone and sat up in bed. Her mind felt clearer. The compulsion to cry was gone. The ache in her stomach had ebbed. Perkasa was already en route. She needed to get organized.

She unpacked her bags. She had enough clean clothes for one more day. She dressed in her casual gear, went to the desk, and turned on her computer and iPhone. There was the usual barrage of emails from friends and family. She wrote to them all collectively. I'm going to be out of touch by phone and email for the next few days. I'm involved in some business negotiations that need my full attention. I'll contact you as soon as issues here are resolved. Everything is going very well, so don't worry about me.

Her voicemail was less busy. Maria whispering that she missed her. Sonny telling her that Uncle had gone to the hospital that morning but was now back at home. And Uncle just saying, "Ava, call me."

She knew she had to call Sonny back. He was going to worry and keep phoning unless she did.

"Sonny, it's Ava."

"He went to Queen Elizabeth."

"So you said."

"And the woman thinks he recognized her. She stayed outside but he looked back at her when he went in."

"There isn't any need for her to follow him anymore, is there? We know where he's going. Now we just need to find out why, and Doctor Parker should be able tell us."

"When will that be?"

"I'll be back in Hong Kong in two or three days, so please, Sonny, be patient until then."

"I'll do the best I can."

"Thanks. Now listen, I'm not going to be available to talk until it's time for me to come back. We have some business here that needs my attention."

"I understand."

"Good. I'll let you know when I firm up my schedule."

She sat at the desk, staring at her notebook for a few minutes, after her conversation with Sonny. She was going to phone Uncle; she just needed to figure out what to say to him. Unless she was badly mistaken, he would already know that Perkasa was coming to Surabaya. She had learned over the years that with Uncle's contacts, all roads led back to him. They might be assisting her, but it was because he had done the asking, and he was the man they wanted to please. So there were no secrets between them and her. She assumed that everything she said, everything she did, would be relayed back to Uncle in one form or another. It didn't bother her. She had respect for their loyalty to him, and she was smart enough to know that it bound them to her. Still, if she was correct in assuming that Perkasa had phoned Uncle to say he was heading to Surabaya at Ava's request, Uncle would be calling her to ask why.

Why.

In their years together, personal lives had sometimes meshed with the professional, but usually in alignment with a job. Completely personal matters weren't for sharing. And how much more personal could this be for her?

She was certain, as much as she was certain about anything in her life, that if she told Uncle what had happened, it would not just be a matter of Perkasa coming to Surabaya. It would be Sonny and Uncle flying in from Hong Kong with blood in their eyes. And she didn't want that to happen for any number of reasons, not the least of which was that she had pride in her ability to manage her life, and she wasn't about to cede control to anyone when it came to Andy Cameron. He was hers.

There was also the matter of the humiliation Cameron had imposed on her. She was Ava Lee. There wasn't a man on earth outside of her father and Uncle who could hurt her. Cameron had violated that self-image, not just physically but, more important to her, psychologically. She needed to regain that feeling of immunity, and she was going to do it her way.

She called Hong Kong.

"*Wei.*"

"Uncle, it's Ava."

"How is it going?"

"Good. I had dinner last night with Andy Cameron, the CEO of Bank Linno. He's a sneaky little guy. I tried to get him to open up about the bank and its operations and he was completely evasive. There's something strange going on there, I feel it," she said in a rush, and then immediately told herself to slow down. Uncle was clever at picking up her signs of stress.

"Do you think it will have any relevance to our clients?"

"I don't know. That's the thing, I don't know."

"A British guy running an Indonesian bank is unusual."

"A British guy who was somehow recruited from a job in Rome."

"And the bank's growth is startling."

"He told me last night that he's increased their capital base twenty-fold."

"What else did you get out of him?"

"Almost nothing else. I asked about their international business and he slammed the door on me."

"So what do you want to do?" asked Uncle.

"I've asked Perkasa to come to Surabaya," she said and then paused, giving him the chance to acknowledge that he knew.

"Yes, he told me," he said.

Ava didn't miss a beat. "I think it's time we had a private conversation with Cameron, one in which he'll be more amenable to answering questions. If it leads to nothing, then I'll be back in Hong Kong in a day or two."

"Do you have access to him?"

"I'm arranging that."

"Ava, do you think this is worth that kind of trouble?"

"We have clients; we owe them our best. I don't know any other way of getting to the truth about what happened between Lam, Purslow, and the bank."

"Perkasa arrives today?"

"This afternoon."

"When will you pick up Cameron?"

"I'm aiming for tomorrow."

"Well, if it has to be done, it has to be done. Just make

sure there are no repercussions if Cameron and the bank have nothing to hide. I do not want you being hounded."

"I'll be careful."

"Keep in touch."

"As always."

"And good luck."

It wasn't entirely a lie, she thought as she ended the call.

Ava opened her notebook and starting making a list, a short one, of the things that needed to be done. Indra's information was at the top and she hadn't heard from him.

She called downstairs to the front desk. "This is Ava Lee. Can you tell me if there is a hardware store in the immediate neighbourhood?"

"There's an Ace Hardware in Tunjungan Plaza."

"Thank you, and could you also tell me if Pak Indra is still in the hotel?"

"He's standing next to me."

"Can I speak with him, please?"

He came on the line almost at once. "I assume you're calling about that information you wanted."

"I am."

"I just put it in an envelope. It will be delivered to your room in a few minutes."

"Wonderful. Is it complete?"

"Absolutely... How much longer do you think you'll be a guest in the hotel, Ms. Lee?" he asked casually.

"Another day or two."

"And then back to Hong Kong?"

"Yes."

"Well, I hope you enjoy the rest of your time with us."

"That is the plan."

"But please be cautious. Surabaya isn't a violent place, but young single women need to be careful."

"I normally am," she said.

She waited by the door for the envelope. She had expected it to be hand delivered, but the bellboy slid it under the door. She opened it as she walked back to her desk. Cameron lived in a house in Citraland. Indra had underlined the fact that he had full-time, live-in domestic help. He drove a black Porsche Boxster with a standard plate number. He golfed at a private club, Paradise Run, that had security at the entrance. There were four phone numbers at the bottom of the page, for mobile, home, office, and golf club.

Ava went online and searched for Citraland. There it was, "the Singapore of Surabaya," a large high-end, affluent community in the western part of the city, home to Surabaya's professional class. Paradise Run was also in the west, farther out from the city by about ten kilometres. It advertised itself as East Java's finest and most exclusive golf and country club. She had no doubts that the security Indra had mentioned would be tight.

She copied the information into her notebook and then began to detail the options they had for getting to Cameron. She wondered how capable Perkasa's local contacts were. That was a question that was going to have to be answered, and answered soon.

(24)

SHE HEARD FROM PERKASA AS SHE WAS WALKING OUT of Ace Hardware with a bag holding two rolls of duct tape.

"I'm here," he said.

"Where exactly is 'here'?"

"The lobby of the Sheraton Hotel."

Ava checked her location in the plaza. The hotel was no more than a five-minute walk away. "Wait there for me. I'm on my way. I'm wearing a black T-shirt and black Adidas training pants."

She liked him the instant she saw him. Young, tall, athletic, dressed in black jeans and a dark blue cotton shirt. He stood with his back against a pillar, his eyes darting right and left, attentive without being obvious. *He looks like Derek*, Ava thought — the same build, the same confident way he carried himself. When he saw her, he smiled and gave her a little wave. *That's like Derek too — easygoing, relaxed, even when going about the hard part of a job.*

"I didn't expect someone so young," he said as she approached, her right hand extended.

"Me neither. Uncle's contacts are usually older and usually policemen or army officers. You aren't army or police, are you?"

He took her hand and shook it firmly. "No, I'm not military or police. As for Uncle, he's known my family for a long time. He and my grandfather left Wuhan around the same time and they've kept in touch ever since. We owe him a lot of favours."

The Wuhan link again, Ava thought. It spanned decades, thousands of miles, and all of the adopted cultures.

Ava looked around the lobby. It was quiet, and she motioned to a nearby seating area. "Let's sit and talk," she said. "Time is working against us."

He was about a foot taller than she was, and close up she saw that he was far more muscular than she had thought. He had two knapsacks with him; he tossed one over each shoulder.

"Have you checked in?" Ava asked.

"Yes."

"Do you want to take those to your room?"

"They can wait. I came to work, so let's get started."

They found two chairs in an alcove and settled in. "Did Uncle give you any idea what I want you to do?"

"The only thing he said was that it would probably be something physical."

"There's a bank president here by the name of Andy Cameron. I want to get him someplace private and secure so I can talk to him. We'll need to use a couple of locals. We'll need two vehicles, preferably SUVs—something large. We need a place to take him where we don't need to worry about him making a racket. And we'll probably need weapons," she said. She waited for his reaction.

He just shrugged as if he'd heard it all before. "My *jawara* have guns. One of them drives a Pathfinder, and I'm sure we can find another car without any trouble. I'll call them as soon as we're finished here and ask about a place to take your banker. If they don't have one, they'll get one."

"You trust them, do you?"

"I've worked with them many times before. The older one is a policeman, the other is his brother. They don't speak English, which under these circumstances is probably a good thing, because we won't have to guard our words. But even if they understood everything we were saying, it wouldn't bother me. They're reliable, very professional."

"And they know you're here today?"

"I had them on standby after talking to Uncle the first time, and I called them this morning right after talking to you. I asked Waru — he's the older one — to find the picana you wanted. They're waiting for me to contact them for a meeting. I wanted to talk to you first so I could give them some idea of what we were up to."

Ava said, "Uncle told me your name was Perkasa, but I don't know if that's your first name or last name. What should I be calling you?"

"Perkasa — that's it. Like many Indonesians, I have only the one name."

"Well, Perkasa, I'm going to leave you to call Waru and his brother. Let's confirm the car and find out about a secure holding area for the banker. When that's done, arrange for them to meet with us around here somewhere. I'm completely available, but the sooner we can talk, the better. My objective is to have this job wrapped up by Monday morning, because that's when people are going to start missing him, at least his colleagues at the bank. Your locals should be a lot of help from a planning viewpoint."

"It won't take long with Waru. Do you want to wait here while I make the call?"

Ava wasn't used to this level of efficiency, even from Uncle's men. "Sure, why not?"

He took a BlackBerry from the top pocket of one of his knapsacks. Two flicks of his finger, a ten-second wait, and then Perkasa began speaking in Indonesian. Ava listened, not understanding a word, but guessing from his nodding head and occasional smile that it wasn't going badly.

He put the BlackBerry in his shirt pocket. "Okay, we're set," he said.

"Everything?"

"I told you, these are capable men."

"The cars?"

"They have matching Pathfinders."

"A place to take the banker?"

"Waru's house is outside the city. His nearest neighbour is several hundred metres away. He's going to phone his wife and tell her to take the kids to her mother's for a few days, starting tonight."

"And the picana?"

"He bought one."

Ava was impressed. "Whatever you've been paid, I'm going to give you extra for yourself and the two men."

"That's not necessary. Uncle sent more than enough."

"I insist, so please don't argue with me."

Perkasa conceded with a nod. "After he gets his wife settled, Waru will drive into the city. I told him to come here to the hotel. They should be here by six."

"Perfect. That gives me time to get organized," she said and then paused. "You said Waru is a policeman."

"Yeah, he is."

"When he freelances, does he mind using that to his advantage?"

"What do you have in mind?" Perkasa asked carefully.

"I'm not entirely sure yet. We'll need to go over the plan, such as it is, before we see if there is any need."

"Then that's when we can ask him."

"Fair enough."

"Now what?"

"I'm going back to my hotel. Call me when they arrive."

(25)

AVA KNEW SHE SHOULD EAT BUT SHE WASN'T THE LEAST bit hungry. Her body was numb, her mind falling back into the depression she'd felt after her run. The meeting with Perkasa had brought Andy Cameron front and centre, and she couldn't control the thoughts that washed over her.

She made an instant coffee and sat at the window, looking out on gardens that were familiar and unfamiliar at the same time. The street fronting the hotel was busy now, and Ava tried to focus on watching people going about their everyday lives. It was a wasted effort. Cameron intruded. Ava pushed him aside, willing herself to think about what lay ahead. It worked for a few minutes but then he was back — an image of him walking down a golf course sharing a joke with his buddies, telling them about the good piece of ass he'd had the night before.

Ava got up from her chair and looked aimlessly around the room. *I should have changed hotels*, she thought. The idea occupied her for a moment, until she realized she didn't have the energy to pack and move. *What am I going to do to fill this afternoon?* she thought, almost in a panic.

Her room phone rang and she stared at it. She didn't answer, and a few seconds later the red message light began to blink. *I should find out who called*, she thought, but then her cellphone came alive.

"Ava Lee," she said.

"Ava, this is Fay."

"Hey, Fay."

"Where are you?"

"In my room."

"You changed rooms. They told me when I called in."

"Yes, I did."

Fay paused as if waiting for an explanation. When none came, she said, "And you didn't answer your room phone just now."

"I was in the washroom."

"Ava, are you okay?"

"Yes, I'm fine."

"Are you sure?"

"Of course I am. Why do you ask?"

"Because I'm concerned."

"You have no reason to be."

Fay said, "I don't want to be indiscreet, but my sister Vivian called me about an hour ago. She said she visited you at the hotel this morning and that you were not well. She suggested I look in on you."

"It isn't you being indiscreet, it's your sister," Ava said sharply.

"Ava, please, it isn't like that. My sister has a big heart. She's worried about you, that's all. She didn't share any of your medical details with me, if that is what's bothering you."

"Look, I'm fine. I was a bit nauseated earlier, nothing more. I probably shouldn't have called her."

"Well, then, if you're fine, would you like to do something this afternoon?"

"Fay, I'm not sure I'm in the mood for going out."

"I'm already downstairs in the lobby and my car is idling at the front door. C'mon, it will take your mind off your troubles."

Ava looked around the room. Anything had to be better than staying there. "I have a meeting at six, so I'll have to be back here by at least a quarter to."

"Not a problem. We don't have to go far."

What the hell, Ava thought. "I'll be down in a few minutes," she said.

Fay hovered by the hotel's front door. In knee-length pink shorts, a plain white T-shirt, and no makeup, she looked barely out of her teens. She held her arms out to Ava as she crossed the lobby. They hugged. "You look so pale," Fay said.

"Some air will probably do me good," said Ava.

They slid into the Audi, the air conditioning going full blast. "Where to? Do you want to eat? See some more sights? Shop?"

"I wouldn't mind going back to Chinatown," Ava said.

Fay made a right turn out of the hotel driveway, drove for about a hundred metres, and then did a U-turn at a gap in the concrete divider that separated the lanes. They hadn't gone more than another hundred metres before they heard a siren. Ava glanced back and saw a policeman on a motorbike bearing down on them.

Fay pulled over to the curb, shaking her head. He parked his bike in front of their car and walked towards them. He was short and pudgy, a look accentuated by a tight grey shirt and black jodhpurs. Fay rolled down her window and then reached into the compartment between the two front seats and pulled out a piece of paper. He began waving his finger the moment he got to the window. Fay spoke to him in Indonesian and handed him the paper. He read it and then lowered his head. She took back the paper and handed him a ten-thousand-rupiah banknote. The policeman took the bill and then spoke rapidly to her in Indonesian, pointing in the direction they were going. Fay shook her head.

"What was that about?" Ava asked when he had left.

"I made an illegal U-turn."

"So I gathered, but the rest of it? The only word I understood was *Allah*."

Fay laughed. "My piece of paper says I am a special friend of the police department and to be granted every consideration. I gave him ten thousand rupiah — that's about one U.S. dollar — to apologize for inconveniencing him. He thanked Allah for my generosity and asked if we wanted him to give us a police escort to wherever we were going."

"How civilized," Ava said.

"Yes, for those of us who warrant that kind of treatment. Not everyone is so fortunate."

Traffic was heavier than it had been the day before, but Fay made it seem more obvious than was needed that she was concentrating on the road. *She wants to ask me about Cameron*, Ava thought, a bland reply forming in her mind.

"So, Ava, how did you find my sister?" Fay said, glancing slightly sideways.

"She's wonderful," Ava said, pleased at the reprieve.

"I know, and it hasn't always been easy for her."

"Why is that?"

"Well, she's the oldest of four sisters — there's twelve years between me and her. My parents were harder on her than the rest of us. Their expectations were very high."

"She's a doctor. They must be pleased about that."

"Of course, and in this country that's no small feat."

Ava saw a sign written in Chinese characters. They were only three kilometres away from Chinatown. "Does Vivian have children?"

"She's never married."

"That couldn't have pleased your parents."

"It's less of an issue than the fact that she's a lesbian."

Ava didn't think she had overtly reacted until Fay said, "Don't look so shocked. I'm surprised you couldn't tell."

"I beg your pardon?"

"I mean, you didn't think she looked like one?"

"It never occurred to me. And tell me, what is a lesbian supposed to look like anyway?"

"A bit masculine, wouldn't you say? It was worse a few years ago, when she wore her hair shorter. My parents wouldn't be seen in public with her then. It didn't bother my sisters or me — God knows we love her — but my parents found it very difficult."

They reached the outskirts of Chinatown. Fay parked the car in a no-stopping zone and put her piece of paper on the windshield. "We'll walk from here," she said. "Is there anything in particular you'd like to see or do?"

The sidewalks were crowded but the women were able to walk side by side. "I'd like to go to the temple again," Ava said.

"I'd like that too," said Fay, reaching for Ava's hand. She held it as they walked, as women friends did in many parts of Asia, Ava knew.

It was hot, the sun naked in the sky, and they kept close to the buildings, grateful for whatever shade they cast. They passed a variety of stores, their names written in both Chinese and Indonesian; Ava wondered if the translations were more accurate than they were in Canada.

When they reached Kong Co Kong Tik Cun Ong, they had to stop. People were thronging around the entrance, blocking passage. "They're mainly onlookers," Fay said, tugging Ava to the right. They hugged the wall, inching forward until they reached the courtyard.

Ava bought six joss sticks, an orange, and a mango. She went to the Taoist altar and placed the fruit at its base. She put the smouldering sticks between her palms, her fingers pointing upwards, bowed her head, and began to pray. She asked for good health and peace in the lives of her mother, Marian, her nieces, Mimi, and Mimi's unborn child. She prayed for Uncle, that his life continue free of illness, free of worry, until he had no desire to continue.

And then Ava prayed for herself.

She knew she could not forgive. She would have her revenge, she confessed, an eye for an eye. And when that was done, she asked for the strength to let go, to accept what had happened to her, to start the process of forgetting. She needed Tao's harmony and balance, but first she had to purge. *Help me get through to the other side*, she prayed. Unlike the day before, she shed no tears.

Fay waited for her near the wall. "Me praying twice in two days — my grandfather must be proud," she said.

"I'd glad we came here. Thank you for coming to the hotel," Ava said.

"My pleasure. Now what?"

"I'm famished."

"Chinese food?"

"What else? We are in Chinatown."

"There's a seafood restaurant close by that my grandfather used to take me to."

"I would like to go there."

"Perfect," Fay said, reaching for Ava's hand again and guiding her back through the alleys.

The restaurant was between the lunch and dinner crowds, so they had their pick of tables. Fay chose one that gave them a view of the street. "Is there anything special you would like?" she asked.

"Order what your grandfather liked."

"Yes, that's a wonderful idea."

It wasn't until they were halfway through a plate of fried noodles with shrimp and squid, served with a thick, salty soy sauce that Fay called *kecap asin*, and a platter of curried crab, the curry blended with lemongrass, cilantro, and red-hot green chilis, that Fay mentioned Cameron. "Did he get you home safely?"

"Of course."

"And Andy behaved himself?"

Ava sucked the roe from the inside of a crab shell, her attention on the food. "About as much as you would expect," she said.

Fay began to ask another question but Ava interrupted. "Tell me about Vivian. How long has it been since she's come out?"

"Out? She has never been out. What made you think that?"

"Well, earlier —"

"That's just family business," Fay said quickly. "We're the only ones in Surabaya who actually know, and it's something we keep tightly inside the family."

"I won't discuss it with anyone."

"I wasn't suggesting you would. It's just that this city is so parochial, so bigoted about people like Vivian, that it's best for all concerned for the family to be discreet. About once a month Vivian goes to Jakarta for a weekend or maybe flies to Hong Kong or Manila, and what she gets up to no one asks."

"Isn't that a little backward?"

Fay shrugged. "Maybe for our generation, but it's difficult for my parents. They can't imagine a woman not needing a man, and they can't imagine a woman not being completely subservient to a man. That's why men like Andy Cameron revel in this culture. In their own countries they need to work at getting a woman. Here, all it takes is the right look and some poor girl who's been brainwashed into thinking she's subservient. After a while it becomes expected on the part of the man, and any pretence he used to have about actually wooing a woman disappears. When you hear the way they speak to women, it's enough to make you throw up. I can imagine Cameron saying 'on your back' to a woman the same way he'd say 'roll over' to a dog."

"I don't want to talk about or hear about Andy Cameron," Ava said quietly. "It's enough to say that I won't be seeing him again, and that our company will not be doing business with his bank."

"So he did try something?" Fay asked, with more interest than Ava thought polite.

"Nothing I couldn't handle."

"I did try to warn you."

"And thank goodness you did," Ava said, putting down a crab leg. "This food is excellent, but I seem to have lost my appetite."

The waiter had just brought the bill to the table when Perkasa called her cell. "Waru and his brother are here already," he said. "Where shall we meet?"

"Are you in the lobby?"

"Yeah."

"Can you find a corner where we can talk privately?"

"I'm in one now."

"Stay there. I'll be about fifteen to twenty minutes."

"Who was that?" Fay asked when Ava hung up.

Ava knew her end of the conversation must have sounded strange. "One of my associates from Hong Kong has flown over to assist with this project. We're going to meet and then have dinner."

"That's too bad. John was hoping we could eat together again tonight."

"Give him my apologies."

(26)

AVA TOOK THE INFORMATION THAT INDRA HAD GIVEN her and put it in her bag with her notebook. She had thought about downloading and printing a map of Citraland and the area around the Paradise Run Golf Club, but given that Waru was a policeman she didn't think it was necessary.

It was a ten-minute walk to the plaza from her hotel, and then another ten minutes to find her way to the Sheraton. As she walked, she thought about what she would be asking them to do and knew there would be questions in their minds about the why of it. But if they were anything like the men she usually worked with, no one would actually ask. Still, it would never hurt for them to think they were on the side of the good guys, and Ava didn't want any personal motives clouding the action.

Perkasa stood waiting for her by the front desk. "They're over there," he said, pointing towards a nest of alcoves at the far end of the lobby.

"Are they curious about the nature of this job? Have they asked any questions?" she asked.

"No. We're paying them enough that it doesn't matter."

"You should know anyway, and if you want to tell them it's okay by me. The banker I'm after ripped off thirty or forty Canadian investors for more than thirty million U.S. dollars. Two men who knew how it was done were murdered. A lot of lives have been damaged in one way or another. We need to do what we can to mend them."

Perkasa shrugged. "If it comes up, I'll tell them. Otherwise they don't need to know."

"Then let's go talk to them," she said.

The brothers were of medium height and muscular and had round faces, small noses, and broad, bony chins. They stood up as Perkasa introduced Ava in Indonesian. Waru, the more confident of the two, held out his hand, while his younger brother held back. "His name is Prayogo," Perkasa said.

The alcove held two sofas separated by a coffee table. Ava sat next to Perkasa, opened her bag, and extracted a piece of paper. "Do you want me to go through this bit by bit, or would you prefer for me to explain the whole thing and then you can translate it as you see fit?" she asked.

"Give me the big picture," Perkasa said.

"Well, his name is Andy Cameron and he lives in Citraland, at this address," she began, passing the information to Perkasa. "It seems to be part of a substantial urban development, so I'm sure he has neighbours. He also has live-in domestic staff. So for starters, unless you and the guys think otherwise, I don't think trying to grab him at the house makes much sense unless we want to draw a lot of attention to ourselves — and I can't think of anything positive coming from that," she said. "Now, he's playing golf today and tomorrow at his club, Paradise Run, but there's security there, so I've eliminated that location as well. His office is about two hundred metres from this plaza, which also makes it a non-starter...So that pretty well leaves us with the job of plucking him out of his car."

"Without attracting attention?" Perkasa asked.

Ava heard the doubt in his voice. "Well, with as little attention as possible. Waru should be able to help us figure out if that's at all doable. I figured if we do it tomorrow then we don't have to worry about him not showing up for work at the bank. And if we do it in the morning we can have access to him for the day, and I don't think we'll need more time than that."

"You're sure about his being accessible in the morning?"

"As I said, he's scheduled to play golf. When do most people play in this climate?"

"The morning."

"Exactly. Getting him on Sunday at any time is more important to me than waiting for Monday."

Perkasa said, "Let's make sure about the time if we can. I'll phone the club on some pretext and try to confirm that Cameron is playing and when he's supposed to tee off."

"Good idea," Ava said, realizing she'd been making a lot of assumptions.

"Regardless of when he's scheduled to play, you want to grab him somewhere between his house and the club?"

"That's my idea, but I don't know how far one is from the other and I don't have a clue about the roads in between. I'm thinking that early on Sunday morning they won't be that busy, but we need Waru to check all that out."

"Won't Cameron be expected at the golf club?"

"You or Waru can call and tell them he's had to cancel."

"What was the name of the course again?"

"Paradise Run."

He picked up the paper with Cameron's address on it. "Excuse me for a minute while I talk to the guys," he said.

Ava watched the brothers as Perkasa spoke, his tone completely matter-of-fact. Their facial reactions were equally neutral. The minute turned into something approaching five; then Waru interrupted and Perkasa passed the piece of paper to him. He and his brother looked at it together and then had their own quiet discussion. Waru finally handed it back with his own monologue and what sounded like a question.

"They want to know if the banker has a driver or not. It isn't unusual for that to be the case, and if he does, then in all likelihood the driver will be doubling as a bodyguard and could be armed."

"I don't know anything about a driver. All I know is that he drives a Porsche 911 Targa."

Perkasa smiled and spoke to Waru, who smiled back. "There's no chance he has a driver for that car," Perkasa said to Ava.

"I didn't think so. Now, how about the house? Do they know where it is?"

"Yeah, Waru used to patrol the area. The house and the golf course are both in west Surabaya, about twelve kilometres apart. Waru says the banker has about a two-kilometre drive from his house, through a residential community, to the highway, and then about an eight-kilometre drive on the highway to the cut-off for the golf course. The road going to the course is only two lanes, and very winding. He says it isn't developed around there. The course is quite isolated."

"That sounds like the ideal spot, doesn't it."

"That's what Waru said."

"Then that's the plan. How do you want to coordinate it?"

"Let me call the golf club first," Perkasa said.

He walked over to the hotel desk and started a conversation with the concierge. She punched some information into her computer and then turned the screen for Perkasa to look at it. He spoke to her again and she reached for a phone and made a call while he watched. When she was done, Ava saw him slip a banknote across the desk to her.

"He's playing tomorrow and he's supposed to tee off at seven thirty," Perkasa said when he returned.

"What did she tell them?" Ava asked.

"She said she was calling for a hotel guest who has some paperwork he needs to get to Cameron first thing in the morning. She said the guest wanted to meet up with him before he started to play."

Ava looked at Waru. "Is he willing to wear his police uniform tomorrow?" she asked.

Perkasa repeated the question in Indonesian. Waru nodded.

"Great," Ava said. "Then I suggest that we position one of our vehicles — you and I should be in it — near the banker's house very early tomorrow morning. The other one, with the brothers, should be on the golf course road; we can leave the exact location to Waru. You and I can tail the Porsche after it leaves the house. We'll need to be in phone contact with the other car so they'll know when he's left and just in case he changes his route. When the banker exits the highway, he'll be only a minute or so from our second car. Waru can block the road then. If he's wearing his uniform, he should be able to get the Porsche to stop without any fuss."

Perkasa looked at the diagram she was drawing in her notebook as she talked. "And we'll come from behind and seal off any chance of him reversing," he said.

"Exactly. Then, one way or another, we get him out of the car. Hopefully Waru can talk him into doing it peacefully. If not, then we'll do it forcefully," Ava said. "Now, I want his wrists, eyes, and mouth taped as quickly as possible. There isn't any point in giving him time to memorize faces or licence plate numbers."

"Okay."

"Then we bundle him into the trunk of Waru's Pathfinder and off we go."

"What about the Porsche?"

"Obviously we're not leaving it there. One of us has to drive it back to Waru's."

"Let me explain all of this to them and then we'll figure out who drives what," said Perkasa.

"While you're doing that, I need to use the washroom," Ava said.

She scrubbed her hands with soap and then splashed cold water on her face. *These are good men*, she thought as she looked in the mirror. *Not too many questions, not at all concerned about the why of it all.* It was just a job, a well-paid job, that needed to get done. She'd been lucky with Uncle's men over the years, and it felt to her that she'd drawn well again.

Her opinion didn't change when she returned to the lobby. The three men had moved to one sofa, her notebook in front of them, their faces calm, focused. Perkasa looked up. "They like this plan, and the early morning timing is good."

"Who'll drive the Porsche?"

He smiled. "We all want to, but given that Waru is going to be in uniform and I think I should stay with you, Prayogo is the choice."

"That's fine with me. How about any questions they have?"

"Waru did ask how long you think you'll have to hold the banker at his house."

"Not past Sunday, I hope."

"And they suggested that we drive the routes tonight, the one from the house to the cut-off and the road to the golf course. It will give us a better sense of the time involved, and Waru would like to pick out in advance the best place to intercept the banker."

"Of course," Ava said. She had taken that for granted but was pleased to agree to it as their idea.

"Well, then, we should get going," Perkasa said. "It will be dark soon enough."

(27)

THEY DROVE TWENTY KILOMETRES, ALMOST STRAIGHT west of the city, in Waru's Pathfinder, Perkasa and Ava riding in the back, Prayogo up front with his brother.

CitraLand — "the Singapore of Surabaya," as sign after sign proclaimed — was a grouping of developments. Cameron's house was in CitraGarden, Lampung. The roads were beautifully paved, divided by landscaped meridians that must have taken an army of labourers to keep so immaculate.

Ava looked out at row after row of white stucco houses with red-tile roofs, wooden trim, single-car driveways, and small front lawns. She had seen developments like this outside of Bangkok. It was the Asian interpretation of a North American subdivision, its focus on clean, new, and organized.

Waru led them through the grid, the houses getting gradually larger and beginning to show some variety in architecture. When they reached a street where the houses sat on quarter-acre lots, he slowed down but didn't stop, pointing left to a two-storey building behind a four-metre brick wall. Ava glanced at the pale blue stucco house with its swooping red-tile roof. Then her attention was drawn to the interlocking stone driveway, where a black Porsche Targa was parked. It was the only car in sight. The licence plate matched the number Indra had given her. *The son of a bitch is home,* she thought. The wrought-iron gate fronting the driveway was agape. How easy would it be?

Perkasa looked out the back window in the direction they had come from. “There’s only one road out of here that leads to the highway. We can wait for him at any spot between here and there.”

“I don’t want to take the slightest chance of losing him,” Ava said. “So we’ll wait down there, at the end of this road, with the car facing him. We should be able to keep him in sight without getting too close.”

“Ava, have you given any thought to what we’ll do if Cameron doesn’t follow our script?” Perkasa asked.

She glanced at him. He was looking out the window. “What do you mean?”

“What if he has a passenger in the Porsche? What if he leaves the Porsche here and takes a cab or limo? What if he catches a ride with a buddy?”

“All I care about is that he leaves the house to go to the golf course. How he gets there doesn’t matter. Ideally it’s by himself, in the Porsche. If some other scenario presents itself, we’ll deal with it. You’re okay with that, I hope.”

“I’m okay, but I know the boys will ask the question and I didn’t want to guess at an answer.”

“We’re going to get Cameron one way or another.”

“Like I said, I’m okay with that, and they will be too.”

He’s only being thorough, Ava thought, aware that she might have sounded defensive, and worse, as if she hadn’t thought things through. “I don’t mean that I would ask anyone to do anything reckless," she said. "We'll get here early tomorrow and see how Cameron intends to get to Paradise Run. If there's any dramatic change, we'll discuss it before committing."

"That's fine. Now what?"

"Let's drive the route to the course. We need some idea of timing, and I'd like to see where Waru intends to intercept him."

Perkasa spoke to the men in front. Waru nodded and drove back the way they had come. When they reached the highway, he took a cut-off about halfway back to the city. There was a service station and a cluster of small houses near the exit, and after that nothing but rice paddies on both sides of the road. The road was straight for the first half-kilometre and then began to wind. About another half-kilometre along, Ava saw a small hill. It wasn't much of a rise, just enough to hide a car on the other side. Waru drove over it and then stopped about fifty metres further on. He parked by the roadside.

They all got out of the vehicle. Waru pointed at the hill and then turned and looked in the other direction as he spoke to Perkasa.

"He thinks this is the best spot," Perkasa said to Ava. "The banker won't see him until he comes over the rise, and if he blocks the road here, Cameron will still have time to stop. The good thing is that it won't give the banker time to think about anything other than stopping." He looked down the road. "And we can't see the golf course from here, so no one is going to see us from there either."

"I like it," said Ava.

"We still have to worry about other cars on the road."

Ava shrugged. "It will be early. And even if someone does see us, Waru will be in his uniform and it will all look official."

"When should we be in place?"

"I think we need to be at Cameron's house before dawn."

"Okay."

Ava asked, "How far is it from here to Waru's house?"

"About a thirty-minute drive straight west."

She looked at the hill, at the cars. "I have a good feeling about this."

"Yeah, it seems to hang together."

"Well, if you can't think of anything else for us to do, I guess that's it for today. I'd like to go back to the hotel," Ava said.

"Dinner?"

"If you want to take the guys, go ahead. I had a very late lunch and I can't eat another thing."

Perkasa's eyes shifted away from her, and she sensed he was disappointed. "I may do that," he said.

"My treat."

"That isn't necessary."

Ava shrugged. "Let's head back, shall we? I have some phone calls to make."

"Do you want the boys to meet us at the hotel in the morning or do you want them to come directly here?"

"We'll meet at the Sheraton. Say, five a.m.?"

"Perfect," he said.

"And make sure they have the picana."

"It's at their house. They told me it came with a transformer of some kind."

"It sounds like they bought the right thing. They can leave it at the house — I won't need it until I get Cameron there."

(28)

AVA HAD NEVER BEEN UNCOMFORTABLE WITH BEING alone, but as soon as she got to her room she began to feel unsettled.

Perkasa had driven her to the Majapahit and asked her again to join him for dinner. She couldn't eat, she repeated, and that was the truth. Her body felt disconnected from her mind, which was wandering in unaccustomed patterns.

She lay on the bed, turned on the television, and searched for something that might distract her. She watched *Moonstruck* with Indonesian subtitles for about fifteen minutes and then gave up. Andy Cameron kept intruding, and the initial image was always the same: him walking so cockily towards their table at the restaurant, a sly grin fixed on his face.

Ava went to the bathroom and turned on the tap, slapped her face with cold water. *Focus,* she muttered. *Treat tomorrow like any other job. Get organized.*

The game she was playing, she knew, had its limits in terms of credibility. She wanted to hurt Cameron. She was going to hurt Cameron. But in Perkasa's eyes, and therefore in Uncle's, it had to be seen as a necessity. And that could be made believable, or at least believable enough, only by keeping Cameron under control. Ava did not want him talking about that night — not a word. She did not need any weeping, pleading, or heart-rending and completely self-serving bullshit confessions and apologies. All she wanted him to do was talk about the bank, about Fred Purslow, about Costa Rica and the Emerald Lion Fund and Lam Van Dinh. Or rather, not talk about it — not at first, anyway.

Ava left the bathroom and sat at the desk. She opened her notebook and began to list the questions that under normal circumstances she would want answered. Who owned the bank? How had it accumulated such a huge capital base in such a short time while operating from Surabaya? Why those overseas offices? Why was the Toronto office closed? Where were Muljadi and Rocca? Was there ever a Surabaya Fidelity Security fund? Who killed Purslow? Why kill Purslow? Each question begot more questions, the complexity compounding, the purpose of her search hardening. She tried to imagine how Cameron would react.

The room telephone rang. It startled her and she looked at her watch. It was past ten o'clock; she realized she'd been sitting at the desk for more than an hour. She didn't want to answer, but it could be Perkasa.

"Hello?" she said.

"Ava, this is Vivian Ho. I apologize for calling so late, but I just got back from dinner and I wanted to make sure you were okay."

"You spoke to your sister about me," Ava said coolly.

"Only in the most general way," she said, stuttering softly. "I didn't tell her what happened. It's just that I know my sister, and I know what a good friend she can be, and I know how loving she is. I thought you could use that kind of support."

"How would you know what kind of support I need?"

She hesitated. "Well, you aren't the first victim of this kind of abuse I've attended to. I think I have some understanding—"

"Understanding?"

"Yes, exactly."

"Fay told me you're gay," Ava said.

"I'm not sure my sister has the right—" Vivian began, sounding distressed.

"I am too," said Ava.

There was only quiet from the other end of the line. Ava imagined Vivian gathering her senses, gathering her words. She readied herself for the platitudes that would end their conversation. Then she heard a sob, and another, and then a stream, interrupted only by gulps for air.

"Please," Ava said, almost unaware of her own voice cracking, of her own tears returning.

They cried wordlessly together, Ava's tears coursing down her cheeks and falling onto the notebook. She wiped at them blindly, blotching the questions that only a few minutes before had seemed so clever.

"I am so sorry..." Vivian was finally able to say.

Ava pushed her chair away from the desk and turned towards the window. She wiped at her eyes with the sleeve of her T-shirt. "I really appreciate that you called," she said.

"Is there anything I can do to help?" Vivian asked, still sniffling.

"No, you've done enough."

"I've done nothing."

"That's not true. You were wonderful to me."

"If only I had known..."

"Known what, that I'm gay? What difference would it make to what was done to me?"

"I still think you should go to the police."

"I have... in my own way."

"What do you mean?"

Should I tell her? Ava thought. *To what end?* "Look, Vivian, I need to get some sleep now. I want to thank you again for calling and for all your concern. Chances are I'll be out of Surabaya sometime tomorrow, so we should treat this as goodbye."

"Goodbye then," Vivian said slowly.

"Goodbye," said Ava.

She sat there, still facing the window. The drapes were open, a full moon illuminating the treetops that waved in the nighttime breeze.

(29)

THE HOTEL LOBBY WAS ALMOST DESERTED WHEN SHE came down the stairs. The doorman-cum-security-guard standing by the reception desk flirting with the clerk was the only sign of life. He looked at Ava, then at his watch, and said, "Early start, Ibu."

"Yes, I have an early breakfast meeting."

"A very early meeting."

It was ten to five. She had slept badly, waking every hour, her mind a whirl, not able to settle on the day ahead, not able to settle on anything. She gave up at four fifteen, cancelled her wake-up call, washed, brushed her hair and teeth, threw on casual clothes, had two quick coffees, put her notebook into her bag, and then left the room with the bag in one hand and a roll of duct tape in the other.

"Do you want a taxi?" the doorman asked.

"No, I'm going to the Sheraton. I'll walk."

He left the desk. "That isn't a good idea, Ibu, not alone in the dark at this time."

"I can look after myself," Ava said, going through the door.

"Maybe so, but I'm going with you anyway," he said.

She started to argue but he was already walking beside her, a look of determination on his face. "Did Pak Indra mention me to you or any of the other security staff?" Ava asked.

"No, why?"

"No particular reason."

The streets were still; the only noise she could hear was an insect chirping. "It's like everyone's left the city," she said.

"In about half an hour you won't think so. The muezzin will start the *adhan*, and everything will spring to life."

The walk to Tunjungan Plaza was quick and uneventful, although twice Ava saw figures lurking in doorways. When they reached the Sheraton entrance, she tipped the guard ten dollars. "That isn't necessary, Ibu," he said.

"I know. Take it anyway."

She saw Waru first. He wore a uniform she'd seen the day before, on the policeman who stopped Fay. "Hey, Ava, over here," Perkasa called. He was sitting off to one side with Prayogo. They were both dressed in jeans and black T-shirts, and Ava wondered if that was deliberate.

"Is Waru a motorcycle cop?" she asked as she drew near.

"Yeah."

"You don't think it will look strange, him stopping Cameron in a Nissan Pathfinder?"

"Nah. Around here a cop is a cop is a cop."

"If you say so…"

"Ava, don't worry."

She nodded.

"We're ready to roll whenever you are."

"Well, then, let's hit the road."

They rode the elevator down two levels to the underground parking garage. Both Nissans were parked beside the elevator doors. "The boys were here at four thirty," Perkasa said.

"Let's hope Cameron is as punctual," she said, handing the tape to him. "Please tell Waru that as soon as he cuffs him, I want his eyes and mouth taped. He can throw him in the trunk then."

"He knows." Perkasa passed the tape to Waru and then spoke to the brothers in Indonesian. They listened carefully, nodding and then smiling.

"Well, that's it. They're as ready as they're going to be," Perkasa said to Ava.

The cars separated along the highway, the brothers heading towards the golf course, Perkasa driving the other Nissan to CitraGarden. There was hardly any traffic on the road, and as they entered the development there was no sign of life. The ride had been quiet, and that pleased Ava. She had worked with people who needed to talk incessantly in the hours leading up to a job, as a way to deal with their nerves. The only noise coming from Perkasa was a quiet humming as he accompanied music from a soft-rock radio station.

When they reached Cameron's street, Ava felt a touch of concern. As they drove past his house, she looked anxiously at the driveway. The Porsche was still there, and she drew a calming breath. They drove to the end of the street, made a U-turn, and then parked the car pointed in the direction Cameron would be coming from. "Now the worst part — the waiting," Perkasa said.

The first sign of dawn appeared on the horizon, the sun not yet visible but its advance light beginning to colour their surroundings. The houses on Cameron's street were similarly if not identically constructed. Whatever real differences existed among them lay in the shades of pastel blue and pink and green the owners had chosen for their exterior walls.

Perkasa turned off the car engine and rolled down the windows. Ava could feel the heat start to encroach. In half an hour it would be like sitting in a steam room. She was about to ask him to turn on the air conditioning when she heard the faint voice of a muezzin.

"The call to *salah*, to *fajr*, the first prayer," he said. "The neighbourhood will be coming to life in a few minutes."

It took longer than a few minutes. In fact it was close to six o'clock, the sun now completely visible, the heat building, before there was any activity on the street. It looked as if the domestic staff were arriving. Twice Perkasa turned on the car and drove it to the end of the street, turned the corner, and idled there for a while so they wouldn't be a constant presence near Cameron's.

He was driving past the house, going back to their original watch location, when Cameron's gate swung open. "Finally," said Perkasa.

They parked and waited, both with their eyes locked on the gate. A short, dark man came out of the house and stood on the sidewalk. He looked up and down the street and then turned back towards the driveway. He reached for the gate and held it. The black Porsche backed out onto the street and stopped. The man went to the passenger-side window and said something to the driver. Then he waved and turned back towards the house, pulling the gate closed behind him.

Perkasa started the Nissan and reached for his cellphone. He didn't begin to drive until the Porsche had cleared the corner at the end of the street. Then they followed, keeping it barely in view, confident about where it was headed. He called Waru as they left the development and trailed the Porsche onto the highway.

"We'll need to call him again once Cameron exits," he said.

The Porsche drove in the left-hand lane of the three-lane highway. Perkasa kept to the right one, making it impossible for Cameron to see them in his rear-view mirror. A sign for the road leading to Paradise Run came at them while Cameron was still in the left lane. The exit was on the right, and for a second Ava thought he was going to drive right past it, but at the last minute the Porsche careered across the highway and headed down the ramp.

"We've got him," Perkasa said.

Not yet, Ava thought. *It's never that easy.*

Perkasa talked to Waru again and then turned to Ava. "He says he's seen only three cars since they've been there. There's nothing visible in either direction right now."

Ava looked behind the Nissan. The road ran straight and empty. Could they be so lucky?

Perkasa kept the Porsche in plain view now. Cameron was driving quickly, the car hugging the curves. When it reached the rise beyond which Waru waited, Perkasa gassed the Nissan. Ava counted. She got to ten before they crested the hill and saw the Porsche.

Waru had positioned his Nissan sideways across the right-hand lane. He was walking on the left side of the road towards the driver's-side window of the Porsche, which was still closed. Perkasa stopped at the top of the rise, ready to move if needed.

"He's carrying a radar gun," Ava said, noticing the device in Waru's right hand. "Nice touch."

When Waru reached the Porsche, he looked in the window and then lightly rapped it. It slid down. Ava could see him speaking and shaking his head. Then he reached for the gun in the holster at his right hip.

"Move," she said to Perkasa.

He drove the Nissan directly behind the Porsche to block any chance of retreat. The Targa's door swung open just as they arrived. Ava lowered herself in her seat, not entirely trusting the tinted glass to do its job. "He's out of the car," Perkasa said.

She couldn't help but look. Cameron was wearing tartan shorts, an untucked black golf shirt that hung loose around his belly, and a pair of cheap rubber flip-flops. He had his face close to Waru's and he was yammering away. Ava couldn't hear much of it, just enough to know that Cameron thought he was untouchable. The policeman remained calm until Cameron got too close, until his verbal abuse began to get shrill and he was showering Waru with a spray of spit. That's when the policeman grabbed the Scot by both shoulders and spun him around. He tucked one hand into the waist of Cameron's shorts, the other grabbed the collar of his shirt, and he slammed Cameron face down onto the hood of his car. The cuffs were on almost instantly.

Prayogo had left the other Nissan now, the roll of duct tape in his hand. When he reached the Porsche, Waru turned Cameron around and held him while his brother taped the banker's eyes and mouth. The policeman quickly marched the Scot to the Nissan, its rear door already open. He bundled him inside, slammed the door, and then climbed into the driver's seat. Prayogo was already at the wheel of the Porsche.

Waru turned the Nissan into the left lane and started up the hill. Prayogo followed. "Off we go," Perkasa said.

Ava looked in the direction of the golf course. There was no one in sight. As they drove back over the hill, she saw one car approaching from a distance. It couldn't have gone any better. "That was beautifully done," she said.

"I told you they were good guys."

They drove straight west, past the CitraLand exits, until the highway gave way to a two-lane road and countryside. The few houses they saw were set back from the road, most of them on stilts and with shutters rather than glass windows — no more than small square boxes, places to sleep and eat and stay dry in the rainy season. Waru turned off the paved road onto an unmarked dirt path that was full of potholes. The Nissans handled it easily, but she could see that the underside of the Porsche was taking a beating.

Waru's house was a slightly larger version of the square boxes on stilts. It stood about twenty metres back from the road, the nearest neighbours about two hundred metres away in either direction. "This was a farm," Perkasa said.

The lead Nissan parked in front of the house. Prayogo drove the Porsche to the rear. Waru waved at Perkasa to park alongside him and then walked towards the back of his vehicle.

"I'd like to see the house first," Ava said quietly.

Perkasa spoke to Waru. He shrugged and led the way up six wooden steps to the front door. It was unlocked, and he opened it with one light twist of a knob. There were six rooms: three bedrooms, a bathroom, a kitchen, and a living area. The living room had a wicker couch and chair with cushions that looked as if they had been bleached by the sun, a television, and a coffee table. The kitchen had a dark wooden table with six chairs.

"We'll put him in the kitchen," Ava said. "His wrists should be cuffed to the back of the chair and his ankles taped to the two front legs. Waru should move the table and the other chairs out of the way in case Cameron starts flailing about. I wouldn't want him to do any damage to the furniture." As Perkasa translated, Ava began to move the chairs to one side.

Prayogo had now joined them in the kitchen, carrying the picana and the transformer. "The transformer can go on the floor near the chair where we'll seat Cameron," she said.

The policeman and his brother left the house to get the Scot. Ava leaned back against the sink. "They don't have to be here while I'm questioning him," she said.

"I'll give them the choice, if that's okay."

"Fine."

She heard a noise from the front door and went to look. Cameron's legs weren't supporting him all that well, and the brothers were half carrying, half dragging him up the steps. He also seemed to be trying to talk through the tape. To Ava it sounded like he was saying, "I'll pay, I'll pay." *Yes, you will,* she thought.

They sat him down roughly on a chair that was now situated by itself in the middle of the kitchen. As Waru adjusted the cuffs, Prayogo knelt and taped Cameron's ankles. Ava expected him to strain, but he sat slumped, turning his head from side to side as if he was trying to sense where his abductors were. Whatever cockiness he possessed had disappeared.

"Leave him with me for a few minutes," she said to Persaka.

Cameron's body twitched and his neck stiffened. She knew he had heard her.

Perkasa spoke to the brothers, who nodded and turned to leave. "I'll be outside when you need me," he said to Ava. "The boys are going to drive over to Waru's mother-in-law's house. It's only ten minutes away, so they can come back in a flash."

She waited until the front door closed.

"Hi, Andy," she said.

(30)

THE HOUSE WASN'T AIR-CONDITIONED, AND ALTHOUGH some of the windows were open there was hardly any air flow. Cameron was sweating badly. Ava didn't know if it was because of fear or the heat. The sweat gathered at his hairline and on his brow and trickled around the tape on his eyes, coursing down his cheeks and settling around his collarbones. She looked down and saw moisture on his shins and the tops of his bare feet. She wondered if he had peed himself already, but there was no odour.

"Andy, this is Ava Lee, though I imagine you've figured that out already."

He tried to speak but she reached out, grabbed his knee, and squeezed. "No, don't say anything yet. You need to listen to me first."

He nodded.

"Good. Now the first thing you need to understand is that this isn't personal. I know that may be hard for you to believe, but it's the truth," she said as calmly, as softly as she could. "This is business, Andy. You are here because of the bank. I have clients in Canada, in Toronto, who lost more than thirty million dollars doing business with your bank branch there. So I'm here and you're here because we need to talk about the bank and the branch and the way you conduct your affairs.

"That doesn't mean that I'm not angry about what happened two nights ago, but you know what, Andy? I'm a big girl, and I'm prepared to put personal feelings aside as long as we can have an intelligent discussion about Bank Linno. Nod if you understand."

He nodded, without conviction.

"Okay, that's good. Now I'm going to start telling you about my clients and the fund they invested in, and the cretin who worked for your bank who made off with their money. Do you have any idea what I'm talking about?"

Cameron shook his head.

Ava moved away from him and began to walk in a wide circle around the chair. "The fund was called Emerald Lion and it was operated by a guy called Lam Van Dinh. Have you heard of it, or him?"

He shook his head again.

"Well, it wasn't really a fund, was it. More like a bank account at Linno that was opened for Lam by Fred Purslow. You have heard of Purslow?"

There was slight hesitation and then a slight nod.

"The thing is, Purslow seems to have conned Lam into opening the account on the pretext that the money was going into a fund operated by your bank, a fund called Surabaya Fidelity Security. It paid a modest and steady rate of interest on the money until about six or seven months ago, when the payments stopped. Purslow seems to have left the bank and Toronto at the same time. Now, Lam was understandably upset and paid a visit to the branch, where he met with a man called Muljadi, who as far I know was the Canadian operations president, and another guy, named Rocca. They told Lam in reasonably quick order that they thought Purslow had scammed him and asked him to back off while the bank looked into it. They even paid him a month's interest on the fund's money to buy some time—as good as an admission of liability in my mind. What do you think of that? Is the bank liable?"

Cameron shrugged.

"We can come back to that," Ava said. "Let's finish the story first. So a couple of weeks go by and Lam doesn't hear from your guys. He's about to take matters elsewhere when he is informed that Purslow and a friend of his have been killed in Costa Rica...rather nasty deaths at that. Panicked, Lam runs back to the bank and finds it closed. No one. Nothing. As he's leaving the building, he's picked up by a couple of thugs—hired by the bank, I'm presuming—who tell him that if he wants to end up like Purslow then he should keep pursuing the money. Lam is no hero, far from it. He leaves town too, although not to anywhere as exotic as Costa Rica."

She paused and stood still behind Cameron. She saw him tense. "It's only fair to tell you that I've made several assumptions about this mess. I believe, first of all, that it's entirely possible Purslow orchestrated this fraud on his own and without the knowledge or consent of the bank. I believe that when he left the bank, he took the money with him, probably to Costa Rica. I believe that the bank found both him and the money, in no particular order, and had him killed. I believe that the bank then decided to treat the money as its own and to screw over Lam and my clients."

Ava began circling Cameron. "Now, obviously I want the money returned. But before we get into the mechanics of how you're going to make that happen, I want you to talk to me about Bank Linno. I'm curious—no, actually, more than curious—about how a backwater Indonesian bank managed to build such a large equity base in such a short period of time with a Scotsman running it. I'd like to know who owns the bank. I'd like to know why you opened a branch in Toronto, of all places, and how a bank from Surabaya thought it could compete and make money in New York and Rome and wherever else you are overseas."

Cameron sat still. Ava knew she'd thrown a lot at him and it was time to back up. "Andy, I'm going to take the tape off your mouth. When I do, I'm going to start asking you specific questions and I expect you to start giving me specific answers. If it goes well, then you can take your Porsche and be on your way." She reached from behind and ripped off the tape.

The first words from his mouth were, "This is fucking crazy."

"That's not a good start," she cautioned.

"I don't know half of what you're talking about," he said, his voice hoarse.

"Well, let's talk about the half you do know about. Fred Purslow, for example. Were you acquainted with him?"

"No."

"You've never heard the name?"

He hesitated.

"Don't think you can lie to me," Ava said.

"I heard the name."

"That's all?"

"He was an employee, low-grade. I had no reason to know him."

"Are you saying that when he took off with thirty million dollars, Muljadi didn't brief you?"

"That's when I heard the name, but it was almost in passing. Muljadi said he had things under control."

"And it seems he did. I mean, he took care of Purslow, he recovered the money, and he scared off Lam. That leaves the rather obvious question of what he did with the money. So what did he do with it?"

"I don't know."

"I don't believe that."

"We were closing the Toronto operation, things were in a state of flux—"

"That is a pathetic explanation," Ava said.

Cameron shrugged.

"Who owns the bank?" she said sharply.

"We have a large number of investors."

"And they don't care about thirty million dollars, plus or minus?"

He didn't answer.

"And tell me, just how did you create all those billions of dollars in equity?"

"Our investors put a lot of money in and there was good management."

"Of course, good management. I'm told you were a major player in the Toronto real estate market."

"We're a commercial bank overseas. We invested heavily in real estate and other safe business opportunities in Toronto and New York and everywhere else."

"So why leave Canada?"

"My board doesn't like to be overcommitted to any one market. I operate under a set of guidelines, investment limits. Once I reach a certain threshold in one market, we move on to another."

Ava noticed that the tension in his voice was easing. He was obviously comfortable talking in generalities about the bank. She switched gears. "I want the thirty million dollars returned."

He rolled his head back, twisting his neck. "How do you expect me to do that?"

"You're the president."

"Get real. I'd have to go to my board to get their approval."

"So how much can you transfer on your own authority?"

"Things are very tightly controlled."

"How much?"

"No more than a million."

"Well, if that's true then you're going to have to get creative," Ava said.

"I don't understand."

"No matter. Look, Andy, I'm going to tape your mouth again and I don't want you to resist. Then I'm going to get my associate and we'll resume our questioning."

He stiffened again. "This is a waste of time," he said. "There's no way I can get you thirty million dollars. A million, yes, that I can do. And that I will do. You can split it among your friends here and tell your clients whatever story you want."

She taped his mouth and left the kitchen.

Perkasa sat in the Nissan, the door open, the air conditioning thrumming. "He isn't being cooperative. I'm ready to use the picana," she said.

Ava had seen a picana used only once before. She had been in China with one of Uncle's men and had located a scam artist who had a lot of local protection. They had a limited amount of time to find out what they needed, and Uncle's man had suggested using a picana to speed up the process.

The electric prod was about half a metre long, with a bronze tip and an insulated handle. It could be plugged into a control box with a rheostat, used to raise or reduce voltage, and a transformer connected it to any ordinary electric wall socket. Uncle's man was quite expert with it. He stripped the scammer and then wet the target to reduce the electrical resistance of his skin. He had Ava adjust the rheostat control while he applied the tip to various parts of the guy's body. She was worried they might actually kill him, but Uncle's man explained that although the current was high-voltage, the amperage was low. It took less than fifteen minutes for them to get all the information and cooperation they needed.

Cameron hadn't moved while she was gone from the room. Perkasa took a disinterested glance at him. "Take his pants down while I hook up the machine," Ava said.

Cameron squirmed, rocking his body back and forth. "Be still," she said.

The picana looked new, the current range higher than she remembered. In China the prod had delivered between twelve and sixteen thousand volts. This one promised to go all the way up to thirty thousand. Ava plugged it into the wall socket and turned up the rheostat. When she turned back, Cameron's shorts and underwear were already dangling around his ankles. She looked at his penis. It was fat and stubby and he hadn't been circumcised, so flesh hid the head. She thought it was one of the ugliest things she had ever seen. His testicles sat on the chair, spread out by the contact. Ava thought about wetting him but figured he was sweaty enough.

She set the picana at twenty thousand volts and moved closer. "Lift his penis," she said to Perkasa.

He reached down and grabbed it, averting his eyes. As he raised it, the testicles went along for the ride. Ava moved to one side, slipped the picana underneath, and then placed the tip hard against them.

Cameron's body contorted so violently that he raised the chair from the floor. Ava kept pressing up. His head was rolling from side to side, screams audible even through the tape. She pressed harder.

Ava wasn't aware how much time elapsed. Even when he emptied his bowels, the excrement spilling over the chair seat, she kept the prod in place. It wasn't until Cameron began to convulse that she slid it out from under his testicles.

"Sorry about the mess," she said to Perkasa.

He grimaced.

"No reason to clean him. He'll just do it all over again when I zap him again."

"I know."

"I'm going to pay Waru a bonus when this is done. I'm sure he wasn't counting on this."

"Neither was I," he said, matter-of-factly. Perkasa looked at Cameron. "Do you think he'll be more cooperative now?"

"One more time and then we'll ask," Ava said.

She wasn't sure how much damage she had done. He wouldn't be fit for any sexual activity for a while, but with one more treatment maybe she could make that closer to permanent. She turned the rheostat up to thirty thousand volts. She looked down at the chair and saw that Cameron's testicles were half hanging over the edge, so she wouldn't have to ask Perkasa to expose them. She slid the picana tip just under them and then pulled it high.

The chair came off the ground again. Cameron's body twisted left and right as if he was trying to shake something off. The chair teetered to one side and Ava thought for a second he was going to fall over, but Perkasa reached out and steadied it.

He had screamed when the jolt first hit him, but as she continued to press, the noise lessened until it became not much more than a whimper. His body became less active as well, the contortions becoming twitches, his legs shaking less violently. She knew he was almost unconscious and retracted the picana.

"Let's give him a few minutes to recover," she said. "Then I'll ask my questions again."

They went outside, the morning sun now high in the sky and the heat bearing down on them. "It might be a good idea to clean him up a bit," Perkasa said. "It's going to smell something awful in there in a few minutes."

Ava nodded. "Take him and the chair out the back door and hose them down. I'll join you in a few minutes."

(31)

TAKING THE MOLESKINE NOTEBOOK AND PEN FROM her bag, she reviewed the questions she had written the night before. Most of them had been asked earlier, although not as methodically as was her pattern. She'd been too eager to get to the picana.

Ava walked through the house and out the back door of the kitchen onto a small veranda. Perkasa stood over Cameron with a bucket in his hand. "No hose," he said, as he threw water at Cameron's groin.

She leaned against the wall of the house, in the shade. The Scotsman sat in the sun. "That'll do," she said. "I might as well talk to him here, assuming he's prepared to talk." She reached out and peeled the tape from his mouth.

"Are you prepared to be more forthright, Andy? Because if you aren't, I'm telling you, that rod that's been frying your balls is going to go up your ass. And if we have to do that, the pain is going to be indescribable."

He was starting to revive, drawing deep, ragged breaths. His voice cracked. "Don't hurt me anymore."

"That's all up to you."

"I'll tell you anything you want to know."

"And the money?"

"I'll do everything I can about the money. Just don't hurt me anymore."

Ava opened her notebook. "What actually happened to the money?" she asked Cameron.

"Can you take the tape from my eyes?"

"No, you talk to me first. The money — what happened to it?"

"Much as you thought," he croaked.

"Much or exactly?"

He paused. "My mouth is really dry. Can I get something to drink?"

She looked at his mouth and saw a light crust at the corners. "Could you bring a glass of water?" she asked Perkasa.

"Much or exactly?" she repeated to Cameron.

"They found Purslow first. Neither he nor his boyfriend had taken any real trouble to cover their tracks. He must have thought he only had the Vietnamese guy to worry about. Once they got him, the money wasn't hard to retrieve."

"And then they had him killed?"

"Aye."

"So where's the money?"

"It was absorbed into the bank."

"Where?"

"Here, as always. All the money flows into Surabaya."

"All the money?"

He began to answer but Perkasa emerged from the kitchen, closing the door behind him. He walked to Cameron and rested the glass of water against his lower lip. Cameron slurped, licked his lips, and then slurped again.

"And who are 'they'? Who ordered Purslow dead?" Ava asked.

"Rocca."

"Rocca? Not Muljadi?"

"Rocca ran the show."

"Muljadi was president."

Cameron's lips pressed together. Ava could sense him calculating how much he should say. "This is beginning not to work for me," she warned. "Either you stop making me guess or I get the picana warmed up again."

He groaned. "No, don't do that. It's just difficult to explain things in a way that doesn't seem crazy."

"Try me."

"With Rocca and Muljadi, that's the way they set it up. It was the same everywhere. The presidents of all the branches are Indonesian, except for me here, but there are Italians like Rocca in every one — in supposedly lesser positions — who actually call all the shots. I have two of them in Surabaya. They don't have any titles; they don't show their faces at the bank. We meet offsite. We communicate by phone, by computer. The Indonesians, me, the office here — we're all window dressing."

Ava stopped taking notes. She stared at Perkasa, who stared back. This wasn't what she had expected. "Italians?"

"Aye."

"I'm confused."

"It isn't going to get any simpler," he said.

"Who are these Italians?"

"The 'Ndrangheta."

"The who?"

He spelled the name.

"That doesn't help me any."

"They're like the Mafia on steroids."

"Sicilian?"

"God no. They think the Sicilians are sissies."

"Where are they from?"

"Calabria, Reggio Calabria."

"How did you connect with them?"

He shifted in the chair, then gasped. "You understand that I'm telling you this only so you'll understand why the idea of getting your thirty million back is impossible?"

"Let me make that decision. Now, how did you get hired?"

Cameron shrugged. "I was working in Rome and had some clients who needed some cash moved around. I made it happen, for a fee, of course. After about a year of this, one of them asked me if I would consider changing banks. When I said it would depend on the money I was paid, he said that wouldn't be a problem, and asked if I was willing to go to an interview. I said I would be happy to do that.

"This was June, but I didn't hear from them again until September, when I got a visit and an invitation to go to a town called San Luca, near Calabria. There was a festival on, celebrating Our Lady of Polsi. I met the contacts from Rome and four other men near the sanctuary for the Lady. They described what they wanted me to do and offered me the job as president, at four times the money I was making in Rome, plus bonuses that could double that again."

"Just what were you supposed to do to make that kind of money?"

"Run the bank."

"I thought you said they called the shots."

"I meant that I was to pretend I was running the bank."

"I don't understand. Why would Italian gangsters want to buy a bank in Indonesia, in Surabaya?"

"To launder money."

"But how? How could that work? What did you have to do to make it happen?"

Perkasa moved closer. Ava had been so intent on listening to Cameron that she had forgotten he was there. He seemed as drawn into the story as she was.

Cameron said, "Can I have some more water?"

Perkasa still had half a glassful in his hand. He held it to Cameron's mouth.

"They had everything figured out by the time they hired me," Cameron said. "They had established contacts with senior Indonesian customs officials and had worked out a system for moving cash into the country. They had bought off senior banking regulators and inspectors so they wouldn't ask too many questions about the bank's growth. They had figured out how they could move money out of the country and put it to work safely and for the long term, but what they still needed was bank systems, the nuts and bolts of the loan process. That's what they wanted me to do—provide the paper trail, make everything look above board and legitimate."

"Fuck," Perkasa said.

Ava shot him a glance that said, *Be quiet*. "How do they move the cash in?"

"By the planeload."

"You're joking, right?"

He shook his head. "They pack the bills in bales, like hay. The charters arrived about once a month at first, but during this past year we've been up to a plane a week. They aren't huge cargo jobbies, mind you, just mid-sized private jets that are stripped to the walls, but you can get a lot of money in them. Most of the planes came from Italy at the start, and then Venezuela came online. It's one or the other since then."

"Do these charter planes have a company name?"

"Brava Italia. I think one of them owns it."

"And now one comes every week?"

"Aye, usually Tuesday nights. That's usually when I can count on seeing the Italians. They're always there to meet the plane. They park it in a hangar and then unload the money into a panel van. We take it to the bank, count it, and record it."

"What are their names?"

"Foti and Chorico."

"They go alone?"

"Them and me."

"Who's on the plane?"

"The pilot and co-pilot, no one else."

"And Customs turns a blind eye?"

"The planes land and are taxied directly to a hangar at the far end of the airport that we rent as we need it, and unloaded without a single question in all the years up to now."

"Then what?"

"We drive the money to the bank, count it, register it as a foreign investment, and then convert it all to rupiahs."

"Again no questions?"

"The provincial bank officials in East Java and the national ones in Jakarta have been happy to play along."

"Then you move it out?"

"Aye. Initially we put a ton of money into the Bali region—you know, to establish a local base. Then gradually we expanded outwards. They choose the markets and the investments. Italy, of course, but never Calabria; Rome mainly, but we financed a lot of construction in Milan as well. Then New York. Caracas and Porlamar, on Margarita Island, in Venezuela. A lot of them retire there. And Toronto, of course."

"What kinds of investments?"

"Real estate. Office buildings, apartment buildings, shopping centres, subdivisions—you name it, we finance it. About the only thing they won't go near is casinos and casino-hotel complexes. They don't like the attention they attract. They don't like the idea of having to get licensed, of questions being asked, of all those regulators."

"Who owns the real estate?"

"Them."

"The Italians?"

"Yeah. They set up a web of companies as fronts everywhere, but at the end of the day they own or control them all and they're funnelling money to themselves."

"Those companies have names, yes? And officers? And shareholders?"

"I have no idea who the people are who are listed as officers and shareholders. I assume the Italian powers keep themselves hidden and use friends, lawyers, accountants as the official faces. But I'm not sure. I never asked. I was never even curious. I knew what the reality was; I didn't need unnecessary detail."

"So the branches you set up in places such as Toronto and New York were for the sole purpose of returning money to the 'Ndrangheta?"

"Yeah."

"And those branches make loans to those companies?"

"Yeah, and to some individuals."

"How do you know they're connected?"

"I don't. There's someone in place at every branch. In Toronto it was Rocca, who was a member of the gang or involved with it in a serious way. He gave instructions on how much money was to go to whom and for what. We just do what we're told."

"And then you paper them all as loans?"

"Aye, although in reality they aren't loans, because none of them are ever repaid. Not even a penny of interest finds its way back."

"How do you explain that?"

"Explain to who?"

"Bank authorities."

"I told you, some of them are getting paid off, but just to be safe we run two sets of books. One set shows that the loans are performing and giving us a profit, which we declare and pay taxes on — modest taxes, but it makes us look legitimate. The other set of books is run for the Italians. All they show is money in, money out, and what we have on account."

"And the real estate holdings?"

"They don't care who actually owns what, just how much money was given to whom. The real estate records I maintain for bank records and for the other set of books."

"So the equity base we saw when we looked into the bank is real?"

"On paper it is."

"How does the…," she said, checking the name again, "the 'Ndrangheta generate so much cash?"

"Drugs, knock-offs...you name anything illegal and they're probably into it."

"So all this real estate investment is—what, an attempt to go legitimate?"

Cameron began to laugh. "Hardly. They just have too much cash to leave it lying around. After they put what they need back into their core businesses, they need to do something with the excess. That's why we exist. We're a dumping ground. Can you imagine how much money they have in total if we're just handling what they don't need?"

Ava returned to her notebook. The thirty million dollars now seemed like small potatoes. "Then why did they have to screw around my clients?"

"They don't give a shit about your clients."

"They took thirty million dollars from them."

"No, Purslow took the thirty million."

"They got it back."

"You need to understand how they think," Cameron said. "In their minds, Purslow stole thirty million dollars from the bank. How it got there didn't concern them. It was there; therefore it was theirs. And even if it wasn't, they're the ones who retrieved it, and in their minds it's always finders, keepers. They are the greediest people I've ever met."

"What about closing the branch office. Was that related to this?"

"No, not at all. The decision was made months before. They felt there was only so much money they could put into any one market before they would start to attract attention to themselves, and they're absolutely paranoid about attracting attention—to themselves or to the bank. We had reached a threshold in Toronto and they decided to pull out for at least a while."

"So that part was true."

"Aye, we were only weeks away from closing when Purslow did his thing. I've never seen them quite so angry. Like I said, they thought he was stealing their money. And just as bad, he was potentially the cause of some unwelcome publicity. So they found him and they killed him."

"What about Lam? Why didn't they kill him if they were so concerned about publicity?"

"They talked about it."

"And?"

"Rocca convinced them not to. He was worried that Lam might have spoken to some people after their first meeting or had written stuff down, and that if something happened to him the problem would just get bigger, with more people involved, more questions being asked. He said Lam was a coward and that it would be more effective if they just scared him into keeping his mouth shut. And he was right. At least I think he was right... but then Lam talked to you, didn't he."

Ava ignored the implication. "Why didn't they just give him his money back and send him on his way?"

"They didn't have to, did they. Scaring him was more effective."

She thought of the terrified little man she'd met in Ho Chi Minh City what seemed like a very long time ago. "So where does this leave things with the thirty million?" she asked, knowing the answer.

Cameron drew a deep breath. "You need to forget about it."

"There's nothing you can do?"

"I can give you my own money, what I have, and that's about a million dollars in ready cash. But as for the bank, nothing. No chance. They control every dollar in and out. They'd kill me for trying. Then they'd find you and kill you too. Believe me, they'd find you."

Ava heard the words and believed he meant them. And she believed them too. "What time were you supposed to play golf this morning?"

"Eight."

She looked at her watch. It was just past seven thirty. "Who were you supposed to play with?"

"Friends, just friends."

She turned to Perkasa. "Call the golf club. Tell them you're calling for Mr. Cameron. He's feeling ill and he's headed to the hospital for a quick check-up. He won't make the game. Send his apologies and say he'll call his friends later in the day."

Perkasa nodded and headed into the kitchen.

"Is there anything else I need to know about today? Did you have any other appointments? Are there any other people who will be concerned about your absence?" Ava asked.

Cameron shifted in the chair again, a grimace crossing his face. "I'm not sure I'll be able to walk," he said. "The pain is unbelievable."

"I asked you about other appointments."

"I meet the Italians every Sunday night for dinner at an Italian restaurant in CitraLand."

"What time?"

"Seven."

"You shouldn't have a problem making it," she said.

"You think?"

No, Ava thought, *I don't think that at all, not yet, anyway.* "Listen, I have to go and chat with my man. You'll be here by yourself for a few minutes so I have to tape your mouth again."

"Could you move me into the shade?"

"No, I like you where you are," she said as she tore a strip of tape from the roll.

She walked into the kitchen to see Perkasa closing his phone. "That was the golf club," he said.

"Any problem?" she asked.

"No."

Ava went to one of the other kitchen chairs and sat down. "Well, what do you think?"

"About his story?"

"What else?"

"It's crazy, but that doesn't mean it isn't true. Do you believe him?"

"I think I do," she said. "It isn't exactly something anyone might come up with on the spur of the moment, especially with a picana as a distraction. So, yes, I believe him."

"Me too."

"Tell me," Ava said, "is it really that easy to bribe your way into that kind of setup in Indonesia?"

"That depends on how much money you have to throw around. In this country it isn't a matter of whether someone can be bribed, it's just a question of how much it will take. And these guys are moving their own money around, so it isn't like they're hurting anyone here. Paying taxes on a phony set of books is pretty smart."

"He's supposed to meet with the Italians tonight," she said. "If he doesn't show..."

"I know. We were lucky to grab him this morning."

Perkasa looked down at her and she saw a question in his eyes. It was the same as the one in her mind.

"I need to talk to Uncle," she said.

(32)

SHE LET THE CAR RUN FOR FIVE MINUTES WITH THE AIR conditioning on full blast as she gathered her thoughts. The problem she had now was that the secondary objective of recovering some money had gone sharply sideways. If everything he'd said was true, there was no way she was going to get her hands on the thirty million unless she was willing to take on the Italians.

So what if she took the million he had offered and left with it? Even that wasn't without its problems. Would he be able to get his hands on the money today? And if he couldn't, did that mean he would meet with the Italians tonight? How much trust could she put in him? She would have to talk to Uncle about the Italians and about Cameron's offer.

For once he answered the Kowloon apartment phone himself. "*Wei.*"

"Uncle, it's Ava."

"How did it go?"

She paused. She hadn't told him the schedule. "Well enough," she said, realizing that he and Perkasa had probably talked the night before.

"No problems picking him up?"

"No. It was easier than I would have thought possible."

"Good, good."

"No, Uncle, not quite so good. I've just finished questioning him and things aren't what we supposed. In fact, things are a lot more complicated than I ever imagined."

She could hear Lourdes puttering around in the background, then Uncle saying thank-you to her for his tea. "What is the problem?" he finally asked.

Ava began to explain. She spoke for almost twenty minutes, uninterrupted, only hesitating when she heard him cough and then later, when she said the word *'Ndrangheta* and Uncle seemed to stop breathing.

When she was finished, Uncle didn't say anything right away, but she could imagine him sitting in his easy chair, a tray by his side holding the teapot and his morning newspapers, his eyes hooded, lips lightly compressed as he absorbed what she had related. "I know of them," he finally said.

"The Italians?"

"Yes. A hundred families bound together by money and blood — and oaths that they value above their lives. When they first came here, to Asia, for drugs mainly, we did not know what to make of them. Some of my colleagues thought they were like the other Italians: open to side deals. They soon learned differently. There is a hardness, a dedication, a viciousness to them that makes them difficult partners. I am not surprised they have done so well. I am surprised that they are so clever. That Indonesian bank setup is brilliant."

"Assuming it's real."

"You doubt the banker?"

"No, but I still want to confirm what I've been told."

"And then?"

"And then we'll know for sure. And then we can decide what to do."

"How can you confirm?" he asked.

"Well, I'm not going to talk to the Italians. In fact I wouldn't even risk talking to anyone about them," she said. "But Cameron told me that all the loans the bank has made have been to various companies registered to the Italians and their relatives and friends. One of his major jobs is to paper those deals, make them look legitimate. I want to have a look at them, see who we're actually dealing with."

"Ava, you said the banker is supposed to meet the Italians for dinner tonight," Uncle said slowly.

"Yes."

"How quickly can you access that information?"

"If I have Cameron's passwords and he tells me where to look in the bank's database, I don't see why I couldn't do it in the next few hours."

"Could you download it all?"

"If I can access it, I can download it," she said. "Why?"

"I am thinking, that is all, and I need to think some more. The thing is, I do not want you to stay in Surabaya. I want to you to get out of there today."

"Let me confirm what I've been told."

"Not if it means you cannot leave today."

Ava did some rough calculations. "Uncle, if I can't get the information by noon, then there is something wrong with either me or the information."

"You call me back by then."

"I will."

"And in the meantime I am going to hold a seat for you on a flight to Hong Kong."

There it is again, Ava thought, *caution gone to excess.* They had always been careful, but this was more than that. "How about Perkasa?"

"You need to tell him what I said about the Italians. He is a good man. He knows how to keep his mouth shut. He also knows how to disappear."

"And Uncle — the banker?"

"That will depend on what you find out, I think."

"I was thinking the same."

"We have some time," he said. "You go discover what you can. Me, I want to consider this thing in more detail. With these Italians you cannot afford to make mistakes; you cannot afford to leave loose ends."

Perkasa was where she had left him in the kitchen. "I think you should phone Waru and Prayogo and ask them to come back. I may need a drive to my hotel and we can't leave Cameron alone."

"What did Uncle say?"

"The Italians are trouble. We need to be careful."

"I'll call the boys," he said, his face impassive.

Ava grabbed her notebook and walked through the kitchen and out onto the back porch. Cameron was slumped forward in the chair, the sun beating down on his naked legs, his head, the back of his neck. Even after being washed down, he still reeked of excrement. She stood a few metres away and shouted, "Cameron, wake up. I need to talk to you."

He raised his head. "I'm thirsty again," he moaned.

"In a minute. First we talk."

"About?"

"I want to access the bank's computer system."

He shook his head. "I told you, they control the money. They're the only ones who can transfer it. And even if they weren't and you found a way to do it, don't think they wouldn't find out who did it and where it went."

"I have no immediate interest in moving money from the bank. I spoke to my partner about our conversation this morning and he doesn't quite believe you. He wants me to confirm your story about the loans and real estate transactions. Those are recorded somewhere in your system, I'm assuming."

"Yes, of course they are."

"And you have access to them?"

"They are my records."

"Then this should be easy, shouldn't it."

"Why would—"

"My partner wants me to confirm your story. That's all you need to know," Ava said.

"I'm thirsty," he said again.

She was tempted not to concede him even that, but time was passing. "I'll get you something," she said.

When she walked into the kitchen, Perkasa was already seated in one of the chairs, waiting for her. "He needs another glass of water," she told him.

"The boys are on their way here," he said.

She opened her notebook and reviewed the details. When she went back outside, Perkasa was giving water to Cameron. When he was done, she asked, "How do I get to the bank records?"

"Go to www.regcalindo.com."

"Not the bank's site?"

"We have several."

"Okay," she said, spelling the web address back to him.

He nodded. "I have three passwords. The first one is 'andycolin' — all lowercase. That'll get you into the main directory and let you access all kinds of general information, including some financials — mainly the bullshit ones. Within the directory you'll see a tab for assets. Enter 'chriskaren' — again lowercase, and 'chris' with *ch*, not *k*. Under 'Assets' there are, I think, eight headers. The one you want is at the bottom and it's called 'Projected Income.' The password to get you in is 'karenchriscolin.'"

"One word, all lowercase?"

"Aye."

"And this will show me the loans?"

"All of them."

"Are they referenced?"

"And fucking cross-referenced," he said, as if she'd doubted his professionalism.

The things people cling to when they're in trouble... Ava thought. "That should satisfy my partner," she said.

"Then what?"

"Then we talk about your million dollars, and if we can work something out you should be free to join your Italian friends for dinner tonight."

He groaned. "You don't need this tape or handcuffs anymore."

"No, we need to conclude our business first."

Waru came out with Prayogo. The brothers looked at Cameron and then glanced quickly at each other.

"Apologize to Waru for the mess," Ava said to Perkasa. "And tell him that we're doubling his fee to make up for it."

The men spoke among themselves. When they were finished, Perkasa said to Ava, "No problem with Waru. He just wants to know if you want to leave the banker out here like this. Or can they wash him off properly and move him back indoors?"

"Leave him here," Ava said. "But get one of the boys to fish Cameron's wallet out of his pocket. I may need it later."

(33)

PERKASA DROVE HER BACK TO THE MAJAPAHIT. Traffic was still light and they made great time. He had the radio turned low, and he glanced at her several times during the ride as if he wanted to start a conversation. Ava looked out the window at the passing city. She knew what he wanted to discuss. She just wasn't ready to discuss it.

"I don't know how long I'll be," she said, when the Nissan pulled up in front of the hotel.

"I'll wait right here. No rush."

She was greeted by the same doorman who had walked her to the Sheraton that morning. He gave her a big smile. "How was your meeting?"

"Just fine," Ava said.

She walked up the stairs to her room and went directly to the computer. It took a few minutes to connect to the Internet and then seconds to get into regcalindo.com. She followed the directions Cameron had given her and found herself looking at a list of loan transactions.

They were grouped by branch and listed by date. Under the date was the amount of the loan followed by the company it was loaned to, with an address and contact names, titles, and phone numbers. There were at least two names, and sometimes more, attached to every company. Virtually every one of the names was Italian. None of them were familiar to Ava, but then there was no reason for them to be. Some names appeared several times, and some names were attached to more than one company.

Every building or piece of property being acquired was described in incredible detail. The first group of properties was listed under the Rome branch. Initially the purchases were concentrated in Rome, but as the dates progressed the acquisitions spread to Milan, Florence, and Parma. The companies receiving the loans were almost as diverse, with home addresses spread all over Italy.

New York was next, and two parts of the pattern changed. The companies getting loans were registered in the New York area and nearly all the individuals attached to them had U.S. addresses. The Toronto office had opened only six months after New York. Ava couldn't believe how many properties were listed, using the New York model of local companies and addresses. It seemed that a lot of Woodbridge and Vaughan, two new high-end Italian suburbs in Toronto, was owned by the 'Ndrangheta, or at least by local Italians somehow affiliated with them. She searched again for names she could recognize. She thought a couple of the companies sounded familiar, and the name Rocca popped up repeatedly, although it was attached to Luciano, Alfredo, and Joseph, not Dominic.

There were more pages outlining activity in Venezuela, but Ava had already seen enough to know that Cameron had been telling the truth. She scanned the pages a second time. There had to have been more than five hundred transactions. She quickly calculated their value — more than five billion dollars.

Ava dug into her bag and found two USB drives. She downloaded the files onto one memory stick for herself and then onto the second as backup. When that was done, she phoned Uncle.

"*Wei.*"

"I got the passwords and I got into their system. He wasn't lying about all the money they've been ploughing into real estate. It's at least five billion," Ava said.

"How much information is there?"

"More than I would have thought prudent," she said. "Dates, company names, company officers and directors, addresses, and phone numbers for every company receiving a loan. Payment schedules, copies of corporate and personal guarantees — on and on it goes. And then enormous detail about every property being financed."

"Just what you need to record if you are really running a banking operation."

"Exactly."

"And all of which would look completely above board unless someone knew specifically what you were really doing."

"Yes."

"How are the loans grouped?"

"By date, by branch."

"The Italian ones — where were the companies incorporated?"

"Seemingly everywhere but in Reggio Calabria."

"That is not surprising," Uncle said.

"I downloaded it all, twice. I'll keep a stick with me and arrange to have one sent to you before I leave here."

"Ava, we have booked you on a Cathay Pacific flight leaving Surabaya at six tonight."

"Okay."

"And I think Perkasa should get back to Jakarta tonight as well."

"I'll tell him."

"The locals he hired, how good are they?"

"Excellent."

"Will they keep their mouths shut?"

"I think so, but you should ask Perkasa that question," Ava said, not willing to vouch for people she didn't know, hadn't hired, and couldn't talk to.

He became quiet and she wondered if she'd offended him. Instead he said, "The banker is a problem."

"I know."

"He seems to like to talk."

"He was coerced," Ava said.

"No matter. If they suspect anything, they will make him talk as easily. He knows your name, yes?"

"He does, and he knows people who are friends of friends — friends who know me very well."

"So the question is, can you trust him not to go to his employers and tell them that a young woman named Ava Lee has been sniffing around the bank? Believe me, he does not have to tell them any more than that to make them paranoid. And they are relentless. No one would be safe."

"I don't trust him at all," said Ava.

"So, what to do?"

"I was thinking about it during the car ride to the hotel. He has a meeting scheduled with the Italians in Surabaya tonight, at seven. If he doesn't show, from everything he's told me, they're going to go nutty. The last thing we want is them running around digging into his past twenty-four to forty-eight hours."

"You cannot let him go to the meeting," Uncle said quietly.

"No, of course not," said Ava. "The thing is, we can't just dump his body and his car somewhere. Sooner or later they'll be found. And even if they aren't found right away, he can't just go missing. We need to make them think he's done a runner on them. We need them to think that Cameron is their problem. We need them to focus entirely on finding him."

"You obviously have some idea of how to do that."

"I've been thinking about it and I've come up with something that might work, but I really need the help of Perkasa and his two men here to make it happen."

"Do you need me to talk to him? Do you need more money?"

"No, let me handle it."

"Ava," he said quietly, "no matter what, I want you on that six o'clock flight. I know those people. They are to be taken seriously."

"I'll be on the plane."

"And I will be at Chek Lap Kok to meet you."

"I'll call you after I check in at the airport here."

"Be careful," he said.

"As always."

She phoned Perkasa as soon as she ended the call with Uncle. "We need to figure out what to do with the banker," she told him before he could speak.

"Do you have anything in mind?"

"Yes, I want him to go to Singapore or Manila or KL."

"Okay," he said.

"Tell me, how tough is it for anyone to fly directly from Surabaya to any of those places?"

"There are all kinds of direct flights."

"That's what I thought, but that's not what I meant. How difficult is security? Could we book a flight in Cameron's name, get a ticket in his name, and then have someone else check in using his name?"

He said, "I'm glad to hear you say he's not the one actually flying." And then he added, "You would need to know someone working at one of the airline check-in counters."

"Does either Waru or Prayogo?"

"We have to ask. If they don't, I can make some phone calls to Jakarta."

"How about at the gates? Do they double-check ID here?"

"If they check a boarding pass, it's normally just to make sure you're getting on the correct flight."

Ava said, "Call the boys and see if they know anyone who can help at the airport."

"They may ask for more details," he said. "Like, if one of them gets on a flight, how do they get back?"

"I was thinking more of you getting on a flight. Do you have your passport with you?"

"I do. But I think I'd like more details."

She said, "I haven't thought it all the way through yet. The only thing I know, and Uncle agrees, is that we don't want the Italians chasing after us. Look, you talk to Waru while I check today's flight schedules."

She hung up the phone, went online, and did a quick scan of airlines flying from Surabaya to other major southeastern Asian cities. There was a host of them: Cathay

Pacific, Malaysian Airlines, Garuda, Singapore Air, and two airlines she'd never heard of. If the Indonesians had a contact, she thought it was likely she'd find a flight.

She phoned Perkasa. "Did you get Waru?"

"Just finished with him. Between him and his friends, they have contacts at virtually every airline that flies out of here. As long as you're willing to pay enough, there won't be any problem."

She ran through the flight schedules. "There's a Malaysian Airlines flight to Kuala Lumpur at five thirty and a Singapore Air flight to Singapore at seven. Call Waru back and tell him to make arrangements for the one that works best. And tell him I don't care how much it costs, I just want it done right. If we have to pay ten people, then I will."

"Okay, I'll tell him... Then what?"

"Call me back with the details so I can make the booking."

"Five minutes."

"Good. Then get over to the Sheraton, pack your bags, and check out. Then come back here and pick me up. I'm going to be packed as well and ready to go."

"Where are we going?"

"Away from Surabaya, but first back to the house. We need to look after the banker," she said, and hesitated. "Will this be an issue with the brothers?"

"I thought it might come to this," Perkasa said. "Uncle thinks it is best?"

"He thinks it's the only sensible thing to do. He also wants me out of here today and you back in Jakarta as fast as you can get there. So will any of this be an issue with the brothers?"

"No. We'll pay them a bit more."

"They may have to do more than keep their mouths shut."

"No problem. It's all about the money."

"I have lots of money."

"No need. Uncle sent me enough for a small army."

"Fine. Then I'll see you in about twenty minutes," Ava said.

She looked around the room. She'd be leaving Surabaya without any money for Theresa Ng. She couldn't remember the last time — actually, any time — she had been happy to leave a place without collecting any money or even having any hope of collecting it. There was Cameron's million dollars or so that she might be able to get her hands on, but she was sure it could be tracked. Even if he had ten million, it wasn't worth the risk.

(34)

PERKASA PHONED BEFORE SHE EVEN HAD TIME TO GET her toilet kit packed. "Singapore Air," he said.

She went back to the computer and, using the Visa card she'd found in Cameron's wallet, bought a one-way ticket for him, business class, to Singapore.

Ten minutes later her bags were at the door. She took a last glance around the room, feeling that she had forgotten something. She did a quick search of the bathroom and double-checked the dresser drawers. They were empty. Then she remembered what it was she was looking for — her green jade cufflinks.

Ava carried her bags into the lobby and went to the front desk. She asked for her bill and for an envelope. While the clerk fussed with her computer, Ava wrote Uncle's name and Kowloon address on the envelope and slid the USB key into it. If she didn't make it back to Hong Kong, the information would.

Perkasa walked through the front door as she was settling the account. She waved him over. "When you get back to Jakarta, I'd like you to send this by courier to Uncle," she said.

He stuffed the envelope into a front jeans pocket and reached for Ava's bags.

Traffic was now as bad as she'd seen it all week. As Perkasa eased onto the road, Ava began to calculate the time they had left. If things went smoothly, she figured, they'd be at the airport by five.

"When do we kill the banker?" he asked.

"We have some business to finish first. Not much more than a few hours from now," Ava said.

He nodded.

"We need to keep the Italians off-balance," she said. "I want to make it look as if he's still alive and has left Surabaya for reasons unknown. So we'll drive the Porsche to the airport and park it there. We'll have you board the plane as Cameron. I'd like for us to be able to check a bag in his name and have the bag picked up in Singapore; I think I may have a way we can get that done. When the Italians go looking for him, which they will, it would be helpful to have someone point them in the direction of Singapore."

"The car and the ticket shouldn't be a problem. As for the other two —"

"How close would he be to his housekeeper?" Ava asked.

"What do you mean?"

"Would the housekeeper be privy to his schedule?"

"Yeah, by and large."

"So it wouldn't be unusual for Cameron to tell his housekeeper he was going to Singapore on a business trip and that he needed to pack a bag."

"Of course not, but how are you going to get him to do that without him getting completely paranoid?"

"We'll have to side-door it."

"I don't understand."

"Let's wait until we get to Waru's house," said Ava, closing her eyes and putting her head back on the seat.

Prayogo was standing outside when they arrived. He approached the Nissan as it drove up to the house and began to speak rapidly to Perkasa when he got out of the car.

"The banker has passed out a couple of times since we left. They've been throwing water on him to revive him, but they're not sure what's going to happen if we leave him in the sun," Perkasa said to Ava.

"Then we'll move him into the shade and they can give him all the water he needs," Ava said, climbing the stairs into the house.

She stood inside the kitchen while the brothers moved Cameron into the shade. Perkasa stayed with her, leaning against the sink, looking outwardly calm. "Who is going to kill him?" he asked, his voice even.

"I am."

"Do you think—" he began.

"No, there's nothing to think about. It's my job, my choice. Will Waru object if I use his gun?"

"Of course not."

"You still need to explain our plan to them and why we think it's necessary to eliminate him. And Perkasa, you can't emphasize enough our concerns about our collective self-preservation. They can't discuss this with anyone, not even their wives."

"I'll make sure they understand."

"Good. While you're doing that, I'm going to have another chat with Cameron."

The brothers had moved the chair against the back wall of the house. It was in the shade, but that hardly made an impact in the heat. Cameron was wet from head to toe, his hair flat against his head, the golf shirt stuck to his chest, his belly protruding like an upside-down bowl of jelly, his shorts and underwear heavy with water and lying in a lump at his feet.

"How are you doing, Andy?" she asked.

He grunted.

"This will be over soon enough," she said, as Perkasa led the brothers back into the house for their talk. "Now there's a personal matter I want to go over with you."

He stiffened, and Ava knew he was imagining the worst.

"I'm going to take the tape from your mouth. When I do, I want you to stay quiet until I have a chance to ask my questions. And then all I want you to do is answer me. Got that?"

He nodded.

She reached out and stripped the tape from his face. He threw his head back, gulping in air through his open mouth. "I checked your story and I discussed things with my partner, and it appears you were telling me the truth about the bank. So that's a good thing. We're also prepared to work a deal for your million or so dollars. That's also a good thing. What's not quite so good is that I think you stole a set of green jade cufflinks from my hotel room."

Cameron started to protest and then clamped his jaw tight.

Ava waited for a few seconds and then said quietly, "Don't make me ask again."

"I took them," he said, his voice hoarse and breaking.

"What were they to you, Andy, a trophy of some sort? Is

that how you immortalize your conquests? Do you have a large collection of date-rape mementos?"

He shook his head. "It isn't like that."

"I don't care what it's like. What I need you to tell me is where they are."

"At my house."

"I want them back."

"Yeah, yeah, yeah, I'll get them back to you," he said quickly.

"I know you will, and you'll do it today. In fact, you'll do it before you leave here and before we transfer that million dollars you say you have."

"But how can I do that?"

"Where are the cufflinks?"

"On my dresser."

Ava sat quietly, letting him worry about what was coming next. "Is there anyone at your house?" she said.

"I have staff there."

"And who runs the staff?"

"Yannie, my housekeeper."

"Does she speak English?"

"She has to. I have hardly any Indo."

"That's good. Now, Andy, tell me, is your mobile phone in the Porsche?"

"Aye."

"Good. So here is what we're going to do. My friends will get your phone and you'll tell us your home phone number and we're going to call it for you. You will ask to talk to Yannie. When you get her, you will tell her that you're at the golf course, in the middle of your game, and that you'll be there until dinner time. Then you'll say you forgot to bring the jade cufflinks with you. Tell her you bought them as a gift for a business associate and that you're meeting him for dinner. Ask her if she could wrap them for you and then tell her you're sending one of the security people from the golf course to pick them up. What do you think, Andy? Does that sound reasonable?"

"Yeah, it does."

"She wouldn't find it unusual?"

"No."

"And do you think you can make that call without causing a fuss? I mean, can you do exactly what I just outlined, that and nothing more?"

"Aye, I can do it."

"Because if you can't, Andy, I have to tell you that what you received earlier will seem like a tickle."

His head bobbed up and down as if it were on a string. "I'll do it, word for word."

"That's good to hear. And if you do, then we'll figure out something about the money and send you on your way, in time to make dinner with your Italian friends. How does that sound?"

"Great, just great," he said, his brogue thickening.

"Good. Now you wait here and I'll be back with your phone."

Ava walked back into the kitchen. The three men standing near the stove turned simultaneously. There was no hesitation in their manner, no doubt in their eyes. Uncle had a good man in Perkasa, and Perkasa had good men in Waru and Prayogo.

"We need to get the banker's cellphone from his car," she said.

Perkasa spoke to Prayogo and then said to Ava, "What did you arrange?"

"He's going to call his housekeeper and tell her he's sending someone from the golf course to pick up a gift for a friend. You're going to be the someone."

"Okay."

"When you get there, tell her that Mr. Cameron might have to leave on a business trip to Singapore that evening, and he asked you to ask her to pack a suitcase for him with just enough things for an overnight stay. He will want his passport put into the case. Tell her that if he is going, he'll go to the airport directly from dinner and he'll call her and update her on his schedule."

"Do you have the housekeeper's name?"

"Yannie."

"Good. And this gift, do I need to know what it is?"

"It's small and it will be wrapped. Bring it back to me. I want it."

"Okay."

"And when you get back, we'll settle things with Cameron," she said. "The boys are onside?"

"No problem."

"Would Waru be okay with our burying Cameron in one of his back fields?"

"Shouldn't be an issue," Perkasa said without hesitation.

"Then could you ask the brothers to dig a hole — a deep hole — while you're off getting Cameron's things?"

"Sure."

"Thanks."

"I have to say, Ava, you've made quite an impression on them."

"That wasn't the intention," she said.

Prayogo came back into the house carrying the mobile in his hand.

Ava looked at her watch. "Let's get started."

(35)

CAMERON WAS SLUMPED IN THE CHAIR, HIS CHIN REST-ing on his chest. Ava shook him. "I need water," he said, twitching as he woke.

"After you make the phone call to Yannie, you can have all the water you want," she said. "Now what's the number?"

She punched it in as he recited it. She held off hitting the last digit and she said, "Andy, remember what I told you — no funny stuff. You're sending someone from the golf course to get the gift. Just tell her where it is and tell her to get it ready for pickup. Nothing more. Not one word extra."

"I know," he said.

Ava hit the last number and held the phone loosely to his ear so she could hear it ring. On the third ring a woman picked up. "Hello, Pak Andy."

He spoke quickly. "Yannie, I'm at the golf course and I have to go back to play in a minute, so listen carefully. I left a pair of green jade cufflinks on my dresser. They're a gift for a friend's birthday. He's here with me and I want to give them to him later this afternoon. I've asked one of the men from the golf club to come by and pick them up. Could you wrap them, please?"

Ava heard Yannie's voice and knew she was asking a question.

"No, I don't need a card. Just the gift," Cameron said.

The housekeeper spoke again. Cameron looked up at Ava. "She's asking the name of the person going to the house," he said.

Ava glanced at Perkasa.

"Tell her Tedjo is coming," he said.

"He's called Tedjo," Cameron said.

Say goodbye, Ava mouthed.

"I have to go now. I'll talk to you later," said Cameron.

Ava hung up the phone and put the tape back on Cameron's mouth. "Well done." She motioned for Perkasa to follow her into the kitchen. "Who is Tedjo?" she asked.

"A guy in Jakarta I don't like."

She smiled. "How long do you think it will take you to get back and forth from Cameron's house?"

"About an hour, give or take."

"Call me as soon as you leave there, as soon as you have the gift and the suitcase."

"I will."

"And talk to the boys about digging that hole."

"Right now."

Perkasa called to Waru and Prayogo to come into the house and Ava replaced them on the porch. Cameron was slumped over again, unconscious or close to it. Ava wondered if he was playing possum and nudged his naked knee with the toe of her shoe. He didn't budge.

She looked at him and wondered what Fay would think

of him now. Without the gel in his hair, the fashionable spikes were gone, exposing balding temples. The wet shirt pressed against his torso, and the fact that he was sitting made his belly look twice as big as it probably was. His legs were thin, white, the knees knobby. Then there were his genitals, shrunken now, as if retreating inside his body to avoid any more pain.

He's pathetic, Ava thought. The cocky, sneaky little Scotsman reduced to a whimpering mess with two flicks of the picana. It shouldn't have been so easy. If he had any guts he would have resisted for longer. But then, if he had any guts he wouldn't have drugged her.

Waru and Prayogo came out of the house, nodded at Ava, and then went around the side. When they re-emerged, they were both carrying shovels. They walked in a straight line away from the house towards a cluster of palms and stopped in the shade of the trees. Waru dragged the tip of his shovel across the surface of the earth, making a rectangle. They began to dig, the soft reddish brown soil flying in the air.

In a few hours she'd be on a plane back to Hong Kong, back to a different reality. Surabaya and Andy Cameron would be behind her. But had she really purged herself of him? Maybe not completely, but enough that she knew she could move on.

Ava looked at her watch. If Perkasa's schedule was accurate, she could get to the airport with enough time to get caught up with the rest of her life — a life she hadn't thought about since Saturday morning, a life she now felt the strongest urge to reconnect with. She needed things to be normal; she wanted to be surrounded by familiarity.

Then, as if on cue, her phone sounded. The caller ID showed a Chinese area code — Wuhan. May Ling Wong. Ava let it ring through to voicemail. *The job isn't done*, she told herself. May would have to wait until the job was done.

In the distance she could see the brothers in the hole, their heads bobbing up and down as they bent to dig and then popped up to toss dirt over the side. She thought about telling them that the hole was deep enough, but then realized they might know more about that kind of thing than she did.

She closed her eyes and thought about Hong Kong. She'd spend a few days there. See her father. Congratulate Amanda and Michael. See Uncle. Should she contact his doctor? If she did, what story could she possibly tell that would get him to disclose Uncle's medical condition? The last time she had talked to Sonny, it seemed clear enough that it was the right thing to do. Now she wasn't so sure. Everyone had secrets, and they were entitled to keep them.

Her attention was drawn to the sound of voices. She looked up and saw Waru and Prayogo walking back towards the house. They had left the shovels by the side of the hole. Then her phone rang and she recognized Perkasa's number.

"I have the gift and the suitcase," he said.

"Passport?"

"It's in the case."

"Any problems with the housekeeper?"

"No."

"Good," said Ava. "The boys have just finished here with that piece of work we needed done and are almost back at the house. I'm going to pass my phone to Waru.

Tell him to give me that equipment I need."

He hesitated. "Ava, are you sure you want to do this? I don't mind doing it myself."

"My job, my decision," she said.

"Then give him the phone."

As the two men spoke, Ava approached Cameron. He wasn't moving. She shook him by an arm until his head lifted from his chest. "Can you hear me?" she said.

He nodded.

"Okay, we're going to be leaving here in a minute. We all can use a little air conditioning. I have to keep you blindfolded but I'll take the tape from your mouth, and I'm going to free your legs so you can walk. When we get to where we're going, we'll get your money organized, and then we'll be on our way," she said, reaching out and tearing the tape from his mouth. "Now, Andy, you aren't going to do anything stupid, are you?"

"What do you mean?" he croaked.

"Go to the police."

"And tell them what, that I was kidnapped by the police? Good luck with that."

"Or talk to your bosses."

"Never," he said.

She believed him, or at least she believed that in that moment he meant what he said.

Waru stood in the doorway, the gun in his hand. The sight of it made her shudder. A memory from Macau crashed into her head. She went to the door and took the gun from him. It was a Glock 22, as close to standard police issue as you could get. She'd fired one before, but never in these circumstances.

"I'm going to sit inside for a moment," she said to Waru, gesturing to make herself understood. "Watch him until I come back."

She sat at the kitchen table and tried to steady herself. In Macau she had shot Lok, a Triad member, in the head at close range. It was the first time she had killed anyone for any reason other than immediate self-defence. It had bothered her enormously, but in the months since she had found ways to rationalize her actions. Now she was going to do it again.

The gun lay on the table beside her right hand. Ava watched her fingers tremble. "I'm not sure I can do this," she whispered.

She heard a shout from the porch. She stood up, the gun in her hand. It became quiet outside and she sat down again. *Procrastinating isn't going to make this any easier*, she told herself. There was no choice, she knew. Leaving him alive would put everyone at risk: the brothers, Perkasa, John and Fay Masterson, her, maybe even Uncle. Still she waited, gathering herself.

Then Waru was at the door, shouting at her in Indonesian, pointing back towards the porch. She ran out to him, the gun in her hand.

Waru was standing next to Cameron. The Scotsman's head was slumped onto his chest and he wasn't moving. She walked over to Cameron and held her hand against his mouth and nose. She couldn't feel his breath. She lifted his chin, reached for his neck and searched for a pulse. Then she grabbed his wrist and pressed her fingers into the artery there. Nothing.

"He's dead," she said to Waru.

He ran his hand across his throat in a slicing motion.

Ava nodded.

"What's going on?" Perkasa said.

She turned and saw him emerging from the kitchen. Either the trip from Cameron's house had been very fast or Ava had lost all sense of time while she was thinking about what she needed to do.

"He's dead," she said. "He seems to have had a heart attack or a stroke."

"Fat, out of shape, stressed, cooked by the sun — I'm not surprised," Perkasa said, and then looked at the gun in her hand. "It was nice of him to save us the trouble."

"We need to bury him," Ava said.

"Is the hole dug?"

"Yes."

"Then I'll tell the boys to get him into the ground."

(36)

AVA AND PERKASA SAT IN THE NISSAN WITH THE AIR conditioning running. Neither of them had said much since the brothers left the porch with Cameron. Waru had taken him by the ankles, Prayogo by his wrists, and they had carried him back to the palm trees, where they tossed him into the ground. It took longer than Ava would have imagined to return the dirt to its rightful place.

Perkasa gave her the small wrapped box he had picked up at Cameron's house. She put it into her bag, ignoring the questions in his eyes. He showed her the luggage the housekeeper had packed: a blue nylon suitcase. She checked the nametag. Cameron had been a member of Star Alliance.

When the brothers finally emerged from the house, Ava waved them over to the Nissan. She gave each of them two U.S. hundred-dollar bills. She knew that was probably equivalent to a month's salary. Whatever it was, and whatever else they were being paid by Perkasa, they had been worth every dollar. They smiled at her and then spoke to Perkasa.

"They say thank you very much, and now they want to know what the next plan is."

"You, me, and Waru will drive to the airport in the Nissan. He'd better come inside with us and make sure you have no problems at check-in. Prayogo can drive the Porsche; tell him to put it in long-term parking. Then he can join us inside the terminal. You will get on the plane to Singapore and I'll catch mine to Hong Kong, and we'll try to forget any of this happened today."

It took them an hour to drive back into the city and then south to the airport. Ava had moved to the back seat, her thoughts now on Hong Kong. Perkasa sat in the front with Waru, the two men chatting and laughing as if they were the ones who had just finished a game of golf. Behind the Nissan, Prayogo trailed in the Porsche.

They were ten minutes from the airport when Perkasa turned to Ava. "Do you have a confirmation number for me?"

"Oh, yes, I almost forgot," she said, reaching into her bag.

She passed him the slip of paper she'd written it on. "What are you going to do when you get to Singapore? Get on the first plane back to Jakarta?"

"Maybe, but maybe I'll stay there for a few days."

"Do you need any more money?"

"No, I've told you, Uncle sent more than enough."

Ava looked out the window as Surabaya slid by. She would never come back to the city, she knew. It was going to be struck from her mind, dispatched like Cameron.

"You were great to work with," she said. "So were the brothers. Please make sure they know how much I appreciate everything they did."

"They know. The two hundred dollars you gave them meant a lot."

Waru drove the Nissan into the airport's short-term lot and Prayogo peeled off and headed for the long-term. When they disembarked from the car, Waru reached for Ava's bags. She shook her head but he insisted.

They stopped just inside the terminal, Waru looking around in all directions. The two Indonesians exchanged words. "He's looking for his contact," Perkasa said.

The contact found them — a short, middle-aged woman in a Singapore Air uniform who walked into the terminal through the same door they had used. She tapped Waru on the shoulder and he spun around, to be greeted by a hug. They exchanged words and then she said to Ava, "Are you travelling with us as well?"

"No, I'm going in a different direction."

"Here is my confirmation number and the passport I want to use," Perkasa said to her, handing over the paper Ava had given him. The paper was on top of a stack of rupiah notes.

She put the money in her pocket. "Good. Now follow me over to the check-in counter and we'll get you settled. I'll look after everything personally," she said, looking at the passport, "Mr. Cameron."

Waru spoke to Perkasa. "He says she's the supervisor," Perkasa translated for Ava.

Ava spotted the Cathay Pacific counter further down the terminal. "I'll get my own boarding pass and meet you back here," she said.

Uncle had booked her into first class and there was no lineup at that counter. Within five minutes she was back at the spot where she'd left the men. Perkasa and Waru joined her almost at once. "She's going to take me to the lounge and then wait there with me until boarding. She'll personally clear me at the gate," he said.

"What will you do with the bag in Singapore?" she asked.

"I thought I'd put it in a storage locker at the airport."

"Destroy the passport."

"Of course."

Ava hesitated, trying to think of anything she'd missed, and then she remembered Cameron's phone. It was still in her bag. She took it out and gave it to Perkasa. "Call the housekeeper from the lounge and tell her Cameron just came off the golf course and is going to Singapore. And then lose the phone when you land."

Prayogo came into the terminal and headed towards them. He handed the Porsche keys to Perkasa, who in turn looked at Ava. "Lose them with the phone," she said.

"There could be some noise here about Cameron disappearing. Do you want Waru to keep his ears open and let us know what's going on?"

"The Italians won't go to the police, and they'll discourage anyone associated with him from doing that."

"Yeah, I guess so. Still…"

"If he hears our names connected to Cameron's, call me. Otherwise, let it be."

"Okay."

The supervisor hovered just out of earshot. "It looks like she wants to get you to the lounge," Ava said.

Perkasa nodded. "It's been one helluva twenty-four hours."

(37)

AVA SLEPT MOST OF THE WAY TO HONG KONG, AND when she woke, she knew things were different.

It had started while she sat in the business lounge at Juanda International. She reached for her phone to call Toronto and then realized it was five a.m. there. No one would be answering.

She thought about calling May Ling, then hesitated. Things would get personal — they always got personal. Ava wasn't sure how well she could handle that. Not now, anyway.

So she phoned Uncle and, almost to her relief, went to voicemail. "It's done. I'm at the airport in Surabaya and my flight is on time," she said.

She had a glass of champagne when she boarded the flight and then downed two glasses of a French white burgundy as soon as cabin service began. She refused dinner, reclined her seat, put on an eye mask, and fell into a dreamless sleep.

She woke about half an hour out from Hong Kong, a flight attendant hovering over her, offering a hot towel. Ava took it, laid it over her face, and scrubbed, lightly at first and then vigorously, as if trying to wipe off any last remnants of Surabaya. The South China Sea glittered below, her familiar pathway to Hong Kong. Toronto was only a few days away.

The job had been a bust, but she didn't care. She hadn't wanted it in the first place and had taken it only to placate her mother, and maybe to occupy Uncle. And maybe she'd taken it to avoid making a decision about what she wanted to do with her life. Once she'd taken it on, though, it had been like being on autopilot, going through the motions like the professional she was... like the professional she'd been.

Autopilot — that's what she'd been on since waking on Saturday morning in Surabaya with Andy Cameron's semen encrusting her body. All she felt was numbness when she thought about it, the same numbness she'd felt when she slid the picana under his genitals, the same numbness when she saw him slumped dead on the chair. She had gotten her revenge. Why did she feel no satisfaction?

It has nothing to do with Cameron, she thought. He was just another stranger, like so many others over the years, who had tried to do her damage as she went about her job. He had just been more successful.

"I'm so tired of strangers," she said quietly to herself. They had filled her life for the past ten years. The clients and the thieves, and all the people along the way who had helped her connect the dots between one and the other. All of them strangers who had to be manipulated, brought onside, urged to do the right thing, forced to comply to her will. Cameron had been no different than any of them. And neither were the Indonesians who had worked alongside her, contributing to a man's death without any real interest in the why of it. All of them had taken a piece of her.

"I think I'm done," she whispered.

She deplaned and, ignoring the bustle around her, walked slowly through the airport, a bag in each hand. Uncle hadn't told her where he would be, but he usually sat in the Kit Kat Koffee House, and she headed there without glancing at the designated arrivals area.

He was there, an unlit cigarette dangling from his lower lip, one of the Hong Kong racing papers open on the retro-style round laminated table. He looked up, and when he saw her, he smiled, put down the cigarette, and stood to greet her. "My beautiful girl," he said.

She thought he looked almost gaunt, and then wondered if her imagination was working overtime. She leaned forward and kissed him on the forehead. "I'm happy you came."

He seemed surprised by her response. "There were other problems in Surabaya?"

"No, no, I'm just pleased to be out of Indonesia, and happy to see you."

He folded his newspaper and put it into the side pocket of his black suit jacket. "I am sorry you went there in the first place, and I am sorrier about the way it ended. Perkasa, he was a good man?"

"He couldn't have been better."

He began to say something else and then caught himself. "Well, then, let us go. Sonny has the car parked at the VIP curb. We got here early, so I imagine the police are getting impatient with us."

"Hardly."

"Maybe not," he said, "but I do not like to take things for granted."

He reached for one of her bags. "No, Uncle, I can manage," she said.

"I put you in the Mandarin Oriental," Uncle said as they walked through the terminal, "and I made a dinner reservation for us at Man Wah."

It was Ava's turn to be surprised. "Man Wah?"

"I know you like it."

"But you don't."

"They fuss too much."

"And I'm not in the mood for a fuss. So if you don't mind, I'd rather eat noodles."

He slipped his hand around her forearm and squeezed. "Noodles, then."

"I still need to shower and change," Ava said. She was wearing the same clothes she'd started the day in.

"Who is rushing?"

They went through a door marked PRIVATE. The Mercedes was parked no more than ten metres away. Sonny stood by the front bumper talking to a policeman as if he was an old friend. Uncle said, "Help Ava with her bags."

Sonny stared at her, his eyes pensive. Had he found out something else about Uncle?

The policeman put a fist inside his opposite palm and then lowered his head and moved his hands up and down in a sign of respect. Uncle acknowledged him with a nod.

It was almost ten o'clock when they left the airport, the evening traffic light and moving fast. In less than half an hour Sonny had the Mercedes at the entrance to the

Mandarin. The talk en route had been casual, Uncle asking after her family and Ava telling him about Amanda and Michael. He seemed overly attentive when she explained her role in the wedding party, and Ava found that strange. Usually when a job went sideways, Uncle took it even harder than she did and was always eager to pick apart the details. Now it seemed to be the furthest thing from his mind.

He waited in the hotel lobby while she checked in, quickly showered, and changed into the only clean clothes she had left, a pair of slacks and a pale blue shirt. She was just about to leave the room when her cellphone rang. When she picked it up, she saw she'd missed two calls while she was in the washroom. They were both from Sonny. So was the incoming.

"Sonny?"

"He went to the hospital again yesterday," he said quickly.

"I'll try to see his doctor tomorrow. Hopefully he'll tell me what's going on."

"You won't see him."

"Why not?"

"I had my woman call his office Saturday. She got a message saying he was going to be away from the office for the next week."

"Great."

"Ava, you will stay in Hong Kong until he gets back?"

She hesitated. "If I have to, Sonny, I will. The other option is for me just to talk to Uncle, but I'm not sure how he would react."

"We need to know what's really going on first."

She thought about spending a week in Hong Kong waiting for a doctor who might not talk to her anyway, and then balanced that against questioning Uncle about his health when he had made it clear he didn't want people prying. "You may be right," she said.

"I know I am. If he's trying to keep this from me, you, and Lourdes, he won't say anything. He'll just get angry."

Ava knew how true that was. They each had their secrets, she and Uncle, and they each guarded their privacy with a passion that bordered on obsession. They rarely spoke about personal matters; when they did, it was so awkward that it was almost painful. But not sharing secrets didn't lessen the intensity of their relationship, didn't detract from the strength of the commitment they felt towards one another. If anything it made those feelings all the more powerful, because they were based on something that didn't need to be said, something that was permanent, accepted. In her mind—and, she thought, in his—it was something as close to unconditional love as possible.

Ava said, "Let me sleep on whether I stay or not. You know Uncle is waiting for me to go to dinner. I'd better get downstairs."

It was now past eleven o'clock, but the streets in Central were still crowded. Sunday was family day for the Chinese, the traditional day off for the hundreds of thousands of Filipino housemaids and *yaya*s who lived in Hong Kong, and just another business day for the retailers and restaurants that stayed open late to service them.

Uncle looped his arm through Ava's and let her navigate. She led them to the same noodle restaurant they had sat in five days before... a lifetime ago.

The owner saw them at the entrance, and before a word could be spoken he was already moving other customers around so he could accommodate them. Most of the other tables were occupied by families having a late-night snack. At one, four heavily tattooed men, two of them with their hair pulled back in ponytails, were drinking beer and sharing platters of grilled squid and snow-pea tips fried in oil and garlic. When the men saw Uncle and Ava, they began to talk among themselves, and then they stood as one and walked over to the table.

"It is an honour to see you, to meet you," the oldest said, bowing his head to Uncle. The others followed suit.

"Where are you from?" Uncle asked.

"14K Wanchai."

"Send my regards to Mountain Master Chen," Uncle said.

"And he would want to send his deepest regards to you."

"Thank you," Uncle replied, with slight dip of his head.

The man stared at Ava. "Are you Ava Lee?"

"I am," she said, taken aback.

"We know who you are too," the man said. "Everyone has heard about Macau."

"You are famous now," one of the others said.

Ava lowered her eyes, embarrassed, confused.

The men hovered for a moment and then bowed to Uncle again before going back to their table.

"You have become something of a legend," Uncle said, seemingly pleased.

"For what? Storming a house and shooting an unarmed man in the head? Hardly a contribution to mankind."

"Every society has its own morality, its own code of ethics."

"I never thought I was part of that society," Ava said.

He glanced at her and she saw a hint of disappointment

in his eyes. She hoped it was only because of her tone. "You are a brave girl. Just think of it in that light," said Uncle.

"I didn't feel so brave the way I left Surabaya," Ava said.

"There was no choice."

"I wonder if our Vietnamese clients would look at it that way," Ava said, refusing to concede her fallibility.

"They may not have to," Uncle said.

Ava looked across the table at him and saw a little smile playing on his lips. "I have no idea what you're talking about," she said as the owner arrived, ready to take their order.

"I feel like eating tonight," Uncle said, ordering a plate of noodles with beef drenched in XO sauce, steamed broccoli with oyster sauce, and a San Miguel beer.

"Bring extra noodles — I'll share, and jasmine tea," she said. When the owner left, she turned back to Uncle. "What did you mean about our clients?"

He shrugged, still looking mischievous. "After we talked earlier today, I did some thinking and then I made some phone calls. I spoke to an old friend on the Hong Kong police force, and he put me onto a mutual friend in the Security Bureau... Men I trust, you understand. Men I really trust."

"Men you trust," she repeated as their drinks arrived.

Uncle took a deep swig of his beer, like a man who hadn't had a drink in months. "I mentioned the 'Ndrangheta to them and their interest was immediately piqued. When I explained — very generally — what you had uncovered, they became quite excited. I then put a proposal to them, and while their reaction was not exactly what I expected, it was close enough to make things interesting," he said, and took another pull of beer.

Ava sipped her tea. She had no clue where he was headed.

Their food arrived, the noodles on one of the biggest platters she had ever seen, slivers of beef piled high, almost glittering under the combination of XO sauce and overhead lighting. The owner stood to one side, admiring his kitchen's handiwork. This wasn't a normal serving, Ava knew, not even a normal double serving. And the ratio of beef to noodles was outlandish. Uncle nodded his thanks and then said, "I will have another beer."

"Should you?" Ava asked, and instantly regretted it.

"It is that kind of night," he said.

They dug into the noodles. Uncle filled his bowl, extracted a slice of beef, and held it in the air, examining it as if it was a rarity. His second beer arrived before he had finished his first mouthful. "We may not have to abandon our clients," he said as he set the empty beer bottle to one side and picked up the other. "At least, that is the message I got from my friends."

"I don't understand," Ava said, helping herself to noodles and beef, her appetite surfacing despite her discomfort with the way the evening had gone thus far.

"The information you got from the bank — it has value."

"Value to whom? We're going to blackmail the Italians?"

"Of course not. We need to stay far away from the Italians. The information, according to my friends, has the greatest value to police. They think — in fact, they are convinced — that we should be able to sell it to a police organization."

Ava said, "Why would the Hong Kong police have any interest?"

"Everyone is interested in the 'Ndrangheta, although not that much is known about them, I was surprised to learn. There was an assumption, certainly among the Hong Kong police, that they are not that well organized. When I started to talk about the bank, about the transfers, about the real estate business, it really intrigued my friends. They thought — and they told me the assumption is commonplace — that the 'Ndrangheta was a hundred or so loosely knit families. They had no idea there was this kind of structure to them."

"And they are willing to pay for this kind of information?"

"No, not them. They think we need to talk to the police forces in the countries where you have found proof they are operating — Italy, of course, and then the U.S., Venezuela, Canada, Indonesia."

Ava poured herself more tea, noticing that Uncle had almost finished his second beer. "Even assuming that we have something worth paying for, how do we keep the information secure?" she asked.

"Do you mean how do we keep the 'Ndrangheta from knowing who passed on the information about the bank and the cash, the real estate holdings, and — probably the most important thing of all — the people and companies whose names are attached to those holdings?"

"Exactly."

"That is the problem," said Uncle.

"And a big one," said Ava. "I don't know about you, but I wouldn't feel safe with anyone in Indonesia, Italy, or Venezuela, and when I say anyone, I mean *anyone*. The U.S. makes me almost as uncomfortable, unless you know someone there you trust the way you trust your friends here."

"I know a couple of people, but the problem in the U.S. is that you would have to involve so many police forces. With all that overlapping, it gets tough to get a decision made and it is even tougher to keep things quiet. I do not think they could be bought off as easily as, say, the Italian cops, but with all the competing jurisdictions, things could get very sloppy. And we do not need sloppy."

"So where does that leave us?"

"Canada."

"Aside from the fact I live there, what else recommends Canada?"

"It was not my idea, actually. It came from my friend with the Security Bureau."

"And does he know about me?"

"No, I never mentioned you. But I did explain a little bit about our clients and about the bank's involvement in Toronto. That's when he said the Mounties should be contacted. He spoke highly of them — one force, acting independently, less chance of breaches. And that is where our clients live, in Canada, so it would be logical to go to the Mounties. And also it would not be far-fetched to ask for the money our clients lost as compensation for providing them with the information."

"So we're simply seeking justice for our clients, not trying to extort money for information."

"True enough, is it not?"

"In a rough way, yes, it is."

Uncle drained his beer. "And in the process, my friends said, the Mounties would raise their profile in international law enforcement. If we can provide them with the means to bring down even part of the 'Ndrangheta in Canada, the U.S., Italy, Venezuela, and if we give them the levers they need to stop such massive money laundering, they can only gain in prestige. There is no way to judge how much that would mean to them. Maybe it is thirty million dollars' worth."

Ava nodded, more out of politeness than in agreement. *Why*, she wondered, *does he want to do this? We're out of Surabaya without the Italians on our tail. We don't need the money. Could he really be that concerned about our clients in Toronto?*

She looked across the table at him. He was signalling for a third beer, a slice of beef wrapped in noodles balanced on his chopsticks. There was a sheen on his face, and Ava thought she could detect a hint of yellow in his complexion. There was something else too. He seemed anxious — not in any fearful way, more like nervous — as if he had doubts about his ability to convince her of his position. And why should that matter? She nearly always did what he wanted. She didn't need elaborate explanations, and he had never been a man to provide elaborate explanations. So why now? Did he suspect she wanted out of the business? Was he trying to hang on to it for some other reason? Ava remembered what Sonny had said to her when she'd first arrived in Hong Kong. Maybe that was it; maybe Uncle needed a reason to get out of bed every morning and didn't want to let go of the one reason they had left.

"I know some Mounties," Ava said, frowning at the owner as he brought another beer to the table. The man caught her look and signalled with a raised eyebrow that he understood.

"I know you do," said Uncle.

"But that doesn't mean I'd trust any one of them with what could be our lives."

"How do you figure?"

"If we do this thing and the Italians find out, they'll kill us."

"No," Uncle said, putting down his chopsticks, his bowl still half full, "what I mean is, how do you know those men are not trustworthy?"

Ava shrugged. "The Royal Canadian Mounted Police are as much a big government bureaucracy as they are a police force. It's unrealistic to think they'd even consider handing over thirty million dollars without some kind of committee getting involved and without their doing due diligence on us and on our information."

"Are you concerned about the quality of the information?"

"No, not in the least."

"Then it comes down to credibility and to trust."

"I know."

He put the beer bottle to his mouth, paused, and then set it down. He reached across the table and placed his hand on hers. "The only way I think this could work is if you have one person you really trust, and you deal only with that person, and you deal with him completely anonymously and isolated from everyone else. He has to be your shield. Do you know any Mountie you would trust that much?"

"Perhaps."

"Is he a senior officer?"

"No, so we have to assume he has the ability to get the right people to listen to him."

"And is that likely?"

"I think so."

"Still, you would need to be very careful about how you approach him and what you say to him initially. You could not tell him the entire truth, of course, and you would need to rely on him to parse it with regard to his superiors. At the start he would need to feel them out to see if a deal would even be contemplated. So no names at that point, just a sort of general outline, but with enough bait to see if they are willing to be enticed."

"Uncle, I'd rather do the parsing myself until the level of interest can be gauged. I mean, I think I do trust this man, but I still need to confirm just how much."

"That is wise."

"One step at a time, eh? That's what you taught me."

He sat back, his eyes raised towards the ceiling. Ava thought she saw tears in them, and turned away. "How soon do you think you can contact him?" he asked.

"It's Sunday morning where he is and he won't be at work, but I have his private number. I'll call him when I get back to the hotel. But, Uncle, I'm still nervous about this. You're right when you say we need maximum distance between the information and ourselves... And you know, an idea just came to me that might help us achieve that," she said. "Tell me, could we open a numbered bank account with our friends at the Kowloon Light and Power Bank?"

"Of course."

"But could we open one that wasn't impossible to trace? One that anyone with any savvy could find their way into and locate the real account holder?"

"Why would we do that?"

"I would want the name Andy Cameron attached to the account."

"The banker who is dead?"

"Yes."

Uncle smiled. "Yes, I think the Kowloon bank could arrange all that."

"Well, I think we've just acquired a new client."

(38)

THEY LEFT THE RESTAURANT WITHOUT PAYING FOR their meal. The owner had refused to give a bill to Uncle, and after a few minutes of protest, Uncle thanked him and left an HK$200 tip.

The streets had calmed down. It was getting too late for families and it was still too early for most of the nightclubs and karaoke bars to open. They walked downhill towards the Mandarin, Uncle's arm again looped through Ava's. They had gone only about half the distance when he stopped and took a deep breath. She looked at him and saw that he was pale. As she started to say something he lurched towards the street, stopped at the curb, and bent over. Ava reached out to give him support, but he threw one arm back as if to fend her off. Then he coughed, took a couple of rapid breaths, and threw up on the road. Ava watched in horror, not sure what to do, not sure if there was anything she could do. After several heaves his stomach began to empty, and though his body still racked, he had nothing left to throw up.

Ava went over to him again. She looked down at the mess on the pavement and saw streaks of red.

He slowly raised himself, wiping at his mouth with his jacket sleeve. Ava grasped his arm and squeezed as reassuringly as she could. Uncle shook his head as if he was trying to clear it. "I cannot handle some kinds of food anymore," he said.

There was a 7-Eleven two doors from where they stood. "Wait here," Ava said. She bought a bottle of water and a sleeve of tissues. When she came back, Uncle was leaning against the wall, his face ashen and gaunt. She opened the water and passed it to him. He sipped lightly, no more than wetting his lips. When she gave him a tissue, he patted his sweaty brow. "I'm worried about you," she said.

"No reason to be. I am just an old man having an old man's aches and pains."

"Uncle, you would tell me if it was more than that, wouldn't you?"

"Of course," he said.

He held her arm the rest of the way to the hotel. Neither of them spoke until they saw Sonny standing by the Mercedes. "I will go straight home. You call me there after you talk to your Mountie," Uncle said.

"Okay, I'll call. Even if I don't reach him, I'll let you know."

"Good. One way or another we need to close this case. We owe it to our clients to do the best we can for them."

"Yes, Uncle, we owe it to our clients."

(39)

AVA HAD MET MARC LAFONTAINE ON A JOB IN GUYANA, where he worked at the Canadian High Commission in Georgetown. He was a sergeant, divorced, with three daughters living in Ottawa. He had made a play for Ava. When she turned him down, he handled it with grace and actually showed concern for her well-being in a country where homosexuality was a crime punishable by a jail term, or worse.

She had met him only briefly but under difficult circumstances. At the time it would have been easy for him to fob her off or pass on her story and situation to local authorities to win their favour. Instead he had been honest, supportive, and steadfast — the stereotypical Mountie of dime novels and movies. None of that meant he would still be in Guyana. None of that meant he would remember her. None of that meant he would be prepared to step outside the normal parameters of his job. And even if he was, none of that meant he would know whom to call or be smart enough to sell what Ava was offering.

But she trusted Lafontaine, and that was the overriding priority. He wouldn't lie to her. If he couldn't or wouldn't do what she wanted, he wouldn't string her along or misuse whatever she told him. She just wished she hadn't made it seem so sure to Uncle that Lafontaine was a viable contact. What was worse, she had no backup — it was Lafontaine or no one. And if it turned out to be no one, then the job was over, and she would be left kicking her heels in Hong Kong while she waited for Uncle's doctor to return.

She went into her computer to find Lafontaine's number. She opened her phone, removed the Toronto SIM card, and replaced it with a Hong Kong card that would read simply UNKNOWN CALLER on the other end. She phoned Guyana.

"Hello?" a tentative voice said.

"Is this Marc Lafontaine?"

"Yes. Who is this?"

"Ava Lee. I hope you remember me."

"Under most circumstances you would be a hard woman to forget. Considering what went on here, you can be certain I remember you," he said.

"I'm not disturbing you, am I?"

"It's Sunday morning and I'm sitting on my apartment balcony with a beer in my hand, watching the Demerara River sludge by."

"Some things don't change."

"In Guyana nothing ever changes that much. Is that why you are calling? Has the dreaded Captain Robbins resurfaced in your life?"

"No."

"Good, because right now he's being particularly nasty, and I wouldn't like to think you were one of his targets."

"He and I reached an understanding."

"I don't think I want to know the details."

"I wasn't going to tell you."

"No problem. It's enough to know that someone fought him to a draw."

"Actually, I think I did better than a draw."

Lafontaine laughed. "So here it is Sunday morning, and I'm sitting on my balcony with a beer in my hand, and Ava Lee calls me from — where?"

"Hong Kong."

"I don't imagine this is social."

"No."

"What could possibly be going on in Hong Kong that's connected to Guyana? Or what's going on here that's caught your attention?"

"Neither of the above. I have a proposition to make that involves you on a personal level."

"Ava, how on earth can that be possible?"

"It's a bit complicated."

"Everything about you is complicated."

"I have to say that in this case, you're not wrong."

"Are you going to make me guess?"

"No, because you couldn't. And until two days ago I couldn't have thought up this situation myself, even if I were chemically stimulated."

"Have you ever been chemically stimulated?"

"No, I make do with wine, but I hope you get the picture."

"I make do with beer, and speaking of which, I need another. Give me a minute."

She heard footsteps, a fridge opening and closing, a bottle being uncapped, and then more footsteps, followed by a sigh. "Okay, just so I'm absolutely clear, you're calling me on a personal matter?"

"No, it's business, and I'm sorry if I'm being vague. What I meant by involving you on a personal level is that I need someone to act as a go-between, a negotiator, if you will."

"I'm an RCMP officer. I don't freelance."

"I know. What I need you to do is negotiate with the RCMP for me, on behalf of a client."

"Do you have any idea how strange that sounds?"

"A bit."

"Okay, that aside, negotiate what?"

"My client has some information that he wants to pass along — actually, information he wants to sell."

"Ava, what could that possibly have to do with me? I'm a one-man band in a South American backwater. What kind of authority or influence do you think I have?"

"Marc, the client has hired my firm to represent his interests. Our firm has decided that the RCMP are the best fit for the information he has to sell. You're the only Mountie I trust enough to have even a preliminary discussion with. That's the reason for the phone call."

"You've met me exactly twice."

"I know. But my partner, who is an elderly Chinese man with a colourful past, has often said to me that when it comes to trust, there is no test. If your instincts tell you to trust someone, there should be no degrees. Naive or not, I trust you."

"And I like to think — egotistical or not — that I am worthy of that trust."

"So can we talk with the understanding that whatever I say will be kept strictly between us, unless I decide otherwise?"

"Sure," he said softly. "You've already spiced up what would have been a hot, humid, and empty Sunday. You have my attention and my word, although I have to be truthful and say I'm not sure what benefit you can expect from sharing confidences with me."

"Let me be the judge of that."

"Obviously. I just don't want you to have unrealistic expectations."

"Point taken — and this phone line is secure?"

"Worried about Captain Robbins again?"

"Yes."

"The line is secure."

"Okay, so let me try to explain as simply as possible what's happened. Like I said, we have a client, whom I can't name right now, who has been managing a bank in Indonesia. There's been a rift between him and the bank's owners, and he's decided to resign his position and move to a safer environment."

"What did he do, abscond with bank funds?"

"No, nothing like that."

"So why did you use the word *safer*?"

"Because if the bank owners find him, they'll kill him."

"Ah, now that's something I didn't expect to hear. What could your Indonesian banker have done to justify that?"

"He isn't Indonesian; he's Scottish. And the bank owners aren't Indonesian either. They're Italian."

"Jesus Christ."

"I know, it sounds convoluted, but it really isn't."

"So far I'm not convinced."

Ava had been sitting at the desk. Now she moved to the bed, propped up the pillows, and lay back. She drew a deep breath. "Have you heard of the 'Ndrangheta?"

"Of course."

"What do you know about them?"

"They're a mob — a big, powerful Italian mob."

"They're the bank's owners."

Lafontaine went silent. She heard him breathing, and then what sounded like a beer bottle being placed on a glass table. "Did you hear me?" she asked.

"How in hell do you know something like that?"

"My client managed the bank for them."

"And you believe him?"

"When he left Indonesia, he was carrying with him enough information to convince anyone of that fact."

"You said earlier there was a rift between him and them. What happened?"

"He was indiscreet and they found out. He managed to leave before they could get their hands on him."

"So he's in hiding?"

"Yes, and he approached us to help him find a way to make that permanent."

"How could you do that?"

"He needs to start a new life. He needs to relocate his family. He knows he'll never be able to work again, so he needs money."

"And he hired you to find him the money?"

"Yes, that's what we do — find money. This case is a bit different than most, but money is money."

Lafontaine became quiet again. Ava was wondering if he had gone to fetch another beer when he said, "I'm still not sure what you're trying to tell me."

"I understand it's a lot to wrap your head around. I had the same problem. Let me put things into context."

"Please."

"This bank in Indonesia was purchased six years ago, using a local law firm as the cover, by the 'Ndrangheta for the explicit purpose of laundering money. They shipped in cash and the banker took in the cash as equity, converted it to the local currency, and then loaned it out in some very specific markets — Rome, Caracas, New York, Toronto — to buy real estate. The loans went to companies, families, and friends who were associated with the 'Ndrangheta. The loans were completely phony, of course; nothing was ever repaid. The banker ran several sets of books to keep the Indonesian authorities satisfied, but the reality was that it was strictly cash in, cash out. The gang ends up owning a worldwide real estate empire bought with laundered money."

"Holy shit."

"It isn't something that could be invented."

"And let me guess," Lafontaine said slowly. "Your client has a copy of the bank records."

"He does indeed."

"How much detail?"

"Every single transaction is recorded — who bought what, where, when, and for how much."

"And you're convinced the information is legit?"

"I've gone through it in detail with him. I'm confident it will stand up to any level of scrutiny."

"So?"

"So?"

"Now he wants to sell the information."

"Exactly," Ava said.

"This is about as far off my watch, my expertise, my rank, as you could possibly get."

"Let me clarify something right away," Ava said. "My client has no interest in shopping this information around. He isn't interested in getting into bids. He initially told us to stick to the countries that were directly involved, then thought better of that and forbade us from talking to the Italians, the Venezuelans, or the Indonesians. That left us with the Americans and Canadians. My partner didn't feel that the Americans could keep their information sources secure. So, Marc, we're talking to you, and you alone."

"You mean you're talking to me as a member of the RCMP?"

"That's exactly what I mean. It starts and ends with you. If you feel that you can't contact the force, or that you can't fairly represent our position, then you and I will forget we ever had this conversation. My client will have to figure another way—without my being involved—to meet his future needs. Because, Marc, this is as far as I take it."

"You want me to negotiate a deal with the force on your behalf?"

"I want you to open some doors for me and at least initiate discussions."

"Under what pretext?"

"Pardon?"

"Why has a humble sergeant in a lonely outpost been chosen to be the messenger for this blockbuster deal?"

"Marc, this is the point where the trust we talked about earlier becomes paramount."

"Meaning?"

"The client came to us because that's how he wants all communication handled."

"He won't talk to anyone but you?"

"Yes."

"They won't like that."

"We believe the information he has can speak for itself. They won't need him."

"That still doesn't explain how I was brought into the loop. If I approach Ottawa—and I emphasize the *if*—they're going to ask me why I was chosen to be the conduit."

"About nine months ago you met a woman in Guyana named Jennie Kwong. She came to the High Commission for help, help that you provided. She remembered you. You're the only Mountie she knows."

"Jennie Kwong?"

"I have a Hong Kong passport in that name."

"Ava Lee?"

"As of now, between you and me, and you and them, there is no Ava Lee. Only Jennie Kwong. If you can't go with that, we can stop talking right now. What I need you to promise, regardless of what you decide to do, is that my real name will be kept entirely out of any conversation."

"I gave you my word."

"I know, and I'm sorry if I seem paranoid."

"You're really afraid of those Italians."

"Absolutely."

"So this Jennie Kwong contacts me on behalf of this Scottish banker and asks me to do what?"

"Help her get to first base—put her in contact with people who can start a decision-making process."

"To buy the bank records?"

"Of course. That's what it's about from my client's side."

"Does he have a number in mind?"

"Thirty million U.S. dollars."

"You have got to be joking!"

"Of course not. And let me say I think he's being generous at that price. We're talking about billions of dollars that have been illegally laundered and used to buy real estate. I'm quite sure that if the authorities in most of the countries I mentioned had access to the records we have, they could seize nearly all those properties and turn around and flip them for a profit. On top of confiscating the properties in Canada, the RCMP could also do well by selling the information to other jurisdictions."

"That sounds terrific, but we aren't in the real estate business."

"I don't mean to overemphasize the money side of things; I'm just trying to justify the thirty million dollars. The main reason, of course, that the RCMP would want to get their hands on this information is that the records my client has identify every single person and company that owns a piece of real estate as a result of this fraud. Everyone named is either 'Ndrangheta or affiliated with them in some way. The records would give complete access to their membership and their support system on a worldwide basis. What kind of value does that have to the RCMP? What kind of brownie points would that earn the force with the Americans and Interpol?"

All she could hear was the buzz of the phone line. "Are you there?" she asked.

"I'm processing."

"Take your time."

"I have a buddy I can talk to in Ottawa. He's attached to the organized crime unit, and he's senior enough," he said. "We went to the RCMP Academy in Regina together, so we go back a long way. He'll at least take my call, and he knows me well enough that he won't completely blow me off when I start to tell him this story."

"It isn't a story."

"I get that. I'll need to get him to get that too."

"Listen, Marc, I don't want to say too much until I know there's some interest. And when I say interest, I don't just mean they would like to get their hands on the information; I mean they're willing to pay thirty million dollars for it. So if that's understood, and if your friend says that under the right conditions the money could be available, then I'm prepared to give them the name of the banker and the bank and whatever else they need to confirm my client's credentials."

"Assuming I can reach him and if I get that far, I'll let him know."

"Then call me back, please. I'll stay up until I hear from you," Ava said.

"Okay, I'll try to reach him. If you don't hear from me in a few hours it will be because I didn't."

"Marc, if you do get hold of him, the other thing he needs to know is that we have to move quickly. My client is in extreme peril. He can't hang around waiting for the government to make a decision."

"What's your time frame?"

"A few days, no more than that."

"Ava..."

"Yes, Marc?"

"This is real, right?"

"As real as it gets."

(40)

AVA ENDED THE CALL AND THEN CLOSED HER EYES. She had just put a lot of trust in a man she barely knew. It was the kind of thing she knew Uncle did from time to time. He had a sense about people, not based particularly on what they said but more on how they carried themselves. He believed you could tell a lot about a person through body language and eye contact, and he told Ava that it was often more productive to observe than to listen. It was something she now practised without really thinking about it.

She thought back to meeting Lafontaine at his office in Guyana, sharing dinner with him, and the conversation she had just had. Her instincts told her she had called the right person. Still, it came down to how well he could sell the story, and though she thought it hung together quite well, she wasn't sure it would under intense scrutiny. The thing was, she had no intention of putting herself in a position where there would be that risk.

She turned to look at the clock. It was past midnight but she had promised Uncle she would phone. She punched in his number. Lourdes answered.

"Let me speak to Uncle, please."

"He's sleeping."

"Ah."

"Do you want me to get him?"

"No, leave him be. But if he wakes before I get the chance to speak to him again, let him know I did call."

"He didn't look very good when he got home."

"I know. I had dinner with him."

"What are we going to do?"

"His doctor is back in Hong Kong next week. I intend to speak to him."

"Someone has to find out what's going on."

"I will, Lourdes."

She put down the phone, the memory of Uncle retching on the sidewalk unsettling her. Needing a distraction, she reached for the television remote. She couldn't find anything she wanted to watch on regular programming and clicked on the pay-per-view. *Election 2* was listed. Ava bought it, and despite her worries about Uncle and her concerns about Lafontaine, she was soon immersed in the film's machinations. She was so completely absorbed in it that when her phone rang, she forgot where she had left it and had to rifle though the folds of the duvet to find it. The incoming number displayed the Guyana area code.

"Marc. That was quick."

"You told me to make it fast."

"Did it go well?"

"Well, it obviously got an immediate reaction."

"Is that good?"

"I don't know. My friend was very interested in what I had to say. In fact, I had to repeat the story several times.

Then I had to tell him five times that I thought you were serious and not some scam artist trying to leverage money out of us. When I was done, he asked me to keep my phone on. He said he would get right back to me."

"And did he?"

"Yeah, and not just him. Half an hour later I found myself in a conference call with two higher-ranking officers. There were a lot of questions about Jennie Kwong."

"I can imagine."

"I tried to keep the focus on the bank manager and the financial information."

"Good."

"It wasn't easy. They were skeptical, and at times almost hostile. They wanted to know why we were chosen to be the recipients of such a windfall. I told them about meeting Jennie Kwong in Guyana and that you were Canadian. I said coming to us was almost patriotic of you — I hope that was okay."

"I guess it is."

"But then they really focused in on the banker. They want to know who he is."

"I said I would tell you."

"And they would like to speak to him."

"No."

"I told them that was your position. They then asked if they could speak directly to you."

"Not unless I have to. I'd rather keep talking through you."

"I told them I thought that was the case."

"What else do they want?

"The name of the bank."

"Does this mean they've agreed to the thirty million?"

"There's some reluctance to agree to any amount until they can verify what kind of information the banker has."

"I'm prepared to send them a sample."

"That will help."

"But if I do and I give them the names, what are they prepared to give me in return?"

"Nothing just yet."

"That doesn't work."

"What do you want?"

"First we need a commitment that the sum we're talking about will be paid, and paid quickly, if the information proves to be genuine and as comprehensive as my client claims."

Lafontaine paused. "Truthfully, they asked me if the number was negotiable."

"It isn't. It's thirty million or nothing. You need to tell them that."

"Okay, and if they agree, are you prepared to give them the names and a sample?"

"Maybe, but they also have to agree to keep the banker's name confidential. It has to be kept just as secure internally, and not shared with any other jurisdictions."

"Ava, you do realize that once the bank's name is known it won't take long for everyone to figure out who he is."

"I know, but we're trying to buy as much time as we can. He needs to make himself invisible, and the money he collects from the Mounties will go a long way towards helping him do that. So if we cut a deal, I expect your guys to sit on things for at least a couple of weeks. They will need at least that long anyway, to go over the data I send them."

"I understand. I'm not sure they'll agree, but I'll put it to them."

"Good. If they do agree, I'm prepared to give you the name of the banker and the bank, and I'll email a sample of the deals that were done."

"That was another question they had. How many Canadian and U.S. transactions are we talking about?"

"About two hundred in North America, with close to half of those in Canada, involving well over three hundred people."

"Could you make some of the Canadian information part of the sample?"

"Of course. If I want them to verify the information it's better for us to give them something they can run quickly."

"Okay, I'll pass that along."

"Marc, I'm not finished yet."

"What else?"

"After I give you the information, they have twenty-four hours to get back to me. If they don't, the offer comes off the table."

"Twenty-four hours?"

"That's my time frame."

"They won't like that."

"Tell them anyway."

"Okay, I'll tell them."

"They're waiting for you to get back to them?"

"Yes."

"In that case, I'll stay up as well. Call them and then get right back to me."

She placed the phone on the bedside table and made a quick run to the bathroom to pee, brush her teeth, and wash her face. Despite the hour, she was completely awake. The nap on the plane had helped, but she could also feel the adrenalin pumping through her system. She hadn't felt this engaged since... since she could remember.

Back in the bedroom, she went to sit at the desk. She opened her computer to read the emails that had been cascading into her iPhone. Her last message from Surabaya, saying she would be out of touch for several days, had triggered an outpouring of concern from everyone in her life. Her mother and May Ling had both written four times, Mimi and Amanda twice; Maria had sent five emails in less than two days.

I am back in Hong Kong and safe and sound. Uncle and I have a project we need to finish. I'll contact you all individually when it is done. Until then, I still need to concentrate on the job at hand. Love, Ava, she wrote and then sent it to all of them.

She perused the other emails, deleting most of them. The television was still on and *Election 2* was coming to an end. As she settled back on the bed, her phone rang. She got to the table by the third ring and was about to answer when she saw Maria's number on the screen. She let it ring out, and as she did the memory of Andy Cameron saying "I don't do ugly" flashed in her head. She suddenly felt nauseous. She knew she wasn't ready to talk to Maria, her mother, or May Ling — all the women she felt the strongest emotional attachment to. She had to get herself under control. She needed to act as if everything was normal.

She was not about to share what had happened in Surabaya with anyone, but she wasn't sure what impact her mother's voice might have on her. She didn't know how she would react to Maria's tenderness. All she knew was that she wanted to be spared their emotions, and the only way that could happen was for Ava to be her normal calm self. She didn't know if that would be possible if she spoke to them right now. Aside from the dull ache that hadn't left her since Surabaya, there was the matter of the bouts of anxiety that seemed to attack her without warning. *I need to get my imagination under control*, she thought.

Ava walked over to the bed and slipped to her knees. She pressed her hands together and began to pray to Saint Jude, the patron saint of lost causes. The phone rang before she could finish.

She looked at the incoming number. It was Marc Lafontaine. She felt a touch of relief.

"That was even quicker."

"You have their complete attention."

"What did they say?" she asked.

"It wasn't easy."

"Marc, what did they say?"

"They're agreeable to everything except the deadline."

"No. The deadline is necessary and I won't change it."

He hesitated, and she wondered if the Mounties were now lost to her.

"In that case you should give them your client's name and the name of the bank and arrange to send the sample information to Ottawa via email. They'll work as fast as they can."

"I'll need about half an hour."

"They will want the deadline to start when they actually receive the information."

"Of course."

"Here is the email address they want it sent to..." he said.

Ava walked back to the desk and opened her notebook. "Go ahead," she said. He recited three addresses. "Thanks, Marc. I really appreciate your help with this. If things go well we should be talking in less than twenty-four hours."

"Let's hope so, because I can tell you, Ava, if things don't go well I'm facing a lifetime posting in Guyana."

"Stay positive," she said, reaching into her bag for the USB drive containing the Bank Linno loan data. Then she headed for the door.

She took the elevator to the Mandarin's business centre on the second floor. The place was deserted except for a clerk. Ava signed in and took a computer in the far corner. She logged on, opened the USB directory, found the Toronto records, printed three pages, and scanned them. She then accessed a Gmail account she had had for years under "slauming" and began to write. The banker's name is Andrew Cameron. He is originally from Aberdeen and worked for a British bank in Rome before being recruited about six years ago by the 'Ndrangheta to be front man for their Bank Linno in Surabaya. I attach three pages of Canadian real estate deals. I hope to hear from you shortly. Jennie Kwong

(41)

AVA SLEPT SURPRISINGLY WELL AND LONG. IT WAS past nine o'clock when she woke. She blinked at the clock, hardly believing it was that late. She reached for her phone, turned it on, and saw that Uncle had called twice, the first time just after seven. She knew he would have been up for a while by then, worrying about what was going on.

"*Wei,*" he said.

"Sorry to call so late. I just woke. I was up half the night negotiating with the Mounties."

"Lourdes told me you tried to reach me."

"I did after my first contact, and then there was another call quite a bit later."

"So where are we?"

"Waiting. We have an agreement in principle for a thirty-million-dollar payment if the information proves to be accurate, but they insisted on having the names of the banker and the bank and some snippets of what we had. I sent it to them and gave them twenty-four hours to get back to us. If they don't, I told them we'll walk."

"You gave them the banker's name?"

"Why not? As far as anyone knows he flew from Surabaya to Singapore yesterday afternoon. I told them he was in hiding and that we'd been hired by him to negotiate a deal."

"And if we reach a deal, how does it conclude?"

"Did you speak to Kowloon Light and Power about opening that numbered account?"

"The account was opened an hour ago. It is controlled by one of the bank's directors, but anyone who digs into it will find the name Andy Cameron attached. The director will do whatever we ask with the money when or if it arrives."

"Will the money be traceable?"

"After it reaches Cameron's account it will begin a remarkable journey that no one will be able to recreate."

"Then the deal will conclude with me sending the Mounties all the information on the USB and them sending thirty million dollars to Andy Cameron, care of the Kowloon Light and Power Bank."

"What are the chances we can close?"

"Uncle, I have no idea. This isn't really about whether our information is accurate or not. It's all a question of what value it has to the Mounties."

"Still, I like it that we are trying, and I have to say that it is quite an ingenious approach."

"What, having the Canadian government in essence pay back thirty million dollars to Canadian citizens who lost the money in the first place because they were trying to avoid paying Canadian taxes?"

"That too, though what I meant was using a dead man as the vehicle."

The urge to pee hit Ava and she slid out of bed. She thought about carrying the phone into the bathroom with her and then decided some things needed to be kept private. "Uncle, I want to apologize if I seem rude, but I really need to go to the bathroom. And I need to get some coffee in me."

"Go ahead. We will talk later."

"I might go for a run as well."

"I have no plans. Call me whenever you wish."

Ava put down the phone and sped to the bathroom. She peed, washed her face, brushed her hair and teeth, and wandered back into the suite. She made a cup of coffee and fetched the *South China Morning Post* that was outside her door. Sitting down by the window looking out onto Victoria Harbour, she was reminded of the garden view at the Majapahit. She shuddered and moved back to the desk.

Two coffees later she had finished the newspaper and began to get dressed for a trip to Victoria Park. She was tying her running shoes when her cellphone rang. Ava looked at the screen, expecting to see Maria's or May Ling's name, but instead she saw Amanda Yee's. She hesitated about answering and then felt foolish. Amanda was no May Ling. She was more eager to please than to pry.

"Hey, is this my little half-sister-in-law-to-be?" Ava asked.

"God, that sounds so complicated."

"Blame my father for that."

Amanda laughed. "I was surprised when I got your email about being in Hong Kong."

"Just passing through."

"What are you up to?"

"I'm getting ready for a run."

"Where are you staying?"

"The Mandarin Oriental in Central."

"Do you have plans for lunch?"

"Not yet."

"How about meeting me? I stayed at the apartment last night, so I'm close to the Oriental. I could walk down for dim sum."

"That sounds perfect."

"What time works for you?"

"I should be finished my run and back here by eleven. How's eleven thirty?"

"That works. I'm planning on coming alone — no Michael. I hope that isn't a disappointment."

"Truthfully I'd rather it be that way. I've been seeing too many men on this trip."

"Good. I'll see you at eleven thirty," Amanda said, and then hesitated as if she wanted to add something.

Ava waited for a second and then said, "Look, I'd better go if I'm to get my run in."

She caught the MTR in Central and rode it to the Causeway Bay station. It was the last gasp of rush hour and the trains were still jammed. In her shorts and T-shirt, Ava drew a few stares. *More than normal*, she thought, and then just as quickly wondered if she was being overly sensitive to the attention.

The weather was perfect for a run, the temperature in the low twenties, a light breeze coming in from the bay. Victoria Park was mercifully quiet; the early morning crowd had finished with their tai chi and their group exercise classes and had retreated to the apartment towers and office buildings that circled it. The inner jogging track was six hundred metres around. Most of the time when Ava came to the park, she was forced to walk as often as run. This morning it offered a clear path and she took advantage of it, putting in eight quick laps, until her thighs felt like rubber, her breath came in gasps, and sweat flew off her body.

She took the train back to the hotel, the other passengers giving her a wide berth as the sweat kept pouring off her. By the time she walked into the Mandarin lobby, she had cooled off, and as soon as she was in her room she hit the shower.

She dressed in the clothes she had worn the night before: black linen slacks and the blue Brooks Brothers shirt. She fastened her hair back with the ivory chignon pin and then stared down at the green jade cufflinks that sat on her dresser. She hadn't worn them the night before, almost subconsciously avoiding them. Now she reached for them.

The two women had last seen each other the day before Ava went to Macau to invade the house in which Michael's partner was being held captive. They had communicated only by email since, and as Ava rode the elevator down to the lobby she wondered what changes the past few months had wrought in Amanda.

Ava saw her first, standing by the concierge desk, as slim as ever. She wore black Versace jeans, her hair was tied back in a ponytail, and there wasn't a trace of makeup on her face. When she saw Ava, she held out her arms and ran towards her. Ava was taken aback by the display of emotion and recoiled ever so slightly. That didn't deter Amanda, who wrapped her arms around Ava and hugged her with more force than Ava thought that slight body could generate.

"I'm so happy to see you!" Amanda said.

"Me too."

"How is your leg?"

"Like new, except for the scar."

They walked together to the elevator for the ride up to Man Wah. "My father sends his regards," said Amanda.

"And how is Jack?"

"Happy as can be. He's already talking about having grandchildren, even though he wants me to take over more and more of the business. I don't think he sees the conflict there."

"And how does Michael feel about both those things — children and your career?"

"I don't think he's ready to start a family, and truthfully neither am I. We both still have some figuring out to do."

Michael more than you, Ava thought as she said, "Not everyone is cut out to be a parent."

They were just ahead of the lunchtime crowd and were able to get a table near the window. As the waiter poured jasmine tea, Ava scanned the menu and felt her appetite kick in almost at once. "I do like this place," she said.

Amanda looked around the restaurant. "It hasn't changed in years. This is the restaurant my father used to take me to on special occasions. I have so many good memories of it."

"Is there anything in particular you'd like to eat?"

"They have *siu mai* with pork and black truffles that I love, and they do a deep-fried green chili with garlic and soy sauce that's great."

Ava ticked those boxes on the dim sum order sheet and then added crispy diced codfish, a shrimp dumpling with chives and mushrooms, and a dumpling stuffed with barramundi, thousand-year egg, and cilantro. She handed it to the waiter and then looked across the table at Amanda.

"I'm not used to seeing you dressed quite so plainly."

"I decided to abandon my Hong Kong princess look— not entirely, of course, but at least most workdays. My father's office is rather mundane and I got tired of looking out of place."

"Well, it suits you. You look so young and fresh, like a first-year student at the Polytech."

"I'm not sure that's quite the impression I want to make, but thank you anyway," she said with a laugh.

Then Ava realized she hadn't mentioned the wedding. "My God, Amanda, I'm sorry—I haven't congratulated you yet."

Amanda gave a little shrug. "All we did was fix the date."

"Still, you're going ahead with it."

"Did you doubt that we would?" Amanda asked.

It was Ava's turn to shrug. "I wasn't sure... That was a traumatic experience you both went through, and things like that can change the way people look at their lives and each other."

"You're always so honest."

"Not always."

"Well, you're right about it changing the way we view each other. Michael was always so sure of himself before, and Macau rattled him. Now he doesn't take things so much for granted; he's not so cocky. I kind of like that vulnerability in him. And as for me, I surprised even myself with how strong I was during that time. Michael saw that too, of course, and now he takes me a lot more seriously."

The first wave of food arrived, and the talk idled as both Amanda and Ava plucked shrimp-and-chive dumplings from their bamboo nest. Ava slathered hers in red chili sauce while Amanda opted for the hot mustard.

"Is your father really ready to retire?" Ava asked. Her eyes wandered to the next table, where a diner was biting into a piece of puff pastry that even from a distance smelled disturbingly aromatic. "What is that dish?" she asked Amanda.

"The wagyu beef puff. It comes with a black-pepper sauce. We should have ordered it."

"Not too late," Ava said, waving at their waiter.

When he left, Ava turned back to Amanda. "I was asking about your father — is he ready to retire?"

Amanda looked slightly uncomfortable.

"Sorry, I don't mean to poke my nose into family business," said Ava.

"No, it's not that," Amanda said quickly. "It's May Ling."

"May Ling is involved with your business?"

"Not really, although she has been tremendously supportive over the past three months and has thrown all kinds of deals my way. It's more that she wants me to leave the family business and join her."

"To do what?"

"She won't say specifically."

"You're confusing me," Ava said, biting into a slice of crispy cod.

"Maybe because I'm confused myself... Tell me, has May Ling discussed the possibility of you joining with her in some business ventures?"

"Yes, she's been at it constantly, but I've put her off."

"You have no interest?"

Ava hesitated as she saw Amanda's eyes boring into her. How well did she really know this young woman?

Not well enough to be completely forthcoming. "Amanda, after Macau I took a break from my own business. I'm on a job now but I was sort of tricked into it. The truth is, I don't know if I want to keep doing this thing. That's what I spent the summer trying to figure out, and I'm no closer to making a decision in September than I was in July. If I do decide I've had enough, then I have to make another decision, about what it is I want to do instead. And God knows how long that might take."

"So you haven't discounted the idea of working with May Ling."

"That's fair to say."

Amanda poured tea for the two of them and Ava tapped her middle finger on the table in a silent thank-you. "I have to tell you, Ava, I do want to work with her," Amanda blurted.

"What about your father and his business?"

"It's a trading operation — just deal to deal. You can't build any equity that way. It makes money, of course, and enough that my father could retire tomorrow. But then what? I do more of the same, flipping this and that? That's not where my interest lies. I want to build something more permanent, or at least I want to be part of something permanent. That takes working capital and patience and contacts and smarts. And May Ling has all those things."

"She also has a husband as a partner."

"That's the thing," Amanda said as the wagyu beef puffs arrived. "She keeps telling me she wants to do something separate from him, something for just us girls."

"Just us girls?"

"Me, you, and her, with the idea of bringing more women on board."

"She's never discussed anything like that with me," Ava said. She bit into the puff, the black-pepper sauce exploding in her mouth, the meat so tender it almost melted on her tongue.

Amanda ignored the food, her chopsticks waving in the air as she became more excited. "And with me she's been vague about the details, just saying that she wants us to be in business together. When I pressed her for information, she sidestepped the questions, saying she wanted to make sure you were on board first. I just assumed she'd talked to you about it — whatever it is."

"No, nothing."

"That's strange."

"Not really. I've been evasive from my end. Maybe she wanted to wait until she knew she had my attention."

"Will she get it?"

"Yes, soon enough, I think. I'm beginning to sort things out."

Amanda reached for the last puff. "Ava, if you go into business with May Ling, I'm going to leave my father's firm and join you."

"You'd better not make that commitment until you know what sort of business she has in mind."

"No, it doesn't matter. The most important thing for me is the people I'm in business with. Everything else will sort itself out."

Ava sat back and stared at her. "How can someone so young be so wise?" she asked.

Amanda waved off the compliment, but a smile played at her lips and a slight flush had crept into her cheeks. Then she said, "Ava, do you mind if we change the subject now?"

"What do you mean?" Ava asked, surprised.

"The wedding. We need to talk a bit about the wedding."

"Of course we do," Ava said, just as her cellphone rang. It was her mother. Almost without thinking she answered. "Hello, Mummy."

"Ava, is everything all right?"

Ava could hear voices in the background and the fearsome click of mah-jong tiles. "Yes, I'm fine, but why are you calling me from a mah-jong game?"

"Theresa Ng just phoned. I should say, just phoned again — it's almost harassment at this point. She says all those Vietnamese people you spoke to are calling her every day to find out what's going on. At least, that's the excuse she uses to justify her calls."

"I told them when I met with them that I don't give progress reports."

"I know that, and Theresa is always apologetic about asking for one, but then her apology turns into fifteen demanding questions that I can't answer. I have to tell you, I'm sorry I ever asked you to get involved in this."

"It's a bit late for that."

"What can I tell her?" Jennie asked, ignoring the mild reprimand.

"Do you mean what can I tell you so she'll get off your back?"

"You don't have to put it in such a mean way."

"I don't know how else to put it."

"Look, I'm sorry I asked, but please be a bit more understanding about what it's like from my side."

"God."

"Please."

"Okay, you can tell her this. I found Lam in Ho Chi Minh City and I'm currently in Hong Kong working on another lead. I expect to have some hard information by the end of the week."

"She'll ask me what you mean by hard information."

"I'll know by the end of the week whether or not they will get some money back."

"What chance is there that you will be successful?"

"Ten percent."

Ava heard her mother sigh and knew she didn't like that number. "Maybe I'll skip that part."

"It's your choice. But, Mummy, either way, tell Theresa not to call you anymore, because you won't have anything else to tell her, because I'm not going to tell you any more until this job is finished."

"I understand, Ava."

"I'm sorry if it sounds rude."

"No, don't be. I know your job is stressful and I shouldn't have bothered you."

"Thank you."

"Sweetheart, is everything else okay? I have to say I was worried when I got that email from Indonesia."

"Yes, Mummy, everything is just fine. I'm sitting in the Mandarin having dim sum with Amanda. We're just about to talk about the wedding plans."

(42)

THE AFTERNOON WAS ALL LOOSE ENDS FOR AVA. Amanda left Man Wah just after one thirty after filling Ava's head with details about the wedding. Ava had been to one other wedding in her life — her sister's, which had been held, out of deference to Bruce, in a Unitarian church in Ottawa.

Amanda's was going to be a different animal, as befitted the only child of a wealthy Hong Konger marrying the oldest son of one who was probably richer. A large bridal party, various gift registries, pre-wedding events, the Catholic cathedral, the Grand Hyatt. At first Ava found it distracting, but then it became mind-numbing and she found herself tuning out, until Amanda asked, "Is it possible you could come to Hong Kong a while before the wedding to help?"

"Was that implied when I said I would be maid of honour?"

"Sort of," Amanda said, looking away from the table.

"Then I'll try to organize myself to make that possible," Ava said.

After saying goodbye to Amanda, she had returned to her room. The lunch had gone well in that it hadn't generated any unexpected emotions, and she had been able to handle the call from her mother. Maybe she was getting a grip on herself. She thought about calling Maria and then put the notion aside. It was the middle of the night in Toronto. There was no one more tender, more vulnerable, more loving than Maria when she had just woken up, and Ava wasn't sure how she would react to that.

Maria was Ava's first real girlfriend. There had been relationships before, but none that she had ever thought of as permanent...Ava paused at the thought. She had never discussed the future with Maria.

She went to the desk, opened the computer, and began to write to Maria. I am sitting here in my hotel room and all I can think about is how much I miss you and how much I love you. When I get back to Toronto, we need to sit down and talk about us. Then she stopped. What did she actually mean by "talk about us"? Was she prepared to make a commitment to live together, to marry? She didn't know. Then she imagined Maria reading those words and the meaning she might ascribe to them. She deleted the message and started a new one. I miss you and I love you. See you soon.

Ava walked over to the window and looked out at Victoria Harbour. The afternoon was going to drag and the room was beginning to feel like a prison. She phoned Uncle. Lourdes answered, her voice again filled with worry. "He is sleeping," she said.

"Don't bother him. I'm going over to the Kowloon side to shop, so if he wants to have dinner with me, tell him to call me on my cell."

She left the hotel and walked to the Star Ferry terminal. At mid-afternoon it wasn't that busy, and she was able to get a seat in the rear that gave her a clear view of the Hong

Kong skyline. When she stood among the skyscrapers that lined the harbour, she felt overwhelmed, almost oppressed, by their size and number. As the ferry moved across the harbour, the density and variety of the buildings changed and they became less ominous. They ringed the harbour in a solid line, most of them soaring sixty storeys or more, reflecting the energy and ego of the new China, each built to draw one's eye through clever combinations of steel and glass and colour. Ava thought of them as sentinels, projecting power, protecting the city.

The ferry berthed at Tsim Sha Tsui. She strolled over to the nearby Harbour City shopping centre and began to explore its more than seven hundred shops. Three hours later she re-emerged with a pair of Ferragamo shoes and two new Brooks Brothers shirts. It had been an afternoon of complete calm. The centre, like all the others in Hong Kong and the New Territories, was swamped with people on weekends, but on this Monday afternoon Ava had been the lone shopper in many stores, and she never felt hurried or crowded. Her sense of calm was enhanced by the fact that her phone didn't ring. Twice she checked it to make sure it was on.

Near the Ocean Terminal part of Harbour City was a row of restaurants, including a McDonald's and a congee shop that Ava and Uncle had eaten at many times. She went into a coffee shop, ordered a plain black coffee, and checked her voicemails — none — and emails — all spam.

She called Uncle's apartment again. Lourdes answered. "He's gone out with Sonny," she said.

"Did you tell him I called?"

"Oh, Ava, I'm sorry, I forgot."

"Never mind, I'll call his cell."

Uncle's phone rang four times and cut off. She tried Sonny.

"Hey," he said.

"Is everything okay?"

"I think so. He called me about an hour ago saying he wanted to get a massage. I took him to this place close to the Peninsula Hotel. They really baby him there."

"I'm in Tsim Sha Tsui. Maybe we can hook up for dinner."

"He just went in. He'll be at least two hours."

"How was he when you went to get him?"

"Not bad," he said carefully. "His colour was better, and he seemed to have more energy."

"Good, that's encouraging. Now, Sonny, I'm going to head back to Central. Tell him I called. I won't have dinner until I hear from him."

She left the coffee shop and walked the two hundred metres to the ferry terminal. Rush hour was on and the boats going in either direction were jammed. Ava had to wait fifteen minutes before squeezing onto one. It was close to seven o'clock when she stepped off in Central. She was halfway to the Mandarin when her phone sounded. *Uncle,* she thought, and then saw that the originating number was blocked.

"Hello."

"Jennie, this is Marc Lafontaine."

Jennie? "How are you, Marc?"

"Well enough. I've just finished speaking with Ottawa."

"And how did that go?"

"To be frank, Jennie, they have some problems."

"Marc, I sense that you have someone there with you. Is that right?"

"No, I'm alone."

"But there is someone else on the line listening to our conversation."

"There are two of us, actually," a new voice said.

"And who are the two of you?"

"My name is Kevin Torsney and my colleague is Peter Valliant. We're senior officers in the organized crime unit here in Ottawa."

"It would have been nicer if you'd announced your presence before I asked."

"Apologies. We didn't know if you would speak to us."

"I told Marc I didn't want to talk to anyone but him."

"Again apologies, but if you want to do a deal, one way or another you have to speak to us."

Should I hang up? Ava thought. Marc had called her Jennie. He had given her fair warning, and she was sure that at least so far he had protected her real name. It was almost too late to care anyway. "It is very early in the morning where you are."

"We've been working nonstop, all night in fact, since we received your information."

"And?"

"We have some problems with it."

"How so?"

"We need more time."

"You still have another six hours before my deadline."

"We'll need a lot more time than that."

"No."

"Ms. Kwong, if you want your thirty million dollars, you have to give us more time."

"Mr. Torsney, there was a reason for the deadline."

"We aren't stalling, if that's what you think."

"Why would I think that?"

"I imagine you might think we're taking the extra time to find out enough about Cameron, the bank, and the transactions you sent us so that we won't need you."

"That did occur to me."

"That's not the case."

"So what is the case?" There was a long silence, and Ava thought she heard muttering. "Don't talk behind my back," she said.

"Ms. Kwong, this is Valliant. I've been trying to run down the people behind the transactions you sent us. That's what's causing the delay. Each of the deals is supported by a complex structure — numbered companies turning into law firms holding assets in trust; individuals, Canadian citizens with spotless records but no apparent means, who own real estate worth millions and tens of millions of dollars; and so on. The only things we can find in common are that everyone who is involved is Italian and appears to have connections to Calabria, though not to any criminal organization."

"Bank Linno?"

"Undoubtedly a curious success story with its remarkable growth and its rather suspicious non-Indonesian customer base."

"You mean Italian customer base."

"Yes, that is what I mean."

"Andy Cameron?"

"Curious and suspicious as well," Valliant said.

Torsney interrupted. "And, Ms. Kwong, we have confirmed that he left Surabaya on Sunday for Singapore."

"Just so no one gets any ideas about looking for him there, I do have to tell you he's already left."

"I would hope so. The trail he left was rather obvious."

Ava was approaching the hotel. This was not a discussion she wanted to pursue in the lobby, and at that time of the evening the streets were so crowded she could walk only at quarter speed. "Look, this is really inconvenient for me right now. Is it possible you could call me back in about fifteen minutes?"

"Ms. Kwong, we aren't going to change our mind about needing more time," Valliant said.

"And what do you mean by more time?"

"Several days at least."

"That is quite open-ended."

"I'm sorry, but we can't be more specific."

"Well, I can. I'm not going to give you more time, so I guess you have fifteen minutes to work something out."

"And then what? You'll really walk away?"

"Maybe I'll go to the Americans."

"What makes you think they'll react any differently?"

"They have RICO. The money they can claw back from the real estate deals in and around New York City will pay me what I want and will leave them with a ton of cash and the credit for shutting down at least part of the 'Ndrangheta."

"But will they give you and your client the level of security we can?"

Ava didn't answer.

"Ms. Kwong, the information you gave us does have interest. What it doesn't have right now is any credence," Torsney said. "Two names and some copies of financial transactions do not justify sending you a thousand dollars, never mind thirty million. We need time to verify that what we have is exactly what you claim it is."

"Call me in fifteen minutes," Ava said, ending the call.

She walked into the hotel lobby, saw a vacant chair in a corner, and headed for it, dialling Sonny's cell number as she went.

"He's still in massage," he said.

"I don't care. Take your phone to him. We need to talk."

"Ava—"

"Do it."

She sat down, her mind churning. It was the Canadians or nothing, and nothing was beginning to look like the best option.

"Are you all right?" Uncle asked.

"No. Things are getting complicated. I've just heard from the Mounties. They want more time."

"Why?"

"They're having problems getting to the bottom of the real estate deals I sent them. There are layers upon layers. They say they need time to get to the roots."

"Is that true?"

"Probably."

"So what to do?"

"The way I see it, the longer this gets stretched out, the greater the risk. The Italians will know by now that Cameron's gone to Singapore, and they'll already be assuming he's done a runner. I'm sure they're trying to track him down."

"Never to find him."

"True, but my fear is that in a few days they might be paranoid enough and smart enough to figure out he never left. If that happens, and if they happen to talk to a certain

Singapore Air supervisor at Juanda Airport, their attention would switch to Surabaya and to how Cameron spent his time after leaving work on Friday. That is something I don't want to happen."

"It seems unlikely."

"But not impossible. And if I give the Mounties more time, who knows who they'll start talking to. Uncle, I think our only chance to get our money and to get distance from this entire affair is to push for a quick resolution."

"All we have are the bank records. If that is what is causing the delay, that is not going to change. What surprises me is that they have not insisted on meeting or having direct communication with Cameron."

"That, I think, will be the next thing they want."

"What do you want to do? End it?"

"No, I would like to have the money. But I'm beginning to think that what I want even more is every law enforcement agency in the Western world hounding the 'Ndrangheta. I want the Italians to be focused on that and not on hunting the ghost of Andy Cameron. A good offence is often the best defence."

"But you do not want to give the Mounties the time they say they need to establish that what we are telling them is accurate."

"Not if it involves days or weeks of work going through bank records. We simply cannot give the 'Ndrangheta that kind of time."

"I am beginning to wish I had not called my friends at the Hong Kong police. I should have thought this through better."

"There is nothing wrong with your plan if we can move fast enough."

"Is there anything we can do to make that possible?"

"There is one thing. It's a bit of a gamble, but it has the main advantage of providing positive proof in the quickest way possible and the secondary advantages of giving the Mounties the money they need to pay us and taking the Indonesian-based Italians out of the game. It would most certainly get everyone's attention."

She heard Uncle inhale. He would be smoking a cigarette; she imagined the tip held delicately to his lips, his eyes hooded as he considered what she had said. "Are you talking about the airplane?"

"Yes."

"The airplane with money that the banker said arrives every Tuesday in Surabaya?"

"Yes."

"How can you confirm that it will come tomorrow night?"

"I would have to talk to the Mounties and they would have to have conversations with the Indonesians. Flight plans have to be filed. A plane can't just show up at an airport."

"You said the customs people are being paid off."

"That doesn't mean air traffic control is. And besides, this can't be done without Indonesian involvement, so at some level it has to be opened up. All I can do is stress to the Mounties how compromised Indonesian Customs is and ask them to find other ways to get the information we need."

"You will also need the Indonesian police or military."

"I know. In this case I think it will most definitely be military."

"And you have to hope that the Canadians have strong enough connections in Jakarta to make that happen."

"I have to assume that they do. If they don't, we'll know soon enough."

"Ava, what have you told the Canadians about the planes?"

"Absolutely nothing. The word *plane* was never uttered."

"Good. That at least gives some negotiating room."

"That's what I'm thinking."

"And you want to do this with tomorrow night's flight?"

"Yes. I don't want to wait another week."

"If they cannot organize it that quickly, or if they say no?"

"Uncle, what is there to organize? We're talking about one smallish commercial jet with only a flight crew, which is being met, as far as I can tell, by two Italians. We don't need an army."

"Do not minimize the politics that will have to be managed."

"That's out of our hands."

"All right, but what if, with every good intention in the world, the Canadians cannot make this happen the way you want?"

"Then I believe we should send all the information to the Mounties and walk away from the money. Whether we get paid or not, we still need them to harass and occupy the attention of the 'Ndrangheta."

"What about your friend — the one who knows who you are?"

"I can only hope that, once they get the information, his superiors will stop caring how it found its way to them."

"I think that is entirely likely."

"Me too. Now let me go and see if I can swing a deal."

"Ava, even if the Canadian side is secure, are you sure you covered your tracks in Surabaya?"

"As sure as I can be," she said.

"You do not say that with as much conviction as I would like to hear."

"It has been a difficult case—" she began, and then saw the familiar 613 area code light up her screen. "Uncle, the Canadians are calling. I have to go."

"Ava, one last thing. Have you thought about what might happen if they go for your plan and that airplane does not arrive?"

"There are so many possible consequences. I wouldn't know where to start."

"Call me as soon as you have things sorted out with them, one way or another. I will not sleep until I know what has happened."

(43)

SHE MANAGED TO CATCH THE INCOMING CALL BEFORE it went to voicemail.

"It's Torsney and Valliant," Kevin Torsney said.

Ava paused. "Where is Marc?" she asked.

"Ms. Kwong, we don't need Sergeant Lafontaine anymore, do we. He opened the door. You really can't expect any more than that from him. We certainly don't."

"No, I guess not."

"Good. Now to get directly to the point, have you thought about our request for more time?" Torsney said.

"I have."

"And?"

"No."

"That is rather disappointing."

"And also, if you don't mind me saying, quite counterproductive," Valliant added.

"We have differing views on what is productive," Ava said. "For me, it's getting things done quickly; for you, it's crossing every *t* and dotting every *i*."

"We're hardly being that unreasonable."

"Perhaps not."

"Ms. Kwong, is there some middle ground we can agree on?"

"Do you have any suggestions?"

"No, not really. We were hoping for some flexibility from your side."

"Well, actually I have been thinking about another way to approach this," Ava said. "My client needs his money and he needs it quickly. You need verification that everything we have told you is true. What if there's a way to accomplish both of those things?"

"How could that be possible?" Torsney said.

"Do you have an interest?"

"Of course we do."

"Are you prepared and are you authorized to make a commitment?"

"We would need to know what you have in mind."

"There's a shipment of cash scheduled to arrive in Surabaya tomorrow night. It will be delivered to the two Italians who run the 'Ndrangheta's operations there."

"How do you know that?"

"My client has the information."

"How much money?"

"I don't know, and he never knows, but certainly it will run into many millions. At least thirty, I hope."

"Where and when will it arrive?"

"I'm not prepared to tell you yet."

"What are you proposing?" Torsney said.

"We meet the shipment. We take the cash."

"Jesus Christ," Valliant said.

"That isn't the kind of rational response I expected," Ava said.

"What did you expect?"

"I'm giving you the means to prove that the money is being shipped in and laundered. I'm giving you two men you can connect to the 'Ndrangheta. I am also giving you the means to pay our thirty million dollars without it costing the Canadian taxpayers a dime. So what I expected you to say was something more along the lines of 'What do we have to do to make this happen?'"

"Ms. Kwong, you're talking about Indonesia, not Canada. And even if it was Canada, I'm not sure we could do what you're suggesting," Torsney said.

"I'm not recommending that we do it without the Indonesians. They would obviously have to be involved and, for all practical purposes, be in the lead. And tell me, why wouldn't they jump at a chance to end an international money-laundering scheme being run through one of their banks?"

"I'm not saying they wouldn't."

"Good. Go cut a deal with them. You and the Indonesians can split anything over and above what I need to take off the top. If it's less than thirty, I'll take whatever it is and not ask for another dollar. And when I get the money, however much it is, I will immediately send you all the other bank records in our possession. That's fair, don't you think?"

"You would actually trust us to tell you how much money was seized? And you would expect us to trust you enough to send you money before we have the complete bank records?"

"Mr. Torsney, none of this can happen without trust, and so far it has been a one-way street. You know who my client is, you know the name of the bank, you have partial records, and now you know about an incoming shipment of cash. When do we get some in return?"

"You said the money will arrive tomorrow night?"

"Yes."

"You're sure?"

"As sure as I can be."

"But you won't tell us where and how?"

"Not until you decide that you're onside."

"How large an operation do you think we're talking about?"

"I'm told that two people, unarmed civilians, accompany the shipment. They will be met by the two Italians. You have to assume that they will be armed and resistant."

"Ms. Kwong, I have to say that your proposal does have some appeal," Valliant said. "It would certainly confirm your client's credibility."

"And give you the money to pay him."

"Yes, I did understand that part of it. And yes, it would certainly be appreciated by our budget-conscious masters here."

"Assuming we can get the Indonesians to agree to it," Torsney said.

"There's no point in discussing that point with Ms. Kwong," Valliant said. "Ms. Kwong, would you mind if we took a five-minute break?"

"To do what?"

"Discuss your proposal."

"Five minutes?"

"Maybe ten. But it's just Kevin, myself, and our boss who need to review it."

"Do you want to call me back or put me on hold?"

"We'll call you."

Ava sat at the desk as five minutes turned into ten and then fifteen. She had no idea what they might do, but to her surprise she didn't feel the least bit anxious. There would either be a deal or there wouldn't be. It wasn't going exactly the way she and Uncle had planned it, but whatever choice the Mounties made, she and Uncle would be ending this job in the next twenty-four hours.

When the call came in, she let the phone ring four times before answering. "Yes?" she said.

"We have decided we're onside as far as Ottawa is concerned," Valliant said.

"Good."

"But now we need to talk to the Indonesians before making a final commitment."

"Of course."

"You know that it can't be done without the Indonesians," Torsney said.

"So we're not making any promises," Valliant added.

"I understand. Now, about the Indonesians — whoever speaks to them should keep in mind that at least some customs officials are being paid off by the Italians. Some central bank regulators are on the take as well, so at all costs those two groups have to be kept entirely out of the loop."

"It won't be anyone here speaking to them, but I will pass that information along," Torsney said.

"Thank you."

Half an hour later, Torsney called again. "You will be dealing with Ryan Poirier. He is our senior man at the embassy in Jakarta. He's feeling out the Indonesians as we speak. You can expect to hear from him before the night is out."

"Is he RCMP or Canadian Security Intelligence Service?"

"He's the assistant commercial minister at the embassy."

"Marc is the assistant trade commissioner at the high commission in Georgetown."

"Ryan also wears several hats. It's up to him if he wishes to expand on that."

One more twist, Ava thought. First, so much for Marc Lafontaine, and now, so much for Ottawa. She couldn't help but feel that whatever control she thought she had was slipping away as she got passed along the chain of command.

(44)

RYAN POIRIER CALLED HER TWO HOURS LATER. WITH A name like Poirier, Ava had expected at least a hint of a French-Canadian accent, but if anything his deep, rumbling voice contained traces of a Scottish brogue.

"Well, you've turned my Monday evening into an adventure," he said. "That is quite the story that Ottawa relayed. I can only hope it doesn't turn out to be a pig in a poke."

"I'm impressed that you think enough of it to work late on a Monday night."

"If it's real, it warrants the effort."

"It's real enough."

"Ms. Kwong, what kind of business do you run that brings in clients like the one you have now?"

"My name is Jennie. I'm an accountant, and my partner and I have a debt-collection business."

"This is a little different, no?"

"Not as much as you might think. At the end of the day, it's all about getting paid. We negotiate settlements all the time in the course of our business. This one is a bit odder than most, but money is money."

"Yes, the money does seem to be your primary motivation."

"Do you have a problem with that?"

"Not as long as the rest of the story holds together and we can capture some bad guys."

"Like I said, it's all real."

"Well, real or not, it's going to be you and me who carry the load now—along with the Indonesians, of course," he said.

"Does that mean you've struck a deal with them?"

"A tentative one. They won't sign off completely until they have all the details about the shipment, but assuming there isn't any dramatic change from what I've been told, there shouldn't be a problem. They were more reluctant to commit to turning over as much as thirty million dollars to a third party."

"Were?"

"They have now been persuaded."

"Mr. Poirier, you did keep Customs out of this?"

"I spoke to a senior military officer. No one else is involved or needs to be involved."

"So where does that leave us?"

"We need to get prepared for tomorrow night, and that starts with you telling me absolutely everything you know about the shipment."

"The money will arrive by plane, a private jet owned by or registered to a company called Brava Italia."

"What time?"

"I don't know, but they will have had to file a flight plan. They've been arriving every Tuesday night for some time now, so we should be able to run a background check and see what's normal."

"Always into Surabaya?"

"Yes. They have some kind of deal with the Customs people there."

"Just the pilot and co-pilot on board?"

"That's what I'm told."

"And not armed?"

"Correct."

"What happens after it lands?"

"It's taken to a hangar. The Italians meet it there to unload the money. They use a panel truck to transport it to the bank."

"How many guards?"

"I'm told it's just the two Italians. Normally my client would be there as well, but obviously he isn't available."

"Do these Italians have names?"

"Foti and Chorico."

"And we should assume the Italians are carrying weapons?"

"Definitely."

"Do they always use the same hangar?"

"I don't know."

"Ask your client."

"He's out of reach right now. He's paranoid about getting in touch with anyone until he gets his money. I have a prearranged time to call him tomorrow night."

"Out of reach?"

"He's in hiding."

"Get him out of hiding. I need him to be at the airport tomorrow night."

"Not a chance," Ava said.

"That represents a problem for me," Poirier said slowly.

"Why?"

"The plan is to have a squad of Indonesian security forces there to meet the plane. They're superbly trained professional soldiers and will be led by a captain who happens to be a friend. So it will be them and me. And if, for whatever reason, the plane doesn't arrive, or if it arrives carrying a shipment of Italian silk scarves, or if it arrives and we end up in a gun battle with ten Italians... Do you understand?"

"You don't want it all on you."

"I don't want any of it on me, or the Canadian government."

"The plane will be there as described."

"If you're that convinced, why won't your client agree to be there? He can confirm the amount of money it's carrying. He can positively identify the Italians. And he has absolutely nothing to fear, given that an elite squad of Indonesian soldiers will be protecting him."

"I'll try to reach him."

"Yes, please do that."

"But I can't promise—"

"Ms. Kwong, I want the man there."

"I will do what I can."

"No, you are not hearing me correctly. I want him there."

"And I will do what I can," Ava said.

"Okay, and while you're doing that, I'm going to be talking to my friend the captain. Assuming your client agrees to make an appearance, his squad will fly into Surabaya tomorrow on a military plane."

"And if I can't reach my client?"

"Then no one will be going anywhere. We'll wait until you can."

"I think it's important to move quickly."

"That isn't my problem."

This man is not going to bend, Ava thought. "Mr. Poirier, given the problematic circumstances, would you be prepared to accept a substitute?"

"Who?"

"Me."

"Are you serious?"

"Entirely. I mean, if the sole purpose of his being there is to have someone designated accountable if things get fucked up, then what difference does it make if it's him or me? In fact, if you think about it, it's more logical to have me there. I'm the one who's been in contact with the Mounties and who's passed along all the information they and you have."

"I'm almost glad to hear you say that."

"Why?"

"It gives me more faith that what you've been telling us may indeed be true."

"I didn't realize you doubted me."

"You aren't naive enough to think that I didn't."

"True... Now, how about my offer?"

"Are you guaranteeing I will see either you or your client tomorrow in Surabaya?"

"I am."

"I have a strong feeling, Ms. Kwong, that it's going to be you."

"That won't be such a bad thing," she said.

(45)

IT WASN'T UNTIL SHE WAS IN LINE AT PASSPORT CON-trol at HKIA that she felt a stab of doubt about her Hong Kong–issued Jennie Kwong passport. She had renewed it without any bother two years before but hadn't used it in more than a year, and she had never used it to enter or leave Hong Kong. This time she had no choice. Ryan Poirier had her flight schedule, and she wasn't taking any chances that he would check the manifest and not find Jennie Kwong on it.

There were twenty people ahead of her but the line moved quickly, the customs officer barely glancing up as he scanned passport bar codes and stamped documents. When it was her turn, he looked at the passport photo and then stared at her. She felt discomfort but held his gaze. Five minutes later she had cleared security and was walking to the Cathay Pacific business-class lounge. As she neared it, her phone rang and she saw Uncle's number. She let it ring out. He was worrying, and she had enough worries of her own.

She had called Uncle late the night before to tell him the Canadians had bought into their deal and that the

Indonesian government was willing to take the lead role. Their conversation went well enough until she told him she had decided to fly to Surabaya the next morning. She did not mention Ryan Poirier's demand.

"I do not think you should go," he said instantly.

"We have money coming in on that plane. Someone from our end needs to make sure it's counted properly and signed for. A few days from now, when the Canadians have their information, I don't want to get into arguments about how much money actually arrived and how much we're to receive."

"I would rather trust them than have you go back there."

"Uncle, I also feel I have an obligation. I've initiated this entire series of events. The Canadian government on two levels has responded in a supportive and responsible way. I feel that the least I can do is be there."

"And if the plane does not arrive?"

"Or if it arrives and is full of Italian silk scarves...? Well, I'll look stupid."

"Or worse."

"Uncle, I wouldn't feel right doing this any other way."

"The other side — the Indonesians and the Canadians — they are all right with it?"

"Yes. They didn't think it was necessary, but I persisted."

"I wish you had not."

"I did and I'm going. I've booked a morning flight out on Cathay Pacific and a return flight early the following morning. I intend to be on both."

"I am going to send Perkasa."

"Uncle, please. He has no role in this now. His presence will only raise questions that none of us want to answer."

"You need to keep in touch with me. If things go badly and the Indonesians become difficult, then we will need him. He has contacts that reach deep into that government."

"I'll keep in touch."

Uncle paused. "There is, I admit, one good thing about your being there."

"And that is?"

"You will know for sure that they get the Italians."

"Yes, I thought of that too," she said.

It was just past ten o'clock when she reached the lounge. She found a Balzac chair off by itself in a corner and phoned Ryan Poirier. "It's Jennie Kwong. I'm at the airport in Hong Kong. My flight is on time."

"Thanks for the update. I leave Jakarta at noon. Our Indonesian friends left an hour ago. Overall, it's been a good morning."

"How so?"

"We ran a very discreet check on your Italians, Foti and Chorico."

"Who is 'we'?" Ava interrupted.

"My local very official and close-mouthed contacts. According to them, the two men arrived in Indonesia about six years ago, so your banker's timeline is credible. They've been renewing visas every six months since then. They list Reggio di Calabria as home."

"Why would they do that?"

"I guess they figured no one in Indonesia would see any significance in it."

"True enough, until now."

"And then we nailed down your Brava Italia jet. It's been going back and forth between Surabaya and various

European airports for about the same time, infrequently at first — I guess they were trying to make sure there weren't any flaws in their system — and then gradually increasing. In the past few months they've been landing once a week, on Tuesdays, as you said."

"What times does it land?" she said, annoyed that Poirier was making it seem as if nothing she had said the night before could be trusted.

"Anywhere between seven and nine."

"Is there a flight plan registered for tonight?"

"Not yet."

"Shouldn't there be?"

"Yes, but the Indonesians aren't fussed about it yet. Surabaya isn't exactly a hub for private jets, so incoming flights don't have to reserve landing times quite so far ahead."

"Do they use the same hangar every time?"

"Evidently they do, according to our sources."

"Mr. Poirier, I know you said your inquiries were discreet. Are you sure your sources are?"

"I trust the man I'm dealing with. There's nothing else you need to know or be concerned about."

"Yes, of course."

"Our associates will be staying in a barracks close to the airport until we have some indication when the plane will land. When I get in, I'm going to join them there. You should call me after you arrive and have cleared Customs and Immigration."

"Fine."

"Jennie, in case I didn't make it clear — I probably seemed less than ebullient about your coming here — I just want you to know that I think you're doing exactly the right thing."

You mean exactly the only thing, Ava thought. "Thanks for that. I'll see you sometime this afternoon," she said.

She rested her head against the back of the chair and opened the email on her iPhone. Maria had written, When will you be home? and nothing else. It filled Ava with guilt. She didn't reply.

Her mother had also written. Her message heading was "BITCH." Theresa Ng called me again tonight, and this time all she did was complain about the way you work, and then she suggested that maybe you weren't working on the case at all. She said she thinks you might have pretended to take it on to get me off your back. She says we have put her in a difficult position with all of the Vietnamese. I don't know where you are with the job, but wherever it is, feel free to stop. I'm sorry I involved you. I will never ask you to do anything like this again. Love, Mummy

A bit late for that, Ava thought, not answering that email either.

She went to the newspaper rack and came back with the *Wall Street Journal* and the *South China Morning Post*. She tried to lose herself in the economic death spiral of Europe, managing to pass enough time that the announcement to go to the gate came before she reached the editorial page in the *Post*. She left the lounge carrying her bag. In it she had her computer, her phone, a small toilet kit, and one change of clothes that she hoped she wouldn't have to use. She had no idea how long it would take from the time they seized the plane to counting the money that would be on it. Hours, she presumed. If it went on long enough, she could forego a hotel, staying at the airport to catch her plane back to Hong Kong.

The CX flight was already boarding when she got to the gate: a long line of Bali-bound tourists waiting to board the economy section. There was no one in line for business class, and Ava was swiftly ushered to her seat. As she settled into it, the realization that she was actually returning to Surabaya took hold. *I hope this isn't a mistake*, she thought. *Please don't let this be a mistake.*

She searched the in-flight entertainment list to find something that would distract her. She was hoping to find a Gong Li film but saw there was a Maggie Cheung movie. Cheung was her mother's favourite actress. And as with Anita Mui, her mother's favourite Cantonese singer, Jennie bore a physical resemblance to her — lean and languid, with a long face and large eyes filled with emotion. Maggie Cheung Man Yuk had Shanghai roots like Jennie, and she spoke English, Mandarin, Cantonese, Shanghainese, and French with almost equal ease. She was a great actress, a star of close to seventy films, with a particular ability to convey vulnerability and heartbreak. Even if there hadn't been a physical resemblance, Ava now wondered if her mother would still have identified with Man Yuk because her movie loves were often unrequited.

Ava started to watch a film in which Cheung played a drug addict in an unstoppable downward spiral, but the futility was too sad to bear. In its place she found a replay of that year's Miss Hong Kong contest. The final group of contestants included a woman from Vancouver and another from Toronto. The woman from Toronto played the cello; Ava rooted for her even though she had no idea how well she was actually playing.

The plane landed five minutes early, but the extra time was immediately swallowed up by a long line of arrivals waiting to buy visas. Ava got in behind some Australians who, thankfully, were so merry that the thirty-minute wait passed quite quickly. At quarter to four she cleared Customs, bypassed Baggage Claim, and walked into the main terminal.

She turned on her phone and called Poirier. His cell rang four times and then went dead. *Shit*, she thought. She was about to redial when her phone sounded.

"Hello, I'm in the terminal," she said.

"What?"

The voice sounded familiar, though she couldn't put a name to it. "Who is this?"

"It's John Masterson."

"Oh, hi."

"Is this Ava Lee?"

"Yes, John, this is me."

"Where are you?"

"I'm back in Hong Kong."

"Do you have time to talk?"

"Yes."

"Ava, have you heard from Andy Cameron?"

"No, why would I?"

"No special reason."

"Then why do you ask?"

"Because I received a very strange phone call earlier today from a man who claims to be his associate."

"What was his name?"

"Foti, Emilio Foti."

"What did this Emilio Foti want?"

"He was looking for Cameron and thought I might know where he was."

"Why should he think you would know?"

"He said Cameron left the bank on Friday and they haven't heard from him since. His calendar showed that he was having dinner with us that night."

"Didn't he have a golf tournament on the weekend?"

"Yes, but evidently he played on Saturday and then didn't show up for the Sunday match."

"Foti told you that?"

"Yes."

"What else did he say?"

"He asked me if Andy had mentioned going to Singapore on business. I told him Andy never discussed his business plans — or his personal plans, for that matter — with me."

"Why would he think Andy went to Singapore?"

"That's where Andy's housekeeper said he had gone."

"Well, she would know more than anyone, don't you think? Maybe Andy flew there for a dirty weekend and decided to stay for a few extra days."

"That's unlikely, knowing Singapore, and knowing that Andy can get all the dirt he needs here."

"Well, it isn't our problem, is it."

"No, not at all. But I have to say this Foti guy was quite persistent. He asked me all kinds of questions about what I do, and then he grilled me about you."

"How did he know about me?"

"You were in the calendar."

"What did you tell him?"

"Nothing, other than that you were a Hong Kong accountant looking for a bank for a client."

"John, I'm sure you've heard from Fay that my after-dinner drink with Andy didn't turn out so well."

"She did hint that he was typically boorish."

"Yes, he was, and I was quite firm in my rejection. He left the hotel in a huff. I never want to speak to him again. In fact, I never want to hear his name mentioned again."

"I get the picture," Masterson said.

"Good. Now I'm sure you've heard the last of Foti, but in case he does call again, I would appreciate it if you kept my name entirely out of the conversation."

"There's really no reason for me to hear from him."

"Of course not," Ava said. "John, I have to go now. Please pass along my warmest wishes to Fay."

"Will do, and make sure you call us next time you're here."

Ava ended the call and glanced around the terminal. No one seemed to be paying her undue attention. *Don't start getting paranoid*, she told herself.

She tried Poirier's phone again. This time it went directly to voicemail. Where the hell was he?

She was standing in the middle of the floor, and suddenly she felt very visible. There was a row of benches along a wall and she headed for them. She sat down with her phone face-up on her lap. There was nothing she could do but wait. She was certain Poirier would call. And after that talk with John Masterson, she was equally certain that coming back to Surabaya was the best thing she could possibly have done.

The Italians were on the hunt for Andy Cameron, and she knew they wouldn't stop at one chat with Masterson. It sounded to her as if they were focused on Surabaya, or at least as focused on it as they were on Singapore. One thing would not lead inevitably to another unless the pursuers were suspicious, smart, and totally committed to finding him. And she had no doubt these men were. It was all about time; her sense that events needed to be propelled as quickly as possible was proving right. Every day that went by added to the risk that the Italians would stumble onto something or someone. Taking them out of play this way and this quickly had been a correct call. That alone would be worth the return trip.

But what if Foti and Chorico had called in outside help? If Ava were in their place, she wouldn't have done that immediately. They were Cameron's caretakers, and for six years the relationship had worked. They had no real reason to suspect that things had suddenly disintegrated. Cameron was missing, not locked up in a police cell, not dead. They would spend at least a day or two — and that's all it had been — trying to sort out the disappearance themselves before reaching out for help. He had been lost on their watch. Why would they make themselves look stupid or incompetent? They would want to exhaust all the local possibilities before panicking. Or so Ava thought. So Ava hoped.

Her phone rang, startling her. The incoming number was blocked. "Yes," she said.

"This is Ryan Poirier. I got your message. Sorry I couldn't pick up earlier."

"Where are you?"

"Five minutes from the airport. I'm on my way to meet you."

"I'm sitting inside the terminal on a bench. Obviously I'm Chinese, and I'm wearing black linen slacks with a white shirt and my hair is tied back."

"I have red hair. I don't think you need to know anything else."

"No," Ava said, laughing. "I'll see you."

"You're ready to go, right?"

"Of course."

From the bench she could see two of the three entrances to the terminal. He walked through the middle one. Poirier was not only instantly recognizable to her but drew stares from most of the Asians nearby, people whose only concept of natural hair colour was shades of black. He was smaller than she had expected — about five foot nine, she guessed — with a slim build. *Too small to be a Mountie*, Ava thought as she eyed his designer jeans and bright green short-sleeved silk shirt. *And too hip.*

She stood and waved in his direction. He saw her, nodded, and walked towards her, his eyes flickering around the terminal. His hair was indeed red, parted down the middle and grazing the tops of his ears. He looked young from a distance, but as he drew closer she saw that the skin around his eyes and mouth was etched with lines. He was fifty, she guessed, maybe even older.

"You're obviously Jennie," he said, holding out his hand.

She looked into a pair of the brightest blue eyes she had ever seen. "Hello, Ryan."

"Can I see your passport?"

Ava hesitated and then realized he was serious. She took it from her bag and handed it to him.

He held the page with her picture up to an overhead light and then twisted the passport so he could examine the seams. "It seems fine," he said.

"Why wouldn't it be?"

He held out the passport. As she took it, he held on and pulled her gently towards him. "We need to go. Things are moving much faster than we expected."

"What—"

"I'll explain as we walk," he said briskly, though he didn't say a word until they exited the terminal. "That's our vehicle," he said, pointing to a grey Daihatsu van with tinted windows that was parked at the curb.

The back door opened as they drew near. Poirier stood aside to let her climb in. There were two soldiers sitting in the front, staring straight ahead. "We're going to the barracks," he said to her.

"What's going on?"

"The plane will be landing in about an hour and a half."

"You finally got a flight plan?"

"They radioed for permission to land only twenty minutes ago."

"How did you find out?"

"You sound suspicious."

"I'm just concerned about leaks."

"So are we. The captain stationed two men in the control tower as soon as he got here. No one has been allowed to leave. Every single communication has been monitored."

"Now what?"

"That depends on what you want."

"What do you mean?"

"You can wait at the barracks until the plane lands and we seize it."

"What are you going to do?"

"I'm going to be at the hangar with Captain Aries."

"Then that's where I want to be."

"It isn't necessary. You've already played your part just by being here in Surabaya."

"I want to be at the hangar."

(46)

CAPTAIN ARIES WAS ABOUT THE SAME HEIGHT AS Poirier, but larger and barrel-chested. He met them at the door to the barracks. The other men sat behind him, occupying half the beds in the sixteen-bed unit. They were all dressed in olive T-shirts, khaki pants, and brown running shoes.

"So you're the young woman who's bringing us all this excitement," he said, looking Ava and down. Then he smiled. "My friend Poirier is not so happy to see you; he would have preferred your client. But me, I prefer pretty women."

"She wants to go to the hangar with us," Poirier said.

"I don't think that's such a good idea," Aries said.

"You brought me here. The least you can do is let me see how things conclude."

"I have no objections," Poirier said.

Aries shrugged. "Ryan will be staying in the background, a safe distance away. I would expect you to do the same."

"Okay."

"Even so, not dressed like that."

"I have some black training pants, running shoes, and a black T-shirt in my bag," Ava said.

"Ryan will be wearing a bulletproof jacket and a balaclava, as will the rest of us. Do you object to those?"

"Not at all."

Aries turned. "Do we have a spare bulletproof jacket and balaclava?" he asked.

"No jacket small like her," the nearest man said.

"I'll tie it tight," Ava said.

"There is a washroom at the other end of the barracks. You can change there," Aries said.

The soldier reached under the bed and pulled out a box. He extracted a jacket and a balaclava and tossed them to Ava. "Do not lose," he said.

"I won't," Ava said.

The washroom was built for men, with a main door that didn't lock and cubicles that had no doors. She opened her bag first, took out her clothes, and then stripped. She slipped the T-shirt over her head and then quickly pulled on the pants. She had put on some mascara and lipstick in the morning. She imagined how hot it would be under the balaclava, and didn't fancy the thought of runny makeup. She wiped it off with a damp towel, put her shirt and slacks in the bag and her phone in her pants pocket, and walked out into the barracks.

Aries' men were standing in a semicircle facing him and Poirier. Ava could hear the captain talking and hurried to catch what was being said. When his words became distinct, she realized he was speaking in Indonesian. Poirier glanced at her and put his index finger to his lips.

The men, Ava noticed, each had a balaclava stuck in their belt and held rifles, muzzle down, loosely at their sides. There were ten of them, all in their twenties or maybe thirties, and all of them were similarly fit. They listened intently to their captain, eyes focused tightly on him, heads nodding. They gave off an overwhelming sense of competence, not to mention firepower. Ava could not imagine the Italians trying to resist such a force.

When Aries finished, the men dispersed into small groups.

"We leave in ten minutes," Poirier said to her.

"Who are these men?" Ava asked.

"They're a specialized rapid-response unit attached to KorMar, the Marine Corps."

"I've never seen rifles like those."

"You know rifles?"

"Some."

"Those are Pindad SS2 assault rifles. They're Indonesian-made, and very effective."

"They look it."

"We're in very good hands."

"So what's the plan that the captain was outlining?"

Poirier raised an eyebrow.

"I know we're only along for the ride," Ava said. "I just think I would be more comfortable if I knew what to expect."

"We're going to wait at the hangar."

"In the hangar?"

"No. To be more accurate, near the hangar. And that's all I think you need to know," Poirier said, his eyes darting over to Aries, who was now standing by himself in a corner talking into a microphone.

Aries shouted to his men. They laid their rifles on the beds and began to put on their jackets. Poirier followed suit. Ava was already wearing hers but hadn't been able to tighten it properly. She waited until Poirier was finished and then turned her back to him. "Could you finish this off for me, please?"

"The plane is forty-five minutes out," Poirier said.

"I assumed as much."

"Are you nervous?"

"Of course I am," she said.

(47)

THEY LEFT THE BARRACKS IN SINGLE FILE. ARIES AND six of the men climbed into the Daihatsu; the remainder, Poirier, and Ava got into a Nissan Grand Livina that was the same size and also had tinted windows. She put her bag at her feet. No one seemed to think it strange that she had brought it with her.

It was a ten-minute drive to the airport, the Nissan following the Daihatsu. They drove past the main terminal, took an exit that was signed only in Indonesian, and then followed a two-lane road flanked by small office buildings festooned with airline logos, hangars, and what looked like warehouses. Everything was surrounded by uniform wooden fences, two and a half metres high and topped by razor wire. Poirier sat next to Ava in the back of the vehicle, his head turned away, his attention on their surroundings. The men in front chatted quietly among themselves in Indonesian, occasionally chuckling. She knew from her own experience that it was their way of keeping their nerves under control, not a sign that they were taking things for granted.

The road ended at a guardhouse that sat about ten metres in front of a steel gate. The driver's-side window of the Daihatsu slid down, a head emerged briefly, and the gate swung open. "One of Aries' men is in the gatehouse with the regular attendant," Poirier said.

The cars drove onto airport property. The main commercial terminal was in the distance, separated from them by an expanse of runway and swaths of grass, and framed by the hangars and warehouses. The Daihatsu took a left turn and drove towards a line of four hangars. The Nissan followed but then veered right, directly to a small office building that was signed in Indonesian and, in smaller script, English: FREIGHT OFFICE. The Nissan driver backed the vehicle into a parking spot in front. They had a head-on view of the hangars.

Through the front window, Ava saw that the Daihatsu had taken up a position along the far side of the hangar closest to the main terminal.

"Which hangar will the plane go to?" she asked.

"The second one," Poirier said.

"Won't the plane see the Daihatsu sitting there?"

"Maybe, but Aries doesn't care about the pilots. He's more concerned that the white panel van doesn't see them."

"Yeah, they'll be far more cautious."

"Especially now, wouldn't you think?"

"Yes, especially now."

"You never told me, do they have any idea what your client is up to?"

"He hasn't handed in a letter of resignation."

"Just taken a flyer?"

"That's it."

"They must be bouncing off the walls."

"I would imagine."

One of the soldiers in front put his hand to an earpiece and then spoke to his colleagues. "The plane has landed," Poirier said.

"Do we know what kind it is?" Ava asked.

"Do you know a bit about planes as well as rifles?"

"No, I'm simply curious."

"It's a Global Express 5000. It can seat about eighteen people if you want seats, and it can fly at more than five hundred kilometres an hour for more than five thousand nautical miles without refuelling. It's the perfect plane for a nonstop flight from Europe to Indonesia."

"Thanks."

"Don't thank me. I knew absolutely nothing about it until Aries briefed us."

Ava looked down the runway. In the distance she could see commercial planes moving to and from the terminal; three of them, lined up for takeoff, were partially blocking their view. A Boeing 747 that had just landed obscured more of it. The jumbo jet lumbered towards them and then slowly ground to a halt, did a slow right turn, and left the runway for the apron that would take it to the terminal. As it moved out of their line of vision, a small white jet, like a gosling swimming in its mother's wake, popped into view.

The man with the earpiece began to speak again. This time Poirier didn't translate.

The jet rolled slowly across the tarmac until it was almost exactly centred between the two vehicles. It was about fifty metres from the Nissan, and Ava could see the pilot, headset on, sitting in the cockpit. He began to turn the jet to the right. Ava saw that two ground crew had taken up positions at the doors of the second hangar. They reached for the handles and slowly pushed the doors to each side until they were completely open, exposing a large, empty space.

The pilot guided the aircraft towards the hangar, stopped in front, and then gradually inched forward until the plane was completely inside, turning it slightly to the left so that the passenger door faced out. Ava stared at the plane but it was too far away to see what was going on inside the cockpit. The passenger door remained shut.

Now they waited, every eye in the car flickering left towards the gate and then back to the plane.

The two ground crew reached for the doors and pulled them closed. They spoke to each other and then left, walking back in the direction of the main terminal.

Ava glanced sideways at Poirier. His full attention was on the gate. Ava looked down at his hands and saw that they were resting on his knees, palms down and fingers spread. He seemed completely relaxed. *He's done this kind of thing more than a few times*, she thought. The marines were just as calm.

"I'm impressed with the composure of these men," she said softly to Poirier.

"These men have fought urban terrorists and jungle guerrillas. Two Italians in a plane hangar don't faze them."

She saw the soldier with the earpiece nod, then raise his right hand in the air with the thumb extended.

"Here we go," Poirier said.

A white panel van appeared at the end of the road and turned in at the guardhouse. It barely came to a full stop before moving through the swinging gate, then drove straight towards the hangars. It stopped short of the first hangar in the row as if the van's occupants, invisible through tinted glass, were sniffing the air. There wasn't a person in view. The only other vehicles in the area were parked in front of the freight office.

For a full minute the van sat in that one spot. "They might be talking to the pilot," Poirier finally said.

As if on cue, the front doors of the second hangar slid apart and the pilot and co-pilot stood framed by the opening. Then they stepped back and stood to either side.

The van turned left and slowly crossed the tarmac. It paused briefly when it got to the doors but then crawled into the hangar, the doors immediately closing behind it.

The soldiers reached for their balaclavas and pulled them on. Poirier and Ava followed suit. It seemed to Ava that no one in their vehicle was breathing.

She counted under her breath. At one hundred and twenty, the Daihatsu stuck its nose out beyond the front of the farthest hangar. It turned left and began to inch towards the Italians' hangar. It stopped parallel to but just short of the front doors.

"Our turn," Poirier said.

The Nissan drove more quickly, but to the left side of the first hangar in line. It went past it and then turned hard to the right and parked at the rear of the second hangar, next to a small door. The soldiers and Poirier left the Nissan and took up positions on either side of the door. Ava saw that the Canadian had a pistol in his hand—she had no idea where it had come from. The back door of the Nissan was still open. Ava slid out, hugging the side of the car. She began to count again.

At twenty, a gunshot rang out.

At twenty-one, all hell broke loose.

(48)

SHE HAD NO IDEA HOW LONG IT WENT ON OR HOW many shots were fired, but it seemed like an eternity. She felt as if she was listening to a full-scale war.

Poirier and the soldiers standing next to the door didn't move until the firing stopped. Even then, the soldier with the earpiece spoke to Poirier before gingerly turning the knob to open the door. When they started to file inside, Ava left the car and got in line.

The soldiers separated and went to either side of the plane. Ava followed Poirier.

In the gap between the plane and the van, four of Aries' soldiers stood with guns nestled in the crooks of their arms. The side of the plane that faced the hangar doors was pock-marked with bullets that had ripped right through the sides of the van, leaving its walls like white lace.

Poirier walked around the van towards the hangar doors. Then he realized Ava was behind him. "You don't want to look at this," he said.

She moved to one side so he wouldn't block her view. Captain Aries leaned against a wall, the balaclava pulled up over his forehead. He was looking down at the floor. Standing next to him, one of his troops gripped a pale young man by the arm, his gun pressed into his back. The young man wore a white shirt with a bar on each shoulder. He was shaking, his free hand rubbing the front of the shirt as if he could wipe away the blood that drenched it.

"Christ," Poirier said.

There were three bodies on the ground, blood still oozing from their gunshot wounds. Another man in a white shirt with bars on the shoulders lay by himself near the front of the van. Blood pooled around his entire body like a halo. The Italians — the men who Ava assumed were the Italians — had fallen together, one body partially covering the other, and their blood had formed a puddle that was starting to stream across the uneven floor towards the hangar door. The face of the man on the bottom looked skyward. There was so little of it left that it was barely recognizable.

"I thought we were going to try to take them alive," Poirier said to Aries.

"One of them pulled a gun. He fired a shot at my men."

"Did that warrant... this?" Poirier said.

"We defended ourselves. You always knew we would. You also know we don't do things in half measures," Aries said, waving his hand at the bodies on the floor. "And what difference does it make to them if we kill them with one bullet or thirty?"

Poirier shook his head and sighed. "I see only one gun."

"I wasn't prepared to take any chances."

"How did he survive?" Poirier asked, pointing to the young man.

"He fell on the floor, put his hands behind his head, and rolled over to the wall."

"Have you ID'd them?"

"No, we're just about to do that," Aries said, and then turned to speak to his men, who were hovering near the bodies.

"Are you okay?" Poirier said to Ava.

"I'm fine."

"Yes... you actually seem to be," he said, looking closely at her.

"I'm sorry if you expected me to fall apart," she said.

"I just didn't know how familiar you were with blood."

"I didn't—" she began.

"Are you ready to see what this plane is carrying?" Aries interrupted.

"Sure, that's why we're here," Poirier said.

"Then let's go."

The captain led the way, Poirier behind, Ava trailing him. The plane's stairs had four steps from the door to the hangar floor. Aries bounded to the top in two and then stopped, blocking the doorway. He peered inside. "Well, well, well," he said. He looked down at Poirier. "This isn't exactly what I expected."

"What the hell are you talking about?" Poirier said.

"I know you were expecting to find millions of dollars or euros or whatever, but even so, I never thought it would be this impressive."

"Keep moving," Poirier said.

Aries entered the plane and Poirier and Ava squeezed in after him. The passenger cabin had been stripped. Where there should have been seats, Ava found herself looking at a wall of money.

"Jesus," Poirier said.

Ava stepped forward. The bills had been stacked and then banded. Eight stacks were cubed and then overwrapped with plastic. Sixteen cubes were overwrapped again and then strapped around both sides to form large blocks. Ava tried to count how many blocks there were, but she couldn't see how many rows back they went.

She looked at the denominations in the stacks closest to her. Five- and ten-euro notes seemed to be predominant. It looked like a lot of money, but if it was mainly fives and tens she wasn't sure it would amount to thirty million.

"Will you be able to get this on your plane?" Poirier asked Aries.

"I'll find the room."

"This isn't going anywhere until I can count it," Ava said.

"How do you propose to do that?" Aries said.

"I don't know yet. I need to open up some of these blocks and see how the money is organized."

"I'll have one of my men help you," Aries said.

"*Komandan*," a voice said.

Aries went to the doorway and looked out. The voice began to speak, and Ava thought she heard the names Foti and Chorico.

"The papers and credit cards and government cards on the men who are dead suggest they were all Italian," Aries said, turning back into the plane.

"What were their names?" Ava asked.

"The pilot was Bova, the other two Foti and Chorico."

"The one who's still alive?" Poirier said.

"We haven't asked him yet, and there isn't any rush. There will be plenty of time for questions about that and many other things when we get him back to Jakarta."

"He seems to have been the co-pilot," Poirier said.

"Yes, I think so."

"I will be surprised if he knows anything of value beyond what his job required. The other two, Foti and Chorico, those are the ones who we needed to take back with us."

Aries shrugged. "It wasn't meant to be. They chose another fate. Besides, who knows what mischief they might have caused in Jakarta. Men like them would say anything to avoid punishment."

Ava was watching Poirier. She saw his top teeth bite into his lower lip, and then he closed his eyes as if he was trying to chase away an unpleasant memory.

"Now we need to help this young woman count her money," Aries said.

(49)

ARIES ASSIGNED TWO MEN TO HELP HER, OR, AS IT turned out, to watch her. They stood by, doing nothing, as she opened two blocks and worked her way into them, her dismay growing as she did. There was an excess of five- and ten-euro notes, and at the bottom of one block, two cubes of pounds sterling. Each stack was all of the same denomination, thankfully, and after counting five of them it was obvious that they were wrapped one hundred to a stack. It was still going to be a time-consuming job.

She left the plane to look for Aries and Poirier. A police cruiser had arrived and a man with a chest full of medals and an elaborately gold-embellished hat was talking with them. They were standing over the bodies of the Italians, the tips of the policeman's shoes touching the puddle of blood. They began to laugh and then stepped back from the corpses as an ambulance pulled up at the entrance to the hangar.

"Can I speak to you, please?" Ava said to Poirier.

"Sure," he said, walking towards her.

"I can't count the money while it's on the plane. We need to unload it. I need enough space to be able to sort it by denomination and currency."

"When we get the bodies out of here, the van will be leaving. Will that give you enough room to operate?"

"Is someone going to mop up the blood?"

"We can do that."

"And then I'll need a large scale. Once we've got the money sorted, we'll weigh it."

"Okay, if you think that will work."

"It will be accurate enough."

"Give us half an hour to get this place cleaned up, and let me see if I can run down a scale for you."

"Thank you. In the meantime, would you mind if I went back to the Nissan? I have my notebook and iPhone in my bag. I need to make a record of what we count."

"You don't need my permission."

"I also want to make a phone call."

"Your client?"

"My partner."

"Go ahead."

Ava walked through the back door, past a soldier who was guarding it, and climbed into the car and extracted her phone. She tried Uncle's Kowloon number first.

"*Wei*," he said before the first ring ended.

"It's me," she said, realizing he must have been waiting by the phone.

"I have been anxious."

"You can begin to relax; the worst is over. The plane arrived full of money and we secured it."

"The Italians?"

"Both dead, and the pilot."

"So they resisted?"

"There seemed to be one gun and one shot. The Indonesians used that as an excuse to put a hundred bullets in each of them."

"That bad?"

"Maybe not quite that many, but there isn't much left for a mother to recognize."

"Once a man is dead, what does it matter how he looks?"

"Well, there's no doubt they're dead, and not much doubt, I think, that they were going to die anyway, whether a shot was fired or not."

Uncle hesitated. "It is better that way."

"The Canadian doesn't think so."

"Did he react badly?"

"He showed his displeasure in a subtle way. Otherwise he was very professional. He knows the game."

"As do we."

"Yes, Uncle, as do we."

"So what happens now?"

"They're removing the bodies and the van the Italians came in. When that's done, I'll count the money, get as many official signatures as I can, and catch an early flight out of here tomorrow morning."

"I am glad you made the decision to go."

"Me too."

"There is always a risk when you are dealing with so many moving parts, but if you had not gone, it would have been very difficult for us to even start to put the Italians behind us."

"And we have the money."

"I care less about the money. Maybe I did when I first suggested trading our information for it, but as I took more time to think, it was the Italians that weighed on me. That is why I am happy you went. You are too young to have to worry about being pursued by people who never forget that vengeance is owed."

"I'm going to count the money anyway, and I'm going to get them to sign off on it."

"The Indonesians will keep it for now?"

"Yes, but they have their agreement with the Canadians and the Canadians have their deal with us, and we have the information the Canadians are waiting for."

"A few days, then, before we will see it in Kowloon?"

"I would hope so."

"By the way, I got a small package from Perkasa today."

"Stick it in a drawer. It's a copy of the bank records. I wanted you to have it as backup."

"It is nice to know that we should not need it."

"I'll see you sometime tomorrow," Ava said.

"What time do you think you will arrive?"

"If everything goes well, around noon on the CX flight."

"Call in the morning to confirm. If you cannot reach me, talk to Sonny. Either way, he will meet you at the airport," Uncle said. "Now I need to get some rest."

Ava looked at her watch. It was still early in the evening. "See you tomorrow," she said.

She closed her eyes and rested her head against the back of the seat. The van was idling, the air conditioning humming, but she still felt hot. Sweat began to trickle down her face and she felt the onset of panic in her stomach. She sat upright, unstrapped the bulletproof jacket, and threw it behind her. Things had gone well, better than she had any right to expect. Now wasn't the time to let other issues intrude. *I have to get outside myself,* she thought.

Poirier came to the back door of the Nissan and opened it. "The bodies are gone," he said.

"Yes, that's great," Ava said, pulling herself together.

"The van is being hooked up for a tow and I'll have someone get rid of the blood, so you can start emptying the plane anytime you want."

"A scale?"

"They're looking for one. It will take you a while to get the money organized. By the time you do, we should have what you need."

"Thank you very much for being so helpful."

Poirier's hand rested on the door handle. "I am sorry it got so brutal in there."

"You didn't seem very pleased with the way things were conducted."

"I wanted to take the Italians alive."

"Yes, that was obvious. Your friend the captain didn't seem to think it was that important."

"He is his own man. Or at least he's the marines' man, and he knows how to obey an order," Poirier said.

"I don't see how it matters that much anyway," Ava said. "We have the money, the bank will be put out of business, and I'll be sending Ottawa the information that has been promised. What else did you want?"

He shrugged. "I wanted to know the things the Indonesians don't want me to know."

"That's all too confusing and conspiratorial for me. I'm an accountant, and all I want to do is count the money and get on a morning flight for Hong Kong."

Poirier moved away from the car. "Let's get started."

Ava walked with him back into the hangar, just as the white panel van was leaving it. A soldier had started to hose down the floor, the diluted blood flowing towards the tarmac. Aries was in a corner talking to some of his men. The policeman was gone. So was the co-pilot. The two soldiers who had been in the plane with her stood at the bottom of its steps.

"We'll put the money over here," Ava said, pointing to the wall farthest from the blood.

Poirier went over to Aries. A minute later, the two of them came up to Ava. "I'll have my men empty the plane right away," Aries said with a smile. "You won't mind if I watch you while you work?"

"Not at all. I don't want there to be any confusion when I'm done."

He turned to Poirier. "I'm going to send most of the men back to the barracks after we unload. What do you want to do?"

"I'm staying here."

"Naturally."

(50)

POIRIER RODE WITH HER TO THE MAIN TERMINAL AT Juanda International Airport. It was seven o'clock in the morning, and she was on schedule to catch her eight-thirty flight.

They had finished counting the money an hour before. The magnitude of the sum involved had done nothing to make it less tedious, and it was with a sense of relief, not any particular pleasure, that Ava wrote the final figure in her notebook and had Aries and Poirier sign off on it. And then, for good measure, she took photos of that page and of the money piled high on the floor and sent it to her Ava Lee email address.

The night before, it had taken a line of soldiers less than twenty minutes to get the money off the plane. The rest of the time was spent sorting. Her plan had been to bundle and weigh one hundred stacks — ten thousand notes — and then weigh everything else in bulk. This would have eliminated the need to count, and if the block contents had been uniform it would have been a rapid process. But the blocks had been constructed with no rhyme or reason and contained multiple denominations and currencies. They had to be taken apart and then completely reconfigured into bundles of like denominations before she could start weighing.

She explained to Aries and Poirier the process she had decided to use, and they both agreed to it, but when the Indonesian saw the resulting numbers, he made her repeat the explanation. The numbers were not exact, Ava stressed, but they would be a good approximation. He then asked her to reweigh everything while he watched.

The results turned out to be identical. The plane had been carrying just over fifty-two million euros, one and a half million pounds, and six million U.S. dollars.

"That's about seventy million U.S.," Ava said. "Thirty for my client and forty for you guys to split however you decide."

"Very nice evening's work," Aries said.

They drove her back to the barracks, where she showered and changed. Poirier stood by the open door while she was inside to prevent any soldiers from wandering in. She appreciated the gesture, and told him that on the drive to the airport.

"Consider it part of my diplomatic responsibility towards a Canadian citizen," he said, and then paused. "You are Canadian, aren't you? They told me you were, but the only ID I've seen is a Hong Kong passport."

"It's a bit late to ask."

"Does that mean you aren't going to answer?"

Ava smiled. "I was born in Hong Kong but grew up in Vancouver and Toronto. A Hong Kong passport is more convenient and raises fewer questions in this part of the world."

"But you're flying back to Hong Kong?"

"Why does that matter?"

"Ottawa wants to know where to reach you. I spoke to them a few hours ago. They're keen to get their hands on the information you promised."

"Once they have our thirty million dollars ready to transfer, then we'll work out the details of the swap."

"That could be as soon as tomorrow, from what I've been told. They know they'll get the money from the Indonesians eventually, but they don't want to wait. The money will be sent from Ottawa."

"Tell them to call me any time they want. My client has opened an account with a Kowloon bank, so he has things organized at his end."

"Okay, I'll let them know."

The Nissan pulled up at the departures area. Ava opened the door, climbed down onto the sidewalk with her bag in hand, and looked back at Poirier. She was about to say goodbye when the door slid shut. She was still standing there when the car drove off.

The terminal was quiet, at least in contrast with Hong Kong, and Ava checked in, cleared security, and found her way to the business-class lounge with an hour to spare. She had a quick coffee at the bar and then carried a second cup to a sofa.

She phoned Uncle. Lourdes answered.

"Where is he?"

"He just left. He's gone to meet a friend. He said for you to call him on his mobile."

He picked up on the second ring. "Ava, where are you?"

"I'm at the airport in Surabaya."

"And?"

"There was about seventy million U.S. on the plane. The Canadians are ready to send us the thirty million as soon as tomorrow."

"That is fantastic news. Good work, my girl."

"I need the Kowloon banking information."

"Do you remember Mr. Tang?"

"Is he the one who helped us with the phony wire transfers to the British Virgin Islands?"

"That is him. Call him when you get in. He will give you the details."

"Don't you have them?"

"Not with me."

"Well, then, when we meet."

"Ava, I will not be able to see you today. I have a friend arriving from Shanghai. He has a lunchtime meeting here in Hong Kong, and then I have promised to go to Guangzhou with him for a dinner. We will probably stay overnight."

"Is Sonny taking you?"

"My friend has his own driver."

"What did Sonny say about that?"

"Since when do I need to seek Sonny's approval for anything?" he said softly.

"I meant no offence, Uncle. We just worry about you."

"There is no reason for that either."

"I understand."

"Now I see my friend waiting for me. I am going to go and enjoy my day with an old comrade, and that is something I can now do with a clear head and peaceful heart, thanks to you. I told Sonny when I thought you would be arriving, but you should call him and confirm. I will see you tomorrow or the day after."

She stared at her phone, not sure what she had just heard. She went back to the bar for a third coffee, debating whether she should call him back. But if she did, what would she say? *Excuse me, Uncle, did you just tell me a lie?*

Ava phoned Sonny and went directly to voicemail. She left her flight details and nothing else. She was about to open her notebook when she saw that an email had arrived with a familiar name attached. It has been three whole days. You should go to a lab today and submit your samples for STI testing. Give them my email address and ask them to forward the results to me. Hope you are well. You have been on my mind. Vivian Ho

Thank you. I will try to get it done today, Ava replied, and then thought how strange it was that she had been back in Surabaya and had not had the memory of Cameron revisit her.

She finally opened her notebook, turned to the page where she had totalled the Italians' money, and began to calculate just how much she would be able to return to her real clients—the Vietnamese-Canadian ones. She had hardly given them a thought since she had arrived in Surabaya the first time, except when her mother had injected them into the conversation. Now she would be able to divide twenty-one million dollars U.S. among them, and with the exchange rate favouring the U.S. dollar, the total would be close to twenty-two million.

It was eight o'clock in the evening in Toronto. Her mother might not be playing mah-jong yet. She phoned her at home.

"Hello?"

"Mummy, it's Ava."

"Where are you? Is everything okay?"

"I'm nowhere very interesting, getting ready to go back to Hong Kong."

"And you are okay? I've been having these strange dreams."

"I'm fine... What kind of dreams?"

"I don't want to talk about them. I find them too upsetting."

"Well, you won't find this upsetting: I've recovered the money that Theresa and the others lost. We'll start doing wire transfers into their bank accounts in a week or so. After Uncle and I take our commission, they will get about twenty-two million."

"I knew you would do it. When will you tell her?"

"I don't want to tell her anything. You call her."

"I... would like that," Jennie said slowly.

"Rub it in."

"I'll do more than that."

"You handle it any way you want; you can say whatever you want."

"The ungrateful bitch had the nerve to say she didn't think you were taking it seriously, that you were never really working on their behalf."

Ava sighed. "That sort of thing happens more often than you would believe. And then when Uncle and I come through for our clients, they pretend they never doubted us and overcompensate on the thank-you side. By then it's too late, though. There aren't many clients we'd accept a dinner invitation from."

"Come home, Ava," Jennie blurted.

"I can't. Not right away."

"I am worried for you. These dreams are bothering me. Maybe they're affecting me because I don't dream very often, but I want you nearby."

"I'll come home when I can."

"The job is done."

"I think Uncle may be ill," Ava said slowly.

Her mother gasped, and then Ava heard her struggle to find her breath.

"Don't panic. I don't know for sure, but I need to stay here until his doctor comes back next week, so I can find out exactly what the situation is."

"And if it is bad?"

"I may stay longer."

"Why do —"

"I really don't want to talk about it anymore. It's all speculation coming from Lourdes and Sonny. I need to find out for myself."

"But you suspect something?"

"Yes, I do. But he is an old man, and it would be unusual if he didn't become ill sooner or later."

"Ava, in my dream I saw you... I saw you lying in a hospital bed."

"Mummy, please."

"Uncle was there as well. He was by your side, lying next to you, holding your hand. I was sitting in a chair in the room and trying to speak to you. But you couldn't hear me, or you couldn't answer. When I spoke louder, Uncle lifted his head and asked me to be quiet."

"Mummy, they're going to board my plane in a moment."

"You have to call me from Hong Kong."

"I will, I promise."

"I am going to pray for him."

"Yes, Mummy, say a prayer for all of us."

(51)

IT WAS NOON WHEN THE PLANE BEGAN ITS DESCENT over the South China Sea to Chek Lap Kok. The sun was high in the sky and the sea glimmered in shades of gold and green. It was a beautiful day, and down below most people were basking in it.

She sped through Customs and Immigration and turned on her phone as she exited Baggage Claim and walked into the cavernous arrivals hall. She saw Sonny standing under the Meeting Place sign, dressed in his usual black suit, white shirt, and black tie, his face grim. He started to walk towards Ava as soon as he saw her. She reached up and kissed him on the cheek. "Thanks for coming," she said.

"I'm glad you're here," he said, reaching for her bag. "Did you talk to Uncle this morning?"

"Yes, I did. Why?" Ava said, surprised by his question.

"What did he tell you?"

"About what?"

"Why he couldn't come to the airport this morning."

"He doesn't always meet me, Sonny."

"He does if he is able to."

Ava heard the strain in the big man's voice. "He told me he couldn't come because he was meeting a friend from Shanghai today."

"He told me the same story," Sonny said.

"Story?"

"It's a lie. He went to the Queen Elizabeth Hospital. There is no friend from Shanghai."

"How can you be so sure?"

"I followed him this morning."

"Without him seeing you?"

"I borrowed a car."

"He also told me he was going to Guangzhou and that he would probably stay overnight," Ava said.

"He will be staying overnight, but at Queen Elizabeth. He's getting radiation therapy, and they'll keep him for at least another day."

"And how do you know that?"

"My friend, the woman, was with me. When he got out of the taxi, she tailed him inside. He registered at the front desk. When he left, she waited for a few minutes and then went to the desk. She said she was with her uncle, Mr. Chow, and that he had obviously signed in and gone on ahead. She asked where she could find him."

"And they actually said 'radiation therapy'?"

"They did."

"Let's head there now," Ava said.

Sonny turned and walked towards the exit without saying a word. The Mercedes was parked at the curb. He opened the back door for her, putting her bag on the front seat.

Traffic was light, and they sped across the Tsing Ma Bridge. "Where exactly is the Queen Elizabeth Hospital?" Ava asked from the back seat.

"King's Park, in the southern part of Kowloon."

"I need to change before going to the hospital, so we'll go to the Mandarin first. My other clothes are still there. I didn't check out when I left yesterday."

He looked at her in the rear-view mirror, his eyes questioning. "Are you really going to the Queen Elizabeth?"

"I am."

"He'll be angry."

"I don't care."

"Well, he loves you enough that he'll probably forgive you."

"How about you? Do you want to come in with me?"

"Me? No, me he would never forgive."

"That's not true."

Sonny shrugged his massive shoulders. "Maybe it isn't, but I still can't do it."

"Which part of the hospital is he in?" Ava asked.

"R Block — that's where I think all the cancer patients go. It's fifteen storeys high. Hard to imagine how many sick people there are that they need a building that size."

"And you said he was getting radiation therapy?"

"Yeah."

"Then I'll find him."

"Ava, I called the hospital this morning to ask about visiting hours. They're only from five thirty to seven thirty."

"I'm not waiting until five thirty. I'm going there after I change."

He looked at her in the mirror again and then fixed his gaze on the road.

(52)

SHE MET SONNY IN THE HOTEL LOBBY AT ONE THIRTY. She wore a plain white shirt, black slacks, low-heeled pumps, and no makeup. The simple clothing fitted her mood. She still wore her Cartier watch and jade cufflinks, however, and her hair was fastened with the ivory chignon pin. This was Hong Kong, after all. She knew the jewellery signified money, and money meant influence. If the hospital staff knew she had *guanxi,* then they might not be so reluctant to waive visiting-hour rules.

Sonny dropped her off at the main entrance to R Block, on Gascoigne Road. She stood on the sidewalk for a few minutes, looking up at it and gathering herself. Queen Elizabeth was the most massive hospital Ava had ever seen. The main building was thirteen storeys high, and it was surrounded by others even higher, including R Block. Now that she was actually there, some of the bravado that had fuelled her since meeting Sonny at the airport began to ebb. *What's the worst thing that could happen?* she thought. *They won't let me see him until five thirty?*

Ava walked through the front doors into an immense lobby that was almost as busy as an MTR station. There was an information desk directly ahead, with a line of about ten people waiting for help. She saw a hospital directory off to the left and went to it. She had no idea exactly what she was looking for, but when saw "Cancer Patient Resource Centre" on the sixth floor, she figured it was as good a place to start as anywhere.

She rode the elevator with two people in wheelchairs who were surrounded by what looked like anxious family members. Ava hated hospitals — not for what they did, but simply for the pain and suffering they represented. She had never had a prolonged stay in one herself. Even the bullet in her thigh hadn't kept her in the private hospital in Macau for more than a day. Marian had been less lucky. She had had her tonsils removed and then her appendix, and Jennie had insisted on dragging Ava along to visit her sister. It had been more than awkward, with Ava hopping up and down on one leg, hardly able to look at the patient.

The patient resource centre was as crowded as the lobby had been. Ava went to the reception desk and got in line. When she finally reached the desk, she found herself looking down at a small, chubby woman with dark skin and white teeth. "How can I help you today?" she asked in a Filipino accent.

"My name is Ava Lee. I'm here to see my grandfather, Chow Tung. I've just flown in from Canada and came directly to the hospital. I don't know what room he's in."

The woman typed the name into her computer. "Yes, Mr. Chow is here, but visiting hours aren't until five thirty."

"I'm a family member."

"There are no family members listed in his profile," the woman said as she checked her screen.

"Probably because he wasn't expecting me to fly here so soon."

"There are no members listed."

"Please... Margarita," Ava said, reading the woman's nametag. "I'm all the family he has left in this world and I've flown all the way from Canada to see him. Please don't make me go back to my hotel. Please don't make me wait."

She returned to her computer. "He was scheduled to have brachytherapy this morning at nine. He could still be feeling the side effects."

"I thought he was getting radiation therapy," Ava said.

"Don't be alarmed. Brachytherapy is just a specialized form of radiation therapy."

"Just?"

The woman looked up at Ava. "I'm not trying to scare you."

"I don't know enough about this kind of thing."

"No one really does until it's necessary."

Ava looked around the resource centre and said, "I feel so bad for all these people."

The woman nodded. "Your grandfather may not be completely alert."

"I need to see him. Even that would be enough."

She looked back at her screen. "He's in the patient ward on the seventh floor."

"Can I go there?"

"I'll have to clear it with the nursing station first."

"Please."

The woman pointed to a vacant chair by the wall. "You wait over there."

Ava sat, her eyes fixed on the woman, who made one phone call, then quickly hung up and began to speak with the person who'd been in line behind Ava. She waited, trying not to stare at the other people in the resource centre, trying not to imagine why they were there.

After five minutes she began to steel herself to the idea of just leaving the area and taking the elevator to the seventh floor. Then the woman picked up the phone again, spoke rapidly to someone, and motioned to her. Ava walked back to the desk.

"Okay, you can go upstairs, but you need to check in with the nursing station."

Ava exited the elevator on the seventh floor. An arrow on the wall directed her to the station. She walked down the hallway past open room doors, the only person not in some kind of uniform, feeling like a trespasser. The nursing station was bursting with activity; it took Ava a few minutes to get someone's attention. When she did, the nurse said, "Why are you here?"

"I was sent here by Margarita from the resource centre downstairs. She spoke to someone here by phone and said it was okay for me to come. I'm Chow Tung's granddaughter."

"Wait a minute," the nurse said.

She disappeared behind a wall in the middle of the station, and when she re-emerged, another nurse was with her. "You're here to see Mr. Chow?"

"I am."

The nurse was stout and grey-haired and had two red stripes on her uniform lapel. She looked Ava up and down. "This is unusual."

"I know, and I can't tell you how much I appreciate it. I've just flown in from Canada. I had no idea he was so ill until yesterday."

The senior nurse came through a gate in the counter. "He's down at the end of the ward. I'll walk you there," she said.

"How is he feeling?" Ava asked.

"He's just had a round of therapy, so he'll be feeling a bit beat-up, but other than that he's an ideal patient. Never complains."

"How many rounds has he had?"

"This was his fourth. The others were in the day-patient clinic."

"Why is he staying in hospital this time?"

"I can't discuss that. You'll have to speak to him or his doctor."

"I understand."

The nurse stopped at a closed door. "This is his room." She looked at her watch. "I'm going to give you ten minutes. Don't make me come and get you, and check in with me before you leave."

"I will."

"And, Ms. Lee, don't expect to be able to do this again."

Ava nodded.

The nurse opened the door. Uncle lay on his back, his eyes closed. His face was pale and drawn; he had lines under his eyes and beside his mouth that seemed to have sprung from nowhere. His mouth was slightly open, the skin under his chin hanging loose. Ava gasped. She had never seen him look so old. She had never once imagined him to be so frail.

The nurse walked to the bed and checked the intravenous tube. As she did, he turned his head towards them and opened his eyes. When he saw Ava, he closed them again but didn't move his head.

"He's all yours," the nurse said.

There was a chair in the corner of the room. Ava lifted it and carried it next to the bed. She sat and put her hand on top of his. She then lowered her head onto the bed, her eyes tightly shut. She invoked St. Jude in a whisper, and as she did she felt tears trickle from the corners of her eyes. She began to sob.

"I will not be able to bear it if you cry," Uncle whispered.

"I can't bear the thought of your being here," she said, raising her head to look at him.

"When I spoke to you this morning, I thought, *She does not believe my story about a friend from Shanghai*," he said, his eyes still closed.

"I wanted to, but other thoughts kept intruding."

"We know each other too well."

"How can that be a bad thing?"

He opened his eyes and she saw they were gleaming. Her spirits rose.

"So your flight was on time?"

"Of course."

"Did Sonny get you?"

"Yes."

"He has been following me, he and that woman of his. He thinks I did not notice."

"He thought you might have."

"Well, I give him credit for that."

"He's just worried. We all are."

"Who are 'we'?"

"Him, me, Lourdes."

"Anyone else?"

"No."

"I want to keep it that way."

"Yes, Uncle."

"Did they tell you what I have, the nurses?"

Ava stroked the back of his hand. The skin was soft and clear, his nails manicured. "No, but I know you've been getting brachytherapy, and I've been hearing about and seeing the stomach problems you've been having. When you threw up blood last week on the street... Well, I assumed the worst."

"It started about six months ago, and fool that I am, I ignored it for three months. And then I could not let it go anymore."

"Stomach cancer?"

"Yes."

"What caused it?"

"Smoking, they think."

"But you're still smoking."

"Yes. I went to a *gweilo* doctor named Parker when I first became aware of my symptoms. I figured he would not know who I was, and so there would be no gossip. When he gave me the diagnosis, I asked him if I should stop. He said, 'Why? It won't reverse the damage. And after all these years, the withdrawal would only cause you extra stress.'"

"But they're treating the cancer."

"There is not much they can do," he said, his eyes closing again as if the words pained him. "It is into my liver and pancreas. They cannot perform surgery, and even if they could, at my age it would not be wise. They offered me chemotherapy, but after Parker described it to me I decided to pass. So I am taking the radiation treatment. It buys me some time."

"Is there some treatment available anywhere else, like the United States?"

He placed his free hand on top of hers and squeezed. "Ava, I am eighty-four years old. Why would I want to become a desperate man now, when I have spent my entire life being in control? No, this is the process I have chosen, and I am going to see it through my way. I value my dignity—maybe even too much—and I have a reputation that I intend to uphold. So Ava, I am telling you, as much I respect you, do not try to do anything else, and please keep the rest of the world at bay. I understand about Sonny and Lourdes, and I also know them well enough to know they would not dare talk about me to anyone else. You are not quite so afraid of me."

"Amanda gets married in January," Ava said softly.

"What does that mean?"

"She needs me here, so I'll be staying in Hong Kong until then at the least."

"I am sure she will appreciate that."

"When I'm not working on the wedding, I can spend time with you. I should be able to visit every day. We can meet in the mornings for *jook*."

"I do not intend to live only on congee," he said, a tiny smile playing on his lips.

"You know what I mean."

"I think I do." He opened his eyes and gazed at her.

She felt a flutter of panic, a fear of what she would see in them. But she saw the same resolute eyes she'd been looking into for more than ten years.

"There are some things I need to discuss with you," he said. "If we do it now, then we never need to discuss these things again, do we."

"Do we have to now?"

"It would give me some peace. I have been thinking about these things for some time now."

"Yes, Uncle."

"You know I have no family left."

"Yes."

"And I have been in Hong Kong for so many years that my ties to Wuhan are more wishful thinking than real."

Ava nodded.

"I met with a lawyer two months ago and did my will. I named you as executor."

"Uncle, I do not want to talk about your will," Ava said.

"Perhaps not, but I do. And then, as I said, it will be done, and it will be one less thing for me to worry about."

"Uncle, please —"

"I am going to leave ten million Hong Kong for Lourdes, and I am also going to give her the apartment. If she wants to sell it and move back to the Philippines and live like a millionaire, she can do that. I am also leaving ten million to Uncle Fong. He did not save enough for his retirement and he does not have any children to care for him. So I am giving him the ten million and asking you to look in on him from time to time to make sure he is okay. He has been a good friend."

Ava said, "Yes, he has been a good friend."

"Sonny is a different matter," Uncle said hesitantly. "I am leaving him the car and some money as well, but we need to do more than that for him."

"Like what?"

"You must hire him."

"Uncle, I have no need—"

"Listen to me, Ava. Sonny is not a man who can be left to his own devices. He needs structure; he needs to feel that he belongs to something, to someone. If he is on his own he will get into trouble, and the kind of trouble Sonny can get into is not the kind that will earn him just a slap on the wrist... Ava, no one could be more loyal."

"I know that, Uncle, but I have no plans to live in Hong Kong."

"That is not what I hear from Wong May Ling."

"May Ling is saying what?" Ava said.

"Actually, it was the husband, Changxing, who has been telling me things. He says May Ling has a plan to start up a business with you, and she has put aside a hundred million U.S. dollars to fund it. He is not happy about it but he will not oppose her, because he is afraid of losing her."

"I know nothing about any of this."

"Now you do."

"Uncle, I have no plans to live in Hong Kong, so I don't know what you expect me to do about Sonny."

He shook his head. "Anything will do. Tell him he is working for you but you need him to look after that half-brother of yours, or you need him to chauffeur your father or Amanda Yee. Come up with something, anything. We need to keep Sonny occupied."

"All right," Ava said, knowing it was useless to argue. "But about May Ling—she's never discussed any plans with me. As far as I'm concerned I have only one partner, and that's you."

"I know, but as I told you months and months ago, I am not going to be around forever, and May Ling is a powerful and very intelligent woman. And as you found out in Macau, she is a woman with *guanxi*... Ava, what will you do when I am gone? Take vacations?"

"I don't know what I'm going to do."

"You would make a strong team."

"If she puts up a hundred million dollars, we won't be a team. She'll be the boss. I would never work with her unless we were on an equal footing."

"Why is that not possible?"

"I don't have a hundred million dollars, or anything close to it."

"When I die, you will."

Ava lowered her head, her teeth biting into her lip. "I can't talk about your money."

"You need to talk to Parker. He brings clarity to things," Uncle said. "If I had gone to a Chinese doctor who knew me or had heard about me, he would have given me two bags of herbs and told me what he thought I wanted to hear. When I asked Parker what he thought I should do, he told me I was an old man who had incurable cancer and that I should get my affairs in order. I appreciated his honesty and I have taken his advice. So, like it or not, you are going to inherit the bulk of my estate. What you do with it is up to you. All I ask is that you look after Uncle Fong and keep Sonny out of trouble."

Ava felt tears well in her eyes again. She wiped at them with her loose hand. "Uncle, I don't want any of this to happen."

"Neither do I, but here we are."

She felt herself starting to come apart. The feeling of helplessness that had overcome her in Surabaya was back. *This isn't my life anymore,* she thought. *This has to be happening to someone else.*

"Ms. Lee," a voice called.

Ava thought she was hearing things.

"Ms. Lee, I gave you ten minutes and it's up. You need to leave now."

The nurse stood in the doorway, looking severe.

"I'm sorry. I lost track of time," Ava said.

"You're abusing our kindness."

"I'm sorry," Ava said, standing.

Uncle looked up at her with what she could only think of as contentment. "I am glad things are settled," he said. "I was worried about how I was going to tell you. You have made it easier for me."

"I'll be back tonight."

"At regular visiting hours," the nurse said.

"At five thirty," Ava said to Uncle.

"I am out of here tomorrow."

"And I'll be here to get you."

"Ms. Lee..." the nurse said.

Ava bent over and kissed him on the forehead. "I love you," she whispered.

She was walking towards the door when she heard him say her name. She stopped and turned. "Yes, Uncle?"

He was on his back, his eyes closed. "Nothing, my girl, nothing at all."

COMING SOON
from House of Anansi Press
in February 2014

Read on for a preview of the next thrilling Ava Lee novel, *The Two Sisters of Borneo.*

(1)

AVA LEE SENSED SOMETHING WAS WRONG THE INSTANT she saw May Ling Wong standing alone at the entrance to the Cathedral of the Immaculate Conception.

It was the second Saturday in January, and the sky was overcast. It was cold and dank, typical weather for the middle of a Hong Kong winter. Ava was in a Bentley limousine with Amanda Yee, the bride-to-be and her future sister-in-law, and three bridesmaids when she spotted May Ling. Amanda was about to marry Ava's half-brother Michael, and Ava was the maid of honour. They had driven from Sha Tin, the town in the New Territories where Amanda's parents lived.

The five women had been up since six that morning, getting coiffed, made up, and dressed by some of the most expensive hairstylists and makeup artists in Hong Kong. Ava had resisted having her shoulder-length black hair twisted and sprayed into an elaborate updo. She had declined to have her face slathered with foundation and powder. But she had no choice about the sleek lavender silk dress that Amanda had chosen for the bridal party. The tight strapless gown fell to Ava's knees and made her feel as if she was enveloped in coloured plastic wrap.

Ava was in her mid-thirties but this was only the third wedding she had attended. The first had been her older sister Marian's, when she married a *gweilo* civil servant named Bruce. The previous August her best friend, Mimi, had married Ava's best guy friend and occasional work associate Derek Liang, at Toronto City Hall in front of ten friends and family members. Mimi was pregnant with Derek's child, and the wedding had been little more than a formality. They had already started their life together, recently moving into a house in Leaside, one of Toronto's more affluent neighbourhoods. Afterwards Derek had treated everyone to lunch at a nearby Chinese restaurant. The Hong Kong wedding, in contrast, would be going from the splendour of the cathedral to an eight-course feast in the ballroom of the Grand Hyatt Hotel.

When the limousine arrived at Immaculate Conception, three photographers and two cameramen were waiting for the bride and her bridesmaids. Twenty or thirty of the several hundred wedding guests were huddling together on the sidewalk for a last-minute cigarette. May Ling stood to the side, apart from the others. She wore a fitted coral and pale green Chanel suit, the skirt coming to just slightly above the knee. She stared vacantly, her face impassive, her back pressed against the grey stone church wall.

"There's May," Ava said to Amanda. "She looks a bit troubled."

"Huh?" Amanda said, her attention focused on gathering up the metre-long train of her ivory Vera Wang wedding dress.

"Nothing," Ava said, knowing the word *troubled* shouldn't have escaped her lips. The wedding might be taking place in Western fashion in a Roman Catholic church, but Chinese superstitions couldn't be that easily dismissed. Even a negative word, let alone deed, was viewed as having the potential to jinx the married couple. As the maid of honour, part of Ava's role was to make sure that Amanda stayed protected inside a happy bubble.

When Ava got out of the limo, May Ling took a step forward and waved. She smiled, but her brow was furrowed and the smile was fleeting.

Amanda slid from the car, posed for the cameras, and was then surrounded by the bridesmaids for more photos. The plan was for them to escort her to a small room just inside the main entrance, where she could make any last-minute adjustments and prepare for the walk down the aisle. As the bridal party started towards the church, Ava moved next to Amanda.

"We have about twenty minutes before the ceremony starts," Ava said. "I'm going to have a quick chat with May Ling and then I'll meet you inside."

"Where is May?"

"Over there," Ava said, pointing, and realized with relief that Amanda hadn't heard her earlier comment.

Amanda glanced at May. "I'm surprised she's here."

"Why?"

"She phoned me a few days ago to say she might not make it."

"Why not?"

"She didn't say. She just said she had some issues in Wuhan to deal with."

"Well, she's here, so I guess the problem has been resolved. Now you'd better get inside."

"Don't take too long. I'm more nervous than I thought I would be," Amanda said.

"I'll be there shortly."

Ava turned and walked towards May Ling. The two women had met the previous year, when May and her husband, Changxing, had hired Ava and her partner, Uncle, to help them locate and recover the millions of dollars they had lost purchasing forged paintings. Ava and Uncle were then in the debt-recovery business. The case had not gone smoothly, and the relationship between the two women had degenerated into betrayal and mistrust when May had used and deliberately undermined Ava. But a short time later May had come to Ava's assistance in a case that involved Ava's family — specifically her half-brother Michael — and the two women had found common ground and begun to build a friendship.

May took a step forward and held out her arms. Ava slid into them and the two women hugged. "You look absolutely gorgeous," May said.

"I spent last night and this morning with Amanda and those twenty-something friends of hers. They made me feel old, not gorgeous."

"You're only in your mid-thirties. I'm in my mid-forties, so imagine how I feel."

"May, men adore you," Ava said.

"Changxing does, anyway."

Ava took a step back. May was the same height as her — five foot three inches — and weighed maybe five pounds less at 110 pounds. She was slim, fine-boned, and, like Ava, had an ample bosom that she didn't hesitate to show off. Her hair was straight and cut short in a fashionable bob. Physically she gave off a sense of vulnerability, but she had a sharp mind and a quick tongue that could be raw and cutting. And she could be highly charming and subtly seductive. Uncle said that men were torn between wanting to protect her and wanting to impress her.

"Where is Changxing?" Ava asked.

"He doesn't like weddings and he hates churches. He's spending the afternoon with Uncle. He'll meet me later at the Mandarin Oriental to get dressed for the dinner."

"Uncle didn't mention anything to me about Changxing."

"He called Uncle this morning to see if he was up for a visit. He said he was, although I did tell Changxing he should have checked with you."

Uncle, like Changxing and May Ling, was from Wuhan, in Hubei province in central China. He had fled when he was a young man to escape the Communists. After he landed in Hong Kong, he had became prominent in the Triad society before retiring as its chairman and starting the debt-collection business that Ava later joined. Changxing liked to emphasize the Wuhan ties between the two men. Uncle's interest in the wealthy businessman, who was known as the "Emperor of Hubei," had always been in his *guanxi*, his connections, and in his ability to deliver favours.

Ava and May Ling's relationship stood separate from that of the men, a situation that Uncle endorsed. Though her feeling was unsubstantiated by word or deed, Ava had a sense that Changxing didn't share Uncle's enthusiasm for the women's increasingly tight friendship, which was further emphasized by the fact that they had set up a business together. The Three Sisters was the name of their newly formed investment fund. May Ling and Ava were the majority shareholders and Amanda had a minority stake. The fund was now Amanda's full-time occupation; May Ling was splitting her time between their new venture and her business interests with Changxing; and Ava had committed herself to the business after Uncle gave her his blessing.

"I'm not Uncle's nurse or his secretary, and he hates it when I start acting like one."

"How is he?" May asked softly.

"As well as anyone can expect. The cancer has travelled from his stomach to his other organs. While the doctors don't like to talk about time frames, I don't think I'll be needed in Hong Kong for much longer."

"It's been four months now?"

"We're in the fifth month. He's better than I thought he would be, though. Most days I meet him in the morning, for congee, and if he's up to it, for dinner somewhere in Kowloon. The dinners are becoming rarer these days; there are only so many things he can eat. That irritates him, and not many things do. But he seems to accept what's happening, and we manage to spend our time enjoying each other's company and talking about other things. My mother flew over from Toronto for two weeks in early December. She was a blessing in terms of supporting me and taking Uncle outside himself. She makes him laugh."

"Ava, in these talks you've had with Uncle, have you kept him up to date on our business?"

"I've kept him briefed. I told him you and Amanda are running things until I'm ready to join full-time."

"Good." May hesitated, her eyes wandering past Ava towards the church door. "I think one of the bridesmaids is looking for you," she said.

Ava turned and saw the one named Camille standing in the doorway. "I'll be right there," she shouted.

"I can't help but think how strange this situation is," May said, looking around at the guests, who were now filing into the church.

"What do you mean?" Ava asked, again surprised by May's vagueness.

"Sorry. I meant your being the maid of honour," she said, and then put her hand to her mouth. "Oh, Ava, I'm sorry again. I don't mean to offend; it's just that people are talking."

"I know. This morning I met Michael's three brothers — my half-brothers — for the first time. At first they were distant, tentative. Then we chatted a bit and, truthfully, they couldn't have been nicer. But I know what some people are saying about the daughter of a second wife having such a major role in the wedding of the eldest son of the first wife."

"It is unusual."

"The way I look at it, I'm a friend and now a business partner of Amanda. Her father, Jack, was Uncle's and my client, and we even saved his life. If she had been marrying anyone else I'd have the same role. I'm here for her."

"Ava . . ." Camille's voice could be heard from the church doorway.

"I have to go," Ava said to May.

"Tomorrow can we meet for breakfast? We can have dim sum at the Mandarin."

"Sure, that should be fine," Ava said, and then realized May was looking past her again. "Is there a problem?"

"No, not really. We just have some things we need to go over."

"Ava, Amanda is almost ready," Camille said, appearing at her side, a hand reaching for her elbow.

"Tell her I think she's the most beautiful bride I have ever seen," May said.

"Yes, I will," Ava said, and then turned and walked into the church with the bridesmaid.

What a strange day, she thought. *First meeting all my half-brothers, and then May acting so anxious. And now I'm going to walk down the aisle right behind Amanda, knowing that most of the people in this church think it's scandalous for me even to be in the building.*

What Ava didn't know was that the day was about to become stranger still.

ACKNOWLEDGEMENTS

I want to thank Sarah MacLachlan and her team at House of Anansi Press for their continuing support.

My agents, Carolyn Forde and Bruce Westwood, for their commitment and dedication.

My wife, Lorraine, and my children — Jill, Ian, Stephanie, and Alexis — all of whom beat the drum and cover my back.

My daughter-in-law, Jane, and my sons-in-law, Todd Howell and Brian Moniz, who are there for me whenever I need them.

My editor, the great Janie Yoon. This is our fifth book together, and her insight is as sharp as ever and her contribution perhaps even more impactful.

There were also a number of people who helped me form *The Scottish Banker*. Among them: Robin Spano, a friend and a fine crime writer in her own right; Catherine Rosebrugh, a lawyer and another good friend; John Paterson, former business partner and a resident of Bali; and Kristine Wookey, the wife of Bruce Westwood, but more important to me, someone who understands Ava.

Last, I want to thank book clubs. Over the past few years I have made it a point to accept every invitation I have received from book clubs. I have never been disappointed. There is something refreshing, almost affirming, about meeting people who love books — even if they don't always love mine — and aren't hesitant about expressing their opinions about them. I have made changes to manuscripts and reprints on the basis of book club input.

One club in Richmond Hill has been particularly supportive. That seems uncannily appropriate since that's where Ava was raised and her mother still lives. That club was my first, and those women of Richmond Hill have stuck with me through every book. I almost consider them my good-luck charms: a book launch without them wouldn't feel the same. So my thanks to Samantha, Kim, Sherri, Ann, Kristine, and the rest of the women of Richmond Hill.

IAN HAMILTON is the author of *The Water Rat of Wanchai*, *The Disciple of Las Vegas*, *The Wild Beasts of Wuhan*, *The Red Pole of Macau*, and *The Scottish Banker of Surabaya*. *The Water Rat of Wanchai* was the winner of the Arthur Ellis Award for Best First Novel, an Amazon.ca Top 100 Book of the Year, an Amazon.ca Top 100 Editors' Pick, an Amazon.ca Canadian Pick, an Amazon.ca Mysteries and Thrillers Pick, a *Toronto Star* Top 5 Fiction Book of the Year, and a *Quill & Quire* Top 5 Fiction Book of the Year. The sixth book in the Ava Lee series, *The Two Sisters of Borneo*, will be published in February 2014.